THE ANCIENT NINE

ALSO BY IAN K. SMITH

The Clean 20

Blast the Sugar Out!

The SHRED Power Cleanse

The SHRED Diet Cookbok

SUPER SHRED

SHRED

The Truth About Men

Eat

Happy

The 4 Day Diet

Extreme Fat Smash Diet

The Fat Smash Diet

The Take-Control Diet

Dr. Ian Smith's Guide to Medical Websites

The Blackbird Papers: A Novel

THE ANCIENT NINE

IAN SMITH

ST. MARTIN'S PRESS NEW YORK

THE ANCIENT NINE. Copyright © 2018 by Ian K. Smith. All rights reserved. Printed in the United States of America. For information, address St. Martin's Press, 175 Fifth Avenue, New York, N.Y. 10010.

www.stmartins.com

Designed by Kathryn Parise

The Library of Congress Cataloging-in-Publication Data is available upon request.

ISBN 978-1-250-18239-5 (hardcover)
ISBN 978-1-250-18240-1 (ebook)

Our books may be purchased in bulk for promotional, educational, or business use. Please contact your local bookseller or the Macmillan Corporate and Premium Sales Department at 1-800-221-7945, extension 5442, or by email at MacmillanSpecialMarkets@macmillan.com.

First Edition: September 2018

10 9 8 7 6 5 4 3 2 1

*To **Jordan R. Dann, Class of '47** (and still kickin'!) . . . mentor . . . gentleman . . . scholar . . . humanitarian . . . uncle . . . industrious . . . a true man of Harvard. A bloodline couldn't make our bond any stronger. I thank you for all that you have been in my life and the unique blessing that you will always be.*

Dana Smith, Class of '91 (Fly Club)
Jonathan Cardi, Class of '91 (Delphic Club)
Kevin McFarlane, Class of '91 (Fly Club)
Ron Mitchell, Class of '92 (Delphic Club)

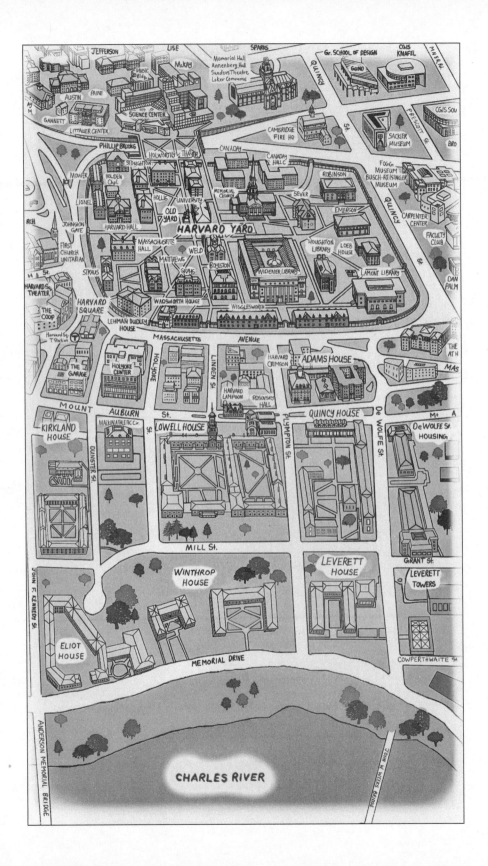

Based on real events

THE ANCIENT NINE

PROLOGUE

✣

Halloween Night, 1927
The Delphic Mansion
Cambridge, Massachusetts

EMPTY ROPES CLATTERED against flagpoles, and street signs flapped helplessly in the shadowy night. Two boys sneaked down a cobblestone path crowded with heavy bushes and enormous signs that warned against trespassing. They stood there for a moment, their bodies dwarfed by the gigantic brick mansion.

"That's enough, let's turn around," Kelton Dunhill whispered. He had large competent hands and knots of compact muscles that bulged underneath his varsity letter sweater. He carried a long silver flashlight he had borrowed from the superintendent's office of his residential house.

"I'm going all the way," Erasmus Abbott said firmly. "I didn't come this far to chicken out. Just a few more minutes and we'll be inside."

Dunhill looked up at the tall wrought-iron fence that had been reinforced with solid wood planks to obstruct any potential view into the rear courtyard. He was a tough, scrappy kid, a varsity wrestler who had been undefeated in almost three years of college competition. He was many things, but a quitter was not one of them. Very little intimidated Dunhill, the son of a banker and elementary school music teacher, but when he looked up at the mansion's towering spires and turrets set against the ominous sky and the royal blue flag that snapped so loudly in the wind, something made him feel uneasy. At that very moment, if Erasmus Abbott had not been standing next to him, he would've turned on his heels and run like hell. The only thing that kept his feet planted was his greater fear of the humiliation he would face once the others got word that the scrawny Abbott had showed bigger nerve.

"If we get caught, we'll be fried," Dunhill said in his most persuasive voice, trying to sound rational rather than scared. "Technically speaking, we're trespassing, and they can do anything they want to us since we're on their property. I don't need to remind you of what happened to A. C. Gordon."

Erasmus Abbott took the milk crates they had been carrying and stacked them in a small pyramid against the fence, then slipped on his gloves and pulled his hat down until it settled just above his eyes. He was dressed all in black. Now completely disguised, he turned and faced Dunhill.

"There's no proof Gordon ever made it this far," Abbott contested. "And besides, I never believed the whole business about his disappearance anyway." Abbott turned toward the platform of milk crates, then back at Dunhill, and said, "So what's it going to be? I'm making history tonight with or without you. The answer is in there, and I'm not gonna stop till I find it."

"Jesus Christ," Dunhill mumbled under his breath before pulling down his own skullcap and stepping up to the fence. It all started out as a dare, but Abbott had taken it more seriously than anyone expected. This would certainly not be the first time a student had tried to break into the well-guarded Delphic mansion. There had been many attempts over the years, but according to legend, the farthest anyone had gotten was the external foyer. No one had ever penetrated the interior. What most worried Dunhill, however, was that few had lived to share their story.

"And what's your plan once we get on the other side of the fence?" Dunhill said.

Abbott ran his hand over the small canvas bag strapped to his waist. "Everything we need is in here," he said. "Once we get to the back door, I'll have the lock open in well under a minute."

Abbott had been practicing on different doors all over Quincy House in the middle of the night. His best-recorded time was twenty-nine seconds with a blindfold covering his eyes and a stopwatch hanging around his neck.

Abbott was not particularly athletic, but he scaled the crates easily and in one motion hoisted himself over the top of the fence and its row of pointed spears. Dunhill heard him land hard on the other side, then made a small sign of the cross over his heart, climbed onto the crates, and hurled himself over the fence. He landed on the firm slate tiles with a jolt.

They stood on the perimeter of a large courtyard dotted with elaborate marble sculptures and a fountain whose water sat motionless in a wide, striated basin. There were no lights to guide them, but moonlight cut through the heavy canopy of trees that towered overhead. A formidable, sturdy brick wall that was even taller than the fence they had just climbed surrounded them on two sides. Abbott had correctly chosen their entry point into the Yard.

A gust of wind sent small piles of leaves flying sideways from one corner of the courtyard to the next. The mansion was eerily dark except for the dull flicker of a light in a small window just underneath the sloping angle of the tiled roof. The enormous building looked cold and menacing and unforgiving.

"She's massive," Abbott whispered. "I didn't think she'd be this big. Must've cost them a king's fortune to build it."

"It's not empty," Dunhill said, pointing at the lighted window. "I still say this isn't a good idea. We've already proved our point. Let's get the hell out of here while we still can."

Abbott pretended he hadn't heard a word Dunhill said. He walked quietly across the courtyard toward a set of stairs that led to a large door with small panes and a brass doorknob that glistened under the moonlight's glow. He cupped his face to the glass and looked inside. He turned and waved Dunhill over, but Dunhill remained motionless underneath the fence, still not believing they had actually gotten this far.

Abbott unzipped the canvas bag, pulled out a couple of tools, and quickly went to work on the lock. That's when Dunhill glimpsed a shadow moving across the courtyard. He looked up toward the lighted window and saw

Harvard College
Cambridge, Massachusetts
October 2, 1988

IT SHOULDN'T HAVE been enough to wake me, but I had just drifted off on the couch in the common room that separated my bedroom from my roommate's. It was a short scratchy sound: a pebble or sand being dragged across the linoleum floor. I looked toward Percy's bedroom. His door was closed and his light off. I sat up on the sofa, swiveling my head in the darkness to see what could've made the noise. Mice were not exactly uncommon sightings in these old Harvard houses, some of which had been built more than a century ago, so I was preparing myself for vermin out on a late-night scavenge. But when I turned on the lamp and looked down at the floor, what sat there took me completely by surprise.

Someone had slipped a small cream-colored envelope underneath the front door. There was no postage or return address, just my name and room number elaborately inscribed.

Spenser Collins
Lowell House L-11

I turned the envelope over, hoping to find some indication of who might have sent it, but what I discovered was even more puzzling.

Embossed on the flap were three torches—so dark blue, they were almost black—arranged in a perfect V shape.

I heard footsteps just outside the door, slow at first, but then they began to pick up speed. I pulled the door open, but the hallway was empty. Our room was on the first floor, so I grabbed my keys and ran a short distance down the hall, jumped a small flight of steps, then rammed my shoulder into the entryway door, forcing it open into the cool night. I immediately heard voices echoing across the courtyard, a cluster of three girls stumbling in high heels, dragging themselves in from a long night of drinking.

I scanned the shadows, but nothing else moved. I looked to my right and thought about running across the path that led to the west courtyard and out into the tiny streets of Cambridge. But my bare feet were practically frozen to the concrete, and the wind assaulted me like shards of ice cutting through my T-shirt. I retreated to the warmth of my room.

Percy's bedroom door was still closed, which was not surprising. He wouldn't wake up if an armored tank tore through the wall and opened fire.

I sat on the edge of the couch and examined the envelope again. Why would someone deliver it by hand in the middle of the night, then sneak away? None of it made any sense. I opened the book flap slowly, feeling almost guilty ripping what appeared to be expensive paper. The stationery was brittle, like rice paper, and the same three torches were prominently displayed in the letterhead.

The President and members of the Delphic Club
cordially invite you to a cocktail party on
Friday, October 14, 7 o'clock
Lily Field Mansion at 108 Brattle St.
Cambridge.
Please call 876-0400 with regrets only.

I immediately picked up the phone and dialed Dalton Winthrop's number. Fifth-generation Harvard and heir to the vast Winthrop and Lewington fortunes, he was one of the most finely pedigreed of all Harvard legacies, descending from a family that had been claiming Harvard since the 1600s, when the damn school got its charter from the Bay Colony. Dalton was a hopeless insomniac, so I knew he'd still be awake.

"What the hell are you doing up this time of the night?" Dalton said. "Some of us around here need our beauty sleep." He sounded fully awake.

"What can you tell me about something called the Delphic Club?" I asked.

The phone rustled as he sat up.

"Did you just say 'the Delphic'?" he said.

"Yeah, do you know anything about it?"

There was a slight pause before he said, "Why the hell are you asking about the Delphic at this ungodly hour?"

"They invited me to a cocktail party next Friday night. Someone just slipped the invitation under my door, then ran."

"Are you fucking kidding me? The Delphic invited *you* to a cocktail party?"

"Unless there's another Spenser Collins I don't know about."

"No offense, Spenser, but don't get your hopes up," he said. "This is probably some kind of prank someone's pulling on you. The Delphic isn't just a club, like any fraternity. It's the most secretive of Harvard's nine most exclusive clubs. They're called final clubs. The Delphic goes all the way back to the 1800s and has some of the world's most prominent men as members. An invitation to their cocktail party is like an invitation to kiss the papal ring."

"So, what you're really trying to say is that they would never give an invitation to a poor black kid from the South Side of Chicago."

"Spenser, you know I don't agree with that kinda shit, but that's how these secret societies operate. They haven't changed much over the last century and a half. Rich white men passing off the baton to the next generation, keeping their secrets shielded from the rest of the world. Yale has Skull and Bones, but here at Harvard we have the final clubs. It's no exaggeration when I tell you that some of the country's biggest secrets are buried in their old mansions."

"If I don't fit their image, then why did someone just slip this invite under my door?" I said.

"Because it's not real," Dalton said.

"What do you mean?"

"Guys joke like this all the time. This is the beginning of what's called punch season, which means the clubs are secretly nominating sophomores to enter a series of election rounds. Whoever survives the cuts over the two months gets elected into the club. You've heard of the hazing they do in fraternities. Well, this is a little like that, but it's a lot more formal with much bigger stakes."

"What makes you so sure my invitation is fake when you haven't even seen it?"

"Are you alone?"

"Percy's here, but he's out cold."

"Pull out the invite and tell me if you see torches anywhere."

I was sitting in the chair underneath the window, still eyeing the courtyard, hoping I might see who might've dropped off the envelope. The ambient light cracked the darkness of our common room. I held up the envelope.

"There are three torches on the back of the envelope," I said.

"What about the stationery?"

"There too."

"How many?"

"Three."

"What color?"

"Dark blue."

"Is the center torch lower or higher than the others?"

"Lower."

Dalton sighed loudly. "Now take the stationery, turn it over, and hold it up to a light," he said. "Tell me if you see anything when you look at the torches."

I followed Dalton's instructions, carefully removing the shade from one of Percy's expensive porcelain lamps that his grandmother had proudly given him from her winter house in Palm Beach. I held the invitation next to the naked bulb. "There's a thin circle with the initials JPM inside," I said. "But you can only see it under the light. When you move it away, the letters disappear."

"Jesus fuckin' Christ, Spense, it's the real deal!" Dalton yelled as if he were coming through the phone. "The Delphic really has punched you this season. I can't believe this is happening. Tell me the date of the party again."

It was rare to hear this level of excitement in Dalton's voice. Few things got him going, and they typically had to do with either women, food, or his father, whom he hated more than the Yankees.

"Next Friday at seven o'clock," I said. "It's at a place called Lily Field Mansion."

"Lily Field, of course," Dalton said. "It's the biggest one up there on mansion row, and it's owned by the Jacobs family, one of the richest in the country. Stanford Jacobs used to be the graduate president of the Delphic, so it makes sense that he's hosting the opening cocktail party."

Secret society, mansions, ultra-wealthy families, an invitation delivered under the cloak of darkness. It was all part of a foreign world that made little sense to me, the son of a single mother who answered phones at a small energy company.

"So, what the hell does all this mean?" I asked.

"That you're coming over here tomorrow for dinner, so we can figure out some sort of strategy," Dalton said. "This is all a long shot, but if things go well for you on Friday night, you might make it to the next round. I'm getting way ahead of myself—but one round at a time, and you might be the way we crack the Ancient Nine."

"The Ancient Nine?" I asked. "Is that another name for the clubs?"

"No, two different things," Dalton said. "The Ancient Nine are an ultra-secret society of nine members of the Delphic. A secret society within a secret society that not even the other Delphic members know much about. Most around here have never even heard of the Ancient Nine, but for those who have, some swear it exists, others think it's nothing more than another Harvard legend."

"What do you think?"

Dalton paused deliberately. "I'd bet everything I own that they exist. But no one can get them to break their code of silence. According to rumors, they are hiding not only one of Harvard's most valued treasures but also century-old secrets that involve some of the world's richest families."

2

✿

EVERYTHING ABOUT ELIOT House was so goddamn superior. It wasn't just one of the river houses; it was *the* river house, prominently located at one of Harvard's busiest intersections, the corner of Memorial Drive and John F. Kennedy Street. Eliot's exalted position in the Harvard housing system was cemented when the architects positioned it so that it's the first house seen when taking the eastern approach to campus over the famed Anderson Memorial Bridge. College brochures proudly displayed the splendid brick mansion with its shiny white tower and the sun lifting softly in the distance.

Like everything else at Harvard, Eliot had its own story. One of the seven original houses at the college, it was named in honor of Charles William Eliot, Harvard's twenty-first and longest-serving president, and modeled after the colleges of Oxford and Cambridge. This particular house had always been shrouded in an air of self-importance, mostly because those who run the house affairs have gone to great lengths to preserve its aura of privilege and exclusivity. According to an underground student survey—one that the administration would never confirm nor deny—Eliot housed the largest percentage of trust fund millionaires and by far the greatest number of prep school graduates. In effect, it had become an extension of Harvard's feeder boarding schools, places like Phillips Exeter, Andover, St. Paul's, and Deerfield Academy.

I flashed my ID to the security guard stationed in front of the main entrance of tall French doors and polished brass. The short foyer then opened into the majestic dining hall. It was one of those typical Harvard affairs, dark expensive wood, sweeping chandeliers, and bigger-than-life portraits of stony-faced white men, deep creases carved into their foreheads and a smattering of rose coloring the paleness of their gaunt cheeks. Every Harvard house had its own *dining hall,* not to be called a cafeteria. I had made that mistake once, in my public school ignorance, never to do it again.

I ate at Eliot only once every other week, as Dalton's guest, and as far as I was concerned, that was more than enough. Most of the residents looked like clones, with their heavily starched oxfords, suede bucks, and that unmistakable air of superiority. The women always seemed to be dressed for a garden tea party, their makeup perfectly applied and their hair coiffed and sprayed into helmets. The guys always looked like they were heading to a polo match on some country estate.

I spotted Dalton sitting alone at one of the tables nearest the window. He acknowledged me with a short wave and went back to reading something he was holding in his hand. I ducked into the serving line just inside the kitchen.

One of the good things about eating in Eliot House was that the line always moved faster. It was an open secret that thanks to a deep-pocketed alumnus, Eliot had been afforded a larger kitchen staff than the other dining halls and a more spacious kitchen. After grabbing my tray and silverware and joining the line, I instantly froze.

The most beautiful girl I had ever seen was standing a few feet away from me on the other side of the serving station. Tall, golden-honey complexion, eyes the color of warm caramel, she had tied her long, curly black hair underneath a crimson baseball cap required of all kitchen personnel. She robotically scooped mashed potatoes and dumped them onto plates as students walked by in assembly-line fashion. She was on autopilot, accepting the plates with her left hand, scooping and dumping the mashed potatoes with her right. She never made eye contact with the students, her blank facial expression that of someone who had a million other places they'd rather be.

I asked the first server for a helping of beef and gravy, and while I normally would have had french fries instead of mashed potatoes, I quickly decided there was no better time than the present for a healthy change in eating habits. I could feel my throat tighten as I neared her station, and I prayed like hell I wouldn't let out a squeaker.

"How's it going?" I managed.

She didn't respond. Instead, she held out her left hand for my plate and looked annoyed.

I held the plate far enough away that she couldn't reach it; then I stood on my toes and looked over the food hood and read her name badge—ASHLEY. Her skin was as smooth as a pebble weathered by the sand, her cheekbones high and angular. "How's everything going, Ashley?" I said.

"Do you want potatoes or not?" she answered, icing me with a stare that only made her more beautiful.

"Not until you answer my question," I said. I felt a soft nudge from the tray of an impatient girl waiting behind me.

"Then I guess you don't want potatoes," she huffed, and looked beyond me.

"And I guess you'll have to serve around me while I stand here," I shot back.

She blew out a long sigh. "Fine, you wanna know how it's going?" she said. "Just peachy. So great that when I get home tonight, I'll be doing cartwheels just thinking how much fun I had standing over these hot plates, serving a bunch of spoiled brats like you." She reached out and grabbed my plate, then dumped an absolutely perfect pile of potatoes. "Next."

I walked out of the kitchen, feeling that if I died that very second, I had at least seen the most beautiful thing God had ever created.

"Her name is Ashley Garrett," Dalton said as I settled into my chair. "Born and raised in Roxbury, parents are divorced, and she's already spoken for."

"Who hit the jackpot?"

"Some guy from Somerville who fixes roofs for a living."

I wasn't surprised that Dalton already had the inside scoop. I forgot to mention that not only was Dalton filthy rich, but he was also ruggedly handsome with the charm to match and had a fan club of coeds that even a rock star would envy. He had a special appreciation of the opposite sex, especially women of color, any kind of color—black, Latin American, South American—so long as they had a drop of ethnicity swirling in their blood. I think a lot of their appeal for him had to do with his eternal rebellion against his domineering, magisterial father, whom he derisively called "the Emperor." Conversely, he despised the blond, blue-eyed WASP types his parents were always arranging for him to meet at parties and other society affairs he was forced to attend on weekends. At the tender age of fourteen, Dalton had unofficially declared war on not only his parents, but also the pretense and elitism of their country-club circuit of friends, and his fellow scions anointed to inherit the world.

"She's amazing," I said. "But not the friendliest girl I've ever met."

"How friendly would you be, standing over those hot lamps all night and serving food to a bunch of rich kids?" Dalton said.

"You have a point."

"But, man, is she gorgeous." He whistled. "I'd crawl on my knees backwards all the way down Mem Drive to the Commons if I could get her out on a date."

"I'd do the same, but on broken glass," I said.

Dalton took a long pull on his iced tea. He had four small glasses sitting on his tray. He wiped his hands, folded the letter he had been reading, and stuffed it back into the envelope.

"What was that?" I asked.

"The Emperor's continuing punishment."

"He wrote you a letter?"

"Are you kidding me? He's never even signed his own name to one of my birthday cards. It's from the trust lawyers. I applied for an emergency loan, but they just flat-out denied me. No extra money for another two years, my twenty-first birthday. Their final opinion was that my being cut off from that heartless bastard doesn't constitute an emergency. Then they had the nerve to say that there are plenty of student jobs that would help me cover my incidental expenses. Assholes. Easy for them to say, when managing the Winthrop money for the last hundred years has made all of them millionaires several times over."

"I've got a hundred and fifty in the bank," I said. "Not much, but if things get tough, what's mine is yours."

"Thanks, Spense, but I can't do that," Dalton said. "That's exactly what the Emperor wants me to do, borrow and beg and be humiliated. Not a chance I'll give him the satisfaction. Anyway, enough about my shitty affairs. Do you have the invite?"

I reached into my jacket and handed over the small envelope. He inspected it carefully, first the envelope, then the stationery, turning it around and holding it up to the light. I felt like someone who had taken a family heirloom to the jeweler to get it appraised.

"It's the real deal, Spense," he finally said, sliding the envelope back to me across the table. "Do you know anything at all about the final clubs?"

"Not till you mentioned them last night."

"Okay, so you're a virgin," he said. "Makes our job a little tougher, but we'll get it done. He drained another glass of iced tea and pushed his tray to the side. "First some important background. As you now know, there are nine Harvard final clubs—the Porcellian, Owl, AD, Fly, Delphic, Fox, Spee, Phoenix, and DU. Each one has a gigantic old mansion here in Cambridge that they use as a clubhouse. They are exclusive, members-only, all-male clubs that date all the way back to the 1700s. Back then, Harvard had three major types of clubs arranged in a pyramid hierarchy. The Dickey was a secret society that evolved from something called the Institute of 1770 and the Hasty Pudding Club. The Dickey was at the bottom of the social ladder."

"Is that the same Hasty Pudding that gives out the awards every year to famous actors?" I asked.

"Exactly. It started out as a secret society, but then it became a theatrical club. About forty years ago, they started awarding a Man and Woman of the Year Award, giving the honorees a parade down Mass Ave into the center of Harvard Square. It's the parade with all the male members of the Pudding wearing drag. Anyway, above the Dickey were what they called waiting clubs.

Students joined these, hoping to one day reach the top of the pyramid—the final clubs.

"The Porcellian, or the Pork, was the first and only final club for several years. Only students from the wealthiest families with the most important pedigree were even considered for the Pork. They held private dinners and outings and played in the most expensive private building in Cambridge. But what set them most apart was how tightly they kept their secrets. Except for the staff, no one including the president of the university could step foot in their mansion. Their rituals and traditions became the stuff of legend. Then, as the years passed, other final clubs were slowly established from some of the old fraternities that were on campus."

"And these clubs have never been coed?" I asked.

"Never. And that's not gonna change. They've stood up to every kind of pressure imaginable—lawsuits, protests, sanctions—and nothing has come close to working. It's only made them stronger. The Princeton eating clubs were forced to open their doors to women, and so were some of the clubs at Yale, but the final clubs remain alone, the oldest, most elite all-male college social clubs in the country."

"So how do you become a member?" I asked.

"In the past, it was all about money and status," Dalton said. "You needed to come from the right prep school, and your parents had to live in one of the big eastern cities like Boston, New York, or Philadelphia. Your family had to do all the society shit, travel to Florida in the winter, then north to Cape Cod or Europe in the summer. The who's who of Harvard were members of these clubs, from President Teddy Roosevelt, who was a member of the Pork, to President Kennedy, who joined the Spee. Teddy's cousin, Franklin Roosevelt, couldn't get into the Pork, so he settled on the Fly Club."

"If you're not a member, can you still go inside?" I asked.

"Definitely not. Male Harvard students who aren't members must enter through the back door. They must stay in the billiards and TV rooms in the basement. They're never allowed inside the main rooms of the clubhouse."

"What about women?"

"It depends on the club. Some let them in, but they're allowed only on certain floors. Some clubs even have these elaborate schedules—what doors women can enter on certain days, sometimes only through the back door, other times through the kitchen. It's crazy."

I looked at the three torches on the envelope, wondering why one of these clubs would invite me to a cocktail party when I seemed to be the opposite of everything they represented. No money, no lineage, and a public school education, I was exactly the type of student they wanted to keep out. The more I thought about it, the less sense it made, but the idea that someone thought I was worthy enough to be part of this privileged world excited me.

"So, what's this cocktail party about?" I asked.

"It's the official kickoff event for what's called the punch season, which lasts from now until the end of November. Just like fraternities have a rush, the clubs have what they call a punch. You can only be punched as a sophomore or junior, but most of the punchees are sophomores. Each club secretly selects about a hundred students to enter their punch. Years ago, it was open only to prep school kids and legacies, but now very few blacks and Jews are being invited. The punch is made up of a series of rounds. Each round has a major event, like a dinner, lunch, or outing. After each round, the membership holds a long meeting in the clubhouse to decide whom to cut from the list and who will continue in the punch. The initial cocktail party is usually held at a graduate member's house or at some fancy hall they rent for the night."

"What's so special about the Delphic?" I asked.

Dalton's eyes suddenly lit up. "The club of secrets," he said. "The stories and rumors are endless. Generations of Harvard students have tried breaking into their fortress of a clubhouse, but no one has ever succeeded."

"If the club is so secretive, how do you know their stories?" I asked.

Dalton leaned across the table. "Because my great-uncle Randolph is a torch man," he whispered. "I haven't seen him in several months. He's holed up in his estate down in New York, dying from some kind of respiratory disease. But when I was a teenager and we were at family events, he'd pull me into his study and tell me these great stories about the Gas House, most of which I was too young to even understand or remember, but he liked telling them to me."

"Why the Gas House?"

"That's what the old-timers call the Delphic. Their mansion was one of the first buildings in Cambridge to have electric lights. Uncle Randolph always wanted me to be a Delphic man and not a Porker like the Emperor. He always said my temperament was much better suited for the Delphic. Of course, the Emperor got me punched by the Pork, hoping I would follow in his footsteps. I flat-out refused to participate in any of the clubs. He was mad as hell. Practically had a seizure. The look on his face and the way his head shook—the sweetest revenge ever. But I'm excited that you got punched. The Delphic is *the* club. It's the richest club by far and has one of the biggest clubhouses. They own that enormous old pile with the Carolina blue door over on Linden Street. You've probably passed it a thousand times heading back and forth to class and didn't even know what it was. It has four big columns in front and a brass nine in the middle of the front door."

I vaguely recalled the building. There weren't many on Linden, since it was such a short street. There were Adams House and Claverly Hall and the Bureau of Study Counsel farther up the street. I remembered this old brick mansion I never paid much attention, because I thought it was just another one of Harvard's administration buildings. Occasionally I would notice a couple of guys quietly going in and out, but there wasn't much else to it.

"What's it like inside?" I asked.

"I've never been, but it's supposed to be complete luxury. No expense spared. They have a collection of cockfight paintings in their first-floor reading room worth several million dollars. Their antique furniture was imported from some English castle destroyed in World War II, and their Persian rugs once decorated palaces as far away as Macedonia. You don't hear so much about the Delphic, because they're very private."

"Do you know what the letters *JPM* inside the circle mean?" I asked.

Dalton picked up his last glass of iced tea and drained it in one tilt. "That's J. P. Morgan Jr. of the famous Morgan banking family," he said. "One of the original members and founders of the Gas. The Pork wouldn't let him in, so he took out his checkbook, paid for the mansion, then started his own club. After Morgan came the Astors and Rockefellers and other big names. Getting into the Delphic became so impossible that by the time the Emperor was a student, some guy who lived down the hall from him committed suicide when he didn't get elected."

My head was spinning as I tried to process all that Dalton was telling me. Secret societies, millionaires, mansions, and private rituals—it was the stuff of movies. Yet of all people, I had arrived at this intersection, a poor kid from the wrong side of a midwestern city, now holding an invitation to peek into this clandestine world.

"I know it's a lot to take in at once," Dalton said. "But there's something else I must tell you. It's the real reason why I'm so excited you got the invitation."

Dalton paused and looked around as if others might be listening, though by now only a handful of people were left in the dining hall. He pushed his tray aside and leaned toward me.

"The Delphic Club stole what people have called Harvard's Holy Grail," he said. "No one's sure exactly what it is, but in the early seventies, at least ten students were arrested trying to break into the club to find it. None of them made it past the first floor, but when they were questioned by police, they all said they were looking for the lost treasure."

"What kind of treasure?" I asked.

"Some think it's a rare printing of Shakespeare's First Folio," Dalton said. "Others think it's the jewel-encrusted tiara worn by Pope Clement V during his coronation in 1305. I've even heard that it's a rare Vermeer painting that once hung in the president's office but was stolen in the early 1700s. Whatever it is or was, no one's talking. But lots of people are convinced it's hidden somewhere in that mansion."

"Who do they think stole it?"

"There are nine special graduate members who supposedly have guarded the grail with their lives. But to this day, no one has been able to prove that they exist. They're called the Ancient Nine. Some people have said they've seen an old man who occasionally leaves the clubhouse late at night."

"What does the old man do?" I asked.

Dalton shrugged his shoulders. "Nobody knows except the guys inside, but people believe he lives somewhere in the mansion and protects their secrets."

"Did you ever ask your uncle Randolph about him?"

"Of course I did. Many times."

"And what did he say?"

"That it's all a bunch of crazy stories made up by kids with big imaginations and too much time on their hands."

"Do you believe him?"

"Not one bit."

"Why not? You believe everything else he told you."

"Because I think Uncle Randolph is a member of the Ancient Nine. That's something he would never tell even me."

3

PRECISELY AS THE Russian church bells began to chime nine o'clock in the Lowell House Belfry, the heavy lock of the polished mahogany door slid back. By the time I turned the knob and had the door open, Adele Kilcourse, the obsessively efficient Lowell House librarian, was already seated behind her maze of connected desks. She watched me with little enthusiasm as I made my way across the enormous Persian rug donated by a former Saudi ambassador who had once lived in the worst room in Lowell House, right next to the dining hall, facing Mill Street. She sat there authoritatively with her stiff spine, square shoulders, and a shock of bright orange hair piled haphazardly atop her head.

"Good morning, Mr. Collins," Ms. Kilcourse said. She never called us by our first names. "What brings you into the library so early in the morning?"

"A little research," I said. "Figured things would be quiet around here this time of the morning."

She responded with a suspicious lift of her eyebrows. Her loose skin was covered with tiny moles except for one big pedunculated growth underneath the right side of her chin that seemed to be growing by the week.

"I need to find out more about Harvard's history," I said, purposely resting my backpack on her meticulous desk and watching the back of her jaw clench.

"Harvard history?" she said, almost as if I had offended her. "That's a lot of ground to cover. Three hundred and fifty years. We have plenty of resources, but without a more directed search, you'll have your hands plenty full. Can you be a little more specific about what you're looking for?"

"I'd like to find out about the final clubs," I said.

Ms. Kilcourse wrinkled her brow. "Is this a serious request?" she said.

"Very."

"And this is related to your course work?"

"Does it have to be?"

"Not at all," she said. "But I'm afraid you have your work cut out for you."

"Why do you say that?"

"Because dealings of the final clubs have never been a matter of public record."

"But after all these years, there must be something written about them."

"There is, but very little that's accessible and nothing with much depth."

"Is there anything here?"

"We have a couple of old texts that might be of some help," she said, pushing back from her desk. "They're in the reading room."

I followed her to a small rectangular room lined with floor-to-ceiling bookcases and a long rectangular table surrounded by deep cushioned chairs. She pulled the rolling ladder along its track, then climbed to its highest point and went directly to a thin, small book with a faded black jacket. She then descended a couple of rungs and reached toward a lower shelf, pulling out a thick book with a bland manila cover that had been wrapped in thick plastic.

"Happy hunting," she said, handing me the books. "This second book really is just a manuscript. It was never published. Professor Waldmeier died before he was able to submit it to publishers. But don't get your hopes up. You're certainly not the first who's been on this hunt. The others quickly learned that there's not much here."

After she left, I spread my notebook and the two books across the table. I decided to start with the big book, *Harvard: Making of the World's Premier Institution.* I figured more pages likely meant more material on the clubs. I combed through the table of contents, but didn't find any mention of the clubs. I searched through the index and still didn't see anything listed. So, I opened my notebook to the names of the nine clubs that Dalton had given me. I checked each one against the index entries, and it wasn't until I reached the last name on the list when I got my first hit. The article originally had been written in *The Cambridge Tribune* on July 26, 1902.

THE PORCELLIAN CLUB
A Word About This Famous and Exclusive Harvard Organization

The club of Porcellians is hardly known except by name ever in Cambridge itself, says the Sunday Post. Although it calls itself "of Harvard University," no non-member is permitted to enter its sacred and secret precincts except as an invited guest, "personally conducted" by a member for a very brief visit.

So exclusive is this aristocratic club of millionaires that in some years three men only have been added to it.

During the period that the clubmen are college undergraduates, they are called "immediate" members, and bear all the expense of the considerable cost of running the club.

Since all the surroundings are of the greatest luxury and lavish outlay of money is made in frequent repairs, the addition of new furniture and the wages of servants, who during term time provide the "dollar dinner" to such as subscribe from day to day for this fare, it will be seen that the limited membership must provide funds liberally.

This fact, in connection with the generally accepted statement that the initiation fee is $1,000, and the periodical dues in sums proportionate to an initiation fee of such magnitude, easily leads to the conclusion, which is not gainsaid, that the Porcellian club comprises only the very innermost circle of scions of family and wealth, and that they are the exclusive faction of such part of the "400" as Harvard holds, and form its very cream.

After graduating from college the Porcellians are known as "associate members." but continue actively to partake of the club functions and privileges, although perhaps not bearing any share in the settling of the current expenses.

The handsome building on Massachusetts avenue, just opposite the Harvard Yard, is their clubhouse, and all except the ground floor is occupied for club purposes. The Porcellian library of 15,000 volumes is one of the most symmetrical collections of miscellaneous books that could be comprised in that number of books, and the best of it is that a large proportion of them are the productions of the brains and pens of its own members.

The earlier and more valuable books are mainly the first editions of our own American authors and the first publications in this country of Scott, Thackeray, and Dickens, and others. Modern books are fully represented.

In the rear of the clubhouse is a spacious court, where "squash" engages a good deal of the leisure of the athletically inclined members, and the banquet room, which occupies the entire top floor of the building, is as luxuriously appointed as one could wish. The fittings are in oak, with the bare rafters showing, as in old English manors.

The fireplace is large enough to hold Yule logs, and its woodwork and the movable furniture are of mahogany, with the boar's head, and the letters "P. C." carved upon them, each chair here and about the various rooms being of the same pattern and the gifts of individual members.

So the "Porcellian Club of Harvard University" is its present name, although at its foundation the young sprigs of American aristocracy forming the club called themselves the "little pigs," of which "Porcellian" is only the adjective equivalent in the dignified Latin as more appropriate to a club attached to a university.

But the pig idea persists, and everything in the nature of bric-a-brac, paintings, bronzes, china, and such like is sedulously sought out and finds a final resting place in the club rooms, and the collection is large and varied. There is a glass cabinet with some hundreds of effigies of pretty pigs, big and little in all conceivable materials in which casts and sculptures are made. There is even a capacious punch bowl in the similitude of a boar's head, and the walls are embellished with the mounted heads of the monarchs of the Black Forest.

The carvings on the keystones of the arches of the dull building and on the gate contributed by them to the new fence also bear the typical pig, and their present book plate is in the style of the coat of arms of Great Britain except instead of a lion and unicorn it bears two wild boars "rampant." The club motto is "Dum vivimus, vivimus."

A portion of its fame is that the president of the United States, "Colonel" Theodore Roosevelt, is a member, and was once the librarian of the club.

The club was founded in 1792 by the Rev. Joseph McKean, of the class of 1794, and while the impression which obtains among the few who have been privileged only to a superficial knowledge of it that it was a place of too convivial habits, others of the reverend clergy besides its founder, have been members, with no qualms of conscience as an aftermath.

In 1812, the order of the Knights of the Square Table was founded, and the two—the Porcellian club and the "Knights"—were distinct organizations until 1831, when the latter was merged with the former.

I searched through the rest of the book, looking for more references to the Porcellian or any of the other clubs, and found one more small mention.

While rules insisted that non-members were not allowed into the clubhouse, there had been rare exceptions. Winston Churchill and Dwight Eisenhower were granted the courtesy, but the honor was on a one-time-only basis, and when President Eisenhower asked if he could come back a second time he was refused. The list of known Porcellian members while difficult to obtain, includes celebrated architect H. H. Richardson, Civil War hero Robert Gould Shaw (leader of the black 54th Regiment), Supreme Court Justice Oliver Wendell Holmes, President Theodore Roosevelt (his younger cousin FDR was rejected), and internationally acclaimed writer George Plimpton.

It's been widely believed that the Porcellian began when an under-graduate, Joseph McKean, Class of 1794, served a group of friends a dinner of roast pig. Its original name was the Pig Club, but this was soon changed to the more genteel, Latin-derived Porcellian.

The gate located at the entrance to the Yard between Wadsworth House and Boylston Hall was completed in 1901 and is called the McKean Gate. The money to build it was donated by the Porcellian Club to honor its founder, who later served (1808–1818) as the Boylston Professor of Rhetoric and Oratory at the college.

There was no other mention of the other clubs, so I turned my attention to the smaller book. It was titled *Memoirs of My Harvard Years.* I opened the jacket and discovered the name of the author, K. Christolph. There was no table of contents or index, just seven small chapters loosely organized in no apparent order.

"What are you looking for?" a voice said, interrupting my thoughts.

I practically jumped out of my seat. I looked up into the sallow face of Gilbert Henning. He stood at the other side of the table, a beanstalk of a man who in his own way had become a Harvard legend. At fifteen years and one month, Gil had once been the youngest student accepted into Harvard. He was the son of Swedish immigrants—his father was a mathematics professor and his mother a prima ballerina. Gil had been a star in the Harvard community, a physics genius who had worked out complicated new proofs to old theorems that had mystified some of the greatest physics minds in the world. Then one afternoon in broad daylight, Gil ran down Mass Ave and into the Square completely naked. Many had thought it was a prank, but when the university police finally subdued him, Gil insisted in fluent Russian, his sixth language, that the spies were coming to get him, and the world was coming to an end. And so ended the illustrious academic career of one of Harvard's most precocious minds, now the assistant in the Lowell House Library.

"I'm doing some research on the final clubs," I said.

"And how is it going?" Gil asked in his typically monotone voice.

"Not great. I've just looked at two books, and together they barely had one page worth of information."

"May I ask how you found the books?" Gil asked.

"Ms. Kilcourse found them for me."

Gil nodded his head and stared blankly at me. He did this often. It was almost as if he were sleeping with his eyes open. But typically, it meant he had something to say and was just waiting to be prompted. Gil might've become withered and withdrawn after his nervous breakdown, but his mind was still as strong and robust as ever, and his photographic memory completely intact.

"Do you know where else I can find information about the clubs, Gil?" I asked.

He looked over his shoulder nervously and started biting the remnants of his thumbnail.

"Gil, it would really help if you tell me if there's more information on these clubs," I said. "This is very important."

He nodded his head slowly. "There were quite a few books written in the 1930s that included several chapters about them," he whispered. "One was an exposé and it even listed the names of some of the members and the rituals they performed inside the clubs."

This was exactly what I was looking for. "Where are they?" I asked.

Gil looked over his shoulder again, then stepped closer to me. "Gone," he whispered with widened eyes.

"What do you mean, 'gone'? As in they're checked out?"

Gil shook his head. "Every book that mentioned the final clubs was stolen from the entire campus library system fifty years ago. No one knows who took them, but I heard a professor say that some of the members from the different clubs got together and decided to purge the system of any information related to their existence. The only two books that remained were the two you have now, and that's because the night they came to steal them, they were sitting under lock and key in Master Tressob's personal residence. We didn't come into possession of them until after he died in 1954. He left them to the university in his will.

4

BY THE TIME I had made it back to Lowell from basketball practice, there were only fifteen minutes left of dinner service. For all my efforts—racing over the river and jumping down a flight of courtyard steps—I was rewarded with a Salisbury steak that looked like a cardboard box left out in the rain. I wrestled with it for a few minutes, sawed off and swallowed a couple of bites to dull the sharpness of my hunger, then hurried to my room to take a shower. Tonight was the cocktail party at the Lily Field Mansion, and the knot in my stomach was tightening by the hour.

I was standing half naked, getting dressed in front of the mirror when the phone rang. It was Dalton.

"How's it going?" he asked.

"I'm getting dressed."

"Good, so everything's on schedule. I was worried your asshole of a coach might keep you guys longer. Remember, don't get there too early. Fashionably late has real meaning in these situations. Fifteen, twenty minutes tops. And just play it cool when you get there. There will be enough other guys kissing the members' asses. Showing that you're too eager in this situation can be the kiss of death."

"Don't worry, I have it all worked out," I said. "By the time I get dressed and walk up there, I'll be fifteen minutes late. And I think you know me well enough to know that there's a lot I'd be willing to do, but kissing ass is definitely not one of them."

"That's why you're my man, Spense," Dalton said. "But I also called about something else that could be really important. I think I can get proof that Uncle Randolph is a member of the Ancient Nine."

I had my shirt buttoned and was taking a second go at knotting my tie. The first one was too small. "What kind of proof?" I asked.

"I saw something in his bedroom when I was a kid. One afternoon, I was hiding in his closet and I found this small wooden box. I was excited because it was a really shiny box, and I thought it might contain something like cigars, which I thought were the coolest. I loved how they smelled and watching Uncle Randolph and his buddies smoke them. His initials had been carved underneath this strange design, which I now realize were torches. So, I opened the box and found this narrow strip of cloth about eight inches long. It had all these diamonds spelling out some strange words I couldn't even pronounce. I thought I'd discovered some lost treasure, so I brought it to Aunt Theodora. But instead of thanking me, she got really upset and told me that I must never tell anyone, not even my parents, what I had found. She made me swear my life on it."

"Swear your life on it?" I said. "That's a little dramatic over some diamonds, don't you think?"

"It wasn't just that," Dalton said. "She had this look of fear in her eyes I had never seen before. I was scared that I had done something wrong and something bad was gonna happen. I cried my eyes out. I'd blocked it out of my mind all these years until late last night when I was reading a chapter on ancient Rome in one of my European history books. I recognized the same words that had been spelled out in diamonds in Uncle Randolph's box were also carved at the base of a sculpture in the Forum. *Serva Sodalitatem.*"

"What does it mean?" I asked.

"It's Latin for 'protect the brotherhood,'" Dalton said.

"There are all kinds of brotherhoods," I said. "There's no proof it had anything to do with the Ancient Nine."

"It wasn't just words alone," Dalton said. "They were flanked by two nines that had also been embroidered in diamonds. Those nines had to mean something."

"So, you're thinking your aunt knew about your uncle's secret and didn't want you to get in trouble by exposing it?"

"It would explain why she was so serious about it all. And I have a gut feeling that tonight you'll be meeting another member of the Ancient Nine."

"What makes you say that?"

"I did some digging around earlier today. Stanford Jacobs and Uncle Randolph are not only very good friends, but Uncle Randolph was also the one who punched Jacobs for the Delphic. I spoke to Muriel, my uncle's chief housekeeper. She said Jacobs has been down to Uncle Randolph's estate a lot over the years. She said they're really close. So, if you get a chance to spend any time alone with Jacobs tonight, you should try to impress him. He has a lot more power than the other graduate members. His endorsement could go a long way in getting you elected into the club."

"How am I gonna impress some seventy-something-year-old gazillionaire?" I said. "All these guys talk about is stuff like the opera, the stock market, traveling to foreign countries, things I don't know anything about."

"Don't worry," Dalton said. "Here's what you do. Introduce yourself, then try to get him alone for a few seconds. Pop him right away with a question about his Chinese art."

"Chinese art?" I laughed. "Have you lost your mind? I don't know a damn thing about Chinese art."

"You don't need to," Dalton said. "Just be conversational. You get the convo going, then let him take it from there. I found out that Jacobs has one of the biggest private collections of Chinese artifacts in the world. If he seems friendly enough, just ask him to show you a few pieces. I've been around these types all my life. They don't love just accumulating wealth, they like to show it. Believe me, get him thinking you're interested in his art, and you'll score easy bonus points."

I had been second-guessing my decision to attend the party all day. It was bad enough I had to figure out how to impress a bunch of preppies who already thought the rest of the world was beneath them. Now Dalton was telling me to bullshit some guy older than my grandfather and richer than God about Chinese art, something I knew almost nothing about. "I hope I don't make a fool of myself tonight," I said. "I'm so far outta my league, it's laughable. But I can't laugh, because I'm too damn nervous."

"You'll be fine," Dalton assured me. "You're a natural charmer. Getting past this first round will be a big test, but I know you can do it. Remember, someone punched you for a reason, so we know there's at least one person on the inside who likes you. If you don't believe in yourself, then no one will."

I hung up the phone and threw on my nicest pair of slacks, a white shirt, and the good-luck tie I had worn to every basketball game when I was in high school. We almost went undefeated with that tie during my senior year, losing only in the state semifinals. I thought the tie would work some magic up in Cambridge, but we had more Crimson losses last year than I had in my entire high school career.

I was brushing my hair when I heard Percy talking to a woman. I walked into the common room and grabbed my only blazer, one handed down from an older kid in my church. I looked into Percy's room and knocked on his door. "I'm heading out to dinner," I said, fishing for an introduction to the girl sitting on his bed. She had short blond hair cut just beneath her ears, big sad eyes, and bright red lipstick.

"Have fun," Percy said, not even looking up from his book. He was nervously working his pinky ring.

"I'll be home late."

"Okay. I'll probably still be up. I have a big paper due tomorrow."

I took one last look at the girl, who gave me a smile that made me think she'd be very adept at loosening up old Percy. I gave her a quick nod, then stuffed the invitation into my coat and scrambled out the door.

The cool breeze sweeping down Mt. Auburn Street felt good. Fall, my favorite time of year in Cambridge, was finally settling in as the leaves turned spectacular shades of red and yellow in their last gasp of life, the resilient ivy strangling the old brick façades. The colorful foliage made the historic campus appear even older than it was. T-shirts and tank tops gave way to chunky wool sweaters and lined jackets. The convertible sports cars that zipped down the narrow Cambridge streets would soon be replaced by Range Rovers and other SUVs better equipped to handle winter snow. The official start of football season wasn't far away, which meant thousands of alumni would be returning to campus for long afternoons of drunken tailgating outside our venerated concrete stadium, the centerpiece of Soldiers Field. Once the game was over, they'd walk back across the river, visiting their old campus haunts, comparing notes on what had changed and what had stayed the same. I sometimes wondered if this would be how I also returned to campus, driving a long, fancy Mercedes with an argyle sweater knotted perfectly around my neck.

I quickly walked through the frenzied activity of Brattle Square, the rotary adjacent to its more famous neighbor, Harvard Square.

I found myself entering a quiet street of colossal houses peering over sleepy treetops, casting long shadows down the dark road. This was not the Cambridge I knew. These single-family homes were expansive and stately compared to the small, crammed multifamily homes in the busier parts of town. Tall maples and wrought-iron fences ensured their privacy. European cars, their back windows plastered with college and boarding school stickers, rested on long gravel driveways.

A quarter of a mile down the street, I saw a gigantic yellow mansion. It was on the right side of the road, sitting back some thirty yards. The closer I got, the larger it loomed. The sign on the gate proclaimed it to be the former residence of the acclaimed poet Henry Wadsworth Longfellow, as well as the temporary home of George Washington at the start of the Revolutionary War. Now a historic landmark, 105 Brattle Street was open to the public for tours. That meant Lily Field Mansion was two houses down on the left. I looked in its direction. Light sprayed into the darkness from the top floor's windows. A wall of trees partially obstructed my view of the house, but it had a massive roofline. I felt as if my heart were climbing into my throat as I neared the property. Between the neatly trimmed rows of hedges shielding the front yard, I could see spotlights lining the lawn and casting their dim glow on the gray sandstone mansion. A black wrought-iron gate with gold fleur-de-lis spears weaved its way along the perimeter, and at the top of the driveway, two large gleaming marble statues protected the auspicious entrance. More of the house became visible, and I noticed hulking white columns and as many as seven chimneys. A colossal nude sculpture with a dense circle of lilies at its base stood in the middle of a cascading fountain.

Cars pulled into the driveway. Groups of three and four, all wearing navy blazers with shiny gold buttons and ties, piling out of BMWs and Volvos before walking up to the front doors. I waited. I rarely felt self-conscious about what I did or didn't have, but it wasn't lost on me that my competitors for a coveted membership were arriving in expensive foreign cars while I arrived in a pair of sturdy five-year-old leather Florsheims that had been resoled four times and polished so much, the white stitching had turned black. I purposely waited for the others to disappear down the long driveway before I turned onto the property. I straightened my tie, buttoned my coat, and took a deep breath. Dalton's reminders played in my head. *Stay away from conversations about politics, religion, or money. Don't be a wiseass. Do more listening than talking. Don't make a fool of yourself by drinking too much. Pop him a question about Chinese art and just get him talking.*

I rang the doorbell adjacent to the massive double doors and cleared my throat. Within seconds, I was staring at a tall, elderly man balancing black horn-rimmed glasses on his arched nose, his black velvet coat and satin-striped trousers perfectly matching the house's splendor. His pair of cotton-white gloves an appropriate accessory to his thinning but meticulously groomed hair.

"Good evening," he said. "May I help you?" His eyebrows slid up to the top of his forehead. He looked American enough, but his accent was distinctly British.

"I'm here for the cocktail party," I said, pulling the invitation out of my pocket and handing it to him.

My stomach knotted as he paused, looked me over, then took the invitation. After a thorough inspection, he handed it back to me, stepped aside, and swung his arm in a wide arc.

"Please, do enter, Mr. Collins, and welcome to Lily Field," he said. "The party has already commenced in the west salon."

5

❧

I TILTED MY head back and took in the cathedral ceiling of the marble-and-stone foyer. An uncanny replica of Michelangelo's Sistine Chapel had been painted across the small tiles. An exceptionally wide staircase wound its way up to a long mezzanine. An immense crystal chandelier hung from the domed ceiling on a cable heavy and long enough to anchor a battleship.

"Your coat, sir," the butler said, head bowed and arm extended. I handed him my overcoat already folded, hoping it would prevent him from seeing the tear in its lining. I had perfected this maneuver over the past year and had yet to be exposed.

"You may proceed in that direction," he said, pointing down the long corridor to a faintly lit room barely visible from where we stood. "Mr. Jacobs has already convened the party."

I ventured down the long hallway, passing gigantic paintings set in baroque gold wooden frames. My incredibly modest knowledge of art had been only slightly boosted by a recent fine arts course I took on the Italian masters, but I knew enough to realize that these pieces were worth a great deal of money and could just as easily have been hung with great fanfare on the walls of the Gardner Museum. According to the metal title plates on the gilded frames, John Singer Sargent had painted all but one of the portraits. I counted ten portraits inscribed with the name Jacobs, mostly sober-looking bald men, gaunt in the cheek, strong in the jaw. Only two women interrupted the line of men, their silver hair austerely coiffed and set back from their oblong faces. They were identically dressed in drab, lace-collared dresses and large double-stranded pearls.

I worked my way down the hallway, and once the butler had disappeared from the other end of the foyer, I sneaked glances through the open doors. Each room was bigger than the last, with grand pianos and their shiny ivory keys, antique furniture, yet more paintings, and what seemed like miles of bookcases. Farther down the hall, marble busts of deceased family members were tucked away in lighted glass wall niches. Most dated from the late 1700s to the early 1900s and bore either the name Jacobs or Billington. The potted plants adorning the hallway were more like trees. How could just *one* family actually live in a house this big?

I finally neared the end of the hall. Billowing clouds of smoke blurred the faces and details of the room's interior. I could make out a receiving line of four guys standing just inside the entrance. They were uniformed in identical navy blue blazers, khaki pants, and loafers. They were shaking hands and making introductions as I entered. They all turned in my direction.

"You must be Spenser Collins," the first guy in line said, smiling as he offered his hand. He was the shortest of the four, with foppish sandy-brown hair and a pair of small oval glasses that sat up high on his long nose. His perfectly knotted bow tie distinguished him from the others, who had opted for long neckties. The same three torches that were printed on the club letterhead adorned all their ties.

We pumped hands firmly.

"I'm Graydon Brimmer, president of the Delphic Club," he said.

"Nice to meet you," I said.

He then pointed to the other three in order. "This is our vice president David Fossi, treasurer Carlyle Emmerson, and secretary Oscar LaValle. Gentlemen, this is Spenser Collins, class of '91, shooting guard from De La Salle Institute in Chicago, National Merit Scholarship Award winner, and premed."

Did he also know my birth date and social security number?

I shook hands with them in order. "It's nice to meet you all," I said. "Thanks a lot for inviting me."

"Glad you could make it," Fossi said. He was the tallest of the four, with wavy dark hair, sturdy broad shoulders, and a narrow waist. His physical build, combined with the hard calluses in his palms, left no doubt that he rowed crew.

"How's the team gonna do this year?" he asked.

"Hopefully better than last year," I said. "We have a freshman in from Long Island, New York, who's really good. He's about six-seven, two-forty. He should be a big help in the paint."

"All you need now is a new coach," Fossi said. "My grandmother could do a better job than what Beasley's done the last five years. Look at all the talent he's recruited, and still no trophy. Any other school would've fired his ass a long time ago."

"Our boosters feel the same way," I said. "But the AD keeps extending his contract. It's a mystery to all of us."

"Well, give 'em hell anyway," Brimmer said, tapping my shoulder. "Plenty of teams have been able to rise above their pathetic coaches."

"On your way in, make sure you sign the register over there," LaValle said, pointing to a large leather book on a wide rolltop desk that looked as if it had been preserved from the turn of the century.

"The full bar is all the way in the back, and the servants are walking around with hors d'oeuvres and champagne," Emmerson said. "Mr. Jacobs is our host for the evening. He's one of our grad members. Make sure you get a chance to meet him before the night's over."

"Forget about basketball and have some fun tonight," Brimmer said. "There should be a really good group of guys here."

"I'll do that," I said, heading to the guest book. I quickly perused the list of signatures in hopes of recognizing some of the names. Half of them were illegible, but of those I could read, none were familiar. I scribbled my name on an open line, then took a deep breath and journeyed into the smoky room.

On my first reconnaissance, I counted about fifty guys clustered in groups of two or three. The room was so enormous, it could easily have fit a couple hundred more. I worked my way around the perimeter, searching for a familiar face or inviting smile. After coming up empty, I looked to my watch for consolation. It was only twenty past seven, which meant there was still plenty of time for a familiar person to arrive.

I stood in a corner, where I could take in the elaborate room. The expansive canvas paintings in their ornate frames and the lustrous marble sculptures gave the room a museum-like feel. Massive blue silk curtains trimmed tall French doors that opened onto a patio whose stairs curved down to a long pool covered for the winter. I could see the gesturing silhouettes of two men with cigarettes in their hands, carried away in conversation.

To my right, standing next to the stone-and-brick fireplace, a couple of guys puffed long black cigars. This was the first time I had seen anyone my age smoke a cigar. In my neighborhood, teenagers smoked cigarettes and marijuana while old men chomped on cigars. But I already knew that most of what I was about to experience that night belonged to a world very different from mine. A ten-piece jazz band in starched tuxedos had assembled in the far corner of the room, their soft music mixing with the aimless chatter. Uniformed staff carried oblong silver platters crowded with crystal flutes of sparkling champagne. It all reminded me of the swinging parties of the twenties I had read about in Fitzgerald's *The Great Gatsby*. The only thing missing was women in fancy hats, elbow-length gloves, and slender cigarettes burning two-inch-long ashes.

I suddenly felt alone and out of place. What was I doing here, so far away from southwest Chicago, where the sound of gunshots was more common than birds chirping at sunrise? These guys had been pampered on gated estates in exclusive suburbs, spending long Saturday afternoons at sprawling country clubs while I hawked candy at city bus stops. It wasn't that I lacked confidence; rather, I lacked an understanding of how all this had happened. If tonight was going to be successful, I'd have to stop thinking about our differences and search instead for our commonalities.

In the midst of the clamor around the bar, I noticed a petite middle-aged woman in a white uniform, hunched at the shoulders and sturdy in her midsection. She was besieged by the constant flow of drink orders. The irony struck me as I watched her scurry frenetically. Women weren't allowed to join the clubs, but they were allowed to serve their members. The feminists on campus would have had hemorrhages if they had been standing there watching the scene before me. I felt guilty.

By seven thirty, the party had grown to over a hundred stiff navy blue blazers. I drained my glass of lemonade, since drinking during the season was something I tried to avoid, and decided it was time to mingle. I headed in the direction of the bar, figuring it would be the easiest place to strike up a conversation. As I made my way across the room, someone tapped me on the shoulder. I turned to find a short, overweight guy with round, scholarly glasses, his wide neck straining his bow tie.

"Hi, my name is Clint McDowell," he said with a slight lisp. Sweat had plastered his hair to his forehead like wet spaghetti on a cold dish. Everything about him was either disheveled or uncomfortable. "What's your name?"

"Spenser Collins," I said. I tried grasping his hand firmly, but his sweaty palm just slipped away. "How's everything going?"

"Great," he said. "Are you a punchee?"

"Yup, class of '91," I said. "What about you?"

"I am too, but class of '90. This is my second party of the week. I went to the Phoenix Club's party a couple of nights ago."

"How was it?"

"Sucked compared to this one. Those guys are social misfits. All they wanted to talk about was school and exams and serious shit. They're the guys the janitors have to kick out of the library at closing time." McDowell leaned closer. A heavy rim of perspiration had soaked through his shirt collar. "The Delphic is a hundred times better," he whispered as if someone were eavesdropping. "The members are a whole lot cooler and relaxed. They don't treat this thing like some goddamn job interview. Is this your first party?"

I nodded. "I don't know too much about these clubs, but I decided why not give it a try? What's the worst thing that could happen? I get some good food in a big fancy house that I probably never would've had the opportunity to see otherwise."

"Well, let me give you some advice," McDowell said. "I was punched by a few clubs last year and didn't make it into any of them. Obviously, which is why I'm here now. But the most important lesson I learned was you have to be really social at these parties and talk to as many members as possible. Make them think that getting into their club means everything in the world to you. The more members you impress, the more votes you get at the election meetings." He rested his hand on my shoulder. "No offense, but my biggest mistake last year was spending too much time talking with the other punchees and not enough time chatting up members. No one likes kissing ass, but believe me, if you wanna make it to the final round, you gotta learn the trade. And fast."

I nodded and forced a smile. I wanted to make it to the next round as much as the next guy, but I sure in hell wasn't about to kiss some blue blood ass just to join some club I wasn't even sure I wanted to be part of anyway. I might not have had the fancy cars and summer houses, but I had my pride. I wasn't above making some minor accommodations, but I wasn't going to pretend to be someone who I wasn't. For good or for bad, I was always going to be the kid from the South Side of Chicago who grew up on South Wabash Avenue.

McDowell pulled back a French cuff that was held together with a shiny gold cuff link and stared into the crystal of his Cartier watch. "Well, it's time for me to find a member," he announced. "I haven't spoken to one in fifteen minutes. Maybe we'll see each other again if we both make it to the next round. Good luck." I slipped out of his hand, then watched him slither toward his next prey.

I continued walking in the direction of the bar and finally spotted a familiar face from my cellular biology class. He was surrounded by three boarding school types raptly listening to his every word. I knew he was telling another one of his jokes, because the others had looks on their faces like they were getting ready to explode. Binky Grunwald was the funniest kid I had met at Harvard, and he loved to hold court. Standing barely five feet with a barrel chest, Binky had the kind of presence that could swallow a room. He was a young Danny DeVito. He had such a run of jokes one night at a seminar that he turned the class out a half hour early because the teaching fellow was laughing too hard to finish the lesson.

"Hey, Binky, what's up?" I said, waiting for a break in his delivery.

"Spenser, how's it going?" he said. "I didn't know you were coming to this. Why didn't you tell me in class last night?"

"I was so bored with all those crazy diagrams, the only thing on my mind was getting outta there," I said.

"No one even understood the damn problems," Binky said. "It was like a Chinese fire drill. Oh, by the way, this is Landon, Nestor, and Duke." Binky pointed to the other guys surrounding him. They were preppie clones in too-short beige corduroy pants, suede buckskin shoes, and tapered haircuts. We shook hands. I recognized Landon, the biggest of the three. He was a varsity lacrosse player.

"Landon, haven't I seen you in the weight room at the ITT?" I said. "You work out with a guy with bright red hair."

"Yeah, that's Pint Stevenson," Landon said. "He's our coxswain on the varsity boat. Coach is on a rampage this month. He has us lifting and running before every practice. He gets in one of his moods every couple of months. You're on the basketball team, right?"

"Yeah, we started our preseason practices a couple of weeks ago," I said. "Beasley's been working us like dogs too. Morning and afternoon practices."

The five of us talked about sports and girls and parties. The conversation was easy, and for the first time since stepping into the mansion, I felt relaxed. Everyone was confident in the unique way that Harvard students can be. They knew that success in the real world was not an "if" but just a matter of "when" and where they wanted to focus their efforts. I was surprised by how easily we found common ground. Duke was heading to the bar, so he took everyone's order and asked me if I wanted to join him.

I followed him as he walked right up to the front of the line, weaving ahead of the punchees clamoring to place their order. "Janice, I'd like you to meet one of our punchees," he said as the harried bartender, ignoring the others, approached us. "His name is Spenser. I'll take two Amstel Lights, a Sam Adams, a glass of red, and get Spenser here whatever he wants." I hadn't realized Duke was a member until he said, "one of *our* punchees."

"Good evening, sir," Janice greeted me in an Irish lilt. "A pleasure to meet you. What will you be drinking?"

"A root beer if you have it," I said.

Duke laughed. "We have a bar full of the best alcohol in the world, and you only want soda? You gotta be kidding."

"Beginning of the season," I said. "Coach will kick my ass if I show up with a hangover tomorrow. He'd have me running wind sprints till I spit up blood."

"See, that's why I swore off all sports when I was a kid," Duke said. "I saw my older brothers come home from practice every day, looking like they had gotten the shit kicked out of 'em. Their entire lives were controlled by games and practice schedules. So, I decided early on that I'd become a writer and dictate my own schedule and have a glass of red wine anytime I wanted."

"Smart man," I said. "This time every year after running the fifth or sixth wind sprint, believe me I start questioning my own decision."

"My point exactly," Duke laughed. "By the way, you came with great recommendations."

"What do you mean?"

"Some of the guys are really high on you," he said. "That's a good thing. We need some fresh faces in the club. We have enough tennis players and heirs. Same shit all the time gets old. I hear you're from Chicago."

"Born and raised," I said. "Where are you from?"

"New York City. Manhattan. You ever been?"

"Not yet, but it's on my list."

"Greatest city in the world bar none," Duke said. "My father works in the State Department, so we've traveled and lived all over the world. Rome, London, Paris, Hong Kong, Berlin, you name it. But every time I go back home, I realize one thing—there's just no place like New York, especially Greenwich Village, where I like to hang out."

"Greenwich Village?" I remembered reading about that part of the city when I was applying to NYU.

"Exactly. Greenwich Village is downtown, west of Broadway. It's more open and artsy and diverse than the East Side. If you're ever in the city over the summer, look me up. I'd love to show you around down there. You'd have lots of fun. The coeds at the NYU summer school are smokin' and very available." He winked confidently.

Janice returned with our drinks. Duke gave her a nod and scooped them up. As we were turning to leave, one of Duke's friends approached us. He introduced me to another punchee, Jason Arnaud from the crew team. He was the prototype crewbie: tall, close-cropped blond hair, sky blue eyes, and strong, callused hands from years of gripping those heavy wooden oars. As he and Duke talked about boats and regattas, I drifted in and out of the conversation, inspecting the room. As I took in the sumptuous décor, I couldn't help but wonder what my mother and grandparents would say if they were standing next to me as the live jazz band entertained and champagne flowed like water. We saw these kinds of homes only in the movies or magazines. I had to keep reminding myself that I was actually an invited guest and not someone who had sneaked in through the back door. I wanted to memorize every detail so that I could share them back home—the silver trinkets lined up on the mantelpiece, the antique guns in lighted cabinets, and the sparkling crystal vases on every tabletop. This one room contained enough furniture to fill our entire apartment twice.

I noticed a regal elderly man with silver hair, working the room. He was dressed in a single-breasted gray pin-striped suit, French blue shirt, and bold red tie. He steadied himself with a long black cane topped with a brass lion's head. Everyone seemed to be falling over each other, trying to meet him. Those who couldn't get close nodded their heads deferentially as he passed. He commanded the room with ease. For a split second, he caught my eye and started to make his way across the room. As he neared, I could see the creases in his tanned, leathery skin.

"Hello, I don't think we've met," he said, switching the cane to his left hand

and extending his right. "I'm Stanford L. Jacobs, class of '47. I'm your host for the evening." He had that distinct inflection in his voice of someone accustomed to privilege.

"I'm Spenser Collins, class of '91," I said, shaking his hand firmly. My stomach tightened.

"Is this your first time at one of these affairs, or have you been punched by any of the other clubs?" he asked.

"This is my first," I said. "I was lucky enough to receive the invitation a few days ago."

"Lucky indeed. The Gas is a very special place. Are you enjoying yourself?"

"Definitely. I'm meeting lots of interesting people."

"Young man, if you survive the cuts, this could be the most exciting four weeks of your life. I remember my days as a punchee. I had the most divine time meeting all those wonderful people and going to all those fabulous parties and dinners. I was eventually elected into the Delphic, Porcellian, and Spee. Choosing between the three was one of the most difficult decisions I've ever had to make."

Suddenly Dalton's parting words sounded in the back of my head. "Your home is amazing," I said. "I noticed the Rembrandt hanging in the front hall. It looked like *Portrait of a Young Girl,* 1645." Thank God for last year's Fine Arts 234b final exam.

"Excellent eye, young man," he said. "One of my favorites. Not one of his best pieces, but in the family for five generations. On that very wall since I was a little boy."

Jacobs had that rich person's way of speaking that I had never heard until I got to Harvard, those punctuated rhythmic fragments instead of complete sentences.

"Made a few important acquisitions over the years, but most of the pieces were here when I inherited the house. Great-grandfather was a big collector. Traveled all over the world, purchasing some of these pieces."

"Did he also live here?"

Jacobs nodded. "Built it in the early 1800s. Father added another wing, but

I've made very few changes since he passed away. Did a little restoring and opened up a couple of the rooms. But the house is basically the same as Father left it. I sense you have a keen interest in art."

I almost fell out right there when he said that. Me with a keen interest in art? It wasn't that I disliked art, but *keen interest* was definitely pushing it. I'd memorized about twelve paintings by some famous artists, just enough to get through an exam and sound like I knew what the hell I was talking about.

"I didn't know much about art before last year," I admitted. "But after studying it second semester, I've gained some appreciation. The more I learn, the more I'm fascinated." I was turning into a goddamn phony right before my own eyes.

"Best time in your life to learn," he said. "Youth is like a clean canvas. So much empty space to paint on, so much time to interpret the meaning of art. A tremendous opportunity to form opinions and appreciate subtleties. Distinguish one artist from another. Father insisted I take an early interest. He'd always say, 'Try to understand the story and intention of every brushstroke.' Can't say I was enthused by the idea at the time. But as I got older, I valued what he had done for me. Opened up the entire world right here in this old house. Do let me show you some of my favorite pieces."

Without waiting for my answer, Mr. Jacobs politely excused us, leading me through the room, shaking hands with others like a politician exiting a victory party. I followed him through a back door and down another long, dark corridor. I couldn't understand why everything was so dark.

"Follow me," he said. I feared I was getting involved in a situation that could prove embarrassing. I silently prayed that he would do more explaining than questioning. As we made our way through the lavish rooms, I thought about what Dalton had said. Was it possible that Jacobs was a member of the Ancient Nine, and if so, would I see something on this private excursion that might confirm that? I kept my eyes open for the smallest clues.

"Let's look in here," he suggested as we entered yet another spacious room with yet another vaulted ceiling. "I'll never forget the day I received my first Delphic invitation," he said. "I still have it in a box in an armoire in my bedroom."

We stood for a moment in the darkness. His words continued to echo somewhere off the marble ceiling.

"Why did you choose the Delphic over the Porcellian and Spee?" I asked.

"Two generations of Jacobs men had worn the torches of the Gas, my father and his grandfather. Other Jacobs men had been proud members of the Spee. But the Gas just had something special about it that I didn't feel with the others. Plus, it was almost impossible to get into at the time. Many of the graduate members had gone on to be world leaders, and the buzz about the club was fanatical. All the rage. Everyone wanted to get into Morgan's mansion."

Jacobs flicked on a wall switch. We stood underneath a large, ornamental Italian chandelier that scattered light throughout the mahogany-paneled room. Three of the four walls were lined with books from floor to ceiling. A sliding ladder leaned against the upper shelves.

"Oldest of the three libraries," he said. "My brothers and I would sit here every night for our French and Latin lessons. Mother was determined her boys would not grow up *provincial,* as she liked to say. She had designs to make us *fashionably international.*" He smiled softly. "Latin would increase our vocabulary and give us a solid command of the language. French for summers on the Riviera." Jacobs sighed as his mind wandered back in time. "Anyway, I brought you here to show you something."

He walked across the room and stopped at a wide cabinet, then flipped a switch that made several rows of lights flash behind the glass windows.

"That entire top shelf is from the Qin dynasty, about 221 to 207 B.C.," he said. "I acquired most of those pieces from a museum in Baoji, a city in Shaanxi."

The first piece was a gold crouching tiger with its mouth open and strange ears. It was only a couple of inches long, and to be honest, didn't look very impressive. I nodded my head pensively as if I were completely overwhelmed by its historical significance.

"An important piece," Jacobs said. "Once used as a harness ornament for horse-drawn chariots. At the back, there's a bar where the leather strap could attach. That and the drinking vessel next to it are two of the oldest Chinese artifacts I own."

"Was it difficult to get them?" I asked, searching for something to say without displaying my complete and utter lack of knowledge.

"Let's just say there was a significant amount of backroom wheeling and dealing." Jacobs smiled.

"You did the negotiating?" I asked.

"Never," he said, as if the mere thought offended him. "One of my dealers handled all the hand-to-hand combat. Sometimes this can be a tricky business. Lots of fakes out there. Gotta be careful. I've got something else you might like."

He switched off the lights and led me out the door. I followed him farther down the hall and into another room with enough space to play a full-court game of basketball. "Mother's sitting room," she said. "Loved to entertain her guests here."

We stepped into the airy room filled with baroque furniture and bright watercolor paintings. This was the first time I had ever seen peach lacquered walls. To my surprise, I actually recognized several of the paintings. It was as if half the works we had studied in our fine arts course were hanging in that room.

"These paintings are impressive," I said. "Many of them masters."

"Indeed," he said. "Mother liked to keep most of her major pieces here despite the best efforts of her interior decorator, who absolutely detested the arrangement of this room. She tried to convince Mother that all these pieces shouldn't be in one room, but rather spread throughout the house. She complained that too many big pieces in one room would cause them to fight each other."

"Then why did your mother still keep them all here?" I asked.

"She was getting older and not moving around the house as much. She wanted all of her favorites in the one room where she did most of her entertaining. Mother could be a very practical woman. But I brought you here to see what she really treasured more than anything else."

Jacobs led me across the room to a long walnut table that was filled with vases and colorful porcelain bowls. He turned on a row of lamps, and I immediately knew what he was talking about. Anyone who knew anything about art could recognize the work of El Greco and his religious imagery, a dead Christ with blue-hued skin lying softly in the arms of Mary.

"*Pietà.* Circa 1592. How ironic that a Greek would become one of the greatest to swing a brush in Spain. Mother acquired this right before she died. She loved his Mannerist style of painting."

"Do you worry about keeping all this great art in the open?" I said. "What if there's a fire or someone breaks in?"

Jacobs smiled. "Art is to be seen, Spenser, not hidden. If collectors lived in fear of destruction, they would never have the opportunity to enjoy the work. Having said that, we are very confident in our security protocol." He winked at me and turned off the lights.

As we made our way back to the gathering, he pointed out the masters— Picasso, Renoir, Monet, Cézanne—and told me brief stories about how a piece was acquired or why the work held such importance in the collection. We passed through one room that had a grand piano with keys made from the ivory of elephants his grandfather had killed on safari in Eastern Africa. Another room in the far corner of the west wing was used only for VIP dinners and was filled with a long table that ran the length of the room and was covered with enough sparkling silver and china for sixty people. We didn't go into the solarium that ran along the back of the house and out into the yard, but he explained how his mother had it built specifically for afternoon tea parties to properly entertain fellow board members of the many charitable organizations she served.

The rooms looked as though they were never used, not one chair or pillow out of place. We walked down another long hall where most of the twenty bedrooms were located. They were all extravagantly furnished, many of them with daybeds and chaise lounges flanking an enormous four-poster bed draped with silk dust ruffles. At least half of them boasted grand marble fireplaces with gold-encrusted utensils. Their lavishness was dizzying.

"Before we go back to the party, there's one room upstairs you must see," he said.

I followed him up two short flights and into a spacious room. Windows filled three of the four walls. He kept the lights off.

"Father renovated this room for Mother on their tenth anniversary," he explained. "The glass in each set of windows has a different magnification that offers a different view of Boston. No building in this city has a better view of the Charles winding its way through Cambridge and into Boston. When the room was complete, architectural magazines across the country ran stories on it. I can remember strangers coming to the door, asking to see 'the room.' It was an amazing time for this old house, like a rebirth."

I looked through one set of windows and recognized the lighted tower of the Prudential standing gracefully above the others. It was at least eight miles away, but the magnified windows brought it within arm's distance, close enough that I could see people moving around in their offices.

"Tonight's a bit cloudy," he explained. "But on a clear night, you can see the Hancock and most of the other skyscrapers in the financial district."

We walked to another window and looked out into the darkness. I could see the old buildings of the Yard and the row of houses along the Charles. There was the famous Citgo sign in Kenmore Square, near Fenway Park, the home of the Boston Red Sox. I couldn't help but think that my friends back home would never believe I had actually stood in a mansion with this view, next to a man as rich and powerful as Stanford Jacobs.

While I was standing there, looking out at the lights of Boston, Mr. Jacobs surprised me.

"How is your mother, Gwendolyn, doing?" he asked.

"Fine," I said. I was too nervous to ask how he knew her name.

"Do you have any contact with your father's side of the family?" he asked.

I shook my head. "My father was killed when I was a toddler."

"Yes, I know that. I'm sorry. He was heading home from work. It's why you've always wanted to be a doctor. You feel like his life could've been saved had someone with medical training gotten to him fast enough."

"How do you know this?"

"We make it a point to learn something about all our punchees."

There was an awkward pause, and Jacobs had a look on his face like he was working through something.

"Family is very important," he finally said. "It often defines who we are and what we'll make of ourselves."

"I have a great family," I said. "My mother and her side of the family have always been very supportive and hardworking. I'm here at Harvard because of their sacrifices. I will give her the life she deserves after I become a doctor."

"And no one from your father's side of the family has ever contacted you?"

"I met a second or third cousin once when I was in second grade. That's it."

"So, you don't know your family's history?"

"My family history is the story of my mother and her family," I said. "Unfortunately, my father's family history remains a mystery. He was a hardworking man who moved to Chicago from Mississippi when he was eight or nine. While he hasn't been with me physically, I feel his presence every day of my life."

Jacobs nodded. "I can only imagine how tough it must've been growing up without a father," he said. "But by all accounts, your mother has done a great job of raising a fine young man," he said. "It's good to have you in the punch. Just think, you would've missed all of this if you had gone to Hobart."

His last comment paralyzed me. Hobart was a small liberal arts college in upstate New York. I had applied to the school only because my high school girlfriend said that's where she wanted to go. But I had filled out and sent in the application secretly, telling no one. My mother would've launched all kinds of protests with the faintest hint that I was considering a school that was so far off her radar. How could Jacobs know about Hobart when it was something I had only secretly discussed with Caitlyn?

He rested his cane against the window and pulled out a black alligator wallet, took out a business card, and scribbled on the back before handing it to me. "This is my home number," he said. "Don't be shy about using it."

"This is really nice of you," I said, looking at the card, then sliding it into my jacket pocket. I tried to hide my discomfort. It was the first time in my life that someone outside of my family had offered to do something for me without asking for anything in return. But I was still confused about why he had decided to pick me out of the group, and why he knew so much about my personal life.

"I think we'd better rejoin the party," he said. "They'll be sending a search and rescue team for us if we don't get back soon."

The jazz band had come to life and the party room was now filled with anxious chatter and boisterous laughter. The free-flowing alcohol had done its job, dissolving tensions and boosting confidence. Brooks Brothers blazers now hung on the backs of the nearest chairs, and the once-starched shirts were wrinkled and opened to the second button. Thick cigar smoke circled heavily in the air.

I walked through the room, catching pieces of conversations, updating my running Rolex count, which already hovered near thirty-five. I passed one group standing around the pool table, talking about a weekend getaway to the Bahamas.

"C'mon, Bernie, we're just going away for the weekend," the tallest of the three prodded.

"I know, Parker, but we flew to Paris last month, and my father had a damn cow," Bernie said. "He told me I was cut off till further notice."

"But this trip won't cost us anything," Parker insisted. "My dad said he won't be needing the plane, so we can use it. And the staff opened our winter house last week, so everything is all ready to go."

"Bernie, how can you say no?" the third guy nudged. "Three days in the sun, and native women running around the beaches. We'll be getting laid forty-eight hours straight."

Bernie rubbed his temples pensively. "What the hell?" he finally relented to a round of high fives. "You only live once." Triumphant, the three raised their glasses of Dom Pérignon in a toast.

I moved on to another group debating the World Series. They were rooting for the Dodgers over Oakland since Oakland had beaten their beloved Red Sox.

And that's how the conversations went. Weekend getaways to private islands and summer vacations to distant continents. Sports, women, family businesses, ski trips to the Alps, powerful relatives who ran multimillion-dollar companies. Who were these guys?

I spotted the first casualty of the evening, a semiconscious punchee lying facedown on the floor. His blazer was half on, and with his free arm he was hopelessly tugging at the knot in his tie. A couple of members came to his rescue, and he looked up into their faces with a pathetic expression. "I'll get in, right?" he stammered. "Please tell me I'll make the cut?" The rest of the party barely took notice of the sputtering drunk as they made their way to and from the bar, stepping over him with more concern about spilling their drinks than the condition of their fallen comrade. The boasting and laughter continued, and the band played on.

By midnight, the party began to wind down. Mr. Jacobs stood in the center of the room, surrounded by the four officers who had greeted me at the door. Glasses were tapped, and once the room was quiet, Jacobs announced, "It has been an absolute pleasure hosting all of you this evening. As I no longer enjoy your youthful stamina, I must retire. But please feel free to carry on without me. My staff and hospitalities will continue to be at your service. Best of luck the rest of the way, gentlemen. And long live the Gas." He bowed his head slightly, and raised his hand to thunderous applause. He turned on his heels and swept out of the room with his butler following behind. It was an exit that Hollywood couldn't have scripted better.

As I walked back to Lowell House that night bundled up against the chill, the conversations and images from the party continued to play in my mind like a movie in slow motion. In one night, I had seen and learned things that four years of Harvard classes never would have taught me. But what weighed most heavily on my mind as I traveled back along those cold, empty streets of Cambridge was my conversation with Jacobs and his line of questions. Something wasn't right. I felt like he was asking me questions not because he didn't already have the answers, but to see if I knew them.

6

I CALLED DALTON as soon as I got back to my room.

"So, how was it?" he asked.

"Ridiculous," I said. "Next to yours, it's the biggest house I've ever been in. It was like walking through a museum. There were paintings and sculptures everywhere."

"The Jacobs family has some serious dough," Dalton said. "At one point, they owned more real estate in the City of Boston than City Hall."

"But the old man was kinda creepy," I said. "He was asking me all these personal questions about my family."

"That's what they're supposed to do, Spense. This is like an audition. Your answers can make the difference when they're deciding who they're gonna cut from the next round."

"But he wasn't really looking for my answers. I felt like he already had all the information and he was trying to find out what I knew."

"You have to remember who you're dealing with," Dalton said. "The Delphic is not only the most exclusive club on campus, but it also has the most powerful membership directory. It matters a lot to these guys the kind of people they let in. They probably ran a background check on everyone."

"It just didn't feel right," I said. "Jacobs was nice, but it freaked me out when he knew things like my mother's name or the fact that my father had been killed. He knew exactly why I wanted to become a doctor. How could he have seen my admissions application essay?"

"Spense, not to make you paranoid, but they probably know the name of your sixth-grade social studies teacher too," Dalton said. "This is serious business for these guys. Did he ask you about basketball? His family once owned half of the Celtics."

"No, we talked about his art collection, then he started with all those personal questions. For some reason, he seemed focused on whether or not I knew any relatives from my father's side of the family."

"What did you tell him?"

"The truth. That I'd only met a cousin once when I was in elementary school. I don't know, maybe it was just my nerves, but I felt like he was trying to make a point."

"You're overanalyzing," Dalton laughed.

"You're probably right," I said.

"This is all great news," Dalton said. "He liked you. It's exactly what you want. Anything that gives you an edge over the other punchees will help you advance to the next round."

I went to bed that night doing something I hadn't done since the night of my seventh birthday—visualizing my father's mangled body on the side of the road and what my life might've been had he not been hit by that car.

IT HAD BEEN almost a week since the cocktail party, and I hadn't heard anything from the Delphic. I tried my best not to think about it, but that was proving impossible. One night I was sitting in the common room, trying to study organic chemistry, but not getting much done. Percy was in his room chatting up a fellow member of the Din and Tonics, an a cappella singing group of fourteen men who ran around campus, singing jazz tunes and other types of music old people listened to on the car radio while kids complained about it from the backseat. The guy's name was Angstrom Hartman, and if you think his name was a mess, you should've seen him. He was a barrel-shaped bundle of physical and behavioral eccentricities, but the kid could really sing. He had a soprano voice like a nine-year-old girl's and sang like that's all he was put on this earth to do.

So, there I was, trying to read about organic synthesis reactions and electron counts and partially listening to Percy and Hartman complain about another member of their group who was nervous he had knocked up some girl from Wellesley. The phone's ring was a welcomed interruption. It was Dalton.

"What are you doing right now?" he asked. He was all out of breath, like he had just finished running a mile up Heartbreak Hill.

"Trying to get some studying done and not doing a very good job," I said. "What's up?"

"These fuckin' stairs are gonna give me a heart attack one day."

"The stairs or the cigarettes?"

"I don't need a fuckin' lecture right now, Spense. Shauna lectured me all damn weekend about smoking."

Shauna Marshall, Dalton's main girl, was a dance student who lived down in New York City and attended Juilliard. She was gorgeous, but most important, at least for Dalton, was that she was a black girl. Born and raised in Detroit, she came from modest means and had risen above it all to earn a free ride to Juilliard. She was as intelligent as she was attractive. Dalton met her on one of his New York excursions about a year ago. She was his waitress at some burger joint he liked in a trendy part of the city called SoHo. Needless to say, Shauna was yet another sore subject between Dalton and the Emperor.

"How soon can you get over here?" Dalton said.

"Depends on the incentive," I said, closing my book.

"I just got back from Uncle Randolph's place about an hour ago."

"I didn't know you were going down there."

"I didn't either, but since I was in the city for the weekend, I decided to stop on the way back and check on him."

"And?"

"He's hanging on, but he's not doing so hot. I don't know how long he has left. I had to keep propping him up in his chair, and he was drifting in and out of sleep the whole time. His nurse had him wrapped in two heavy blankets, and it was already a thousand degrees in the damn house. It was depressing as hell to see him like that."

"What did you guys talk about?"

"Well, if you'd get your damn ass over here, I'll show you what I brought back. You're not gonna believe it. Remember I told you about that box I found in one of his closets when I was a kid?"

"The one your aunt made you promise never to tell anyone about?"

"Exactly. Well, I found it again and borrowed it. There was more than just that cloth with the diamonds. There was his initiation medal and a really old article from some newspaper. It's about some guy who disappeared after trying to break into the Delphic clubhouse."

"I'm on my way."

ELIOT HOUSE WASN'T even a five-minute walk from Lowell. Our houses were separated by manicured lawns and surrounded by old trees, open spaces big enough for the intramural teams to use for football and soccer games. Before reaching Eliot, you had to walk by what once was called the IAB—the Indoor Athletic Building—perfectly located in the center of campus and official home of the fencing, wrestling, and volleyball teams. It housed everything from an Olympic-sized swimming pool, two weight rooms, and an entire floor of basketball courts. It was also the most popular athletic facility for non-varsity athletes and other students who were restricted from using our varsity facilities across the river. The old-timers still called it the IAB, but its name had been changed a few years back to the Malkin Athletic Center. Some alumnus worth a gazillion dollars who set the record for serving on fifteen Harvard committees at once donated a pile of money to have his name plastered across the scrubbed brick. I still don't think he got his money's worth. Instead of calling it the Malkin, everyone just called it the MAC.

Dalton's room was on the top floor, which meant climbing five flights of stairs, but everything else about it was great, including the view his common room had of the Charles River and the old Harvard Stadium over in Soldiers

Field. When I entered, Dalton was in his room, sitting back on his bed with a small box in his lap.

"Where are your roommates?" I asked.

"They all went to the Yard to hear Prim debate some guy from Princeton," Dalton said. "The Princeton guy is supposed to be the best in the country. His dad runs one of those pointy-headed think tanks down in Washington. Prim's gonna get his ass handed to him."

"Let me see what you have," I said.

Dalton brought the box to his desk, then turned on the lamp. I pulled up one of his armchairs and sat next to him.

"Where did you find it this time?" I asked.

"Up on the third floor in one of his studies in the bottom of a desk drawer. It was buried underneath a stack of bird-watching books. Took me damn near four hours before I got my hands on it. I forgot how many rooms there are in that old mansion. Some of them looked like they hadn't been used since I played hide-and-go-seek with Aunt Teddy as a kid."

"Who lives there now?"

"Uncle Randolph and his army of servants."

I looked down at the box. It looked like an old jewelry box with navy blue inlaid leather and dark, polished wood. Three torches had been pressed in the middle of the lid with the initials *R.A.W.* carved underneath. The hinges and hook clasp were rusted. There were multiple compartments. As Dalton lifted the lid, the sparkle was immediate and impressive.

"Damn, those are some serious diamonds," I said, moving closer to get a better look. The strip of velvet had faded from blue to purple. The ends of the cloth were threadbare. The diamonds spelled the words *Serva Sodalitatem*.

"I think this is a garter emblem," Dalton said, carefully pulling the cloth out of the box and laying it out on the desk. It was about eight inches long and a couple of inches wide.

"A garter?" I said. "Like a garter that holds up a stocking or sock?"

"I think that's the origin," Dalton said. "About an hour ago, I went downstairs to the library and looked up garters. I found several books on England's history. One of them had an entire chapter on something called the Order of the Garter. Inside the chapter they had a compilation of articles from different writers and news organizations."

"Never heard of it before."

Dalton reached across his desk and picked up a printout. "It's all right here."

The article was titled "Order of the Garter" and written by some outfit called The Monarchy Today. It explained that the Order of the Garter was the most senior and oldest British order of chivalry, founded by Edward III in 1348. The Order consisted of the King and twenty-five knights, and was intended by Edward III to be reserved as the highest reward for loyalty and military merit. The blue garter was the emblem of the Order. Its origin was unknown, but some believed it was inspired by an incident while the King danced with Joan, Countess of Salisbury. The countess's garter fell to the floor, and after the King retrieved it, he tied it to his own leg. Those who had been watching laughed and whispered about the awkward moment, but the King admonished them and said, *"Honi soit qui mal y pense."* Shame on him who thinks this evil. This became the motto of the Order, and those words had since been embroidered in diamonds on the emblematic garter owned by each member.

I picked up the cloth again and compared it to the picture of Prince Albert's garter in the article. The two were eerily similar, except for the wording.

"And there's more," Dalton said. He reached into the box and slipped back a clasp, then removed the bottom tray. He pulled out a circular silver medallion hanging on a blue-and-gold cloth. The three Delphic torches engraved in the front were identical to the torches pressed into the lid of the box. The initials *R.A.W.* and the date *Dec. 10, 1943,* had been stamped on the back.

"This personalized medallion is given to all new members of the club during the initiation ceremony," Dalton said. "Uncle Randolph never showed me the garter before, but I remember seeing him wear this medallion one night when he and Aunt Teddy had a big dinner at their house. I was ten or eleven. All these old men arrived in limousines, dressed in tuxedos and wearing these medals. I asked Uncle Randolph what they were, and he said all members of the Gas wore them to important functions. He said I would learn all about it one day when I went to Harvard."

"Are you sure your uncle's not gonna be looking for this stuff?" I said.

"He barely knows his own name half the time," Dalton said. "I doubt very seriously he'll be looking for this box."

"If he's that close to dying, maybe you should ask him about the Ancient Nine," I said. "He might be willing to tell you something."

"I did ask him, but he started talking about Aunt Teddy and when they met and how much he loved her. It was mostly gibberish."

"How about that article?"

Dalton reached into a tiny compartment in the bottom of the box and pulled out a tattered newspaper article that had turned sepia with age. It felt like it was going to crumble when he handed it to me. The name of the publication and part of the date had been torn off, but *Boston* and *1928* were still legible.

> Over the winter break, the president of Harvard College, in conjunction with the Cambridge Police Department, issued a press release stating that the missing Erasmus Abbott '28 is believed to be dead. The nationwide search for the heir to the Abbott fortune has been terminated, and plans for a day of remembrance are under way. Abbott has not been seen since eating in the Quincy House dining hall on the night of October 31.
>
> Over the last three months, the Cambridge Police Department has received several anonymous phone calls about Abbott's disappearance, none of which have proved helpful in the investigation. The call that raised the most controversy came from an unidentified man who claimed Abbott had expressed a desire to attempt the Halloween prank of breaking into the Delphic clubhouse on Linden Street to find what many believe to be a secret room with hidden treasures.
>
> Rumors about this room have been circulating for several years on the strength of the rich history of this exclusive final club and its obsession with privacy. The membership, both current and graduate, have steadfastly denied the existence of this room, and have uncharacteristically opened their doors to the authorities. Both the Harvard University Police

and Cambridge Police Departments report no such secret room, nor any evidence that Erasmus Abbott had succeeded in entering the mansion.

Many students, however, continue to support the belief that Abbott's demise was directly related to his quest to break into the storied room. According to one student by the name of————

That was it. The article had been cut off.

"What the hell happened to the rest of it?" I said.

Dalton shrugged his shoulders. "I'm thinking either after all these years, the damn thing fell apart or someone purposely clipped it. But that's why we're heading over to Widener. If we can get some of those archived newspapers on microfiche, then maybe we can try to piece some of this together."

"We don't even know what paper this was in," I said.

"No, but I'm sure there weren't a lot of papers in Boston at the time. It was either a school paper or a city paper. That shouldn't be too hard to figure out."

"It seems almost too coincidental for it to have fallen apart at that precise line," I said. I carefully handed the article back to Dalton.

"Makes you wonder what was really going on," Dalton said.

"Was your uncle around when this happened?"

"Nope. He didn't get to the college until 1932, five years later. But I looked at the family tree. His older brother Cyrus was a student then."

"Was he a member of the Delphic?"

"Yup, the second Winthrop to join the Gas. Their father, Milton, was the first. He was a classmate of J. P. Morgan."

"So, you think Randolph got the article from Cyrus?"

"Possibly."

"And you think someone would actually *murder* another student just because he was trying to get into that room?"

Dalton held up the garter. "It's possible they would've done whatever it took to protect the brotherhood. There must be some reason why Uncle Randolph kept the article hidden in this box along with the garter for the last fifty years."

"The library closes at ten," I said.

Dalton looked down at his watch. "That gives us almost two hours if we run."

7

✣

THE WINDS RATTLED the lampposts as we made our way up Dunster Street, toward the Yard. The cold nights of a Boston autumn were the outstretched hands of an approaching winter. The naked trees cast their long shadows on the frozen ground as brave and determined pedestrians in tight skullcaps jammed their hands into wool-lined pockets, their faces hidden behind knitted scarves. Few words were exchanged between these lonely partners of the night as they stared downward, jackets zipped above their chins, their footsteps marching quickly toward warmer destinations.

We entered the Yard through the Holyoke gate and walked alongside Boylston Hall. A group of ambitious freshmen was tossing a football and attempting to tackle each other on a small corner of grass in front of Wadsworth House. While it was strictly forbidden to ride bikes in the Yard, many were emboldened by the darkness of night and pedaled across the paths that crisscrossed the expansive rectangular lawn.

"Roz Minter lives over there in Weld," Dalton said as we passed the dark residential hall in the southeast corner of the Yard.

Roz Minter was the much-talked-about freshman volleyball player from Santa Barbara, California. She was every bit of six feet, devastatingly gorgeous with warm caramel skin, and the reason why half the upperclassmen walked by her corner of the Yard, even when they didn't have to, hoping to get a glimpse of her. I'd seen her in the training room once and immediately fell in love.

We turned the corner of Widener Memorial Library and scaled the long gray slab steps. Lights beamed from the tiny windows of the upper floors as the brainy seniors worked through the night, researching theses the rest of us could barely pronounce, let alone understand.

Dalton stopped and looked up at the enormous columns fronting the library. "Somewhere on one of those floors, in some corner of this monstrosity, could be our answer," he said, wrapping his arm around my shoulder. "Let's get in there and complete the mission set before us, comrade."

We walked past the security guard, sneaking in three cans of soda, a couple of candy bars, and a wool blanket to battle off the notoriously fierce draft in the bookstacks. Regardless of how many times I clambered up the giant marble steps that led to the second floor, I was always struck by the sheer size of the building. Widener had the third-largest collection of books in the country, outnumbered only by the Library of Congress and the New York Public Library, and like everything else at Harvard, Widener had its own story. Construction of the library began in 1913 with a two-million-dollar donation to the university by Mrs. George Dunton Widener. Eleanor Widener generously donated the money as a memorial to her son, Harry Elkins Widener, class of 1907, who met his tragic fate in the spring of 1912 on one of his many forays to Europe to purchase rare books for his collection. Returning from England on the *Titanic*, Widener and his father went down in the Atlantic along with the many rare books he had just purchased. According to legend, Harry Widener had been about to step into a lifeboat that would have saved his life, when he remembered one of his newly acquired books, a rare 1598 copy of the second edition of Bacon's *Essays*. Against his father's protests, he ran back to retrieve the book and was never seen again. Mrs. Widener, who had also been on the *Titanic*, made it safely to one of the life boats, but her husband and son perished at sea.

Every freshman was told the story of how Mrs. Widener agreed to donate a large sum of money in her husband's and son's memory, but only if Harvard would adhere to a litany of contractual stipulations. The one stipulation that gave the school the most trouble was the "no movement clause." This asserted that once the library was finished in 1914, the outside face of the library could never be changed—"not a brick, stone, or piece of mortar shall be changed," was the legal language. Mrs. Widener even went so far as to have this stipulated in her will, ensuring this restriction would be in place forever.

Some years after her death, the university wanted to construct a breezeway between Widener and the adjacent Houghton Library so that students and faculty wouldn't have to walk outside in the harsh cold to get from one to the other. It was a great idea, except for one obstacle—the Widener stipulation. The dilemma was resolved only after months of brainstorming between a team of legal experts next door at Harvard Law and a group of Boston's most decorated architects. The only way to circumvent the restrictive clause was building the walkway through one of the gigantic windows on Widener's third floor. This way, no brick was moved, just glass, and there would be no violation of the binding will.

After Dalton and I walked up the first flight of stairs to the mezzanine landing, the staircase opened to heavy oak double doors that stretched to the ceiling. This was the Harry Elkins Widener room, dedicated to its namesake. An eerie feeling came over me every time I reached that landing and thought about his drowning on the legendary *Titanic,* his family's incredible wealth, and his mother's obsessive need to immortalize his name with one of the biggest libraries in the country. The room stayed open only a few hours during the day, remaining closed through the evening and holidays. I had once read that the Widener room was finished in English oak, carved in England and brought across the Atlantic in individual panels. An expansive chandelier hung from the domed rotunda, illuminating the antique stained-glass windows that had once been compared to those found at the Vatican.

An enormous portrait of the young, emaciated Widener hung on the back wall, surrounded by glass-encased bookshelves housing his private collection of 3,500 rare books. A small brochure highlighted the literary gems in the room, like copies of Shakespeare's First Folio and a fifteenth-century printing of the Gutenberg Bible the family donated in 1944.

Dalton and I reached the second floor and passed rows of students anchored at computers, furiously typing on their keyboards. We entered the spacious reading room, big enough to host a rock concert. The bespectacled reference librarian sat behind the desk, her wrinkled arthritic fingers gripping the handle of an oblong magnifying glass. The tiny print of a Walt Whitman poem jumped off the page.

"Excuse me," I said. "Can you tell us how we can find out about the newspapers that were printed in Boston in 1927 and 1928?"

She looked up, cupped her ear with her right hand, and leaned forward. Her skin looked like it had expired a thousand years ago. "Excuse me, young man?" she said.

I stepped closer and raised my voice a little. "We're looking for the names of the papers that were published in Boston in 1927 and 1928."

"That could be quite a task," she said. "But if we're lucky, there might be a directory that would have all that information compiled in one place. Are you looking for dailies, weeklies, or monthlies?"

I looked at Dalton.

"All of them," he said.

She shook her head and ran her bent fingers across the keyboard. I was surprised by the speed of her typing.

"Okay, we have something," she said, bending even closer to the monitor. "I'm showing five major directories. First, the *History and Bibliography of American Newspapers, 1690 to 1820*, edited by Clarence S. Brigham."

"No good," I said. "We need 1927."

"Here's another one," she said. "*Working Press of the Nation*. Wait, that's no good either. It doesn't start until 1945." She tapped a couple of more keys. "Here we are," she announced proudly. "*N. W. Ayer and Son's American Newspaper Annual*. Published by N. W. Ayer and Son in Philadelphia."

"What years does it cover?" Dalton asked.

"Eighteen-eighty to 1986," she said. "This says it was published annually as the *Ayer's Directory*, and includes a list of newspapers and periodicals published in the U.S. and Canada and arranged geographically. It also includes subject listings such as culinary and housekeeping, fashion, matrimonial, millinery, woman's handiwork, and women's clubs. Do any of those subjects interest you, gentlemen?"

"Not really," I said. "But if we look through the directory, we might be able to find the paper we're looking for."

"And which paper is that?"

"We're not sure," I said. "We only have the date and part of the title."

"What part of the title do you have?" she asked.

"'Boston,'" Dalton said.

"Good luck," she said, shaking her head. "I was hoping you had a more specific word that might help narrow down the list, but there were many papers at the time with 'Boston' in the title. You'll have to search each one in the directory."

"Where can we find this directory?" Dalton asked.

"On the eighth floor of the stacks," she said, scribbling down the call number on a piece of scrap paper. "Once you get the name of the paper from the directory, then you can go down to the microfilm reading room and see if we have it on film."

"Do you have a list of the newspapers that are stored on film?" I asked.

"Sure," she said, tapping the keyboard. "We have them arranged by state and city. I'll print the list out for you so that you can take it with you and see if what you find in the directory matches the film we have in our collection. If they don't have the film downstairs, they might be able to tell you what other library carries it, and we can make an interlibrary loan request."

Within minutes, we had eight sheets with more than 180 titles of Boston newspapers that were available on microfilm.

"I'm not sure what you're researching, but you also might want to check some of the Harvard papers from that time," she said. "Off the top of my head, I know the *Harvard Gazette* and the *Crimson* were being published. There might've been others. The microfiche room will have a complete listing."

We thanked her and quickly headed to a part of the library that most students dreaded even hearing about let alone entering. To most of us, the Widener stacks belonged in a Stephen King horror flick. Sequestered from the main part of the library, the stacks occupied their own enormous wing. There were ten floors in all with 3.2 million volumes housed in over five miles of bookshelves. Its collection of rare books dated back to the sixteenth century. The stacks were always cold, dark, and damp, and odd sounds echoed down the empty narrow aisles. Some of the floors were encased in a metal fence, and it could take a while sometimes to find an exit that wasn't locked. The Widener stacks were legendary in the academy, serving as the research base for some of the most widely published and internationally acclaimed scholars in the world. While the rest of the library had been renovated with new equipment and material improvements, the Widener stacks were left untouched and distinctly primitive, as if to remind us that true academic rigor should be austere in all aspects.

Dalton and I had to turn sideways to fit into the creaky old elevator that would transport us into the cold dungeon of knowledge. It was one of those antiquated elevators with the sliding metal doors and mesh cage that allowed you to see outside as the car moved between the floors.

"One day someone's gonna die in this damn box," Dalton said as the door barely closed shut.

We finally reached the eighth floor, where Dalton flipped on the switch at the entrance of the passageway, turning on a row of naked lightbulbs dangling from the ceiling. We broke off in opposite directions down the narrow aisles. Many of the books were so old and dusty that their titles had faded into the cloth of the jackets, and the call numbers, which had been stuck on with tape, were barely clinging to the chipping spines.

After almost twenty minutes of searching, I heard Dalton's cry. "Got it! Get over here, Spense!"

I ran down the hallway, almost crashing into one of the bookshelves as I slipped while turning a tight corner. Dalton was sitting on the ground, surrounded by several piles of books. A thick book sat open across his lap.

"Did you have to empty an entire bookcase?" I said.

"I couldn't read the damn call numbers," Dalton said.

"Is that it?" I said, taking a seat next to him on the floor.

He turned to the title page, sending a cloud of dust into our faces. The old typeface confirmed that this was in fact *Ayer's Directory.*

"Where's that list of microfilm titles she printed out?" Dalton said. "Let's see if anything matches."

The librarian was correct. There were several pages of Boston newspapers that had been published in 1927. But what made it difficult was that they had included magazines in the directory and hadn't made any notations that would help distinguish them from the newspapers. We spent the next forty-five minutes cross-referencing the microfilm list with the directory until we came up with a list of five papers that might have contained the Abbott article.

"Let's hope it's in one of these," Dalton said, standing up. We began to replace the books on the shelves.

"When we get downstairs, you start searching those papers, and I'll look through some of the old *Crimsons*," I said.

"Sounds like a plan. If we hurry, we can get this done before the closing bells."

THE MICROFILM READING room was located on the first floor of the library in a meticulously organized area filled with tall metal cabinets and several rows of bulky microfilm readers. All but one machine was occupied. We approached a middle-aged man with a deeply receding hairline and a long angular nose seated behind the information desk. When he turned to the side, he looked like a bird sitting on a streetlamp.

"How can I help you?" he asked.

"I'm looking for early *Crimsons* that might be on microfilm," I said.

He wrinkled his forehead. "I'm pretty sure we don't have the *Crimson* on microfilm," he said. "But let me check to be sure." He played with the computer keys for a few seconds, then shook his head. "As I expected, not on microfilm," he said. "They've been publishing since 1873. I know they keep bound copies of the papers in their offices."

I turned to Dalton. "What should I do?"

Dalton looked down at his watch. "They're definitely closed, but there's usually someone in the newsroom all night, trying to make deadline. Go to the delivery entrance and knock on the side door. The newsroom is in the back of the building."

"I'll give it a try," I said, gathering my backpack. "Give me a call when you get back to your room."

"May the Force be with you," Dalton said before giving me a fist bump, then turning toward the microfilm machine in the center of the room.

8

THE YARD WAS completely deserted as I descended the Widener steps. I cut around the corner of the library and into a dark alley that separated Widener from the more provincial Houghton Library. Light from the occasional lamppost cast long shadows across the pavement. I sensed that the story of Erasmus Abbott might be a loose thread that could unravel the mysterious tale of the Ancient Nine.

As I neared the middle of the walkway, I heard footsteps behind me. Nothing alarming or unusual, but the cold air echoed their rhythmic cadence between the buildings. It was the sound of hard rubber grinding loose sand. I stopped to zip up my coat, and the footsteps fell silent. Was I imagining this? I was tempted to turn around, but instead I started walking again toward the gate that led out of the Yard and into the Square. I walked faster, and the footsteps returned, keeping pace with mine. At the gate, I encountered a line of cars heading into the Square, but I took my chances, found a small gap, and hustled through them across Mass Ave to the opposite sidewalk. The *Crimson* was located on Plympton Street to my left, but instead I took a quick right and walked ten yards toward the heart of the Square. I turned my head slightly and looked back. I picked up my follower out of the corner of my eye—a man, definitely over six feet, wearing a black puffy ski jacket and baseball cap. That was all that I could make of him without committing to a full turn. He continued to walk into the Square but on the opposite side of the street. After several more steps, I made a U-turn and walked back in the direction of Plympton Street. I waited a few seconds before looking to see if he had done the same. He was gone. No sign of him anywhere. Maybe all this talk of a disappearing student and a secret room was really starting to get to me.

I reached the corner of Linden Street, one block away from Plympton. It wasn't until I was passing the windows of the Ferrante-Dege camera store when I saw his reflection. He must've been no more than ten feet behind me, his hands jammed into the pockets of his coat. There were no markings on his blue baseball cap.

I crossed Linden Street and continued along Mass Ave. I passed the Harvard Book Store, then Mr. and Mrs. Bartley's burger joint. I pretended to look in the window, and saw him again, still following at a comfortable distance but steady in his pursuit. Who was this man, and why was he following me? My heart thumped against my rib cage.

I broke into a light jog, then took a hard right on Plympton, a dark narrow street that fed down to Hearst Castle, Cambridge's version of the more famous one in California. After I turned the corner, I kicked into a full sprint. I reached the parking lot of the *Crimson* in a matter of seconds and hid in the shadows of a large dumpster. I had just crouched down when I saw him. He was caught between a fast walk and a jog, like someone trying to disguise their eagerness to reach a destination. He stopped directly opposite the *Crimson*. It was difficult to make out the details in his face because of the cap pulled down over his eyes, but I could tell that he was a slim white man with a hard cut to his jaw. I could see only the bottom of his eyeglass frames. They were wire and rectangular. He stayed there for several minutes, looking up and down the street, then focusing on the *Crimson*. He pulled out a pad from his pocket and quickly scribbled something down. Then he took one last look in my direction before he turned and walked back up the street and disappeared.

I sat there for a few minutes not only to make sure he had truly gone, but also to allow my heart to settle. Sweat poured out underneath my jacket, and

I leaned my head back against the side of the building, the cool wind feeling good against my damp skin. I finally stood up and walked to the door, taking in the building before knocking. The *Crimson* was the nation's oldest continuously published daily college newspaper. Its former editors and writers had become the who's who of journalism, numbering not only many Pulitzer Prize winners in its ranks, but also two U.S. presidents as past editors—Franklin D. Roosevelt '04 and John F. Kennedy '40. Only at a place like Harvard could the competition to join a student newspaper be fiercer than making it onto one of the varsity sports teams. Earning a spot on the *Crimson* masthead was like getting accepted into Harvard a second time.

I banged on the door several times, scaring a homeless man sleeping underneath the fire escape in the alley. The door finally opened. A short girl with curly black hair and eyeglasses thick enough to be bulletproof stared up at me.

"We're not open," she announced in a nasal voice. "You'll need to come back tomorrow morning."

She started to close the door in my face, but I stuck my hand out and stopped her. I recognized her from my Music and Verse class. She was the brainiac who always got Professor Rothman's questions right after the rest of us had made fools of ourselves.

"You're in Rothman's Music and Verse," I said. "First row, third seat from the right. You wear a red coat with a hood."

"That's right," she said, and smiled a mouthful of big, crooked teeth.

"My name is Spenser," I said. "What's yours?"

"Gert Stromberger."

"Gert, I was hoping you could help me with a little jam I'm in," I said. "I'm working on something that's really urgent, and I think my answer is here at the *Crimson*."

"What are you looking for?"

"I need to check out your bound copies from 1927."

"You know the exact date?"

"November 1."

Stromberger looked down at her watch and shrugged. "Well, I really can't help you search them, but I can show you the bound copies, and you can look through them yourself. I have three more articles to copyedit before midnight, and I'm here by myself." She stepped to the side.

"I owe you big-time, Gert," I said. "Just point me in the right direction, and I'll go from there." Little did I know that Gert Stromberger would be just the luck I needed.

She led me down a short corridor and into a small office filled with stacks of newspapers piled almost to the ceiling. There were two metal desks in the center of the room, facing each other. Both were empty except for two Harvard mugs jammed with pens and pencils. Several tattered legal pads sat next to a telephone.

"Make yourself comfortable in here," she said. "I'll go and get the 1927 volume from archives."

Stromberger returned a few minutes later, dropping the thick volume in front of me. "Try to be careful with these pages," she said. "They're kind of delicate, and the preservative they used back then wasn't too good. I'll be in the main newsroom if you need anything else."

"Is there a photocopier I can use?" I asked.

"Sure, two doors down on your right. But don't break the spine of the books when you do the photocopying. It drives our managing editor crazy."

Stromberger went back to her articles, and I quickly dived into the bound newspapers. I flipped to the Halloween paper. The headline wasn't exactly a jaw-dropper: SEEK NEW METHODS OF ORE DISCOVERY. This article focused on graduate students in the engineering school conducting experiments in scientific methods for locating ore deposits. Breathtaking. I moved on to a second article, which was equally thrilling. Three English debaters who recently met the debating team were guests of the liberal club at a luncheon. The last article was about the ticket manager of the Harvard Athletic Association, C. F. Getchell, announcing the order in which the graduate classes would be awarded their coveted seats to the Harvard–Yale football game that year.

It wasn't until I turned to November 2 that I found something. The major articles included an announcement about W. A. Purrington, a New York lawyer from the class of 1873, bequeathing $150,000 to the school for medical research in the field of dentistry. Important sporting news announced that the 150-pound crews from Harvard, Princeton, and Yale would meet the coming spring in a triangular race. On the third page along the right margin of advertisements, I found gold.

ABBOTT POSSIBLY MISSING

Erasmus D. Abbott, a Quincy House senior, was last seen at dinner on night of October 31. His roommates haven't seen or heard from him since. His professors have noted his repeated absences from class.

Earlier, the Dean's office had little to say of Abbott's mysterious disappearance, surmising he had probably gone home for the weekend and was extending his visit. As time progressed, this explanation seemed less likely, and students expressed their concern that something unfortunate has happened.

Calls to Abbott's parents in Newport didn't return any new information about his whereabouts. They reported he hasn't been home since the beginning of fall semester. The only irregularity they noticed in his behavior was a special request to have his monthly allowance sent early. They take comfort in the belief that he went on one of his impromptu vacations to visit friends and decided to stay longer than planned, something he's been known to do in the past.

All parties concerned are sure he will return soon.

I went through every article for the rest of the week, expecting some follow-up on Abbott's disappearance, but couldn't find anything. I slid a bookmark inside the November 2 paper so that I could photocopy it later, then moved to the next week's papers. Monday, November 7, 1927. The lead article was a call to action for students to take on the challenge of social responsibility. It was written by the secretary of service for the Phillips Brooks House, the oldest and longest student-run public service organization at Harvard.

Then I found something buried on the fourth page.

SEARCH CONTINUES FOR ABBOTT

According to a Cambridge Police report, Erasmus Abbott, a physics concentrator from Quincy House, has been officially reported missing. His whereabouts have been unknown since dinner on October 31.

A national search has been under way, but no useful leads have been found. His parents, Collander and Elizabeth Abbott of Newport, Rhode Island, have offered twenty-five thousand dollars for any information leading authorities to his safe return.

Experts suspected a possible kidnapping, as Abbott is the only heir to the famous Abbott fortune. However, no ransom notes or calls have been received.

The President's office, in conjunction with the Cambridge Police Department, has requested that anyone with information pertaining to Abbott's activities on that night please come forward.

My nose was practically rubbing the pages by the time I had finished the article. A nationwide search, fortunes, a Halloween-night disappearance—it was like a movie. I closed my eyes and tried to imagine what the night of October 31, 1927, might've been like, with the Delphic mansion probably empty and locked as costumed students passed by in its shadows.

I continued to search through the rest of the November papers, but there was no mention of Abbott. I double-checked them to make sure I wasn't missing anything, but found nothing, not even a sentence updating the previous reporting. How could the disappearance of a student, especially one from such a wealthy and connected family, not be reported? I took the entire volume to the photocopier. I carefully placed the papers on the glass without breaking the spine. When I was finished, I found Stromberger sitting behind an enormous desk that swallowed her tiny frame. Her face was about half an inch from the screen, and she was surrounded by five Styrofoam cups filled with varying amounts of cold coffee. She was so engrossed in her work, she didn't hear me enter.

"I need some help, Gert," I said.

She jumped at the sound of my voice. "Oh my God!" she said, holding her hand to her chest. "I didn't hear you come in. How's it going?"

"I found some of what I want, but I think I need to look at a couple more months. Can you get me December of 1927, then the first three months of 1928?"

"You'll be here all night," she said. "That's more than a hundred papers. Do you have a specific date in mind?"

"That's the problem," I said. "I had a date at first, but now I'm looking for follow-up articles."

"What are you looking for, if you don't mind me asking?"

"Articles about a student who disappeared in 1927."

"You know his name?"

"Erasmus Abbott, class of '28."

"I can probably help you figure out where those articles are. We just indexed our archives. Give me a sec."

She stood up and walked to another computer along a back counter and began beating the keyboard. She had something in less than a minute. "Three articles," she said. "November second and eighth of 1927 and May twenty-seventh of 1928. You've already got the first two, so let me give you the May volume."

Stromberger disappeared down a dark hallway only to return minutes later.

"Good luck," she said, handing me a large book identical to the one I had just searched.

I went back to my temporary office and jumped in. It didn't take long to find the article plastered on the front page.

ABBOTT PRESUMED DEAD

A joint announcement from the President's office and the Cambridge Police Department acknowledges that missing Quincy House senior Erasmus Abbott of Newport, Rhode Island, is presumed dead. A seven-month search has produced no evidence of the Harvard senior's fate or that he is even alive.

Much had been made of statements from Kelton Dunhill '30, bio-
logical sciences concentrator in Quincy House, who said Abbott had told
him of his plans to enter the Delphic mansion on Linden Street to pull
a Halloween prank. Rumors of a secret room in the club have been ban-
died about for years, but have been staunchly denied by club members
and the university administration.

Abbott was one of the college's lead debaters and very involved in
house activities. The office on academic affairs has decided to decree
Abbott his diploma with the rest of his class in June. The Abbotts have
already donated monies to the college for the establishment of an endowed professorial chair in their son's name.

A memorial service is planned for noon on June 4 in the Appleton
Chapel on what would have been Abbott's twentieth birthday.

I photocopied the article, then returned the book to Stromberger, who was
sitting back in her chair with her feet on her desk, sipping from one of the
cups of coffee. Her eyes were dark and sunken, her hair more disheveled.

"Did you find it?" she asked.

"It was there," I said. "I couldn't've done it without you."

"So, what happened to the student?"

"It doesn't say. He just disappeared, and eventually they presumed him
dead."

"That's kinda scary. Did they ever find his body?"

"Doesn't say anything about that either. Seems like the case was closed and
everyone just moved on. Not a single reference in later papers about what
might've happened."

Stromberger gazed toward the ceiling, strumming her chin. "Reopening
the case of a Harvard missing student sixty years later," she said. "Could make
a good article." She scribbled something on her pad.

I suddenly thought of Kelton Dunhill, who had been mentioned in one of
the articles. "Do you guys keep an alumni directory around here?" I asked.

"Are you kidding?" she said. "You can't walk five feet without bumping
into one. Those things are like gold. Alums are our main funding source." She

swiveled in her chair. "There's one right over there, next to that computer on the back desk."

"Does it say if the alums are still alive?" I asked.

"It tells you everything. Their graduating class year, the last known address, phone number if there is one, and if they died, the year of their death."

It was a long shot, but I had a hunch. I walked over to the corner of the office and flipped through the thick directory until I found the class of 1930. Many of the names had a *(D)* next to them with the date of death at the end of the entry, except for Kelton Dunhill. He was living in the Thompson Home for the Aging in Miami, Florida, and there was a contact number where he could be reached.

9

"**WHERE THE HELL** have you been?" Dalton was on the other end of the phone, trying to crack my eardrum.

"I just got home from the *Crimson,*" I said. I looked at the clock on my nightstand. It was a little past one. I hadn't realized it was that late when I left Stromberger. We talked for about an hour before I left. She turned out to be a lot more interesting than I had expected. We talked sports, movies, campus politics, and agreed that it was strange the *Crimson* hadn't run more stories on Abbott's disappearance.

"I've been calling you for the last two hours," Dalton said. "I found the damn article and almost got my ID taken away in the process, but that's another story."

"Someone followed me from Widener to the *Crimson,*" I said.

"Followed you? Why the hell would someone do that? You're tired. Your imagination is on overload."

"I know what I saw. I'm not crazy. The guy followed me out the Yard and toward the Square. Just to see if it was real, I quickly turned around and started heading back toward the *Crimson,* and he was right behind me. I turned down Plympton, sprinted to the *Crimson,* and hid behind a dumpster. A few seconds later, he was standing across the street. This guy was definitely following me."

"Jesus Christ! Did you get a good look at his face?"

"Not really. It was too dark, and he was across the street. He was white, wearing a plain baseball cap and wire-rimmed glasses, and was at least my height. That's all I could see from where I was."

"Did he do anything?"

"He looked up and down the street, then just stood there and stared at the *Crimson.* He took out a pad and wrote something down. Then he turned and walked away."

"Really weird," Dalton said. "It's late and we're both tired. Maybe you just thought he was following you, but was doing something else."

"Maybe," I said. "Anyway, which paper had the article?"

"The *Boston Evening Transcript.* It was written by some reporter named Archibald Fleming. This guy must've really done his homework. He had a lot of sources and knew a lot about the clubs, stuff only someone on the inside would know."

"You think he talked to some of the members?"

"He must've. Abbott had been planning for a long time to break into the Delphic to find this secret room everyone was talking about. Several guys had tried the year before, but got caught by the club steward before they made it into the club's main rooms."

"Was Abbott part of that group?"

"It didn't say. Everyone figured those guys were from another club like the Pork or Spee."

"Was Abbott a member of a club?"

"Nope. He had been punched by the Fly as a sophomore, but didn't get in. Halloween night, a bunch of guys were eating dinner at Quincy, and Abbott announced he was breaking into the Delphic to find the secret room. He asked if anyone at the table wanted to go with him."

"And they all wimped out," I said.

"Everyone except for a guy named Kelton Dunhill. He lived down the hall from Abbott and was on the wrestling team."

"Holy shit!" I said. "I got the same name. There were three articles in the *Crimson,* two from November of '27 and one from May of '28. Dunhill was mentioned in the third article."

"Did they have all the other stuff I found?"

"No, the last article just had a quote from Dunhill saying Abbott was planning to hit the Delphic on Halloween night."

"Well, Fleming wrote a lot more. He said Dunhill actually walked up to the Gas with Abbott just after midnight."

"Dunhill went in with him?"

"No, Dunhill got cold feet at the last minute and left."

"Did he know if Abbott made it in?"

"That's where the article comes up short. It places Dunhill at the clubhouse, but it doesn't say if he actually saw Abbott enter."

"Something's not adding up," I said. "You have a kid from a very prominent family who suddenly disappears, and only three articles appear in the student newspaper?"

"And no mention of culpability or lawsuits," Dalton said. "How un-American. It's like everyone just accepted the guy disappeared, then announced him dead when they figured enough time had passed and they were ready to move on. It doesn't make sense at all."

We paused and rolled things over in our minds. "So, you think Abbott could've seen or heard something he wasn't supposed to?" Dalton finally said.

"That's what I'm thinking," I said. "And someone from the Delphic decided to keep him quiet. Permanently. Remember the words on that garter."

"*Serva Sodalitatem*," Dalton said. "Protect the brotherhood."

"That's right. And maybe the brotherhood decided Abbott had become a liability, so he conveniently disappeared."

"Sounds pretty good, Spense, but there's just one problem."

"Which is?"

"We don't even know if the Ancient Nine were even around back then."

"That's why we need to track down Kelton Dunhill."

"How the hell are we gonna do that?"

"Pick up the phone and call him." I took out the entry I had copied. "Mr. Kelton Dunhill now lives in the Thompson Home for the Aging in Miami. I got his address and phone number from an alumni directory over at the *Crimson*."

"Nice work, Spense. We'll call him first thing tomorrow. Hopefully he still has his marbles and can talk to us. He must be closing in on eighty by now."

"He's probably one of the only guys still alive who remembers what happened that night," I said. "Unless you can squeeze something out of Uncle Randolph, Kelton Dunhill is probably our only shot."

DALTON CAME OVER TO my room the next morning since Percy left earlier with Hartman to attend some singing retreat up in the Berkshires.

"Who's gonna do the talking?" Dalton said, sitting on our couch, flipping the remote in his hands. Dalton always liked to flip things. If it wasn't a remote or football, it was a pillow or book. Anything to keep his hands occupied.

"Maybe you should do the talking," I said. "You sound more like an innocent college student."

Dalton wasn't fooled for a second. "You mean I sound white, and he's less likely to hang up on me because of that."

"Close enough," I conceded.

"That's fair. Let's talk strategy before we call. What do we want to accomplish?"

"We want him to tell us everything he remembers about that night," I said. "He must know something. Fleming had him not only at dinner with Abbott, but at the Delphic the night of the disappearance as well."

"What if the guy has Alzheimer's?" Dalton said. "More and more old people are coming down with it. So, let's say Dunhill is half out of his mind, then what?"

"I don't know. I guess we're at a dead end. Maybe see if he kept a journal or something that we can look at."

"Sounds good," Dalton said. "What if he wants to know why I'm asking all these questions?"

"You'll figure something out. You're the king of bullshit."

Dalton flipped the remote a few more times, then said, "All right, what the hell, let's give it a try."

I put the phone on the table between us, hit the speaker button, and dialed. A woman answered on the third ring.

"I'm looking for Mr. Kelton Dunhill," Dalton said in his most official tone.

"Is this business or personal?"

Dalton looked at me. I mouthed the word *personal*. "Personal issue, ma'am," he said, keeping his voice low and steady.

"Are you on his call list?"

Dalton shrugged his shoulders at me and said, "No, but I'm sure he'd want to take this call."

"Your name, sir?"

"Dalton Winthrop from Harvard College. I'm calling Mr. Dunhill about an important school matter."

"Is this a solicitation, sir?"

"Not at all. This is for something completely different. We're bouncing around the idea of honoring him at one of the reunions."

The absolute king of bullshit.

"That's such a nice gesture," the operator said. "Mr. Dunhill could use something like that to lift his spirits. What did you say your name was?"

"Dalton Winthrop, class of '91."

"One moment, Mr. Winthrop."

Classical music blared from the telephone while Dalton and I exchanged high fives. "So far, so good," I whispered, feeling a surge of adrenaline.

"This is Kelton Dunhill." The music was gone, and the deep voice boomed over the intercom. "What can I do you for?" Dunhill growled.

"Good morning, sir. My name is Dalton Winthrop, class of '91. Thanks for taking my call."

"What do you want, Winthrop?"

Dunhill was nothing like we had expected. His voice was clear and strong, and he sounded like he could've been sixty instead of eighty and ready to go about five rounds without gloves.

"I was doing some research, sir, and came across your name in one of the archived articles," Dalton said. "I found your contact information, so I figured I'd give you a call."

"What articles were you reading?"

"The articles about Erasmus Abbott, class of '28. I was hoping—"

There was a loud sound, then silence.

"Mr. Dunhill?" No answer. "Mr. Dunhill, are you there?" Dalton looked at me. I shrugged my shoulders.

"What the hell just happened?" Dalton said.

"He obviously didn't like what you said and hung up."

"Maybe we just got disconnected."

"I don't think so."

"Let's call him back."

"He's not gonna speak to you, Dalton."

"He'll talk to me," Dalton said. "Dial the goddamn number."

I dialed the number again. The same lady answered the phone. She put him right through to Dunhill's line. The old curmudgeon picked up on the first ring as if he knew Dalton would call back.

"Dunhill here."

"Mr. Dunhill, it's Dalton Winthrop again. Sorry we got disconnected."

"We didn't get disconnected," Dunhill roared back. "I hung up the damn phone, and I'll do it again!"

"Please don't do that, sir. I just wanted to ask you a couple of questions. It won't take much of your time."

"At my age, I got all the damn time in the world, but I still have nothing to say about Erasmus Abbott or anything connected to his death."

"But you said something to Archibald Fleming."

"That was a long time ago, and it was a mistake. I regret I even spoke to that little weasel. You damn reporters are all the same. You take the information people give you and twist it to fit the angle of your story. Objective journalism, my ass!"

"I'm not a reporter, sir. I'm just a student."

"What the hell does a student care about a story like this? It's been more than fifty-odd years since all that happened."

"It's just one of those stories you hear about, but can't believe," Dalton said. "I was reading what little I could find about the case, and I was surprised at how the investigation seemed to stop so abruptly. I expected a missing student would be a pretty big deal back then, especially when it involved such a prominent family. But there wasn't much coverage in the press. I just find the entire situation fascinating."

"Well, un-fascinate yourself, because I have nothing further to say on the telephone," Dunhill said. "If you're really a student and not some reporter posing as one, and you want to talk to me, then present yourself in person. Once I can make you out, then we might have a little chat. Any other arrangement you might be after, you can forget about it. Face-to-face and nothing else."

Dalton looked at me. I shrugged my shoulders. "When would you like me to present myself, sir?" Dalton said.

"Whenever you want. I'm always here."

"Would you mind if I brought a classmate with me?"

"As you see fit."

"Thanks for your time, Mr. Dunhill."

"See ya around, Winthrop."

And with that, Kelton Dunhill ended the call. Dalton and I sat there for a moment and stared at each other in disbelief.

Dalton smiled. "I hope you haven't put away your swimming trunks for the winter. This weekend, we're heading to Miami."

10

TWO DAYS LATER, I was cursing Harvey "C Minus" Mettendorf as I walked up the back steps of the Coop, Harvard's famed bookstore that anchors the center of the Square. During some lapse of sanity, I decided to take a philosophy course taught by Mettendorf, a renowned professor in the government department who had been on the faculty for almost thirty years and for every one of those years at the center of some type of controversy. Whether it was baiting the Vietnam protesters in the sixties or criticizing the university's efforts at recruiting more minorities and women, Mettendorf used his esteemed tenured position to incite and injure, worrying little about those he harmed, instead finding immense joy in the number of victories he amassed in his ideological wars.

I took Mettendorf's course for two reasons. First, it was the Harvard thing to do. There was an unofficial short list of important professors and courses known throughout the student body. These internationally acclaimed thought leaders, whether you agreed with them or not, were considered to be an integral part of the Harvard experience and essential to a student's intellectual growth while being schooled in the great Harvard halls.

The second reason I subjected myself to the taunts of this ornery spitfire was to prove something to myself. Mettendorf's middle initial was *C,* which had been quickly turned into C minus for his notorious hard grading and reputation of giving out more C minuses than any professor in Harvard's history. Mettendorf was convinced that Harvard suffered from escalating grade inflation despite evidence to the contrary, so he dug in his heels and fought against the tide by giving out grades that sent the ultracompetitive summa cum laudes to University Health Services on the verge of nervous breakdowns.

So, this is why I was cursing "C Minus Mettendorf" as I trudged up the back steps of the Coop. He had already assigned us three books for the semester, and we had just learned he added another to the list—Kant's *Groundwork of the Metaphysics of Morals*. Not exactly beach reading. With my budget for the semester already stretched, I resorted to the "used texts" section of the store, which some considerate soul was kind enough to set up near a back staircase so financially challenged students could sneak into the discount section and quickly disappear without being noticed by our classmates.

But my cursing of "C Minus" didn't last very long that afternoon. Standing in front of the secondhand philosophy shelf, thumbing through a paperback, was Ashley Garrett from the Eliot House dining hall. Gone were the crimson uniform and baseball cap. She wore a pair of jeans that hugged her every curve and a tapered suede coat that couldn't have hung more perfectly.

"Ashley," I said as I approached.

She looked up from the book she was reading and said, "Mr. Cocky Harvard Man." Then she went back to the book.

"What are you doing here?" I asked.

"What does it look like I'm doing?" she said without looking up from her book.

"My name is Spenser," I said.

"I'm overwhelmed," she said, still flipping through the pages.

As I got closer, I noticed she was thumbing through Locke's *Second Treatise of Government*.

"Locke's *Second Treatise*," I said. "That's some pretty heavy reading."

"What's that supposed to mean?" she said, cutting her eyes at me and making me feel three inches tall.

"I'm just saying that Locke isn't . . . well, I've read that book and . . . there's a lot of information that . . ."

"Spit it out," she said.

"It's a tough book," I stammered.

"Go ahead, say what you're thinking," she said, planting a hand on her hip. "Why in the hell is the kitchen help reading John Locke?"

That's exactly what I was thinking, but I shook my head in deep protest. She closed the book, then pulled another off the shelf—Rousseau's *Social Contract.*

"How long have you been working at Eliot?" I asked.

"That was a onetime gig, my first and hopefully last time."

"You quit?"

"No, I'm a floater. I fill in wherever the supervisors need me for the night."

"Where do you work the most?"

"I just started last month. They send me everywhere."

She went back to *The Social Contract,* and I went back to digging for some way to keep the conversation alive. Then out of nowhere, I asked, "Do you like homemade ice cream?"

She looked at me as if I had three heads and said, "Relevance?"

"Emack and Bolio's in the Square is having a special for the rest of this week and next. Buy one cone, get the second free."

"Last of the big-time spenders," she said. "You really know how to impress a girl."

"Why pass up a good deal?"

"I have to get going. I have class in an hour."

"Where do you go to school?"

"Far away from here, thank God."

"What's the name?"

"It doesn't matter. You wouldn't know it."

"Try me," I said.

She sighed, then said, "RCC."

I searched my brain like hell, praying I had heard of it. When I couldn't come up with anything, I nodded my head and said, "Really good school."

"Bullshit," she said. "It's a community college. You need to work on your bluff, Harvard Man." She started walking away.

"What about the ice cream?" I said.

"I like chocolate chip cookie dough," she said. "In a waffle cone with rainbow sprinkles on one side and chocolate sprinkles on the other."

That afternoon I sneaked down the back stairs with two used books and a big smile on my face, grateful for the first time for Harvey "C Minus" Mettendorf.

THE SECOND ENVELOPE arrived as mysteriously as the first. Percy was tucked away in his room, sleeping off a late night of partying at the Hasty Pudding Club, while I was heading out to my morning chemistry lecture. Dalton had told me that if I didn't receive another invitation inside of a week, I should consider myself another punch casualty. Only two-thirds of the punchees would be lucky enough to make it to the next round.

Same envelope and stationery stock. Same meticulous calligraphy. No postal markings.

The President and members of the Delphic Club
invite you to the annual outing. Saturday, November 5.
Please bring a change of outdoor clothes and sneakers.
We will meet promptly in the courtyard of the clubhouse
at 7 AM. Enter through the side gate.
Regrets only 876-0400.

I called Dalton. "Another invitation," I said when he picked up the phone. "Must've come last night." I was standing in the middle of the common room with the invitation held up to the naked bulb.

"And it's legit?" Dalton asked.

"JPM inside the ring."

"What does it say?"

"The outing is next Saturday. We're meeting in the courtyard first thing in the morning."

"They're probably taking you to some alum's house for the day," Dalton said. "This is perfect. We'll have our talk with Dunhill before then."

"What time are we leaving tomorrow for Miami?"

"First flight at seven thirty. I booked us two rooms at the Raleigh. I don't feel like trekking all the way to my parents' place in West Palm. Besides, we'll have a lot more fun in South Beach."

"Do you think Dunhill will have anything important to tell us?"

"A treasure trove," Dalton said. "I found out something else yesterday at the alumni office. Dunhill knew Abbott long before Harvard. They both went to Choate, this exclusive little prep school in Connecticut."

I SLEPT MOST OF THE WAY to Miami, thanks to the thrilling offerings of Immanuel Kant and his meditations on reason and freedom. I was excited to be in Miami for the first time, especially after hearing so much about the occasional topless sunbather and the white-sand beaches. The Florida heat smothered us as soon as we stepped off the plane, and when we walked into the terminal, I caught my first glimpse of the paradise I had always imagined—vivacious, curvy women strolling through the airport in tight shorts and tiny minis with deep tans that glowed like the setting sun. Children frolicked in bright clothes and flip-flops, and I couldn't help but think about the hardened Bostonians back up north, layered in their thick wool sweaters and thermals, hunkering down for another frigid winter.

We jumped in the back of a cab, and Dalton gave the driver the address to the Raleigh. As we set out toward the beach, our strategy session began.

"Dunhill comes from Omaha, Nebraska," Dalton said. "His father was a banker and his mother a music teacher. He had one younger sister who also went to Harvard and an older brother who died in high school from polio."

"How in the hell did you find all this out?" I said.

"There are a few situations where the Winthrop name means something,"

Dalton said. "The Harvard alumni office is one of them, especially while they're in the middle of a university fundraising campaign. They were falling over themselves to help me out."

"I think Dunhill's gonna be a hard nut to crack," I said. "There's no doubt he'll want to know why we're snooping around about Abbott's death. And even if we tell him, there's no guarantee he'll give up anything."

"We'll get him to talk," Dalton said. "Just stick to our story. We're writing a paper on Harvard history. During our research, we came across the Abbott death and got curious about it. How could he resist two charming and studious undergrads?"

"Speaking of charming, I saw Ashley Garrett yesterday," I said.

"The dining hall girl?"

"Yes, my future wife. She was buying books at the Coop."

"Schoolbooks?"

"She's a student at some school called RCC. Ever heard of it?"

Dalton shook his head. "How did you get that out of her?"

"Sure in hell wasn't easy. She's a really smart girl."

"What makes you say that?"

"She was standing there, flipping through Locke and Rousseau."

"Jesus Christ! Looks *and* brains. A double threat. Did you ask her out?"

"Sort of. I asked her if she wanted to go to Emack's."

"And?"

"She really never answered. She had to go to class."

"In other words, you got shut down," he laughed.

"Down but not out," I said. "She at least told me her favorite ice cream flavor."

"Doesn't get rid of her boyfriend."

"She didn't mention him. Maybe he doesn't exist."

"The eternal optimist," Dalton said. "I haven't seen her again in the dining hall."

"Don't worry, I'll find her."

"Be careful. Her boyfriend's from Somerville."

"And I'm from the South Side of Chicago."

"Yeah, but you're a Leaguer now, a long way from the South Side. You study Machiavelli and Rembrandt. That guy probably pounds nails into roofs for a living. I wouldn't want him to do the same thing to that pretty face of yours."

The driver pulled up to a tall art deco hotel on a street full of other gigantic hotels and colorful low-rise apartment buildings that looked like they were stuck in a Cuban time warp. The palm trees soared overhead, and all the hotel workers were dressed in white linen pants and floral shirts with permanent smiles fixed across their heavily tanned faces.

"We'll check in, then get over to Dunhill's," Dalton said. "He's about a twenty-minute cab ride from here. Then we'll come back and hit the beach."

The icy air-conditioning blasted us as we walked into the lobby, but the woman greeting us behind the front desk was anything but chilly. She was Latina, almost as dark as me, and with a body that could stop traffic. I put her somewhere in her twenties, and she had a personality that filled the lobby. Dalton nudged my leg as we approached and wasted no time starting to flirt.

We checked into our rooms, changed our shirts, and met back in the lobby. Dalton was standing outside, talking to the bellhop when I arrived. The Thompson Home for the Aging was not in a heavily traveled area where it would be easy to hail down a cab for our return trip, so the bellhop gave us a card with the name of a car service company. He told us to drop his name, Juan Carlos, and they'd not only give us the friends and family discount, but make sure two beautiful señoritas would accompany us on the ride back to South Beach too. "Welcome to Miami," he said with a wink as he ushered us into the back of a cab. "Anything you need for the rest of your stay, Juan Carlos will take care of it."

THE THOMPSON HOME for the Aging was perfectly situated on Biscayne Bay, nestled between a yacht club and the Crandon Golf Course. It was one of those expansive plantation affairs with sweeping lawns and cascading water fountains fronting an audaciously columned entrance. Several elderly residents sat out on the front veranda in bright-colored cardigans and long polyester pants, canes at their sides, and tall glasses of iced tea sitting atop silver trays.

We walked into a spacious lobby decorated with shiny Italian marble and calming pastels. Two women sat behind a large glass-and-chrome desk underneath a domed roof. One was talking on the phone, so we approached the other, who was typing on her computer.

"How can I help you gentlemen?" she asked.

"We're here to see Mr. Kelton Dunhill," Dalton said.

"Is he expecting you?"

"We have a meeting with him at twelve thirty."

The woman asked us our names, typing something into her computer. She picked up a phone and told someone that Mr. Dunhill had two visitors. When she hung up, she turned to us and said, "Mr. Dunhill will be meeting you shortly under the portico out back. Please follow me."

She led us through a maze of open hallways and cozy sunlit rooms. An army of young Cuban and Haitian women went about their work quietly, arranging vases and dusting ledges. We eventually walked through a set of tall French doors that opened onto a lawn running down to the water. A slightly elevated white columned portico sat at the end of a narrow strip of lawn. She pointed us toward a table and told us that Dunhill would be joining us soon.

"Pretty spiffy place to die," Dalton said as we walked out on the lawn. "Nice view of the water, a bunch of pretty girls in tight uniforms running around. I'm already liking our man Dunhill."

"Seems depressing to me," I said. "Sitting around all day with a bunch of old people waiting to see whose number is up next. Not the way I wanna go."

"But that's why the señoritas are running around," Dalton said. "Keeps the blood rushing through their veins."

Just as we sat on the wicker chairs surrounding a small table that had been set up for lunch, a man in a lime green suit with a towel over his arm approached us, carrying a silver tray of glasses and a pitcher of iced tea. He poured the chilled tea, then left the pitcher and the remaining glass on the table. We were nearly halfway through our drinks when a short, stocky man walked out the back door and onto the path. He had thick silver hair, heavy eyebrows, and deep lines carved into his leathery skin. He wore a pair of khaki pants and a short-sleeved white shirt that was opened wide enough to show a little of what was once a muscular chest. He walked with a slight limp, but he was far from feeble. He shook our hands with a firm grip and took a seat across from us. The stoic expression on his face matched the gruffness in his voice.

"Well, boys, so you made it to Miami," Dunhill said, taking a sip of iced tea and stretching back in his chair. "Shouldn't you be studying for midterms this time of year?"

"They're a couple of weeks away," Dalton said. "We wanted to get down here before things got too busy."

"What's your interest in the Abbott affair?" Dunhill said, getting straight to the point.

"We were doing some research and found some articles about Abbott's disappearance in the *Crimson*," Dalton said, sticking to our script. "It seemed interesting, so we decided to follow up on it and see if there was anything there."

Dunhill looked over at me. "Is that true?"

I nodded my head.

A young boy in uniform approached us with an open box of Davidoff cigars and held it out to Dunhill, who took one, then offered the box to us. When we refused, he waved the man off and then burrowed his eyes into Dalton.

"You're bullshitting me, Winthrop," he said. "And I don't like it. There's no way the two of you would fly all the way down here just because you read some goddamn articles. There are more than three centuries of Harvard history you can dig through up in Cambridge. The Abbott case amounts to nothing more than a footnote. Either you come clean or this little meeting is over before it even starts."

Dalton looked at me and I looked at Dunhill.

"Okay, we're not just doing some random research," Dalton said. "We've been looking into the final clubs and came across an old article about Abbott's disappearance and started looking into what happened. Your name was mentioned in the article, so we looked up your information in the alumni directory. We figured you might tell us in your own words what happened that night."

Dunhill looked at me for confirmation. I nodded my head. He then clipped the end of the cigar, lit it, and relaxed in his chair. He took a long puff on his cigar, then said, "So all of this out of simple curiosity."

"It sounds like a really interesting story," Dalton said. "Mysterious."

"Most people don't even remember Ras," Dunhill said. "We were kids back then. Most of us who knew him are either dead or half out of our minds. I've been lucky enough to keep everything together. My memory is starting to leak a little, but I still have most of my life stored away."

"So, do you remember if Abbott was trying to break into the Delphic's secret room?" Dalton said.

"Is that what the article said?"

"At least one of them," I said.

Dunhill nodded slowly. "That damn room was his obsession," he said. "That's all he ever talked about."

The waiter returned, refreshed our glasses, and took our lunch orders. When the waiter asked Dunhill how he wanted his steak cooked, he said, "I want to see the blood." After we ordered and the waiter had left the portico, Dunhill leaned his head back, blew a cloud of smoke in the air, then said, "Does Aurelius know you're down here, Winthrop?"

We were both startled by that question.

"No, sir," Dalton said. "This trip has nothing to do with him. You know my father?"

"Not personally, but everyone knows *of* him. From what I've heard, he's a coldhearted bastard. No offense."

"None taken," Dalton said. "I couldn't agree more."

"But your uncle Randolph was a different story," Dunhill said. "I met him at a couple of the reunions. He was a complete gentleman in the old tradition, generous with his money and without pretense. Is he still alive?"

"He's hanging on," Dalton said. "He's got some kind of lung disease that's been slowly eating away at him. But he's still with us."

"Sorry to hear that," Dunhill said. "Through the years, he's represented your family with distinction."

"So, what exactly happened that night in 1927?" I asked.

Dunhill put down his glass, twirled the cigar in his mouth, then pulled it out and rested it on the edge of the table. He folded his hands across his stomach and looked out into the water. His eyes were a million miles away.

"It was Halloween night, and our regular crew had gotten together for dinner," he began. "There were five of us. Benny Shelton from Philly, Jasper Cummings from New York, and Thaddeus Arrington from Boston. Then, of course, Ras and me. We ate together most nights. A good group of guys." Dunhill smiled softly as the memories played back in his head. "We had a some good times in those days. Anyway, that night, Ras kept talking about breaking into the Delphic. We never paid him much attention, because he was always going on about finding a way to get in there and penetrating the secret room. But that night, I believed him. There was a look in his eyes that I had never seen before."

"Why was he so obsessed with the Delphic?" Dalton asked.

"Ras was always out to prove he belonged. He was the same way in boarding school. We were hall mates. He wasn't an athlete like the rest of us, so he always felt a little slighted. We'd heard about the Delphic's secret treasure room, and I think Ras felt that if he could break into it, he would prove that he was more than just another trust fund kid waiting for his inheritance to kick in."

"Do you believe there really was a secret room?" I asked.

"That's what was whispered for years," Dunhill said. "Some believed that J. P. Morgan Jr. had it secretly built on the third floor of the mansion and filled it with a lot of expensive paintings and artifacts that he had purchased in Europe. There was also a rumor that they held séances and communicated with the dead in there. Back then, there was so much being said that it was hard to separate fact from fiction."

"But what did you believe?" Dalton asked.

Dunhill took a couple of puffs on his cigar. His face cloudy in the smoke, he said, "I believed there was definitely something going on in that old mansion.

The members were too quick to deny the rumors, and they were overly secretive about their affairs. My club, the Spee, and many of the others would let nonmembers occasionally come in for lunch or dinner, but not the Delphic. Their door was always closed. But secret treasures and all that jazz? I think it's all imagination."

"Did you know any of the Delphic members?" I asked.

"A few," Dunhill said. "And don't think we didn't try to work them over for information. We'd get them drunk till they couldn't stand, and they still wouldn't say a word. But then something strange happened. One of the workers, some little Irish guy, was out one night at a bar in downtown Boston. He had too many shots of Jameson and started blabbing that he knew all the secrets buried in the Delphic mansion, and how if he wanted to, he could bring down some of the most powerful men in the country."

"Did he ever tell the secrets?" Dalton asked.

"Never had a chance," Dunhill said. "Two days later, they found him floating in the Charles down behind MIT."

"Was this before or after Abbott disappeared?" I asked.

"About a year before Ras disappeared."

"That Halloween night that Abbott tried to break in, what did the other guys at dinner think about his plans?" I asked.

"Benny and Jasper told him he was crazy. Thaddeus egged him on. I agreed to go with him because I was afraid he was gonna do something stupid and get in trouble."

"You told Fleming from the *Boston Evening Transcript* that you walked up to the club with Abbott," Dalton said. "But the article never said if you actually saw him go in."

"Archie Fleming was a piece of slime," Dunhill said. "I'd spit on his grave if I could find it. I never should've spoken with him. He was one of those sleaze reporters looking for a big break. He promised me what I said would stay off the record, and then he turned around and twisted almost every damn word I told him. I wanted to strangle him when I read that article. Made me look like a piece of shit."

"Did you tell him everything?" Dalton asked.

"He thought I did," Dunhill said. "But there was something about him that made me reluctant, so I just fed him a little to see what he would do with it. He betrayed me, so I never spoke to him again."

Two waiters arrived with our dome-covered plates, arranged the food in front of us, and at once lifted the shiny domes in grand fashion. I had ordered pasta and Dalton the lamb chops. Dunhill's steak looked as if it had just been killed on the plains and sliced on the plate. He wasted no time attacking the heavy slab of meat.

"So, what did you see?" Dalton said.

"I've shared that information with only one other person," Dunhill said. "My first wife, Eleanor, who I met at a dance at Wellesley. She's long gone, God rest her soul."

"Will you share it with us?" I asked.

"Depends."

"On what?"

"Whether you stop feeding me a load of horseshit and come clean about your reasons for wanting to know about Ras."

Dalton and I exchanged glances. It was time to be honest. Dunhill was nobody's fool.

"I'm being punched by the Delphic," I said.

"Is that so?" Dunhill smiled. "And you want to learn all their dirty secrets behind that blue door."

"I think it's only fair to know what I could possibly be getting myself into," I said. "I want to know everything I can."

"You'll never know everything until you become a member," Dunhill said. "And even then, I'm not sure. How far along are you?"

"We just finished the first round," I said.

"And the outing?"

"I just got the invitation yesterday."

"That's a strong showing, Collins. I don't know if it's the same anymore, but in my day, about a third of the initial list was cut before the second round."

"Hasn't changed," Dalton said.

Dunhill looked at Dalton. "Have you been punched too?" he asked.

"I'm not the club type," Dalton said.

"Must be killing your father," Dunhill said. "He was a Porker, from what I remember."

"Yes, he was. But my uncle Randolph is a Delphic man."

"Have you asked him the questions you're asking me?"

"Some of them, but like I said, he hasn't been doing too well. His mind is in and out."

"That's too bad. He'd know a helluva lot more about this than I would."

"But he wouldn't know more about the night Abbott disappeared," I said. "You were actually there."

"Yes, I was." Dunhill sat back in his chair, his broad shoulders falling to his sides. He played with the cigar in his mouth. "After dinner, I left with Ras. We went back to his room and talked for a bit. Then he changed into a black shirt and pants. He was convinced that he had to wear black for the break-in to be successful. He had read it in some book or something. We walked up Linden Street to the club. The lights were usually on in the Gas, but for some reason, that night they were off. It was all the better so that we wouldn't be seen. We waited for the street to clear and then climbed the trellis on the side of the mansion and dropped into the courtyard." Dunhill stopped and shook his head.

"What's wrong?" Dalton asked.

"Ras had always been clumsy, but that night he was as agile and coordinated as a ballet dancer. He was a totally different person. He finally had his chance to prove himself, and I was his audience. He walked to one of the back doors, opened up his kit, and started working on the lock."

The waiters came to clear our plates and refresh our glasses. The sun was still sitting high in the sky, but out of nowhere, sheets of rain started pouring down. The waves crashed hard against the rocky coastline. We stayed dry underneath the portico and ordered ice cream and cake for dessert. Once the waiters headed back to the main building, Dalton asked, "Did you see him go in?"

"He'd been practicing, and it paid off," Dunhill said. "I couldn't believe he had actually gotten that lock open in under a minute."

"So, you went in?" I asked.

Dunhill shook his head slowly.

"Why not?" I asked.

"'Cause I was scared as hell," he said. "I just knew we'd get caught. There was a new steward living there, a hulk of a man named Moss Sampson. They hired him after the Irishman was found in the Charles. Rumor had it he had done time for killing two men down in Mississippi. Big, dark-skinned ugly man with hands that looked like they could twist steel. I had seen him once carrying firewood into the club. He was massive. But besides being leery of Sampson, I was worried that if word got out that I had broken into the Delphic, I'd get kicked out of my own club. There had been a string of club burglaries, members pulling pranks on other clubs, so the inter-club council put together a very strict set of rules about territory breach. Any club member caught entering another club without authorization was immediately suspended for the rest of the semester. A second offense brought expulsion. Don't get me wrong, I was as interested in the Delphic's secrets as anyone else, but I loved the Spee too much to risk losing my membership. Ras didn't belong to any club, so he had nothing to lose."

"So, you did see Abbott go in?" Dalton said.

Dunhill continued to look out aimlessly into the bay.

"Mr. Dunhill, did Abbott go in?" Dalton asked more firmly.

The two waiters reappeared, walking underneath large umbrellas. They placed our desserts down and disappeared. I still couldn't figure out how it was raining and there was barely a cloud in the sky.

"When are the two of you leaving?" Dunhill asked.

"Tomorrow afternoon," Dalton said.

Dunhill nodded his head as he lifted what seemed like half the slice of cake to his mouth. The rain suddenly stopped as if it had been turned off by a switch. The waves fell down and slid easily to shore.

"That's enough for today," Dunhill finally said. "That's as much as my wife knew and about as far as I want to go. Come back tomorrow morning for breakfast."

11

＊

AT NINE O'CLOCK sharp, we rolled onto the grounds of the Thompson Home. Little had changed since yesterday—majestic water fountains shot toward the sky, Cuban men worked the property in pale blue uniforms, and the same collection of old people sat on the front veranda, dozing off to the chimes knocking softly in the wind. The sun was barely up, but the temperature was already hovering somewhere in the nineties. The heat didn't exactly help the banging in my head, thanks to last night's raucous party at a club that Juan Carlos had recommended.

We entered the lobby and approached the desk, but this time the receptionist was expecting our arrival and escorted us to the other side of the complex and up a winding staircase to a small, ornate dining room surrounded by tall windows that opened up on the bay. A couple of tables were occupied by residents hunched over their plates, being fed by aides who held up their drinks and wiped the corners of their mouths.

Dunhill, however, was a different story. A lion of a man, he was seated at a table on a patio that offered a grand view of the water and the jagged skyline along the beach. He wore a yellow polo shirt and white linen pants. His thick silver hair was wet and combed back into a helmet. The sun made his blue eyes look translucent. He was sipping from a glass of orange juice as we sat down.

"Did you sleep well last night?" he asked with a wink.

"Nothing like falling asleep to the sound of the waves," Dalton said.

"Especially when you have someone sleeping beside you," Dunhill said.

"That doesn't hurt either."

A waiter came, and we quickly ordered breakfast. Our plane was leaving in a few hours, and we had been warned that our ride back to the airport could be long, depending on traffic. We all sat in silence for a moment, looking at the long sailboats and watching the seagulls circling effortlessly.

"I often wondered if things might've worked out differently if I had gone in with Ras," Dunhill said without prompting. "Maybe we could've protected each other. I've gone back and forth about this over the years. It's been one of only a few regrets I've had in my entire life."

Dalton nudged me with his leg under the table before saying, "So you did see Abbott go into the mansion?"

Dunhill nodded slowly. "Yes, Ras went in. I stood right there and watched him with my own eyes. Once I knew he was inside, I felt like my feet were glued to the ground. I didn't know if I should run in to find him or if I should get the hell out of there before someone caught us. Life comes down to a few critical decisions. I decided to leave. Maybe that saved my life, but it probably cost Erasmus his."

"So, all you saw was Abbott go in?" Dalton said.

"Not exactly," Dunhill said. "Before Ras got in, I saw Moss Sampson. He was on one of the top floors, looking out the window. It definitely was him. Looked as mean as a bull with swollen testicles. We had all heard about him, but actual sightings of him outside the clubhouse had been rare. He must've seen us approach. I wanted to scream out to Ras, but he was already inside, so I turned and ran like hell. Jumped back over the fence and didn't stop running till I got back to Leverett House."

"And that was the last time you saw Abbott?" Dalton said.

Dunhill nodded slowly.

"Do you think he ever made it out of the Delphic?" I asked.

Dunhill shrugged his shoulders. "There's not a day that goes by that I don't ask myself that question. I just wish I knew what happened."

"Did anyone question Sampson about Abbott's disappearance?" I asked.

"Supposedly," Dunhill said. "But nothing came of it."

"Why didn't you tell anyone that you saw Sampson in the window after Abbott got in?" Dalton said.

"Because I felt guilty and confused, and I was scared to death. If it had gotten out that I had actually gone with Ras that night *and* I had seen Sampson in that window, then I didn't know where that would put me. But I just knew they would call me a coward for not going in with Ras. Even worse, they might blame me for his death."

Dunhill paused for a moment and clenched his jaws.

"I was just a kid," he said. "If I had to do it all over again, of course, I'd do it differently. I would've gone right to the police and told them everything. I was scared. I had heard all the rumors about the Delphic mansion and their secrets and what they were willing to do to keep their privacy."

"I could understand not telling the police," I said. "But you could've at least told some of the other guys who were at dinner that night."

Dunhill had that distant look in his eyes again. "Not a word."

"You went to Choate with Abbott," Dalton said.

"That's true," Dunhill said. "We had known each other for most of our lives. But we were from very different backgrounds. The Abbott family was extremely wealthy and lived like recluses down in Newport. Ras and I really didn't become friends until we got to Harvard. He was a difficult kid to know. He didn't play sports with the rest of us, stayed to himself most of the time reading books, and he went home a lot on the weekends to see his family. He was an only child and they were constantly after him about everything."

"It seemed like no one really cared about his disappearance," I said. "The *Crimson* ran only three articles the entire time. You'd think the sudden disappearance of a student, especially an heir like Abbott, would've caused a lot more commotion than what was reported."

"It caused plenty of commotion, all right," Dunhill said. "The students were petrified. There were all kinds of rumors going around. Some were saying his body had been found in the Charles like the Irishman's. Others said he had been kidnapped walking home and decapitated when the family wouldn't pay the ransom. It was a wild time. We kept hoping he'd eventually turn up, but he never did."

"Why didn't the papers keep the pressure on?" I asked. "They just let the story die."

"Times were different then. None of the university officials wanted to talk about it. The family and administration put pressure on the paper to back off. A kid who lived down the hall from me was one of the editors. He told me the Abbotts and President Lowell wanted it to go away as quietly as possible. At first the paper refused to keep quiet, but then Lowell called the editorial staff into his office for a meeting. The editors changed their position. That's really the only reason I talked to Fleming. I knew that no one else would touch the story. I'd heard there was this reporter nosing around on campus who said he wanted to help find Ras. He'd been asking students what they knew of that night and giving out his number for people to call if they had something to tell. I got the number and called him. The guilt was killing me."

"What's the possibility that Abbott is still alive?" Dalton asked.

"Slim to none," Dunhill said. "Knowing Ras, if he were still alive, he would've tried to contact one of us over the years. I'm sure of that. None of us ever heard a word."

The waiters arrived with a spread big enough to feed an army. Dunhill dumped every condiment within arm's reach on top of his omelet then attacked it like he hadn't eaten in a year. He chased the first couple of bites with a glass of orange juice and cleared his throat.

"What can you tell us about the Ancient Nine?" Dalton asked.

"You've been doing your homework," Dunhill said, devouring another big bite of the omelet. "The old-timers believed Morgan started the Ancient Nine to build a mystique around the club. Remember, he had been rejected by two other clubs, so he wanted to do something that would make the Delphic stand out from the others. Rumor had it that a bunch of his poker buddies were sitting around the clubhouse after dinner one night when someone came up with the idea to start a small brotherhood within the club. No one was ever able to identify the members, but it was believed they had bonded together to protect a secret. No one knew for sure what that secret was, but some said they had hidden something extremely valuable in their mansion. They called it Harvard's Holy Grail. The less people knew, the crazier the rumors got."

"So, you think the Ancient Nine really exist?" I asked.

Dalton shrugged. "Probably in some form or another," he said. "But it's hard to separate rumor from facts, because no one really knows anything about the members who started the brotherhood. Their identities have been protected for almost a hundred years."

"Let's suppose the group does still exist," Dalton said. "What do you think they're hiding?"

"You name it and I've heard it," he said. "Jewels from one of the early popes, priceless artwork that's been missing for centuries, Egyptian mummies in sarcophagi. Lots of stories, but no one has been able to penetrate that damn fortress up on Linden Street to really know. No member has ever gone on record to talk about it and probably never will. At least not in my lifetime."

"I know you don't have any proof of what happened that night," I said. "But do you think they really *killed* Erasmus Abbott to protect a secret?"

Dunhill worked his jaws hard for a moment and looked out into the water. Then he said, "I think it's possible that night Ras got too close to their secrets. He was alone in their clubhouse in the middle of the night. Moss Sampson knew he had gotten in. Sampson took his orders from someone. You can fill in the blanks."

"Is there anyone you know who might be able to help us find out more?" Dalton asked. "Anyplace where we might be able to go and read more about Abbott or the history of the Delphic?"

"I appreciate your determination, but I think you boys should leave well enough alone," Dunhill said. "You open too many doors and you might find skeletons. You open the wrong door and those skeletons might end up being yours."

12

❦

THE MORNING OF the outing was one of those overcast days where it seemed like the sun just gave up and went back to bed. The campus was still sleeping off Friday night's round of parties, except for a few red-eyed, hungover souls who reported to the Delphic's courtyard at the profane hour of 7 A.M. Linden Street was a straight shot from Lowell, just on the other side of Mt. Auburn Street. When I reached the bottom of the road, I noticed three yellow school buses in front of the weathered mansion parked half on the sidewalk, half in the street.

I wasn't in the best of moods. The week after returning from Miami had been a disaster. Coach ran us in practice like he was training the Olympic sprint team, Harvey "C Minus" Mettendorf decided to tack on a final paper in addition to the final exam, and Percy spent every night in front of the television in our common room with prospective members from the Hasty Pudding Club. On top of everything, I got a call from one of my high school teammates, who confirmed that my ex-girlfriend really was dating Dallas Holton, my biggest rival from Simeon High School, who got me fouled out in a state championship game during my senior year. Now here I was dressed in a blazer and tie, with a sweat suit and sneakers in my duffel bag, heading off for a day of sports and male bonding at some undisclosed location.

The Delphic's garden was located behind the clubhouse, adjacent to the Bureau of Study Counsel building. A tall gate shielded it from the view of passersby on the street, and some fleshy kid in a Delphic bow tie was standing there, greeting people with a smug grin on his face simply because he was a member and we weren't. When I approached and gave my name, he looked down at a small clipboard in his chubby hands and instructed me to put my bag with the others along the far corner of the wall. As I walked through the entrance, he informed me that I would be riding on the second bus.

The courtyard was larger than I had expected, with a palpable air of history and privilege. It was completely enclosed by the mansion and a tall brick wall along the back of the property. A replica of *Manneken Pis,* the famous sculpture of a naked boy urinating in a fountain, stood in the center of the garden, surrounded by a circle of meticulously trimmed rosebushes. A tall row of manicured hedges lined the back. Bagels, doughnuts, and juice had been neatly arranged on one table, while an adjacent table was crammed with the biggest bowls of fruit I had ever seen in my life along with mounds of smoked salmon on bagels. Two uniformed servers stood behind the table, keeping things tidy as everyone picked over what they wanted and ignored any mess they made while doing it. A small bar had been set up adjacent to the back porch, and I noticed the same woman who had been serving drinks at the cocktail party.

Several guys were crowded around a keg, taking turns sipping from the tap, spilling beer all over their ties and shirts, grabbing each other in headlocks, and singing drink songs as they choked back the cold beer. I immediately knew it was going to be a messy day. There must've been about ninety of us, everyone dressed up like we were going on a job interview, most still smelling of last night's alcohol. I scanned the faces, but I didn't see Clint McDowell, the sweaty guy I had met at the cocktail party with the winning formula for making it to the next round. Binky Grunwald was holding court as usual, standing on the top step of the porch, surrounded by a bunch of guys holding up their mugs of beer in a toast.

Then I saw Satch Washington, and my blood froze. Ellis Satch Washington was the most reviled black student on campus. He was no bigger than a finger snap, had skin the color of old pancake batter, and his thick wavy hair looked like it had been professionally relaxed and lightened. Last year he quickly climbed to the top of the Black Students Association's most hated list when he declared in front of a standing-room-only crowd in Sanders Theatre that women and minorities had been given too many allowances in academia and needed to stop using their color and gender as an excuse for their shortcomings. It wasn't that other minorities didn't agree with some of Satch's arguments, but what had sparked instant ire within our ranks was that he had made this proclamation in front of such a mixed audience, airing our dirty laundry right in front of the neoconservatives who were rolling in their seats with glee. Racial treason.

His pedigree was impeccable. His father had gone to Dartmouth, then on to Yale Law School, and was now one of the highest-ranking black judges in the federal appeals circuit. His mother graduated from Harvard, then went to business school at Wharton before joining Goldman Sachs, where she currently had some fancy job in their mergers and acquisitions division. It wasn't that we were jealous of Satch. In fact, it was encouraging to the rest of us that a black family could achieve such greatness in *their* world. What rubbed people the wrong way, however, was that Satch did everything imaginable to deny his blackness. He didn't have any black friends, only dated the palest, blondest white girls, and had officially lobbied the university to exclude him from any institutional accounting that included him in the black student tally. I stood there looking at him with that big phony smile and frosted hair, and couldn't help but think how much I wanted to land a solid right across his thin jaw and watch him squirm on the ground in pain.

"Hey, Spenser, what's up?" a voice called out.

I turned and found Duke McCallister approaching me from across the courtyard. He was the only member not wearing a tie, and he had a smile on his face like we were old friends. I had immediately liked Duke the night we met at the cocktail party, and I strongly suspected he had been my ally in getting me through the first cut and into the second round. We shook hands when he reached me.

"So, you ready for today?" he said.

"I guess," I said. "I'm not really sure what to expect."

"I felt the same way when I was a punchee. It's pretty nerve-racking getting all these cryptic messages and no one's really telling you what's going on. I almost didn't go to my outing until one of the members convinced me I'd have a good time."

"Did you?"

"Let's just say it was a lot different than I expected. But today I think we have a good group going with us. You'll get a chance to meet more members and punchees. We tried to make it a mix of low-key guys like yourself and some of the party animals."

He pointed to the crew standing around the keg. They were now doing keg stands, where the drinker places his hands on the keg and two others pull up his legs and hold them in the air so that he's doing a headstand on the keg. The third person takes the tap and places it in the drinker's mouth; then the fourth guy used his watch to time times how long the person can drink from the open tap without stopping. I had played the game once as a freshman and drank so much, they had to carry me to University Health Services. I quickly retired from the sport.

"How far is the place where we're going?" I asked.

"Shouldn't be more than forty-five minutes away," Duke said. "We go there every year. It's an unbelievable piece of property in the middle of nowhere. And there will be a little surprise for everyone." He winked. "You'll like it a lot."

Another member called Duke over, but before he left, he told me that he had arranged to ride on the second bus with me. There would be a couple of drinkers in our group, but he assured me that it wouldn't be too crazy. After Duke left, I looked up at the gigantic mansion. It was old, but well maintained. Every window, and I must've counted at least thirty, was covered inside by an impenetrable blue curtain. The exterior lighting fixtures were wrought-iron torches. I thought about what Dunhill had described the night he and Abbott had climbed the trellis above the fence. Both were still there. I noticed three small steps that led to the back door and kitchen. Was that the door Abbott used to enter the mansion? I walked into the center of the yard and looked up to the third floor. There were ten small windows just underneath the roofline, and I wondered at which window Moss Sampson stood watching Dunhill and Abbott that night.

My thoughts were suddenly interrupted by the sound of silverware clinking against glass. Graydon Brimmer, the club's president, stood on top of a chair, calling for our attention. He unfolded a small sheet of paper in his hand.

"Cease and desist, you wild beasts," he called out. "Woe to the man who speaketh while I have the stage."

Raucous cheers erupted throughout the courtyard.

"Welcome to the Delphic courtyard," Brimmer read aloud. "A place where boys are made into men, and men are made to bear their darkest secrets. Those of you gathered before me have successfully defeated the less fortunate and made it past the first round. Though your journey remains long and fraught with unpredictable peril, you are at least one step closer to lighting the legendary torches of the Gas."

Wild applause sprang from the gathering and bounced off the brick walls like the sound of a herd of animals stampeding through the gates. Everyone raised their cups skyward and in unison downed the foaming beer.

Brimmer waited for the noise to settle before continuing. "Today we will test the endurance of your wills as well as the endurance of your livers. You shall fight the elements of nature as you battle the duplicity of your fellow man. You've been divided into three groups, which are your assigned teams for the rest of the day. Do not take these assignments lightly, as those who stand shoulder-to-shoulder with you will either help lead you to victory or cause your inglorious demise. As in war, you are only as strong as your weakest man, so find that slimy bastard, beat the shit out of him, and make him commit his life to your survival." The courtyard filled again with laughter. "This will make a big difference at the end of the day when the competition is over, and the prizes are awarded," Brimmer continued. "So, bond well, ye faithful punchees of the Gas—and march on to lands unknown and battles yet to be won."

By the time Brimmer's speech had ended, everyone had been poured a fresh cup of beer, and the first drink song of the day blasted up from the Delphic courtyard and into the languid Cambridge morning.

> *Drink beer, drink beer.*
> *Oh, come drink beer with me.*
> *For I don't give a damn for any old man,*
> *Who won't drink beer with me.*
> *Bring out the old golden goblet*
> *With the Delphic torches on it,*
> *And we'll all kill another keg of beer!*
> *For it's not for knowledge that we come to this great college,*
> *But to raise hell while we're here.*
> *Raise hell while we're there.*
> *Raise hell while we're everywhere.*
> *Oh, we'll drink, drink, drink to the old Gas,*
> *And we will raise our glasses high;*
> *And we'll drink to the beloved torches,*
> *And we'll be loyal till we die.*
> *Oh, how we love our sacred brotherhood,*
> *And we will laud it to the sky;*
> *And when the day is done, we'll drink one more pass,*
> *To that mansion on old Linden, venerable home of the Gas!*

Our bags had already been loaded onto the bus by the time we filed out of the courtyard. Guys pushed and pulled, horsing around in anticipation of the long day ahead of us. Gallons of alcohol had already been consumed, and it was only eight o'clock in the morning.

The bus driver, Franco, was a short man with a hairy mustache, thick forearms, and a floppy French cap that fell halfway down the side of his face. Two extra seat cushions propped him high enough so that he could see over the wheel, and a cigar stub was jammed into the corner of his mouth. I took a seat closer to the front as I noticed most of the hardy drinkers had made their way to the back. Duke sat next to me, and after the last of the five kegs was loaded, the buses began to roll out of Cambridge.

We weren't five minutes into the trip before the kegs started flowing, the drink songs kept coming, and the jokes got raunchier. None of it seemed to bother Franco, who bounced on his elevated seat with his bulging forearms spread across the wide wheel. There was a bus in front of us and one behind—three yellow school buses loaded with ninety future presidents, Supreme Court justices, and Fortune 500 CEOs already wasted on cheap beer and hard alcohol, heading out to the country for a day of drinking and games, freed from the rigors of Harvard life, and now a chance to be ordinary teenagers swollen with testosterone.

The buses finally turned off the highway and onto the wide streets of rural Massachusetts. We were only twenty minutes into the trip, but the dramatic change of scenery made it seem like we had traveled thousands of miles out of Cambridge. The colorful foliage marked the changing of the seasons as we passed through quaint towns with their weather-beaten shingled houses and tidy lawns. Innocent children frolicked with their dogs, jumping into piles of leaves while parents gazed from a distance as they tended to matters about the house.

There were no taxi drivers or city buses or subway platforms. Instead the roads were owned by station wagons with wood side paneling, weathered Volvos and pickup trucks with hardened mud stuck between worn tire treads and U.S. flag stickers peeling off the back window. Cardboard signs hanging on large maples advertised cold apple cider and freshly baked pies. I got lost in the rustic New England landscape a world away from the urban sprawl of Chicago and other cities where concrete buildings clawed the skyline and children played on fractured blacktops.

The buses abruptly pulled to a stop along the side of the road. "Bladder run!" someone yelled from the back of the bus. There was a sudden commotion as the emergency door opened and bodies began flying out the back of the bus. I had to go as well, but I looked out the window at the small houses and their manicured yards and couldn't bring myself to do it. But there they stood, at least thirty of them, in broad daylight, shoulder-to-shoulder with their backs to the road facing a tiny yellow house. I could see the arcs of urine from my vantage point and dared to imagine the view from inside the house. One of the members ran onto the yard with a big, fancy camera and started snapping pictures, and the future leaders of the world stood there, hands on their swords as they posed in midstream. I wondered how many promising political careers could be ruined were these photos to reemerge years later.

After the fertilization of the lawn had ended and the high fives had been slapped, everyone boarded the buses, and we rolled again along the empty roads. The alcohol had finally taken effect and the vomiting began, sometimes between the seats, at other times out the windows onto passing cars. After another ten minutes, we pulled onto a narrow dirt road that ambled across acres and acres of fertile farmland and dense woods in all directions. Eventually an enormous white farmhouse with shiny black shutters and tall brick chimneys came into view. A nearby silver milk silo looked like a rocket sitting on a launch pad. The bus slowed, and we pulled onto the driveway, which ran to the back of the house and into a freshly cut field. We parked in front of a boxy red barn that was almost as big as the house.

A middle-aged man wearing a cowboy hat, jeans, boots, and an oversized apron met us. "Welcome to Milgorn Farm," he said. He was a big, jolly man with a wide neck, heavy beard, and smile that wrapped around his meaty face. "My name is John Milgorn, class of '59," he said. Everyone chimed their greetings. Those standing near him reached out and shook his hand. "The food is on the spit," he said. "You all go out and enjoy yourselves, and everything will be ready in a couple of hours. The place is yours. And I had some of the boys saddle up the horses, if you want to ride the property. Just be careful of Zeus, the black quarter horse. He's been a little cranky lately." He tipped his ten-gallon hat and strolled over to the barbecue pit, which was surrounded by a circle of linen-covered tables and comfortable lawn furniture.

I looked at the gigantic tractor trailers and the clusters of cows that speckled the undulating hills. I had never been on a real farm. I was surprised that a Harvard graduate actually owned and worked a farm, as I always imagined Harvard alumni in fancy office buildings, gated estates, and exclusive country clubs. But not to be disappointed, I soon spotted the Mercedes-Benz and Jaguar parked on the other side of the barn. Even the graduates living off the grid seemed to enjoy the material trappings of success.

We changed out of our blazers and khakis and threw on heavy sweats and sneakers. Some guys started tossing a football while others kicked an old soccer ball. The drinkers made a beeline to the kegs and began pouring pitchers of frothing beer. The sun was still absent from the sky, but the crisp air started to warm, as did the spirits on the field.

Brimmer stood on a folding ladder to use a bullhorn to announce the first competition. "Time to get the games going," he said. "Football first. Divide up into your teams. The members will give each of you a team shirt. Group one is with me. We're the red team. The second group is blue, and the third is white. Rules are simple. My team will play the blue team first; then the white will play the winner. We'll keep rotating till everyone has played the other teams at least twice. Whoever has the best record at the end of the four games will be declared the winner and receive the first prize, to be announced after the game. Each game will be twelve minutes long, two time-outs per team, and ties will be broken by a coin toss."

For the next hour we battered each other, and a game that was only supposed to be touch turned into full-contact with lots of crushing blows and heavy tackling. I decided to play wide receiver to avoid contact during most plays. I figured Coach wouldn't exactly do cartwheels if I showed up to practice on Monday with a broken arm or twisted ankle. Jon Carderro, a punchee who played tennis and lived in Leverett House, shared my injury concerns and chose a position that also prevented him from being trampled. The games started out competitive and surprisingly organized, but as the alcohol began settling in and the testosterone levels rose, it became less a game of football and more an uncontrolled mash to kill the person holding the football. The rules changed every other minute, depending who was in possession of the ball and how loudly he yelled. There was a lot of tumbling and cursing and bloodied knees as we ran wildly over the enormous field. I was doing well until I caught a touchdown pass and someone came from behind and leveled me. That was the last thing I remembered before looking up and seeing what looked like thousands of eyes staring down on me and someone yelling, "Give the man some room!" They carried me off the field, but my team fought on, and we won the game by a last-minute catch in the end zone.

The white team and their bunch of bruisers finished one game better than my team and were declared the winners. We watched as they were taken to the other side of the barn, stripped, then hosed down by two of the members, who then provided them with fresh towels, clean underwear, new T-shirts, and shorts.

"Come with me," Duke said.

We started out toward the front of the property, but before we reached the road, he looped around the perimeter and headed toward a hill behind the football field.

"Where are we going?" I asked.

"I'm going to show you the prize they just won."

We cut across a small stream, clipped our way through a dense patch of trees, and trekked around a long oval horse run. When we reached a clearing between two hills, he said, "There it is over there."

I looked but still didn't see anything. "What am I looking for?" I said.

"See that little house over there behind the fence?" he said.

It might've been little by his standards, but for me it was rather large. It was built out of stone with a wooden porch that wrapped entirely around it. There were three large windows on the first floor and several more above them. Smoke billowed out of the long chimney. I thought I saw someone moving in one of the windows, but we were too far away for me to be sure.

"Let's get closer," he said.

He didn't want us to be seen, so we jogged over another hill and completed a semicircle until we were about fifty yards away from the house but still hidden in the woods. When we had settled into our best viewing positions, I immediately saw the prize. There must've been a dozen of them from what I could see. Most of them were either tall blondes or shapely brunettes. There was one black girl who had a body that looked like it had been cut from rock. None of them were wearing clothes as they walked around in their heels, touching each other's hair and dabbing on makeup. My heart was beating so fast that my stomach started to hurt.

"Not too bad a prize, right?" Duke said.

I was too shocked to answer with anything other than a nod.

"Milgorn is the best," Duke went on. "He lets us ship them here every year for the outing. Most of them are from Boston, but I heard this year they have a couple of girls who just moved here from the Soviet Union."

I could see the white team coming over a hill. They looked fresh and unsuspecting. Two members led the charge. Why in the hell hadn't my team played harder?

"So, what happens next?" I said.

Duke laughed. "To the victor goes the spoils, but don't worry, the day is long. There will be plenty of opportunities for us to make our victory march."

I could tell the moment the white team realized what awaited them, because they started throwing up their arms and whistling and shoving each other. The women heard the noise and started spreading out on the porch, still naked and still in their high-heeled shoes.

"Let's go," Duke said. "They'll be looking for us soon."

I took one last look at the twelve naked beauties, then turned and followed Duke back around the perimeter of the property and to the football field. Everyone was already seated at the tables, eating like they had never seen food before. Milgorn was cooking a full pig, head and all, on the spit, rotating it carefully over the fire and slapping on fresh coats of barbecue sauce. Four older women in uniform tended the eight long tables that lined the lawn. The tables were lavishly decorated with crystal vases of wildflowers, candles, and fine china. The plates had a gold rim and a picture of the farmhouse artfully sketched in the center. THE MILGORN FARM, EST. 1865 was conspicuously painted under the drawing. Platters of burgers and hot dogs had been set down, and most of the guys were already working on their second and third helpings. Enormous bowls of potato salad and coleslaw had been evenly spaced between large bottles of condiments.

The food seemed to settle everyone, and after I had put away my third cheeseburger, I got up from the table and found my way to a big maple far enough from the eating area where I couldn't be bothered by the noise, but close enough that I could see Milgorn slicing away at the pig and dumping the barbecued pork on the waiting plates. The first member of the white team began making his way back toward base camp. You could see his smile all the way across the field, his shirt on backwards. The rest straggled back equally disheveled and content.

Once people had finished lunch, everyone spread out across the vast property. A few guys casually tossed the football, some went back to the stables to ride horses, but most of us found a quiet spot and succumbed to a nap. The wind blew softly, and the birds sang from their branches high in the towering trees. Jon Carderro joined me underneath the maple, and it wasn't long before we were both asleep.

THE SOUND OF THE bullhorn woke me up. Carderro still stretched on the grass beside me. The clouds had broken up and the sun sat alone in the sky, providing unseasonable warmth on what had started out as a crisp day. Brimmer ordered us to take our places in the field. It was time to line up and play a game of stick races. I roused Carderro, and when we returned to the fields, we found four sticks lined up fifty yards away. The game was described like a drunkard's version of relay races. Each team had a keg at its starting point. The object of the game was to drink a cup of beer while touching the keg with our foot. Once that had been accomplished, we had to run down to the other end of the field, pick up the sticks, plant them in the ground, place our hands on the sticks, then our foreheads on our hands. After completing ten circles around the sticks, we then had to run back to our teams and tag the next man in line.

Once each team had figured out the order of their men, Milgorn fired a shotgun in the air to start the game. The first three guys downed their cup of beer and ran to the sticks. All of them fell, trying to maintain their balance as they circled the sticks. When they finally finished, each of them ran off in different directions as they struggled to find their way back to their respective teams. Our guy collided with the lead-off member of the red team, and both crumpled to the ground. The guy from the white team was running in the exact opposite direction, and his team was yelling at him to turn around, which he finally did after going twenty yards out of the way.

We all laughed as they staggered back to the starting lines and collapsed. And this is how the game continued, bodies strewn about the field, lunches returned in nearby bushes, faces and shirts marked with grass stains. I fared a little better because I hadn't had much to drink, but the ten circles around the stick threw me. I was running for a short time, when suddenly it seemed like the ground was sliding up and trying to hit me in the face. Within seconds I tasted grass, and it took several attempts before I could get back up and find my way to my team. After I crossed the finish line, I buckled into Duke's arms and we fell to the ground together and laughed.

We won the game because the last man on the red team got himself disqualified by completing only nine circles around the stick instead of ten. There was an immediate protest and demands for a rematch, but Duke and the other members on our team refused to hear any of it. They led us behind the barn, washed us down with hoses, then handed out clean clothes. The others kept asking what our prize would be, and Duke gave me the signal for silence. When everyone had been cleaned up and outfitted, we headed out to the back of the property. Several minutes later, I could see the stone house on the other side of the hill. The smoke still flowed from the chimney, and there was a flurry of movement in the windows. For some reason I thought of Eppsy, our no-nonsense dean of students and the rage that would fill his face if he ever heard that thirty of his "best and brightest" were trudging over hilly land in tight cotton shorts and loose T-shirts to claim their female spoils after a drunken game of stick races. The image of his contorted face and bulging neck veins brought a smile to my face.

When we had reached a point on the hill where the stone house and its wide porch of naked beauties were visible, a chorus of cheers raced up to the heavens. We ran the rest of the way to collect our prizes.

BY THE TIME THE last man had made his way back to the field, everyone else was drunk again and the sun kneeled on the western horizon. Brimmer announced that it was time to head back to Cambridge. All of us to a man shook Milgorn's hand and thanked him for his hospitality. We loaded back onto the buses, and I caught my last glimpse of the big house and the lush fields of Milgorn Farm. As the buses rolled away, I could hear the roaring silence of the fields blowing in the wind, like a long exhale of relief with our departure.

Unlike the ride out to the country, the return trip was completely silent as those who weren't sleeping stared at the fading mountains. I was tired, but my mind was racing with too much information to sleep. In many ways, I felt like the day had been one big dream of possibilities. Not until I thought about all the term papers, class assignments, and ornery professors waiting for us in those ivy-strangled buildings did I realize that the purpose of these outings went beyond the drunken debauchery and naked romps. Ninety guys who likely would never be together again in the same place had been given eight hours to cast aside the pressures and lofty expectations that often dogged us as Harvard students. We had been allowed to be children again, foolish and politically incorrect without penalty, all on secluded hinterlands that had released yet another class of trapped souls and allowed them to be free—even if only for that one afternoon.

13

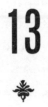

THE LEGENDARY WINTHROP mansion stood on top of historic Beacon Hill underneath the shadows of the gold-domed State House and adjacent to a scattering of other weathered but important Boston landmarks. It had once been the manor house of the enormous Blaxton estate, fifty acres of wooded land and meadows, which now constituted Boston's largest park, the Common. The Winthrop family had lived in the old brick mansion since the early 1700s, and by the looks of it, not much had changed in almost two centuries. Except for a few modern conveniences like central air and electric heat, the house was a testament to colonial Boston and the wealth of the Brahmins who occupied most of the private houses around the Hill.

Dalton hated the mansion for its obscene display of wealth. It was one of the Emperor's showpieces and a reminder to everyone that *his* had been one of Boston's first families. But what I thought was the damnedest thing was how little time the Winthrops spent there. If I had owned a house with four floors, more than thirty thousand square feet, and an adjoining carriage house where many of the staff lived, they'd have to drag me by my ears to get me out. But the Beacon Hill mansion was only one of six they owned around the world, and like everything else in their life, which house they occupied at any given time was planned down to the smallest detail. The Boston residence was primarily occupied between September and November. After Thanksgiving, they moved down to their oceanfront mansion in West Palm Beach, packing up and carrying servants with them like pieces of well-traveled luggage. They spent spring on the family compound in Arizona or at their château on the golf course in Palm Springs, California. Dalton quietly maintained his own apartment in Boston's Back Bay neighborhood as well as a small staff that stayed behind with him while his parents mansion-hopped around the country.

Dalton raced his Aston Martin through the narrow, cobbled streets of Beacon Hill, turning blind corners and ducking into tight alleyways, almost meeting disaster on two occasions when other cars pulled out in front of us without warning. Dalton always drove fast, but it wasn't meant to impress his horrified passengers. Dalton once explained that he equated speed with freedom. I was as big a proponent of freedom as he was, but I much preferred expressing it in ways other than death-defying maneuvers in a car that was barely big enough to fit both of us. But I had given up complaining a long time ago, so before the quarterly pilgrimage to the Winthrop mansion, I said my prayers, strapped in tightly, and left it in God's hands that he would deliver me with limbs intact to the top of Beacon Hill, then back to campus.

We slipped into the open gate along the western side of the house and entered through a side door, something that always annoyed the Emperor. That was the servants' entrance, and it led directly into the back of the smaller of the two kitchens. The Emperor constantly scolded Dalton about using that entrance, insisting that the family and invited guests were to use the front door.

Erma Tillman—an enormous black woman with silver hair and a deep, rumbling voice—controlled the back kitchen. She always had a ready smile planted across her face and a good story to tell if you had the time to listen. Dalton loved Erma more than he did his parents. Erma had been inherited with the house, just like the Monets and Renoirs dotting the walls, and, like the artworks, her value to the house only seemed to increase with age.

She was standing over the oven when we walked in, her hands perched on her wide hips. "I could hear you all the way down on Acorn Street," Erma said as Dalton walked up to her and planted a loud kiss on her cheek. "Lord knows I wish you would start driving like a child with some sense. One day you're gonna crack that car up. Speed kills, Herbie." Herbert was Dalton's middle name, one that he had always despised. Erma was the only one he allowed to call him Herbie. She had been calling him that since he was an infant.

"That's where you're wrong, Erma," Dalton said. "Speed doesn't kill, bad drivers do. I'm a great driver. Right, Spense?"

Erma cut her eyes at me and I begged off, walking up to her and kissing her on the other cheek.

"Evening, Spenser." Erma smiled. "If he doesn't have enough sense to slow down, you should have enough sense not to get in that death trap with him."

I shrugged my shoulders. "Don't worry, he's getting better," I said. "At least he's stopping at red lights now."

"Get out of my oven!" Erma yelled. Dalton had pulled down the lid and was searching for our regular treat. Erma always baked us a pan of buttery, homemade biscuits, the recipe of which, I swear, could have made her rich. "You know better than to touch my pans without washing your hands," she said.

We obeyed promptly, and Erma put the hot biscuits out on the counter next to two glasses of cold apple cider.

"Who did they drag over for dinner tonight?" Dalton asked as he stuffed half a biscuit into his mouth.

"I've never seen them before," Erma said, taking a seat on a high stool. "I think they might have some business with your father."

"Another thrilling night at the old homestead," Dalton said.

"Herbie, you mind your manners tonight," Erma said. "Your father isn't feeling good. He's been fighting a cold for almost two weeks, and he's not in the best of moods."

The door swung open, and in walked a young woman carrying a tray of silverware. She had white-blond hair, a mess of freckles, and a uniform that fit snugly against her compact body. Dalton and I looked at each other and exchanged our approval. Erma instructed the girl to take only the Christofle silver into the dining room and put the rest away.

"I don't believe we've met," Dalton said. "I'm Dalton, the driver for old Spenser here. And you are?"

"Sophia," the girl said, her eyes darting between Dalton and me as she tried to make sense of what he just said.

"And why have we never met?"

"I just started working here a couple of weeks ago," she said.

"Well, I'd have come by sooner had Erma been nice enough to share the news that you'd been hired."

"Now, mind your manners, Herbie," Erma said. "Sophia, this is Dalton, Mr. and Mrs. Winthrop's son. And this here is his classmate, Spenser."

"Pleased to meet you both," Sophia said before walking through another door that led to the main dining room.

"Let me guess who hired her," Dalton said. "At least his taste is consistent."

Erma shook her head. "Please behave yourself, tonight," she said. "I don't want any problems out of you at dinner, ya hear?"

Dalton and I put away the last of the biscuits and headed for the door. "Me, start problems?" Dalton said. "C'mon, Erma. Never in a million years would I embarrass the Emperor."

Erma yelled something after us, but we were already through the door. We hiked up the back stairs to the second floor and walked to Dalton's room at the end of the hall. Our clothes had already been laid out on the bed. A jacket and tie were requisite attire for our dinners at Winthrop House, whether it was just the four of us or a full house. Mrs. Winthrop left little to chance, so one day last year a tailor showed up at my dorm and informed me that he was there to take my measurements for a proper jacket and trousers. From that point on, I had my own closet full of *appropriate* dining clothes waiting for me at the Winthrop mansion.

After changing, Dalton said, "We should just sneak downstairs and cut out of here. Jump in the car and go to Tecce's." Tecce's was Dalton's favorite restaurant, an old-style affair in the heart of Boston's North End.

"Your parents would kill us if we left," I said. "Even worse, they might think I had something to do with it. Hell no, we're going downstairs." The last thing I wanted was to face the wrath of Aurelius Winthrop. It had already taken a great effort to get him to accept my sitting at his table. I wasn't going to undo it all with one impulsive prank.

"All right, we'll stick it out," Dalton said. "At least we get to look at Sophia all night. Did you see the wheels on her?"

"Tremendous," I said. "But I thought you didn't like blondes?"

"Where in the hell did you get that idea? I don't like anything *they* drag in to arrange for me. But what makes Sophia even more delicious is that she's *his*. Flirting with her will be a perfect way to piss the hell outta him."

As I came to spend more time with the Winthrops, I gradually learned that the Emperor, for all his stuffiness and elitism, was really a study in contrasts. He was a grade-A phony in many respects, always preaching to Dalton about responsibilities and the family reputation, then turning around and popping the help right in his own house. Most of the staff under the Winthrop employ were relics, old faithful workers who had traded in their own lives to work for one of Boston's most prominent families. But there was a continuous rotation of young women at the house, each recruit better looking than the last. Dalton told me that once the Emperor tired of a particular girl, he quietly paid her to leave, then had another brought in to replace her. Ironically, he liked them with little in the way of education, but lots of attitude. Dalton's biggest revenge had been flirting and occasionally sleeping with them, knowing that not only did it annoy the hell out of the Emperor, but he also couldn't do or say anything without risking his own exposure.

Dressed and dabbed with cologne, we walked down the dizzying spiral stairwell and entered the front salon, a cold room with stuffed animal heads tacked to the walls and stiff, creaky wooden furniture. Dinners always started here, where the fancy hors d'oeuvres were a lot less satisfying than Erma's biscuits. We also were allowed to drink cocktails, something that always struck me as odd, considering we were underage. But Dalton said it was completely normal. He had been drinking wine at dinner since he was thirteen. I had come to learn that it was quite common for rich people to allow their children to drink with them.

Once we walked into the room, it was immediately evident why the guests had been invited for dinner. The girl standing by the fireplace was the most perfect country-club type you could ever imagine. I at least had to give the Winthrops credit for their eye. There was no doubt that she was a beautiful girl, but she was every bit not Dalton's type. Tall and slender with high cheek-bones, a delicate nose, and doll-like porcelain skin. She wore a long, red plaid skirt and a velvet top with a big satin bow tied about her neck. I knew in-stantly that Dalton wanted to run out of the room. He dug his fist into my side and whispered, "Oh shit."

"Evening, gentlemen," the Emperor said. He was sitting in his favorite chair, one that had resided in the Oval Office at some point and was given to his grandfather by one of the presidents as a gift. The damn thing looked like a throne, square and wooden with a thick leather cushion that lifted him sev-eral inches above the rest of us. He was dressed in his customary charcoal gray pants, navy blue blazer, and a bright yellow ascot perfectly arranged around his eternally tanned neck. He seldom wore socks, preferring instead girly little velvet slippers with the intricate gold Winthrop crest stitched above the toe.

The Emperor was starting to gray at the temples, but his sturdy arrange-ment of black hair looked strong and determined. He was an extremely hand-some man, and it was easy to see where Dalton had gotten his looks.

"Evening, sir," Dalton and I said in unison. We were in the room for barely a minute before one of the servants had a tray of caviar-stuffed pastries under our noses and glasses of red wine in our hands. I never really liked wine, but it was only one of many things I tolerated while at the Winthrops.

"You both made it all right," Mrs. Winthrop said. She said the same thing every time we walked into that room, almost as if she expected us to get lost or killed on the way. It bugged the hell out of Dalton, and it always brought another nudge of his fist into my side.

"All in one piece, Mother," Dalton said. "As always."

"Good evening, Mrs. Winthrop," I said.

Mrs. Winthrop was several years younger than the Emperor, and she was still his perfect match. Pretty in a WASPish way, thin, strong chin, her dyed-blond hair coiffed and sprayed away from her face and flipped at her shoul-der. She wore conservative dresses and simple scarves. Mrs. Winthrop's one extravagance was jewelry. She knocked around in the kind of gems you'd ex-pect royalty to wear to coronations. She didn't wear a lot of it at once, but whatever she had on, you knew damn well that it cost some poor soul his life trying to mine it and Mr. Winthrop a good chunk of his fortune when he bought it. Tonight, she wore a pair of teardrop diamond-and-ruby earrings with a matching cocktail ring that practically blinded me when she lifted her glass.

The Emperor introduced the stiff couple sitting on the couch as Mr. and Mrs. Gilbert Hodge and their daughter standing by the fireplace as Melanie.

"Melanie is a sophomore at Smith," the Emperor seemed pleased to inform us. "She's studying the classics."

Melanie did everything but curtsy, for chrissake, and I expected that Dalton was going to have a field day with her over dinner. We walked over and shook her hand and struck up a mindless conversation while the adults went on about horses and their imminent preparations for opening neighboring winter houses in West Palm Beach. I drifted in and out of Dalton's conversation, throwing in a couple of opinions when he called my name or attempting humor when the awkward silence crept up. I was keeping an eye out for Sophia, but only Tate and Wendell made the rounds.

At precisely eight o'clock, the Emperor stood from his throne, indicating that it was time to move the party along. He led the processional down the great hall into the main dining room, which offered some of the most spectacular views of the city. The long rectangular glass table that was normally there had been replaced with a circular one to make the affair more intimate. Mrs. Winthrop always obsessed over the proper seating arrangement, making sure Dalton and I never sat next to each other. So, I got stuck between the Hodges, while Dalton, as you might've expected, found Melanie planted on his right. Another seating rule was that the Emperor always anchored the table by sitting underneath the Cézanne.

Among other things, Dalton hated the way these dinners always seemed scripted by the Emperor.

"What do you make of this election season?" the Emperor said. It was customary to wait for him to choose the first topic of conversation.

"God-awful," Mr. Hodge said. "Dukakis stands no chance against Vice President Bush. He's a lightweight. Even worse, a card-carrying left-wing liberal!"

"He's even admitted he's a card-carrying member of the ACLU for God's sake," Mrs. Hodges said. "How can he be trusted to run the country?"

Dalton leaned into me and whispered, "Emp just got himself in a big bind."

"But what does Bush really stand for?" the Emperor said. "He sits at Reagan's knee, hasn't really done anything as vice president to strike out on his own."

"Speaking of vice presidents, his own choice of a running partner wasn't the smartest of picks," Mrs. Winthrop said. "Quayle might be handsome and all that, but a brick for a brain. For the life of me, I can't figure out what prompted Bush to make such a silly decision."

"Are you all really considering voting for a Democrat?" Mr. Hodges said, full of indignation. He locked eyes with the Emperor, who then looked down and fussed with his silverware.

"It's a quandary," Dalton interjected. "I'm sure no Winthrop has voted for a Democrat since Grover Cleveland. Maybe even further back when the Dems were the more conservative party, fighting for states' rights and segregation. But the real problem is that Bush created the ultimate sin, Mr. Hodges, and it wasn't choosing a brickhead for his running mate. Bush and his entire family enrolled in that little school down in New Haven, Connecticut. There's nothing that will get you on the other side of the Winthrop fighting line faster than an allegiance or association with Yale." Dalton smiled widely. "It's either pulling the lever for liberal Dukakis or sitting this one out."

The Emperor looked like the he was about to choke. The first shot had been fired. I was surprised it had taken so long.

The staff arrived with the first course, steamed asparagus wrapped in smoked beef carpaccio. I didn't care for vegetables, especially the crunchy kind like asparagus, but I could hear my mother's voice in the back of my head telling me to remember my manners and eat what was put before me. I poured a generous helping of dressing on it to add some flavor and pretended to enjoy it. Sophia finally made her appearance. Dalton winked at me from across the table. I caught the Emperor looking at her as she leaned in to set the plates down. Mrs. Winthrop loudly cleared her throat.

"I'm more concerned about the future of the party," the Emperor said. "We experienced unprecedented economic growth under Reagan. I just don't know if Bush has what it takes to keep the trains rolling."

"And the racist Willie Horton ads aren't a problem for you?" Dalton shot back.

My stomach immediately tightened. I should've expected Dalton to go there, but I was praying like hell he wouldn't. No one would look in my direction.

"Those ads were repulsive," Mrs. Winthrop said. "Completely inappropriate and not at all constructive to the political discourse. Atwater and his cronies who created it are an embarrassment to those of us who maintain our integrity even at the deepest level of disagreement."

"Well said," Mrs. Hodges joined in. Dalton smiled at the Emperor's noticeable silence.

Battle one to Dalton.

"Melanie just became president of the Young Republicans Club at Smith," Mrs. Winthrop announced. "Isn't that right, Melanie?"

I could see Mr. Hodge's chest inflate about six inches over the table. I wasn't exactly a political person. To be honest, I had a lot more important things to worry about other than donkeys and elephants and a bunch of old white guys standing on the floor of Congress calling each other nincompoops and draft dodgers. But as naïve as I was about politics, I sure as hell couldn't align myself with a party that touted the phrases "welfare moms" and "another Willie Horton."

Of course, Dalton's politics were clearly on the left side of the aisle, directly opposite his father's.

"Congratulations, Mel," Dalton said. "So, what exactly does this presidency get you?"

Melanie smiled uncomfortably. "What do you mean?"

"The benefits?" Dalton said. "Surely being the leader comes with its spoils."

"It's not about what the organization can do for us, but what we can do for the organization," Melanie said.

Dalton let go a sly smile. "A Republican quoting a Kennedy," he said. "That's a first."

"You know, Melanie, when I was your age, I took a keen interest in politics," the Emperor said. "It was one of the most important things I did in college. It's good to see a young person taking responsibility for *our* issues." He cut his eyes at Dalton.

"Thank you, Mr. Winthrop," Melanie said. "It hasn't been easy for our club. Our campus tends to be quite liberal. But I think we're starting to get more girls interested in our side of the issues."

"I also hear those *liberal* girls can be really tough," Dalton said. He mockingly made the quotation sign with his fingers. "On another note, Melanie, is it true what they say about you lovely Smithies?"

"What would that be?" she said.

"How much you truly enjoy each other's private company."

"That's enough, Dalton!" Mrs. Winthrop said, bringing her fist down on the table and making the rest of us jump.

The servants arrived to clear the dishes, and I noticed that when Sophia bent over Dalton's shoulder, his eyes didn't miss the opportunity to investigate her ample cleavage. I got the feeling that she enjoyed him watching her. The Emperor could only sit there, boiling.

"Spenser's being punched by the Delphic," Dalton announced.

"Congratulations, Spenser," Mrs. Winthrop said.

"Thank you, Mrs. Winthrop," I replied.

"Do you have friends who are members?" she asked.

"None at all."

"Someone hit you?" Melanie said with great displeasure.

"No," Dalton replied before I could. "Spenser's being considered to join one of the final clubs at school."

"Those kinds of clubs are something out of the Dark Ages," Melanie said. "Run by a bunch of pigs who believe women will always be inferior."

"I couldn't agree more," Mrs. Hodge said. "The time is long overdue to close the doors to those types of gender-discriminating organizations."

"What say you, Father?" Dalton said.

Everyone looked at the Emperor, who was visibly squirming in his chair.

He pretended to be occupied with buttering a piece of bread as we all waited for his answer.

"I think it's a perplexing situation," he dodged. "These clubs have been around for a long time."

"But that doesn't make them right," Melanie said. "Slavery was around a long time too, and that didn't make it right."

I couldn't help but smile. Slavery was always the lowest-hanging fruit. I didn't bite.

"Come clean for Melanie, Father," Dalton said. "Tell her about your years in the Pork."

"Stop being so antagonistic, Dalton," Mrs. Winthrop said. "We're having a conversation here, not a debate."

"Father is a card-carrying member of one of those pig institutions as you describe it," Dalton said, ignoring his mother. He looked across the table at the Emperor, who practically had steam coming from his eyes. "In fact, the pig is your mascot—right, Father?"

The arrival of the entrées turned the conversation to other things, but it was still 2–0 in Dalton's favor. Erma had prepared individual Cornish game hens and some type of vegetable medley. Everything was served formally, polished silver domes and fancy carving knives. Sophia seemed a little uncertain about protocol, and Wendell whispered directions in her ear. When she was standing next to Dalton, I saw him slide his hands up the back of her skirt. She jumped, dropping a spoonful of vegetables all over Melanie's lap. Dalton's howl competed with Melanie's screams, and Sophia's repeated apologies made it a scene never to be forgotten.

The rest of the evening was largely uneventful. Mrs. Winthrop kept highlighting Melanie's résumé, and Dalton found an infinite number of ways to deflect the implications. Sophia continued to serve us, and Dalton's flirtations grew increasingly more obvious, forcing Mrs. Winthrop to clear her throat on more than one occasion and Mr. Winthrop to visibly clench his fist.

Listening to them talk about their possessions and properties and social obligations, I realized that despite all their wealth, they were unhappy people, prisoners of the expectations that come with such overwhelming privilege. I truly believed every single one of them would have traded at least half their old fortunes to have my kind of freedom.

Dalton wanted to cut out right after dessert, so we bade our farewells around the table, walked through the kitchen to say goodbye to Erma, and enjoyed our last look at Sophia. Mrs. Winthrop walked us to the car, and as always, the Emperor stayed behind and continued to hold court.

"We really need to do something about this money situation, Mother," Dalton said as we got into the car. "I can't spend the rest of the semester like this."

"This is between you and your father, dear," Mrs. Winthrop said. "I've already talked to him, but he's not budging."

The Emperor finally got a point on the board, and he wasn't even there to see it. But the score remained 2–1 in Dalton's favor.

"All because I won't live in some crummy house that has his name carved over the archway," Dalton said.

"You knew what the consequences would be prior to making your decision to live in Eliot and not Winthrop House like your grandfather and uncles," Mrs. Winthrop said. "You have to learn how to compromise sometimes, Dalton. That's an important part of negotiating life."

"He doesn't want a compromise, Mother, he wants complete control," Dalton said. "And I'll die penniless before I let him control me. I *hate* him!"

The engine of the Aston Martin roared awake and we shot out of the Winthrop estate and onto the dimly lit streets of Beacon Hill. I looked into my side mirror at Mrs. Winthrop standing there under the shadows of the towering mansion. She waved at us with her right hand, then slowly dabbed underneath her eyes with her left.

14

THE THIRD ENVELOPE arrived. I knew there was still a long way to go before I had made it to the final round, but after reading this new invitation, I allowed myself to consider for the first time the real possibility that I might be elected into the Delphic, and it thrilled me more than I expected.

The President and members of the Delphic Club
cordially invite you to lunch at the clubhouse at 9 Linden St.,
Tuesday Nov. 15. The first course will be served at
12:00 noon sharp. Jacket and tie required.
Regrets only: 876-0400.

"What is that?" I heard someone say. Percy had just walked out of the bathroom in his monogrammed robe and slippers. I didn't even know he was awake. His thin blonde hair flew all over his head like he had gotten caught in a sandstorm.

"Nothing much," I said, not sure if I wanted to get into a long conversation with him about the Delphic Club at eight o'clock in the morning.

"It has to be something," he said. "It must've been slipped under the door late last night, because it wasn't there when I came home from rehearsal."

"It's a lunch invitation to the Delphic," I relented.

"As in the Delphic Club?"

"Exactly."

Percy sighed. "Great, my roommate is being punched by the Delphic, and he doesn't even tell me."

"C'mon, don't get all sentimental on me," I said. "It's not that big of a deal, and I was gonna tell you sooner or later."

"Bullshit it's not a big deal," he said. "It's the number one club on campus. And it's already the third round. How much longer were you gonna hold out on me?"

"How did you know that it was the third round?" I asked.

"'Cause I'm being punched by the Spee."

"Well, this is the first I'm hearing of that," I said. "So why in the hell are you giving me a hard time when you haven't been up front with me either?"

"I didn't say anything, because I didn't want you to feel like you were the odd man out," Percy said. "What's your excuse?"

I couldn't believe at eight o'clock in the morning, Percy was giving me the business about a final club. To be honest, it never even crossed my mind that he would care one way or another that I was being punched. It wasn't like we sat down and had those kinds of conversations about our personal lives. I thought we had carved out a very functional relationship by keeping our distance when it came to these matters. I didn't want to hear about his choir rehearsals or society dances, and I was certain he didn't want to hear about basketball or the newest rap song we were partying to in the dark, sweaty basement of Adams House.

"It just didn't seem real at first," I said. "If it pisses you off that I didn't tell you sooner that I was being punched, then I'm sorry."

I thought that would end it, but instead, he flopped on the couch, put his feet on the end table, and folded his hands behind his head. "So, how's the punch going for you?"

"All right," I said, taking a seat on the other couch. "I made it to the third round, so I guess that's a good sign."

"You know the Delphic is the hardest club to get into," he said. "It used to be the Pork, but since everyone started talking about that secret room, the Delphic has become the one everyone wants."

"How did you hear about their room?"

"From an ex-girlfriend of mine. She used to live in the house next to us out on Nantucket. Her father was a Gas man."

Percy had gotten my attention. "What did she say about the room?"

"That it's all true."

"What do you mean, it's all true?"

Percy crossed his pale, skinny legs. "Morgan had a special room built on one of the floors where only members of his inner circle could enter."

"Her father told her that?" I asked. "I thought they swore an oath of secrecy, even when it came to family members."

"Her father was a member of the club, but he never made it into that room. And he didn't tell her. She read it in his journal."

"Journal as in a diary?"

"Yup."

"What else did he write?"

"I don't really remember much," Percy said. "I was a kid back then. One afternoon after golf lessons, we were sitting around the pool, talking about our parents and all kinds of shit, and somehow she mentioned that she'd snooping around their attic and found his college journal in a box."

"If you were only kids, then how did you know what she was talking about?" I asked.

"Because when she took me to her room and showed me the journal, I remember laughing because he belonged to some club called the Gas," Percy said. "I kept thinking it was a place where guys sat around and farted all day."

"Did you read the entire journal?"

"Hell no. I was scared we were gonna get caught. But she showed me the part where he talked about the Gas House. And there was one section about trying to figure out the location of a secret room. Then he wrote in the margins how he hoped his uncle would admit the truth about the room and be nice enough to give him a chance to see it."

"This is huge," I said. "You're saying there's definitely a secret room at the Delphic."

"I'm not saying it; he did."

"Do you still see that girl anymore?"

"Not for a few years. Her parents got a divorce and sold the summerhouse. Last I heard, she was down at Princeton, rowing crew."

"What's her name?"

"Katie. Katie Huntington. Her grandfather, P. J. Huntington, just donated a hundred million dollars to the school, half of it in Impressionist paintings. That family's been in the Delphic since it was built."

I TRIED REACHING Dalton all day, but he wasn't answering his phone. I wanted to tell him what I had learned from Percy about Huntington and the Delphic's secret room. I stopped by Eliot on the way to practice, but his room-mates said they hadn't seen him since early that morning. I left a handwritten message for him to call me urgently when he got back. I jumped on my bike and raced across the bridge. Coach was a stickler for punctuality, and he blew his whistle at precisely four o'clock. If you weren't dressed and on the court, you were considered late, which meant after practice you owed him three wind sprints for every minute, and each one had to be run under twenty seconds or you had to do them all over again. He ran Markus Hollenstein, our seven-foot center, so hard one night that he collapsed in his own vomit behind the bleachers. That afternoon, it took half the damn team to carry Markus over to the training room, where the doctor hooked him up to an IV and had to dump six liters of saline into his veins to rehydrate him.

When I got into the gym, things were unusually quiet. Typically, a few of the guys would be on the court early, practicing their dribbling, jumping rope, or shooting baskets. But today no one was on the floor. I walked into the locker room, and Mike Geilton, our captain, was standing up at the chalkboard while everyone else sat staring at their lockers.

"Coach is in a really bad mood today," he said. "Lavietes went to the AD and told him if we didn't win it all this year, he was gonna withdraw all his support."

Roy Lavietes was a former hoopster who lived in Connecticut and made a fortune in the concrete business. He must've been somewhere in his eighties, but he was a die-hard basketball fan and easily our most supportive booster. He had already pledged ten million dollars for a new arena to be built under his name, and another ten million dollars if we brought home the championship trophy while he was still alive. One thing I had learned about Harvard was that it almost never responded to whiny student complaints or pressure from the media, but money always got the attention of University Hall. And Lavietes had buckets of it.

"So, everyone be cool today," Geilton said. "No horsin' around. Play the whistle and hustle between drills. He's gonna be looking for anything to punish us today, so let's not give him any excuse."

That was our plan after we gathered in a huddle and left the locker room. For the first half of practice, we stuck to our strategy and things worked out perfectly. Coach was in a foul mood, just as Geilton had predicted. He kicked out a handful of old men who always sat and watched our practices, telling them that today was a closed-door session. When Coach was really pissed, he did just the opposite of what you'd expect. Instead of screaming like a tyrant, he'd keep really quiet, which made everyone in the gym nervous. He had very little to say, speaking up only to criticize a play or call one of us a name. Even the assistant coaches were on edge, cutting us angry looks and not letting us take our usual water breaks. Their jobs were tied to Coach's, so they were threatened too.

We had fifteen minutes left to practice, and the women's team, which was practicing after us that week, was already stretching on the sidelines. Their appearance was always a good sign, because it meant practice was winding down and we had only a couple of easy drills left before surrendering the court. But then Coach blew the whistle and called for us to line up for Box Out. We all looked at each other. He was going to put us through the most physically torturous drill at the end of a long practice.

Box Out is a rebounding drill. One player goes up against another player, and they fight like two rabid dogs to see who will come out alive with the basketball. We line up in a single line, and then one player is called out to take on the rest of the team one man at a time. Coach throws the ball at the rim, purposely missing, and the two players pull and scratch and do almost anything else to get the rebound. The defensive player is responsible for boxing out—which means keeping the guy on offense from getting the ball. The defender must get three rebounds in a row before he's relieved of his duty. Once he accomplishes this, another player gets called out to defend the basket and rebound the ball. Sounds like a simple drill, and it is. But if you don't find success early, fatigue makes it exponentially more difficult. The cruelty of this game lies in the fact that you must get three rebounds consecutively or start all over. The defender is out there the entire time, while everyone else stays refreshed, rotating to the back of the line with each rebound.

The smaller guys who were at an inherent disadvantage especially hated this drill. Coach knew this. The defender would be throwing elbows, kneeing people in the groin, even landing an elbow to the gut if he could get away with it. It once took Tom Morrissey, the smallest guy on the team, twenty-five minutes to get three consecutive rebounds. By the time he was done, he had a bloody nose, scratches all over his neck, and a sprained thumb. He missed the entire next week of practices, which seemed to gratify Coach even more.

Today, we knew the drill would be an all-out war. We were already tired, and the coaches in their foul moods wanted to see nothing less than blood. The first three guys were in and out, and Coach warned the rest of us that if we were trying to take it easy on the defender, we would run after practice until our guts were hanging out of our mouths. We became instant enemies.

Paul Mitchell, a six-foot-seven freshman from Long Island, New York, was up next. Mitch had been an all-star forward at Friends Academy and one of our most highly touted recruits in years. He also happened to be the son of the most successful black CPA in the country, a millionaire businessman who played golf with senators and poker with Fortune 500 CEOs. The older Mitchell had grown up a poor boy in Jamaica and, after moving to the States with his seven brothers and sisters, clawed and hustled his way to the top of the corporate world. Though the Mitchells lived a life of luxury like no other black family I had ever met, Paul inherited his father's toughness. He was a ferocious competitor and fearless protector of his honor.

Mitch quickly disposed of the first two offensive players, grabbing the rebound easily before preparing to take on the third. But the ball took a bad bounce, and Mitch lost the rebound he needed to get out of the circle. And it went like this for the next fifteen minutes, each battle wearing him down to the point that he was barely able to move his legs. The girls were now standing around, watching, anxious to take the court, and Coach was still throwing that ball up, yelling at Mitch to fight like a man and get the damn rebound. Miraculously, Mitch got a second wind, and a couple of lucky bounces of the ball and he had nabbed his second rebound in a row. I was up next. I liked Mitch. In fact, he was my closest friend on the team. But I knew that if he got that third rebound on me, Coach would have my head in a sling. Mitch wore goggles in the tradition of Kareem Abdul-Jabbar, and when he was sweating and tired, they'd fog up and sit askew on his face. I looked in his eyes and could see him begging for me to let him get that third rebound. I had made up my mind to do so and risk one of Coach's cursing sessions. Coach threw the ball, which hit the corner of the rim and backboard and shot to the right of us. I let Mitch get a good jump on me, but when he almost had the ball in his hands, he slipped on a wet part of the floor, his legs buckled, and his tired body slid to the ground. I had no choice but to pick up the ball, which meant his torture would start all over again.

Mitch stayed there on the ground, stretched on his back, gasping to catch his breath. Everyone else, the girls included, started shouting encouragements at him, knowing Coach was going to keep him out there until he was broken. He blew the whistle on Mitch, and yelled at the top of his lungs, "Get up and be a man, you fuckin' pussy!"

The rest of us froze instantly when we heard that. Mitch was the kind of guy you could mess around with and even poke fun at occasionally. Unlike a lot of big guys, he was a pretty good sport about things. But there were a couple of things he didn't tolerate from anybody, and one was being called a pussy. Coach had not only said it, but he did it in front of all of us, including the women's team. I prayed like hell that Mitch would swallow his pride just once. But when he got to his feet, his shirt half torn, his goggles now dangling around his neck, he walked over to Coach and said, "What did you just say to me?"

"I called you a fuckin' pussy," Coach said. Then Coach did something I had never seen him do even when he was in the middle of his worst meltdown. He looked up and pushed Mitch in the chest and knocked him back a couple of feet. Everything from there went in slow motion. Mitch clenched his right fist. Then Geilton and Markus, who were standing closest to Mitch at the time, lunged forward to hold him back. Coach turned his head slightly to say something to the rest of us, and when he turned back toward Mitch, the blow caught him square on the side of his face.

It reminded me of one of those replays of boxing knockouts in which one guy lands a direct hit and the other guy's face seems to bend around the glove. Well, that's exactly what happened to Coach. His whistle flew out along with a couple of teeth inside a thick squirt of blood. Then his knees wobbled, and before anyone could reach him, he crumpled to the ground, his face lying in a pool of bright red blood.

There was instant pandemonium. Markus and Geilton stopped Mitch from continuing his charge. The assistant coaches dropped to their knees to help Coach, and someone yelled out to run and get the trainer. I stood there paralyzed, wondering if Coach had been knocked unconscious and worried that Mitch had just cost himself a Harvard degree. Half of us huddled around Coach, the other around Mitch. The door flew open and two trainers ran into the gym with their medical kit and several bags of ice.

After working on him for half an hour, they finally carted Coach off to the training room and the rest of us walked Mitch into the locker room. No one said much of anything, including Mitch, who at that point realized the gravity of his situation. Everyone showered and dressed in silence, and instead of heading over to Kirkland House with the rest of the team, I rode back to Lowell for dinner, still in shock. I made it into the dining hall just as they were locking the kitchen door.

"We're closed," a voice called out from the other side of the counter.

I looked up into the face of Ashley Garrett. I couldn't help but smile.

"It would have to be you," she said.

"Tonight's my lucky night," I said.

"Why would you come in one minute before the kitchen closes?"

"Basketball practice ran late tonight."

"You play basketball? I'd love to see that."

"Damn right, I hoop. And don't sound so surprised."

"I just can't imagine you getting dirty, on the ground diving for loose balls."

"What do you know about basketball?" I said.

"My first cousin was the captain at Rindge and Latin. He plays for Memphis now."

Cambridge Rindge and Latin School was the former home of NBA star Patrick Ewing and one of the best high school basketball programs on the East Coast. It had sent several players to the NBA and made a star of its head coach, who went on to become a well-regarded college coach at St. John's. By association alone, her cousin was in good company.

"Can you play?" I asked.

"Second team all-state my senior year," she said. "I messed up my ankle halfway through the season."

"Let's close it down, Ashley," a man called out from the back of the kitchen. "I want to get home at a decent hour tonight."

"So, what will it be?" she said to me. "Pizza or meat loaf?"

I looked at both of them and said, "Some real pizza at Tommy's and when we're done, dessert at Emack and Bolio's. I'm buying."

"Are you asking me out on a date?"

"That's exactly what I'm doing."

"Then I won't go."

"Why?"

"Because after five minutes of stepping foot on this campus, I promised myself I would never date one of you Harvard men."

"Fair enough. Have you eaten yet?"

"We don't eat until the kitchen closes."

"Do you want to eat what's left in these trays?"

She looked down at the dry pizza and hardened edges of the lumpy meat loaf. "Not really."

"Well, since both of us need to eat, how about we agree to *meet* at Tommy's and sit next to each other and have a little conversation if the mood strikes. Not a date. A meeting."

She thought it over for a few seconds, then said, "I could live with that, but I've got to clean up my station first."

"I'll meet you there in thirty minutes," I said.

"And I can't be out long," she said. "I have a paper due tomorrow. And no funny stuff."

"I promise," I said, crossing my heart.

"Good." She smiled. "My brother still has friends that live around here. And they hate snobby Harvard people, so you're on notice."

I ran back to my room and jumped in the shower. I felt like the luckiest kid alive.

"SO WHY ARE YOU so aloof?" I asked. We were sitting at Tommy's, a greasy spoon in the middle of campus that had the best New York–style pizza in all of Cambridge. One TV monitor was showing an old black-and-white movie. The other was turned to a hockey game. A blues song scratched from the tired jukebox leaning in the corner. It was early for Tommy's, which usually didn't start rocking till after midnight, so Ashley and I had our choice of seats.

"I'm not aloof," Ashley said. "I just don't fall for you preppie types and your I'm-greater-than-God bullshit."

"I'm the farthest thing from a preppie," I said.

"Yeah, and the pope isn't Catholic."

"I'm from the South Side of Chicago. Trust me, there aren't any preppies living on my side of the city."

"It doesn't matter where you're from," she said. "Just being here at Harvard gives you preppie credentials."

I decided to change the subject since I wasn't going to win that debate. "So why would a smart and pretty girl like you want to work for Harvard's dining services?" I asked.

"I don't *want* to work here," she said. "But I need the job. The hours are flexible, and so far I've been able to tolerate it. But who knows how long that will last."

Our pizza was ready, a large pie with veggies on her side and pepperoni on mine. The two-liter soda came half price with the pizza.

"So, tell me about your school," I said. "I don't know much about it."

"I wouldn't expect you to," she said between bites. "It's a community college in a part of the city you have no reason to visit. Not the best school around, mostly commuters and part-time students. But it's affordable. If I keep my grades up this year, I'll be able to earn a scholarship and transfer to UMass or BU."

"What are you studying?"

"Poli-sci."

"So that explains the Locke book."

"You thought I was just picking it up to impress you?"

"Never," I said, shaking my head. "Why don't you have a boyfriend?"

"Maybe the same reason you don't have a girlfriend."

"I never said that I didn't."

Ashley pushed back from the table and started reaching for her coat.

"Only kidding," I said, grabbing her arm. "I'm completely single."

"Tall and a half-decent smile," she said. "I'd think latching on to a girl here would be easy for you."

"Who said it isn't?"

"Then why aren't you dating anyone?"

"Let's just say I'm in a recovery phase of my dating life."

"Sounds like an ex-girlfriend problem."

"You can say that. She's dating my biggest high school rival."

"Do you still like her?"

"Not like I used to."

"Then maybe it's time to move on."

"That's why I'm sitting here with you."

"Not so fast, Harvard Man. This is just a meeting, remember? Nothing more."

I looked at her sitting there beautiful as ever in that stained uniform. We both knew this was the start of something special.

I HAD JUST fallen asleep after reading the same paragraph in Kant's *Metaphysics of Morals* four times when my phone rang. I looked at the clock on my nightstand. It was almost two o'clock in the morning. It could only be one person.

"It's me," Dalton said.

"Where the hell have you been?" I said. "I called you at least five times today. I even went to your room and left a note."

"I spent all day at the archives warehouse of the Boston Police Department."

"Doing what?"

"Checking out Dunhill's story."

"How did you get access to the files?"

"The Emperor invites the commissioner over to dinner once a year. Says it's good to be friendly with those who protect us."

"What did you find?"

"There's a file about an inch thick on Moss Sampson. He was every bit the brute that Dunhill made him out to be. Supposedly, he killed two guys down in Mississippi who molested one of his girlfriends, then spent ten years in the pen, where he became an ordained minister before his release. He moved up to Boston and lived with some relatives. He worked a couple of odd jobs before the Delphic hired him."

"But why would a club like the Delphic hire someone like Sampson?"

"Nothing in the file explained that," Dalton said. "Just said he worked there fifteen years, then left."

"When did he leave?"

"About two years after the Abbott case."

"Did the cops talk to him about Abbott?"

"Five different times. He never deviated from his story."

"What did he say?"

"He wasn't in the Delphic on Halloween. He spent the night at home with one of his cousins. They were playing cards and drinking. He didn't know anything about a break-in, and he never met anyone by the name of Erasmus Abbott."

"Did they believe him?"

"One of the investigators had his doubts, but the cousin verified Sampson's alibi. Said he beat Sampson for about three dollars, then they went to bed."

"So maybe Dunhill didn't see Sampson in that window," I said.

"No, I think he did," Dalton said. "I think Sampson panicked about everything and lied to the cops."

"What makes you say that?"

"Because they also talked to one of the cousin's girlfriends, who said that Sampson wasn't acting like himself for a couple of weeks. He was quiet and avoiding people. She also said that she had spent Halloween night with the cousin and Sampson didn't come home until early the next morning. She remembers waking up to the sound of him running bathwater."

"Did the cops follow up on her story?" I asked.

"They couldn't. The next day, she and the cousin were found dead on the wharf, a gunshot to each of their heads. They found twenty-five thousand dollars in cash in the cousin's pockets."

"That's a ton of money," I said.

"Especially back then. The detectives couldn't figure out why the killer didn't take the money. It was practically falling out of his pockets."

"The killer was after something other than money."

"And that's where the case went cold."

15

LUNCH AT THE Delphic couldn't have gone better. I met three new members, all with three names each, but who seemed curiously familiar with my background. We ate in a large room in the basement that had been supplied with enough expensive china and glassware to serve a state dinner. Two staff members who seemed as old as the club itself waited on us the entire time, continually filling our wineglasses and attending to every other need that hadn't even crossed my mind. We heard courageous stories of hiking in the Himalayas and white-water rafting in Nepal, mixed with the recounting of late-night escapades into the dormitories of Wellesley College. It was made crystal clear that the Delphic brethren were men of the world whose physical and intellectual brawn were matched only by their voracious sexual appetites.

Later that afternoon, I could feel the tension as I walked into the gym. The early birds were practicing free throws and jumping rope, Coach Beasley's office was dark, and the assistants weren't out chatting up the team as they usually did before the start of practice. Our little fan club of four old men who usually sat on the bleachers near the front door was absent for the second day in a row. The blood had been cleaned up, and the floor had been waxed and buffed to a shine. I walked into the locker room and saw Mitch sitting in front of his locker with his street clothes on, talking to Geilton. It was obvious he wasn't going to practice with us today.

"I've already talked to my dad about it," Mitch was saying. "He was upset that I only had a chance to hit him once."

"Coach's pride is hurt more than anything else," Geilton said. "Just give it some time, and I'm sure this will all blow over."

"Someone said I might have to go in front of the Ad Board," Mitch said.

The Ad Board was Harvard's disciplinary committee, which handled everything from academic violations like plagiarism to charges of sexual misconduct. They make the recommendation to the dean's office of what penalties should be meted out for the offense.

"I wouldn't worry about that," I said. "Coach pushed you first. I don't think he wants to take this any further. Technically, he assaulted you."

"That's what has my father so pissed," Mitch said. "He wanted to fly up here and talk to President Bok but I convinced him to sit cool for a while."

"Good idea," I said. "Let the dust settle. It'll be good for everyone. Who's running practice today?"

"Zimowski," Geilton said. "Coach had some work done on his mouth this morning and is still loopy from the medication."

Mitch grabbed his gym bag and got up to leave.

"Did they say when you could come back?" I asked.

"I'm meeting with him tomorrow morning," Mitch said.

"Hey, look on the bright side," I said. "If basketball doesn't work out, you could always join the boxing team."

It was probably the first time Mitch had smiled since the now infamous punch.

PRACTICE WAS RELATIVELY uneventful, and everyone went out of their way not to mention what had happened between Mitch and Coach. Zimowski took it easy on us, letting us scrimmage most of the day and releasing us fifteen minutes early. I made it back to the dining hall before the kitchen was closed, hoping to find Ashley, but no luck. So, I grabbed a plate of turkey with mac and cheese and headed back to my room.

Percy's door was closed, but I could hear him with Hartman running up and down the scale, then belting out one of their show tunes. I put my dinner in the microwave, poured myself a tall glass of sweetened iced tea I'd smuggled out of the dining hall, and stretched out on the couch. Just as I turned on the TV, the phone rang.

It was Dalton. "We've got a problem," he said.

"What?"

"I just got a call from Uncle Randolph's secretary. He wants to know if I removed anything from the house when I was there last, and if so, I'm to return it immediately. Uncle Randolph was very upset that something special was missing from his study."

"I thought you said your uncle barely knew his own name," I said. "How in the world could he know that you had taken the box?"

"Beats the hell outta me, but we have to return it."

"We?" I said.

"You and me, Spense. I took the damn thing for *us*."

"I can't go down to New York," I said. "I'm way behind in Mettendorf's class and there's a paper due next week. Plus, I have basketball practice."

"Missing one day of classes isn't gonna kill you," Dalton said. "And we'll be back in time for your practice. I give you my word."

I sat there for a minute, thinking of the trouble I'd be in if I didn't make it back in time for practice. Coach would spit fire. After the incident with Mitch, he'd be looking for any reason to explode. But missing a day of classes wouldn't be the end of the world.

"Your uncle doesn't even know who I am," I said.

"Doesn't matter. I could use your company. The drive's pretty long."

"How long?"

"About four hours each way. If we leave at five in the morning, return the box, and get back on the road, we'll be back here by two. You guys have late practice this week, right? So, you'll be back in more than enough time."

"I'll go on one condition," I said.

"What's that?"

"You keep the needle under eighty."

"C'mon, Spense, at least give me eighty-five."

"Why do I always let you talk me into this crazy shit?"

WE BURNED OUT of Cambridge a little after five the next morning and arrived at the gates of the Wild Winds Estate in just over three hours. Dalton pressed the intercom button on the post, gave his name, and the tall wrought-iron gate with two mounted cameras slowly rolled back. We must've driven for another five minutes along a curvy road that carried us through a forest, over a lake, and across a meadow that was as large as any park I had ever seen in my life. I thought we had mistakenly entered a wildlife preserve.

"Is this his property?" I asked.

"Pretty amazing, isn't it?" Dalton said. "It's the largest tract of private land in all of New York. At the turn of the century, his father bought it from some rail-road tycoon who used it as a country home. Wait till you see the actual house."

We drove another minute or so through a heavily wooded area that opened suddenly onto a clearing. A monstrous structure rose up behind a row of tall hedges. Gothic towers, stone archways, peaked windows, pointed turrets, and pinnacled roofs. It was a massive stone castle.

"The views from the second-floor terraces are insane," Dalton said. "Now you can see why this was my favorite house to visit when I was a kid. Every room was a new adventure, and Uncle Randolph and Aunt Teddy would set up all kinds of stuff for me like rock-collecting expeditions and treasure hunts. I never wanted to leave this place."

Dalton pulled around the circular gravel driveway. By the time we reached the top step of the staircase, the doors were already opened. An old tank of a woman with curly white hair and stubby fingers stood there with a crooked but warm smile lighting up her circular face. She wore a light blue dress with a large white apron that had smudge marks along the hemline.

"Good to see you, Master Winthrop," she said in a thick brogue. "What a beautiful morning for a drive, eh?"

"Couldn't be better, Muriel," Dalton said, stepping inside. "This is a friend of mine from college, Spenser Collins."

"A pleasure to meet you, Master Collins," she said with a short bow of her head. "Would the two of you like a bit of breakfast?"

"Unfortunately, we can't stay that long," Dalton said. "We have to get back to Cambridge right away. We just came down to see Uncle Randolph for a few minutes. He's expecting us."

"You picked a good day," Muriel said. "He's really been doing well this past week. Even left his room yesterday for a short trip around the gardens."

"Where is he now?" Dalton asked.

"Finishing up breakfast in his room," Muriel said.

Dalton gave the old woman a peck on the cheek and said, "Good seeing you again, Muriel, and thanks for looking after Uncle Randolph. You know he thinks the world of you."

"If you change your minds about breakfast, there's plenty of food in the kitchen," she said. "Axel can put together anything you'd like."

I followed Dalton through a maze of large, drafty hallways with their Venetian tiled floors and soaring domed ceilings. We passed several uniformed men and women, most of whom called Dalton by name as they dusted and polished the antique furnishings. We approached the west wing of the house and entered a foyer with a grand marble staircase. A short walk down a carpeted hallway, and we arrived at two ornate steel doors that were slightly ajar.

Dalton knocked on one of the doors, then pushed it open. There on an enormous four-poster bed in front of a tall stained-glass window sat Randolph Winthrop. A young black woman was sitting by his side, arranging the food on his tray. She offered us a timid smile and went on pouring milk in his cereal bowl. Uncle Randolph looked up when we entered, but he didn't seem to recognize Dalton until we were standing next to the bed. I quickly took in the room. Gilt-framed paintings hung on the dark walls, and several slip-covered couches and chairs had been scattered about on ornamental Persian rugs. One entire wall was covered with a religious mural while the ceiling had been layered in shiny gold leaf. Several sculptures rested in lighted wall niches, and a row of male busts was perched high up along the far wall overlooking the room.

Uncle Randolph looked like he belonged in this room, ancient and withered, his translucent skin exposing a tangled network of blood vessels. He had a smattering of white hair around his oblong cranium, and dry lips that were slightly open. He moved his head with great effort, and seeing the pained expression on his face even made me wince.

"How are you, Uncle Randolph?" Dalton said. "I hope you don't mind that I brought a friend of mine with me. He's a Harvard man too." The mention of Harvard brought a glimmer of a smile to the old man's craggy face.

He reached up and grabbed the napkin from his shirt collar and pointed at the woman to take the tray and leave the room. When she had left and closed the door, he motioned for us to take a seat on the chairs next to the bed.

Uncle Randolph wiggled the hearing aid in his right ear and said, "Good to see you, Dalty. Who is your friend?"

"His name is Spenser Collins," Dalton said. "He's from Chicago. Class of '91. Lowell House."

"Good to meet you, Spenser," Uncle Randolph said, extending his frail hand. "You look like a basketball player." He lifted his hands up as if taking a shot, and I was afraid the motion might knock him over. "I haven't been to the Windy City in many years," he said. "One of my investment partners lived there. We always enjoyed sailing on Lake Michigan. What a great town."

"I couldn't agree more, sir," I said. "Chicago is one of the country's greatest cities. And better yet, home of the White Sox and Chicago Bulls."

Uncle Randolph smiled with great effort.

"I got the message that you wanted to see me," Dalton said. "Your secretary told me that it was urgent."

Uncle Randolph turned to Dalton, and his expression grew serious. "Indeed, it is," he said. "We need to have a talk, Dalty. I think you might have something of mine that you took without asking."

Dalton reached into his bag and pulled out the small wooden box with the diamond garter. "Forgive me, Uncle Randolph," he said. "I meant to return it sooner. I'll put it back in your study right away."

Uncle Randolph looked at me, then back at Dalton. "I think it's best we have this conversation in private," he said.

I took my cue and left the room. I found a chair at the end of the hallway near a window and sat down. The views were spectacular. A blanket of green treetops descended into the valley, and the mist rose off the Hudson River stretching into the horizon. Sitting there gazing over the estate, I couldn't help but wonder how one family could amass so much money and grow accustomed to living in such excess. I knew all about the Winthrop fortune and how they had accumulated their vast riches, but it wasn't until I was sitting there in that quiet hallway overlooking the spectacular property full of water fountains, rock gardens, and leafy meadows, that I fully appreciated the magnitude of the family's wealth.

Minutes later, I heard the creaking of the heavy steel doors. Dalton poked his head out of the bedroom and waved for me to come back.

"What's going on?" I said.

"He wants you to come in and hear this," Dalton whispered. "Play it cool. I think we might've hit the jackpot, Spense."

Uncle Randolph was now reclining in his bed, his emaciated body enveloped by the wide silk sheets. Light trickled in through the stained-glass window, making him look like a sacrifice on an altar. Dalton and I pulled up two chairs next to him.

"I want you to do exactly as I say," Uncle Randolph said, his voice barely above a whisper. "Go over to that wall over there." He pointed his curved finger across the room. "Lift up the bust of my grandfather. Be careful, it's very heavy. It will take both of you to do it. Underneath it, you'll find a small door. Open it and take out the key inside."

Dalton and I walked across the room and did as we had been instructed. Neither of us could've lifted the bust alone. Dalton grabbed the small gold key and we walked back to the bed.

"That key belongs to a safe-deposit box at the Union State Bank in Tarrytown," Uncle Randolph whispered. "Tell Muriel to give you a tote bag. Put the key and the garter box in the tote bag, then go to the bank. When you get there, ask for Mr. Tippendale, the manager. Be certain you deal only with him. He'll be expecting you. He'll escort you to the deposit box. Make sure he leaves the vault before you open the box. This is very important, Dalty. No one can see what you're putting into the box or taking out."

Uncle Randolph put his head back on the pillows and pursed his lips as he struggled to catch his breath. When his breathing had slowed, he continued with the instructions. "When you take out the safe-deposit box, there will be a small blue book in it. Take the book and put it in the tote bag so that no one can see what you're carrying out of the bank. Put the jewelry box just as it is inside the deposit box, then lock it back up."

"What should I do with the book?" Dalton said.

"Bring it directly back to me. But don't dare open it."

Dalton nodded.

"I'm very serious, Dalty," Uncle Randolph said firmly, lifting his head off the pillow. "You must *never* open that book. You've already seen a lot more than is good for you."

"What's so important about this book?" Dalton asked.

Uncle Randolph waved his hand for Dalton to come to him. When Dalton was by his side, he put his hand behind Dalton's neck and said, "No more questions, Dalty. I'm trying to protect the two of you and correct the mistakes you've already made. Do exactly as I've instructed and never tell a soul, not even your father. Give me your word, Dalty."

Dalton made the sign of the cross over his chest, saying, "You have my word."

Then Uncle Randolph looked in my direction and said, "I need a few minutes alone with Spenser."

Dalton and I looked at each other. "You want to speak to Spenser alone?" Dalton said.

Uncle Randolph nodded firmly.

Dalton shrugged his shoulders, then quickly slipped out of the room and closed the doors behind him.

"Come closer," Uncle Randolph said. "My voice is getting tired."

I walked over to the old man and sat on the bed beside him. I slid my hands under my legs to keep him from seeing them tremble. Then I looked in his eyes. They were large, watery, and pale blue. He had those filmy white rings around his pupils that I had only seen in old people.

"You could be in grave danger, Spenser," he said. "Keep your eyes and ears open and make careful decisions. He took a couple of shallow breaths, then said, "Everything is not as it seems. Think carefully and trust few. You are their biggest threat."

"Threat to who?" I asked.

He grabbed my hand with all his fading strength and put his trembling finger to my lips. "There's no more time," he said. "Get to the bank and do as I've instructed. You stay back in the car, because they might be watching. Don't tell Dalty what I've told you. It's for his own good." He motioned toward the door.

I got up from the bed and slowly walked across the room. Before I opened the door, I turned back toward him. There was such calm in his face.

I met Dalton in the hallway, and we walked to the car in silence.

"What did he say?" Dalton asked.

"He was rambling," I said. I was afraid to say more than that. I needed time to figure out what Uncle Randolph meant.

"Did he say anything about the safe-deposit box?"

"Only that we should follow his instructions carefully."

"I'd bet my life that book contains the secrets," Dalton said.

"You gave him your word that you wouldn't open it," I said.

"Yeah, but he didn't say we couldn't read the title."

"If there is a title," I said. "This whole thing is freakin' me out."

"He knows we're getting close," Dalton said. "He's protecting their secrets with the last bit of life that's left in him."

Dalton pulled over to a gas station and got directions to the Union State Bank in Tarrytown. We drove the rest of the way in silence, both of us prisoners of our imaginations as well as our fears. We pulled into the empty lot of the Union State Bank, a small brick building surrounded by a cluster of towering pine trees on an oval lawn. Dalton parked in the back, and I waited in the car.

After almost thirty minutes, I started getting concerned. Only two customers had come in that time, and both had already finished their business and gone. Then I saw the doors to the bank open and Dalton walk out with the bag slung over his shoulder. A short, bespectacled man in a gray suit and yellow tie stood at the door watching him as he left.

"What took so long?" I asked as he jumped into the car.

"I had to practically give blood to get down there in the vault," Dalton said, starting the car and racing out of the lot. "Tippendale had a security clearance list a mile long."

"Did you get the book?"

"Yup. But I had to ask Tippendale for some privacy. He kept hanging around."

"Did you look at it?"

"I didn't open it, if that's what you're asking. But I looked at the cover."

"And?"

Dalton made sure we were out of sight from the bank before bringing the car to a stop on the side of the road. He opened the tote bag and pulled out a package bundled in tinfoil. He carefully removed the tinfoil and exposed the book. It was small, no bigger than the palm of my hand. The blue had faded with age and the spine was starting to crumble. The images and wording had been pressed in gold ink.

Succession Plan
9

"What if we just took a little peek?" Dalton said. "There's no one here but us."

"I don't think it's a good idea," I said, remembering Uncle Randolph's last words. "He was adamant about what had to be done and we gave him our word."

"You're scared," Dalton said.

"I think we're getting involved in something that's way over our heads," I said. "Maybe we should step back for a minute and think about what we're doing. There have already been two deaths around this stuff, and I don't want to add my name to the list."

Dalton looked down at the book and ran his hand over the cover before sliding it back in the tote bag. "I guess you're right," he said. "Maybe Uncle Randolph will change his mind once we get back. I found something else in the box."

Dalton turned over his right palm and showed it to me. He had written several lines in blue ink. The letters were too small for me to read.

"What's that?" I asked.

"I copied it from a laminated card that fell out of the book. It's some kind of poem." He held his hand closer to me and I read the words out loud. There wasn't a date or name next to the five lines.

> *A son of Waldorf not far from the Rhine,*
> *Brother in the Gas of standing quite fine.*
> *Downed off Newfoundland in waters icy and wide,*
> *Now stands as our protector with loyalty and pride.*
> RMS 240

"What do you think?" Dalton said.

"It sounds like a riddle buried in a poem," I said.

"Poetry isn't one of my strong suits," Dalton said.

"Theirs either, by the looks of this thing," I said. "They weren't trying to win the Pulitzer, that's for sure. Maybe this poem was a way to send a message."

"The first line seems simple enough," Dalton said. "A man who is the son of a guy named Waldorf and lived pretty close to the Rhine River."

"The second line is just as simple," I said. "This man was obviously a Delphic member who others respected and admired."

"And according to the third line, it seems like he was killed in the waters off Newfoundland," Dalton said.

"Either murdered or died in some kind of accident," I said. "That line might be almost impossible to figure out since there's no date. This could've happened centuries ago or last year. And it doesn't specifically say how the person died. It could've been a plane crash, a boat accident, anything."

"Maybe there was some famous accident or murder that has some historical significance," Dalton said.

"Or maybe it was some guy out fishing on a small boat and got lost at sea," I said. "This line won't be easy."

Dalton read the last line, *Now stands as our protector with loyalty and pride.* "What is he protecting?" Dalton asked.

"You're thinking too literally," I said. "If the guy was downed off Newfoundland, then he's dead. It sounds like his protection is more symbolic than anything else. This guy was a member, and his initials are RMS."

"That makes sense," Dalton said. "But the two-forty doesn't fit."

"That has me stumped right now," I said. "But let's divide the lines in half and work on them. You take one and two. I'll take three and four."

We drove along the winding roads of the small town until we had climbed up the mountain where Wild Winds sat overlooking the Hudson Valley. We pulled up to the gate and Dalton pressed the intercom. There was no answer. Dalton pressed the intercom again. Suddenly we heard the loud sound of helicopter propellers overhead. We looked up through the trees and saw a black chopper moving toward the house.

"What the hell is a helicopter doing here?" Dalton said. He pressed the intercom button again.

"May I help you?" a man's voice called out.

"Yes, it's Dalton."

There was no response.

"Hello," Dalton called out, pushing the intercom button. "Is anyone there?"

I looked up and saw the cameras on the gate move and tilt down in our direction. No response. Dalton pressed the intercom again.

"I'm sorry, Mr. Winthrop, but you must come back some other time," the man's voice returned.

"What in the hell are you talking about?" Dalton said. "I need to see my uncle. Open up the gates."

"Please come back later," the man said.

"Who the hell is this?" Dalton screamed.

"It's Mr. Brathwaite, your uncle's attorney."

"Is there something wrong up there, Mr. Brathwaite?"

"Everything's under control," he said. "Please come back later, and I'll explain."

There was the loud buzz of another chopper traveling toward the mansion. I could barely make it out through the trees.

"Something's not right," I said. "Maybe we should get outta here."

Dalton pressed the intercom button again, but there was no answer. "They can't keep me away from my uncle," Dalton said. "I have a right to know what's going on!"

"I think we better leave," I said. "I don't have a good feeling about this."

"What about the book?" Dalton said. "We have to get it back to him."

"We either take it back to the bank or take it with us. But there's no way we're going to get it to him now."

Dalton started to back the car away from the gate, but just as we were about to turn and leave, I saw something coming toward us through the bushes.

"Hold on for a minute," I said. "There's someone coming."

Dalton rolled down his window. "It's Muriel," he said. "What in the hell is she doing?"

Muriel was driving toward us in a golf cart, waving her hand. When she got closer, we noticed that she was pointing at a spot farther along the fence. She made a driving motion with both hands, pointing at the spot again.

"She wants us to drive down there," I said. "Away from the cameras."

Dalton slowly drove along the fence and Muriel shadowed us from the other side. We drove like that for a couple of hundred yards before she signaled us to stop. We pulled the car over and jumped out. Muriel ran to the gate.

"He's dead!" Muriel cried. "Mr. Winthrop is dead!" She kept repeating the same words. She looked nothing like the cheerful woman I met when we first arrived. Her eyes were big and swollen and her skin had turned a ghostly white. Her right leg shook underneath her dress.

"Dead?" Dalton said. "What are you talking about? We've only been gone a little more than an hour. What the hell happened?"

Muriel put her hand to her chest to catch her breath. The tears were coming down harder. "Did you open his window before you left?" she asked.

Dalton looked at me and we both shook our heads at the same time.

"When Selena went back in to get him dressed to take him outside, she noticed the big window next to the bed was open and the room was very cold," Muriel said without taking a breath. "She looked at Mr. Winthrop and he was just lying there with his eyes open, staring up at the ceiling. She called his name, but he didn't move. She did it a second time and he just kept still. That's when she ran to the bed and noticed he wasn't breathing."

"Who the hell is this Brathwaite person?" Dalton said.

"The man with the special number," Muriel said.

"What special number?"

"Mr. Winthrop had given us strict instructions that if something ever were to happen to him, we were to call this number he had written on a card next to his bed. We were not to call the police, 911, or anyone else. He made all of us promise him that we'd follow his instructions. So, when Selena came running down to the kitchen and said Mr. Winthrop was dead, I went up to confirm that was true. Then we called the number, and that's when Mr. Brathwaite came over. He was here in less than thirty minutes."

"How did he come?"

"He drove up in his car."

"Was he by himself?"

"Yes, he came alone."

"Why is he stopping me from going up there?"

"He won't let anyone into the main house," Muriel said. "When he came, he sent all of us to the carriage house and told us to stay there until we were called back."

"So, who's with Uncle Randolph?"

"Mr. Brathwaite and some other men I've never seen before. They arrived in helicopters."

"What are they doing?"

"I'm not sure. I've been in the carriage house. We have an intercom in there also. That's how I knew you were down here."

Dalton buried his face in his hands, then after a few moments said, "You did the right thing by coming down here, Muriel. Now I want you to go back to the carriage house and follow Brathwaite's instructions. But make sure no one mentions that we were here earlier. That's very important."

"Yes, I understand," she said.

"I'm sure someone from the family will be here shortly once the call is made," Dalton said.

"I'm scared, Master Winthrop," she cried.

Dalton put his hand through the gate and rested it on her shoulders. "Don't worry," he said. "Everything will be all right. Just go back to the carriage house and make sure everyone remains calm. You took good care of Uncle Randolph. The family is very appreciative of your service."

Muriel waddled back to the golf cart and sped off into the woods. When Dalton and I returned to the car, we sat in silence for a while. I could see he was fighting back tears, so I gave him time and space to do it.

"I'm good," he finally said. "It's just tough. Uncle Randolph was one of the good ones in the family. I always wondered why I couldn't have a father that was more like him."

We sat in silence for a minute; then Dalton motioned for me to pull out the book.

"What do you think's happening?" I asked.

He pointed to the gold letters on the book cover. "The succession is under way."

16

DALTON AND I drove back to Cambridge, debating whether we should read the book or honor Uncle Randolph's dying words. One minute he would suggest that we pull off at a rest stop and get it over with; then, when I agreed, he'd suddenly get moralistic and change his mind. By the time we had reached the Mass Pike and were seeing signs for Boston, I had an immense headache. I closed my eyes and tried to get some sleep before practice, but I couldn't stop thinking that the book lying only inches away from me might contain all the answers to our questions about the Ancient Nine, the secret room, and the disappearance of Erasmus Abbott. The temptation was unbearable.

By the time we turned into Cambridge, we had beaten the trip down to New York by exactly one minute.

"So, what's our plan?" I said before getting out.

"I'm not going to read the book," Dalton said. "Yet. First, I want to find out what happened at Wild Winds. We can go from there."

"Promise me you'll only read the book when I'm there," I said.

"That's a deal."

We shook hands firmly.

"Something is definitely wrong," Dalton said. "I'm having a hard time processing how Uncle Randolph was alive just hours ago and now he's gone."

Without saying, both of us thought it was possible he had been killed.

WITH ALL THAT WAS going on, I forgot that the Head of the Charles Regatta, a wildly popular weekend of boat races, was being held that weekend. I had never seen people row crew before I got to Harvard. While it wasn't the kind of sport that got the average spectator's adrenaline pumping, it was beautiful to watch, something akin to ballet on water, eight people lifting and planting those long oars in such perfect synchrony, propelling the long narrow boats gracefully through the water.

The Head weekend had become something like a mini Olympics for the rowing world, with more than six thousand international rowers and 250,000 spectators converging on the banks of the Charles for the two-day extravaganza. The campus would suddenly be overrun with prepsters in their L.L.Bean moccasins and tie-dyed ponchos. Travel around the Square was always difficult even during normal times, but with the crush of visitors on this particular weekend, it became virtually impossible. This was also the first time since the race began in 1965 that it was being held in November instead of October. An alum who had rowed on the varsity team had made a windfall on Wall Street trading junk bonds, and donated a pile of cash to give Harvard's venerable boat houses much needed facelifts. The university lobbied to have the race moved back a few weeks so that all the renovation work would be completed in time for the rowing world to admire these architectural gems.

Dalton was spending the weekend at his parents' place on Beacon Hill. He left the book under the mattress in his room for safekeeping.

Saturday afternoon, I built up the courage to call Ashley. A woman, I assumed Ashley's mother, answered the phone.

"May I speak to Ashley, please?" I said.

"Who's calling?" the woman said.

"Spenser."

"Is this the young man from Harvard?"

"Yes, ma'am."

"One moment, Spenser. Let me get her."

I could tell she was trying to cover the mouthpiece, but I still heard her say, "He sounds like a nice young man, Ash."

Then Ashley said, "Give me the phone, Mom." Seconds later I heard, "Hey, Spenser."

"What's going on?" I said.

"Nothing, just catching up on some work."

"What are you doing tonight?"

"Writing a paper."

"You're doing schoolwork on Saturday night?"

"It's due on Monday, and I have to work tomorrow."

"Have you eaten yet?"

"It's a little early for dinner."

"Not if we go to a movie first."

"Do you make it a habit of always asking girls out at the last minute like this?"

"It's not the last minute. The movie doesn't start for another three hours."

"Very cute," she said. "If I come, it's because I'm bored, and it's still not a date."

"Of course not. You would never date a Harvard preppie."

"Exactly."

"Nothing more than a study break," I said, holding back a laugh.

"That's right. And one that doesn't go late into the night."

I WAS SHOWERED and dressed and ready to leave the room when the phone rang. I almost didn't answer it, worried that it might be Ashley calling to cancel.

"Spense, it's me," Dalton said.

"What's going on?"

"The family's flying down to Wild Winds tomorrow for a memorial service."

"Have you heard anything yet?"

"They're saying his heart just stopped."

"Are they gonna do an autopsy?"

"I doubt it. Everyone around here feels like he was really old and sick, and it was his time to go. He left instructions to have his body cremated and his ashes flown twice around the estate, then sprinkled over the lake at the edge of the property."

"Anyone talk to the girl who found him?"

"She said when she left the room, the window was definitely closed, but when she went back in, it was open. She thought she saw the curtains moving, but it might've just been the wind blowing."

"Does anyone else in your family know that we were down there?"

"Not yet."

"When are you coming back?"

"No later than Monday night. And I made a decision about the book. I think we should read it."

"So do I."

"I'll call you when I get back."

I HAD ALREADY calculated the night's budget in my head by the time I had jumped on the T and arrived at the Park Street station. Assuming my expenses would include two tickets, a medium popcorn, two sodas, dinner, one cab ride, and an extra token for her return on the T, I'd have just enough to catch the train back to Cambridge at the end of the night. If there was even the slightest deviation, then I'd have one long and cold walk back over the Charles and down Mass Ave.

Ashley was waiting inside the lobby of the movie theater when I arrived. She was standing by herself against the far window. I stood there and looked at her for a moment. I was on a date with the most beautiful girl in all of Boston, even if she wouldn't call it a date. I enjoyed watching other guys sneak glances at her as they walked past with their girlfriends. By the time I reached her, I was smiling. She wasn't.

"You ready?" I said.

She looked down at her watch. "You're five minutes late."

"The trains were packed."

"You're not off to a great start, Harvard."

"Today was the first day of the Head. I had to wait for three trains before one was empty enough for me to squeeze on."

Her face softened.

"What do you want to see?" I asked.

We stepped back and looked at the listings over the ticket booth. Waves of people were coming and going as the movies emptied.

"No guy movies," she said. "So cross off *A Nightmare on Elm Street* and *Die Hard*."

I really wanted to see Bruce Willis again in *Die Hard*. I had seen it over the summer, but most of my friends had seen it twice and said it was even better the second time.

"*A Handful of Dust* looks interesting," she said. "It's an English film."

I looked at the poster, two men flanking a woman, all stiff and fancy, standing in front of an enormous stone building. The tagline read: "They could afford anything except the price of passion."

"If you really want," I said. "Looks like it could be a little boring."

"Maybe for a jock," she said, nudging her elbow into my side. "There's Forest Whitaker in *Bird*. It's about the famous jazz musician and composer Charles Parker Jr."

"That's a possibility," I said, trying to sound interested. "Forest Whitaker was a great actor. While I wasn't big on jazz, I'd agree to see the movie just because he was in it."

"Look at this one," she said, walking to a poster with two white actors standing in front of a burning cross. "*Mississippi Burning*. This is a special early screening. It's about two FBI agents who go to Mississippi to investigate the disappearance of some civil rights activists."

I looked at the poster. I knew the face and name of one of the actors, but couldn't place him. I definitely had seen this Gene Hackman on the screen.

"I know this guy," I said.

"Of course, you do," Ashley smiled. "He played Lex Luthor in *Superman*."

"I loved that guy!"

"Me too. Let's go."

I bought the tickets and counted my blessings when the cashier handed me a discount coupon for a medium popcorn and soda combination. I was now two dollars under budget. We found a perfect spot along the wall. For the first twenty minutes of the film, I kept wondering what was happening next door in *Die Hard*. Ashley had asked me to hold the popcorn so that if some fell, the butter wouldn't get on her jeans. I obliged, but that meant she had to keep reaching across me. About an hour in, she reached over for a scoop, then changed her mind and let her hand fall, just enough to rest softly on my thigh. I was waiting for her to move it, but she didn't. She just left it there. I developed a quick strategy. I repositioned myself in the seat, forcing her to remove her hand. If she really had meant to leave it there the first time, she'd put her hand back on my thigh once I got settled. If the first touch was just an accident, then she would keep her hand away, and then we'd be back to square one.

I waited five agonizing minutes, then it worked. She rested her hand back on my leg. I shifted toward her so that our shoulders were almost touching; then I caught her, at least twice, looking at me. For the rest of the film, her hand never left my side and I never once gave *Die Hard* a second thought. The movie was dark and sobering as Gene Hackman and Willem Dafoe played two FBI agents sent down to a sinister and corrupt Mississippi town to investigate and discover the truth behind the murders of three young civil rights workers who had come from the north to help local citizens with voter registration.

When the movie was over, there were very few dry eyes leaving the theater. Ashley snuggled under my arm as I presented her with a choice of restaurants within my budget. She decided on the least expensive, a soul food joint at the edge of Roxbury called Bob the Chef's. I wanted to save the taxi fare for her ride home, so suggested we take the T to Mass Ave and walk the short distance to Boston's legendary restaurant, where movie stars sat shoulder-to-shoulder with auto mechanics downing sugary iced tea by the gallons and eating "glorifried" chicken and barbecue ribs.

Our timing was perfect, as most of the tables were paying their checks and many of the waiting customers were ordering takeout. We got a seat along the back wall next to a young professional white couple lifting messy ribs to their mouths and licking their fingers like everyone else.

Ashley and I compared notes on the movie over dinner and wondered how tough life must have been back in the fifties and sixties when our parents' and grandparents' generations fought, marched, sacrificed, and got beat fighting for our rights. All of this happened only a couple of decades ago, but it was a world we could barely imagine, as we now sat comfortably in a calm restaurant, speaking freely and without fear, no worries at all about being abducted by racists or corrupt law enforcement. The movie had put so much of our cultural history in perspective and filled us with a deep sense of gratitude for all of those who had endured pain and sadness and injustices so that our generation would have better opportunities to achieve and transcend.

As in most good soul food joints, our entrées were served in a matter of minutes. I was looking at a plate full of ribs while she eyed two fried golden pork chops.

"So, what do your parents do?" I asked.

"My mother works in one of the university clubs downtown," she said.

"What about your father?"

"He died seven years ago."

"Sorry to hear that."

"Don't be. It saved our lives."

"What do you mean?"

"My father was a raging alcoholic," she said, looking up from her plate. "And the worst kind—abusive. He tortured us every day he was alive. The day he left this world was a blessing." After a brief silence, she said, "What about your parents?"

"My mother's a secretary," I said. "I don't remember my father. He was killed in a hit-and-run walking home from work. I was a baby when it happened."

"That's awful. Did they ever find the person who hit him?"

"Nope. And I try not to think about it."

"You have brothers or sisters?"

"No, it's just my mom and me."

"She must be really proud that you're at Harvard."

"She made me come here."

"Where did you want to go?"

"Georgetown. I wanted to play for John Thompson."

"But Harvard is a much better school."

"You're starting to sound like my mother."

"Lucky you listened to her."

"Why do you say that?"

"If you hadn't, you never would've met me." She crushed me with one of those big smiles, and I was a goner.

ASHLEY WOULDN'T LET me see her house that night, but at least I made her accept cab fare. We were standing on the corner of Mass and Columbus Avenues with cars zipping by and the wind worrying the streetlamps. Her hair blew away from her face and I looked fully into her eyes for the first time. It's amazing how the mind has the ability to block out the physical. I didn't feel the cold at all as we stood saying goodbye.

"I had a really nice time," she said. "Thanks for the movie and dinner."

"So that means we can do this again," I said.

"Probably not."

"Why?"

"Because I might start liking you."

"What's wrong with that?"

"I don't date Harvard preppies."

"Fine, I'll put in for a school transfer tomorrow."

"Where would you go?"

"Boston College."

"Then you might turn into just another spoiled jock."

"Better than a stuck-up preppie."

"I already told you, I don't date spoiled jocks either."

"Then who do you date, Ashley Garrett?"

"I don't." She smiled before getting into the cab. "I take meetings, remember?"

And just like that, I was left alone on a cold Boston corner, wondering how a girl I barely knew could make me feel so delightfully helpless.

17

SUNDAYS IN CAMBRIDGE were always my favorite day of the week. It was my one day off from practice, the dining hall opened later and longer for brunch, and the activity on campus seemed to slow down, catching its breath after raucous Friday and Saturday nights. I slept in a couple of extra hours, got up, and later joined Percy and one of his chums for brunch. We parted when the two of them set off to the Head boat races. I returned to my room and found a message on the dry-erase board hanging on our door.

Spenser give me a call when you get a chance. 8-2357
G. Stromberger

I immediately went inside and dialed her number. Someone with a strong Russian accent picked up and told me she was over at the *Crimson*. So I tried her there and someone transferred me to the newsroom.

Stromberger finally picked up. "It's Spenser," I said. "I just got your message."

"I have something to show you," she said.

"What is it?"

"I remembered you were searching for information about that student that disappeared back in 1927. Erasmus Abbott. Well, I was copyediting a story and came across the name Abbott. I was checking the spelling and one thing led to the next, and I was suddenly reading a 1972 article on Collander Abbott that was in the *Indy*."

The *Indy* was the nickname for the *Harvard Independent,* a weekly newsmagazine that ran longer features than the daily *Crimson.*

"Where's the article now?" I asked.

"With me here at the *Crimson.*"

"I'll be over in ten minutes."

"Come to the same door you did last time."

STROMBERGER ANSWERED the door in a pair of baggy jeans, a ripped Stanford sweatshirt, and a baseball cap. It looked like she hadn't slept in days. She quickly led me into a dark office near the back of the building.

"You look like shit," I said to her as she turned on the light.

"I feel like it too," she said. "And I still have three more articles to get through before midnight."

"Ouch."

"Thank God this is my last week in this rotation," she said. "I couldn't put in another day like this."

"Why are you killing yourself?"

"*Time, Newsweek, The New York Times, The Boston Globe,*" she said. "At some point in the last five years, the top editorial job at all those publications has been occupied by former editors of the *Crimson.*"

"I hope it's worth it."

"Getting your name on top of a masthead of a publication that's read by millions of people is worth every bloodsucking second of it. It's just hell to get there." She handed me the folder she was carrying. "Here's the article from the *Indy.*"

I sat on the nearest desk and started to read a clipping from January 14, 1972.

A NIGHT OF STARS

Last week saw the return of many prominent alumni to Cambridge for what many assumed was a fundraiser for the Harvard College Fund, but instead was the 75th anniversary of the Delphic Club, one of Harvard's oldest and most prestigious final clubs. While details of the event were kept secret in the great club tradition, the *Indy* obtained a copy of the evening's guest list.

Headlining the evening was His Highness the Prince Aga Khan, the wealthy Muslim leader of the Ismailis and a 1959 graduate of the College. Joining him were Nelson Rockefeller and actor Jack Lemmon in an evening of celebration and fundraising for the club's endowment, which is now rumored to be just over $15 million.

Toastmaster for the evening was printing mogul Collander Abbott class of '06 and father of Erasmus Abbott '28. The younger Abbott mysteriously disappeared on Halloween night in 1927 and was never seen or heard from again. Rumors placed Abbott at the Delphic Club the night of his disappearance, something both club officials and the Abbotts have steadfastly denied. A onetime president of the Delphic, Collander Abbott has not only been a major benefactor of the College, but has also made numerous financial and real estate contributions to the Delphic, making it one of the largest landholders in Cambridge. Abbott even loaned his Irish butler, Conor McGee, to serve as steward.

After a dinner in the mansion's upstairs ballroom, past and present members—minus their wives, of course—were chauffeured to Symphony Hall, where they were entertained for the next two hours not only by the Boston Symphony, but some of the most celebrated musical acts of the day. A handful of protesters stood outside of the Linden Street clubhouse, challenging the club's all-male admissions policy. They held signs and heckled the guests as they arrived and left in their limousines.

"What do you think?" Stromberger asked when I looked up.

"Don't you think it's strange that Abbott was trying to break into a club where his father was a member?"

Stromberger shrugged her shoulders. "Depends on the kind of relationship they had. Could've been a father–son competitive thing. Maybe he felt the need to prove something?"

"That's possible, but prove what? Why wasn't there anything more from the parents? Their only son disappears, and they say practically nothing."

Stromberger hiked her shoulders. "Grief can make people behave weirdly. Or maybe Collander Abbott knew a lot more about his son's disappearance than he was willing to let on."

"I wonder if the father is still alive," I said.

"I doubt it," Stromberger said. "He'd be at least a hundred. But let's check the alumni directory."

Stromberger pulled open a couple of drawers and found a directory. We flipped through it and found the entry for Collander Abbott. He died in 1977. His last known address was a law firm in New York City called Wilkins, Pratt, and Dunn. I wrote down the address and phone number and thanked Stromberger for her help. What I didn't tell her was that his Irish butler was probably the same man they found floating in the Charles a couple of days after he had boasted about knowing the Delphic's secrets. Collander Abbott suddenly became a really important piece to this growing puzzle.

MITCH AND I met for dinner that night. No one had approached him about any disciplinary action for "the punch," but he still wanted my take on the incident and advice on how to get everyone to move beyond it. Coach hadn't called him yet for a sit-down, but he was expecting to be summoned to the office any day. Mitch was talking tough, but I could tell that he was a ball of nerves. And rightly so, even if in my opinion Coach got what was coming to him.

We agreed to meet at the Freshman Union dining hall under the enormous chandeliers made from the horns of kudu antelope Teddy Roosevelt had killed on safari. Mitch arrived looking less like a basketball player than a well-off suburban kid who just happened to stand almost a foot taller than everyone else. As he stood there in tortoiseshell glasses, subdued argyle sweater, cuffed slacks, and black penny loafers, you would never guess his right fist had just introduced his basketball coach to the expensive world of cosmetic dentistry.

We grabbed a couple of burgers and found a seat in the small rotunda room where the artists, punkers, and socially awkward tended to hang out. Mitch couldn't walk by a table without some guy yelling his name and making a basketball shooting motion or the girls nudging each other.

"Was I right or wrong?" he said after we had gotten comfortable.

"Both," I said.

"How's that?"

"You were right to square off and slug him, but you were wrong to do it."

"That doesn't make sense."

"This isn't just about what happened the other day," I said, putting on my mentoring cap. "This is about life. Just because something is the right thing to do in terms of justice or fairness, doesn't mean doing it is right. Coach first antagonized you. That was wrong, but acceptable. As players we must be able to tolerate all kinds of verbal abuse, even if it pisses the hell out of us. That's part of the game. But then he pushed you. That's wrong and unacceptable. Any coach that assaults a player crosses the line and should be called on it. Like my grandfather says, 'You can call me all kinds of names, but put your hands on me and you got a big problem.' But the reason *you* were wrong is because the minute you hit him back, you lessened the impact of what he did. You turned his big wrong into a small wrong."

"So, I should've just walked away after he called me a pussy in front of everyone and pushed me?" Mitch said.

"It would've been tough, but it would've been the more effective thing to do. If you would've walked away, we wouldn't be sitting here right now, and Coach would be sitting in University Hall answering to a lot more powerful people than you and me."

"Coach hasn't said anything to me yet. Zimowski talked to me, but he didn't say much."

"Coach will call you up to the office in his own time," I said. "Don't mistake his silence for this being over."

"Everyone thinks he's gonna bench me when the season starts."

"Not gonna happen. He wants to win games. He *needs* to win games. He might be an asshole, but he's not a stupid asshole. There are too many people looking over his shoulder, asking questions about why we're not winning. He won't forget what you did to him, but he'll put his pride away for now, because you're too important to the team."

"I feel like I should say something to him," Mitch said.

I shook my head. "Let him come to you first. He needs time to work it out in his own head. Be yourself, play hard, and don't take any shit on the court. We need some big men on the team who are ready to do battle this year. That's why they brought you here in the first place."

"Everyone keeps saying he's gonna Ad Board me."

"He won't do it," I said.

"Why are you so confident?"

"Because he doesn't want to lose his job. He sends you before the Ad Board, and he knows your father will sue everyone from President Bok down to the janitor who sweeps the court."

A couple of Mitch's friends found us in the rotunda and joined us. We turned our attention to more important matters—the freshman women.

We finished our entrées and moved into the main hall for dessert so that we could do a better accounting of the inventory. We immediately spotted Roz Minter from the volleyball team.

"Now, that is prime choice," Fred Carter said. Carter was the smartest black kid I had ever met in my life. He came from one of the worst neighborhoods in Detroit, son of a city bus driver and a mother who worked in the streets and sanitation department. He was a "perf," which meant he had achieved a perfect score on the SAT.

"Don't waste your time," Alphonse Lewis said. "She's not into the bruthas." I had seen Alphonse around, but had just been introduced to him that night. He had that big New York City attitude with his hooded sweatshirt and red-laced shell-top Adidas sneakers.

"How do you know?" I said. "She has a boyfriend back in California."

"Yeah, and he's about as white as that plate on your tray," Alphonse said. "Someone saw a bunch of pictures of him in her room. She doesn't even try to talk to us. I see her in here at least once a day, and she's always sitting on the other side."

The racial politics at Harvard were complicated. Black students were in a tough position. If we spent too much time with white students, other blacks figured we had sold out. If we spent too much time with other black students, our white classmates assumed we were angry separatists. The dining hall was one big murky fishbowl of social complexities. Everyone looked to see who was sitting with whom and how much time they spent interacting on the "other" side. I was lucky because playing a sport gave me a pass that the non-athletes didn't have. By dint of my team and training obligations, I automatically spent time with both blacks and whites, which gave me immunity.

Mitch said, "Boyfriend or no boyfriend, she's the finest girl on campus."

"Damn right, she is," Carter concurred. "And let me tell you something. Phonso might talk all this shit about her now, but let her give him the slightest opening. His nose would be so wide open, you could see all the way up to his frontal cortex."

We all had a good laugh.

"Damn right." Alphonse smiled. "I might not agree with her social choices, but my daddy didn't raise no fool."

We sat there for the next half hour, comparing notes, making bets, doing what guys do when they've got time on their hands and nothing serious to do with it. Then Carter had to spoil everything. "Let's go up to FBT," he said, looking around the table. "We haven't been there in a while."

The Freshman Black Table was a weekly, two-hour Sunday-night discussion group that took place in a large room on the second floor of the Union. It had been started several years ago by some members of the Black Students Association so that students of color could meet to share ideas, freely express themselves, and simply enjoy each other's company on a campus where it was easy to feel isolated and alone. It was set up as a social support for freshmen, but upperclassmen trickled in occasionally to share their experiences and offer advice.

"I don't know," Alphonse said. "The last couple of weeks, I've been mad as hell when I left there. I was about this close to jumping on Carl's ass."

Carl Johnson was the president of FBT, a buttery-voiced Californian who took himself way too seriously and couldn't hold a regular conversation without seeming like he was stumping for political office. I didn't like him. He was too damn politically correct, arguing both sides of an issue, playing to the majority sentiment when it worked in his favor, then becoming the devil's advocate when he wanted to seem profound.

"C'mon, Alphonse," Carter said. "You sit down here and talk about Minter and how she doesn't relate or hang out with her own people, and now you don't want to go to FBT. Who's being hypocritical now?"

"It won't be all that bad, Alphonse," Mitch said. "We'll hang around for about an hour, then cut out and shoot some pool downstairs."

Alphonse looked at me.

"What the hell," I said. "I'll go."

The meeting had already started when we walked in, and Carl was standing in the front of the room wearing a starched oxford and blazer with a pair of shiny wing tip shoes. There must've been seventy or so people arranged in a semicircle. They all turned as the four of us found our way to the back of the room. Carl was going on about the need for us to keep the pressure on University Hall to hire more minority faculty and the important alliances we could form with the other minority groups on campus.

The discussion was fast and furious, people standing up expressing their anger that a school as rich and powerful as Harvard could offer the excuse that the number of minority faculty was low because it couldn't find enough qualified academics to recruit to Cambridge. Someone had suggested a day of boycotts, while others made plans for a march on University Hall. Carl was in complete control of the meeting, selecting who should speak and in what order, moving the conversation along when he thought new ideas should be infused into the conversation. Then an upperclassman—a husky, dark-skinned guy wearing a brightly colored African dashiki and matching kufi sitting tightly around the crown of his head—stood up.

"We're in the middle of the most sexist, racist season right now, and no one's mentioned it," he said. "The final clubs are in the middle of their punch, picking and choosing who should enter their mansions while at the same time keeping the rest of us locked outside." His voice was deep and full, his cadence dancing like the rhythm of a Baptist preacher. "Many of you, my young bruthas and sistas, may not know about these clubs, but I'm here to tell you that they're a real threat to equality, and regardless of what University Hall says in its official statement distancing themselves, these clubs are every bit a part of the Harvard fabric. Knowledge is power, and you need to know the oppressor is not always out there with bats and bullhorns. Exclusion is quiet and invisible and often a lot more oppressive than a physical beating that everyone can witness in the open."

He didn't mention my name or even look in my direction, but I sank about a foot in my seat. I sat back and listened for the next hour as both men and women stood and told their experiences of white classmates being invited to parties at the clubs while they hadn't, and members sharing old exams and class notes that no one else could access. They discussed incidents of drunken debauchery, specifically one case where a group of members and punchees coming from a dinner had hurled racist insults at a black girl who was walking home alone from the Square. In my zeal to unearth the Ancient Nine and their secrets, I never thought about this side of the clubs. Now I felt awful, a complete traitor. No one looked at me differently, but I felt like every eye in that room was dissecting me. By accepting the Delphic's invitations, was I turning my back on all those generations of brave souls who had fought and struggled for inclusion and justice?

The debate raged on with the guy in the dashiki suggesting we chain ourselves together and sit in front of the clubhouses. A freshman from San Francisco suggested we find out the names of the club members and post them on wanted signs throughout campus. I sat back, trying to reconcile the world they were describing with the one I had witnessed over the last few weeks.

Sure, these guys were big drinkers and loud at times, spoiled brats who had their parents' legacies and bank accounts to keep themselves insulated in privilege. But I had yet to see the racial tension that had made so many people in the room angry. Was it there, but I just didn't see it? Had my desire to join actually become my blinders? Even worse, had I already become one of them and didn't even know it?

Then out of nowhere, a mousy little sophomore raised her hand and stood up in the back of the room. "I'm that girl who was called 'nigger bitch,'" she said. The room fell silent. "At first, I was angry, then I felt sorry for them. I thought it was sad that a bunch of boys who had everything in the world going for them didn't realize what pathetic little fools they were being. The more we protest and argue with the administration to do something about them, the more they're going to taunt other students who don't look or talk like them. I know this might not be a popular opinion, but I think rather than trying to shut them down, change will come faster if we could find a way inside those old mansions and transform their culture."

Her words motivated me, and I left the Union that night with new energy and focus. My mission had now become a lot more than figuring out what happened to Erasmus Abbott or which men held the garter of the Ancient Nine. It was still a long shot, but if I got in, I would try to be that spark for change.

18

BY MONDAY MORNING, the masses who had trampled the Yard had mercifully gone home. Gates that had been locked were reopened, the extra security checkpoints were carted away, and a sense of calm had returned to campus. Dalton hadn't called me, which had me worried. I kept thinking of that little blue book under his mattress. Would it shed any light on Uncle Randolph's death?

I grabbed lunch after classes with a couple of football players at Kirkland House, and then headed back to my room to take a nap before practice. Someone had slipped a large manila envelope with my name on it under the door. Inside, I found a small note written on *Crimson* stationery stapled with two newspaper clippings.

Spenser,

I found these two articles the other night and thought you might be interested. I think your suspicions about Collander Abbott are correct. There's something not right about his son's disappearance and his behavior. Most fathers would be overwhelmed by the death of a young son. He appeared not to be that kind of father. Hope this helps.

G. Stromberger

The first article was dated March 8, 1928, and appeared in the *Newport Daily News.* It was a short article without a reporter's byline. The lead paragraph spoke of a generous donation Mr. Collander Abbott had made to the local horticultural society. It then mentioned the mysterious disappearance of Erasmus Abbott and commented on the shroud of secrecy that had enveloped the case for the last four months. Collander and Elizabeth Abbott had not been seen socially since their son's disappearance, and they denied all requests from the media for interviews. Strangely, the Abbotts never went to Cambridge to meet with police or university officials, choosing instead to handle all communications about their son's case by telephone or through intermediaries. Then the article got interesting. Abbott had been asked if he wanted a search to be conducted of the Delphic Club, the location police believed Erasmus had visited the night of his disappearance. Abbott not only dismissed the search as unnecessary, but actually signed a petition with other Delphic members that was filed in a Cambridge court to block what they deemed to be an unwarranted search of a private institution.

The next clipping was from *The New York Times,* a long obituary and picture of Collander Abbott dated May 1, 1977. It spoke of Abbott's parents, Dr. and Mrs. Geoffrey Abbott and the fortune the family had amassed with their printing concerns around the world. It briefly mentioned Collander's early years before focusing on his time at Harvard, where he was a Phi Beta Kappa and esteemed member of the exclusive Delphic Club. There was one curious paragraph dedicated to Erasmus Abbott.

> Abbott's son, Erasmus, followed in his father's footsteps at Harvard, where he was a noted student in the physical sciences before his disappearance after a prank on Halloween night. The younger Abbott's body has never been found despite a massive manhunt. Questions have always centered on the Delphic Club, a secret society founded by the late J. P. Morgan Jr., of which Collander Abbott remained an active

member after his son's mysterious disappearance. **Reports of a rift between father and son first surfaced when the younger Abbott broke religious ranks with the family and submitted to the Catholic teachings
of a distant cousin who stood at odds with the strong Protestant traditions of the Abbott family.**

The rest of the article spoke of the family's immense philanthropic efforts,
directed most notably to the church he attended. It also mentioned that he
was a prominent member of the Colonial Society of Massachusetts.

Did the religious discord within the family mean anything? Was Erasmus
Abbott really at odds with his father? Did any of this have anything to do with
his breaking into the Delphic?

I picked up the phone and dialed the number to the Thompson Home for
the Aging. The operator put me through to Kelton Dunhill, who picked up
on the third ring. "It's hotter than hell down here," he said. "What's going on
up there in Boston?"

"Just finished Head weekend, sir," I said.

"Now the campus can breathe again," he said. "I attended one of those
weekends in the seventies. One big, continuous party. The only time I'd ever
seen that many people invade Cambridge was for the Game." He referred to
the annual Harvard–Yale football game, always considered to be the most
important social event on Harvard's calendar.

"Things are back to normal," I said. "I can't even tell you if we won any of
the races." I waited for him to finish chuckling before I said, "Sir, I wanted to
ask you another question about Erasmus Abbott."

"You boys still fishing around?"

"Just following up some leads."

"What's on your mind, Collins?"

"Did Abbott speak much of his father?"

"He and his father didn't get along," Dunhill said.

"Do you know why?"

"I don't remember the specifics, but I'm pretty sure it had something to do with religion. The old man was a major capitalist and a staunch Protestant. Erasmus was an atheist."

"Did you ever meet the father?"

"Never."

"What about after Abbott disappeared?"

"Even then," Dunhill said. "No one from the family showed up for the memorial service we held for him in Russell Hall. His parents sent their lawyer and a servant to collect his things from his room. It struck all of us as strange, but the family was known to be extremely reclusive. They didn't like to mingle much outside their small social circle."

"Did you know that Mr. Abbott was a member of the Delphic?" I asked.

"Of course I did," Dunhill said. "And that's what made it all the more tragic. I always thought part of the reason Ras wanted to break into the Gas was to irk his father."

"Did you ever hear the name of the Irishman they found in the Charles?"

"I'll never forget it. Mike Donahue. My third-grade teacher had the same name."

It was starting to sound like Collander Abbott was connected to two deaths, and both had something to do with the Delphic.

DURING AN OLD EPISODE OF *CHEERS,* Dalton finally called. He had just arrived on campus and insisted we look at the book immediately. Some strange things had happened at Wild Winds, and he was wondering if any of it had to do with the book. We agreed to meet in a small study room in the tunnels underneath Lowell.

Dalton arrived out of breath and looked tired. He carried a manuscript box in his hands, which I assumed contained the book. The lights in many of the tunnel rooms were either busted or too dim to see much of anything, which is why I had brought my reading lamp.

"Jesus, it's hotter than Hades down here," Dalton said, pulling off his coat and sweater. His hair was already damp. "There's enough heat down here to melt a polar cap." Once he got himself comfortable, he said, "I think we're doing the right thing. Uncle Randolph trusted me enough to go to the vault. We won't let him down now."

"What happened at Wild Winds?" I asked.

"It felt weird," Dalton said. "I felt like I was being watched the entire time. When the family gathered for the will reading, Brathwaite pulled me to the side and asked me what I was doing at the bank the day Uncle Randolph died."

"How did he know you were there?"

"He didn't say. I assume he spoke to Tippendale."

"What did you say?"

"I told him that I had business there that had nothing to do with him and walked away. He stared at me the entire time. Really creepy guy with his bald head and beady eyes."

Dalton moved the box between us.

"You ready?" he said.

I nodded.

He lifted the lid off the box, unwrapped the tinfoil, and slowly opened the book's cover. His hands trembled slightly. The thick paper had turned sepia around the edges. We stared at the first page.

SIR RANDOLPH T. WINTHROP '36 KG

JULY 15, 1956

No. 4

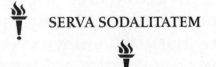

SERVA SODALITATEM

"What do you think that date is?" Dalton asked.

"I'd guess his initiation date into the Ancient Nine?" I said. "At least he picked the best day of the year."

"Why do you say that?"

"Because it's my birthday."

Dalton rolled his eyes and then carefully turned the page.

STEP ONE

CONCEAL THE GARTER IN THE INDUCTION BOX AND PLACE IT IN A SAFE-DEPOSIT BOX AT A REPUTABLE INSTITUTION. INFORM COUNSEL OF THE LOCATION OF SAID BOX AND OBTAIN TWO KEYS. ONE KEY IS TO BE KEPT WITH YOU, WHILE THE OTHER IS TO BE SENT TO COUNSEL TO BE USED FOR THE RETRIEVAL OF THE GARTER UPON DEATH. ARRANGEMENTS MUST BE MADE AHEAD OF TIME WITH THE SELECTED INSTITUTION TO PERMIT COUNSEL OR APPOINTED REPRESENTATIVE IMMEDIATE ACCESS TO THE BOX. THESE INSTRUCTIONS MUST BE FOLLOWED WITHOUT FAIL.

"This is why he was so adamant about us returning the garter to the safe-deposit box," Dalton said. "He knew he might not get there himself, and he wanted to make sure everything was in place."

Dalton turned the page.

STEP TWO

MAKE INSTRUCTIONS KNOWN TO STAFF AND/OR SURVIVING RELATIVES THAT UPON YOUR DEATH, THE FIRST NOTIFICATION SHALL BE GIVEN TO THE DESIGNATED REPRESENTATIVE AT WILKINS, PRATT, AND DUNN. ONCE THIS NOTIFICATION IS MADE, THE FIRST STEPS OF SUCCESSION SHALL QUICKLY FALL INTO PLACE. THE GARTER SHALL BE RETRIEVED IMMEDIATELY AS SHALL THE COAT OF ARMS. A PROPER SEARCH OF THE PRINCIPAL RESIDENCE SHALL BE SWIFTLY CONDUCTED TO ENSURE THAT ANYTHING RELATED TO THE ORDER IS COLLECTED IMMEDIATELY AND DISPOSED OF ACCORDINGLY.

THIS IS A FIRST-RESPONSE SITUATION, AND ALL
MEMBERS OF THE ORDER MUST BE PREPARED TO
JOIN THE RESCUE MISSION IF THE SITUATION CALLS
FOR SUCH ASSISTANCE.

"That explains the helicopters, Brathwaite, and his banning the staff from the main house," I said. "They sealed off the estate while they searched through everything. There's something strange about that name." I concentrated on the page. I had heard it before, maybe on a TV show or in some movie.

"Which name?"

"Wilkins, Pratt, and Dunn."

"Probably a law firm," Dalton said.

I could see the name in typeface, but I couldn't place where I had seen it. Dalton turned the page.

STEP THREE

THE TRANSFER OF $5 MILLION US TO A PRE-SELECTED
OFFSHORE ACCOUNT SHALL BE EXECUTED UPON THE
OFFICIAL CONFIRMATION OF DEATH. THIS CAN BE
ARRANGED IN A NUMBER OF WAYS, BUT IT IS
SUGGESTED THAT A STANDING ORDER FOR TRANSFER
TO COUNSEL BE SIGNED AND WAITING FOR
EXECUTION. THE CHOICE OF TRANSFER MODE
ULTIMATELY REMAINS THE DECISION OF THE
MEMBER, BUT IT IS VITAL THAT COMPLETE
DISCRETION BE MAINTAINED THROUGHOUT THE
PROCESS. IF THE AMOUNT IS NOT CURRENTLY LIQUID
AT THE DATE OF EXPIRATION, THEN ASSETS OF EQUAL
OR GREATER VALUE SHALL BE BEQUEATHED TO
COUNSEL, WHO IN TURN WILL LIQUIDATE THE ASSET
AND TRANSFER THE APPROPRIATE MONIES.

"Five million dollars?" I said. "Jesus Christ!"

"A spit in the ocean for these guys," Dalton said.

"You think there's any way you can find out if this transfer happened?" I asked.

"Doubtful," Dalton said. "Uncle Randolph probably had this set up and ready a long time ago. And if Brathwaite finds out I've been nosing around about a transfer, he'll know I have the book."

"Why would they trust Brathwaite with their secrets?" I said. "He's not even a member."

"But he's a lawyer, which means it's privileged information. By law, he can't reveal anything."

Dalton turned the page.

STEP FOUR

THE CAREFUL RECRUITING FOR NEW KNIGHTS OF THE ORDER IS EQUALED ONLY BY THE NEED FOR EXTREME PRIVACY IN ALL RELATED MATTERS. THEREFORE, EACH MEMBER IS CHARGED WITH PROPOSING, UPON THE IMMINENCE OF THEIR DEATH, A CANDIDATE EITHER WITHIN THE CLUB'S GENERAL MEMBERSHIP OR EXTERNAL TO IT. CAREFUL CONSIDERATION MUST BE MADE WITH THIS PROPOSAL, FOR IT IS ONLY BY THE INTELLECT AND HONOR OF ITS KNIGHTS DOES THE ORDER CONTINUE TO STAND. ONLY ONE CANDIDATE SHALL BE PROPOSED BY EACH MEMBER, BUT PRIORITY WITH GOOD REASON SHALL BE GIVEN TO THE CHOICE OF THE MEMBER WHOSE SPECIFIC SEAT WILL BE VACATED BY HIS DEATH. THIS NAME SHALL BE RECORDED TWICE, ONCE FOR SUBMISSION TO THE SOVEREIGN OF THE ORDER, AND ONCE IN THE TABLET PROVIDED IN THE BACK OF THIS BOOK. ONLY

**IF THE SUBMISSION HAS BEEN RECEIVED AND
VERIFIED SHALL THE RECRUITMENT PROCESS BEGIN.**

"This sounds a lot like the British orders," I said. "The whole Knights of the Garter thing."

"And it was obvious these guys took it seriously," Dalton said. "Muriel told me that Brathwaite was joined later that afternoon by two more men, and they went through the entire house, opening and closing doors as if they were looking for something."

"Do you think the Ancient Nine were doing something illegal?" I asked.

"If so, I'm not sure I really want to know," Dalton said. "Uncle Randolph was very good to me, and that's how I want to remember him."

Dalton turned to the next page.

STEP FIVE

**THIS IS THE LAST AND FINAL ACT. ONCE THE OTHER
STEPS OF SUCCESSION HAVE BEEN COMPLETED, THIS
MANUAL MUST BE PERMANENTLY DESTROYED BY
FIRE. ONLY THE EYES OF THE GARTER KNIGHTS
SHALL SET UPON THE WORDS OF THESE PAGES AND
ALL OTHERS WHO SO TRESPASS AGAINST THE WILL
OF THE ORDER SHALL RIGHTFULLY PERISH IN THE
NAME OF GOD AND CHURCH.**

Dalton and I quietly looked at each other. The message was clear. Murder was fair punishment for those who dared to read the secrets on these pages. Were we now threats and thus foes to the Ancient Nine? Was this why Uncle Randolph was so adamant about our not opening the book? Did he fear for our lives?

Dalton turned to the next page, where we found a mysterious diagram that seemed to be sketched by hand.

"Holy shit!" Dalton said. "It's the floor plan to their chamber!"

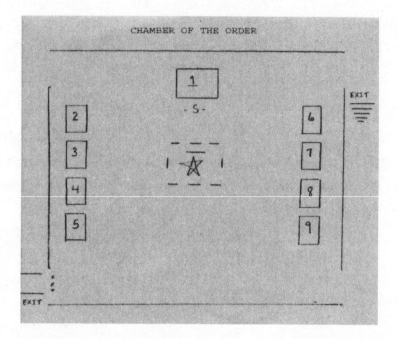

I ran my finger over the page. "There's nine of everything," I said. "Nine positions along the perimeter of the room, and the same around the star."

"What do you think the S stands for?" Dalton said.

"Maybe 'Sovereign,'" I said, remembering what I had read about the titles within the British Order of the Garter.

"I'll buy that."

An image flashed into my mind. "Shit!" I yelled.

"What's wrong?"

"I just remembered where I saw the name of that law firm." I flipped back to step two and took another look at it. "It was in the alumni directory. Collander Abbott's last point of contact."

"Are you saying this firm is the same that represented Abbott's father?"

"A hundred percent sure," I said. "Stromberger and I looked at it together."

"That means Abbott was a Knight of the Order."

"And that could explain why he was acting so strangely about his son's disappearance. He had interests on both sides of the fence. If the investigation pressed too hard, he'd run the risk of exposing the Ancient Nine."

"This connects some of the dots," I said. "We know Erasmus made it into the club that night. Let's say he either came close to discovering the chamber or actually found it, and was murdered as a result of that. His father finds out what happened and is left with two choices. He could push for the investigation, which would eventually incriminate the club and possibly expose the Ancient Nine, or since he already knew what had happened, he could let the whole thing quietly go away, thus protecting the brotherhood."

"So, it was a cover-up," Dalton said. "And Collander Abbott, the supposed grieving father, was behind it all."

Dalton turned to the last page, and things got confusing again.

CREED OF THE ORDER OF THE ANCIENT NINE

WHOSOEVER THEREFORE RESOLVE TO BE GOD'S SERVANTS, MUST MAKE ACCOUNT TO BE HIS SOULDIER ALSO; AND WHILST WITH NEHEMIAH'S FOLLOWERS, WITH ONE HAND THEY PERFORM THE WORKS OF THEIR CALLINGS AND CHRISTIANITY, THEY MUST WITH THE OTHER HOLD THEIR WEAPONS TO REPEL THEIR SPIRITUAL ENEMIES, WHO CONTINUALLY LABOR TO HINDER THE LORD'S BUILDINGS: FOR NO SOONER DO WE BECOME FRIENDS TO GOD, BUT PRESENTLY SATAN ADVANCETH AGAINST US HIS FLAGGES OF DEFIANCE, LABOURING BOTH BY SECRET TREACHERIE, AND OUTWARD FORCE, TO SUPPLANT AND OVERCOME US.

"You're the religious scholar," Dalton said. "What do you make of it?"

"Attending a Catholic high school doesn't exactly make me a religious expert," I said. "I've never seen anything like this before in my life. But it looks and sounds really old. The archaic English and talk of Christianity and Satan make me think these could be the words of a Reformationist. But I can't be sure. There's not enough here."

"It sounds to me like someone heading off to war to save Christianity," Dalton said.

"That's what the Reformationists thought they were doing when they broke from Catholicism," I said. "I'll copy this down and see if I can find out where it came from and what it means."

Dalton closed the book and started wrapping it back up in the tinfoil when I stopped him.

"What's wrong?" he said.

"We forgot to look at the tablet in the back," I said. "The fourth step said that your uncle had to propose a candidate to join the Order."

Dalton carefully turned to the back of the book, and when he flipped over the last page, I felt like someone had slammed a battering ram into my gut and a screwdriver into the base of my skull. The name that had been scribbled across the crumbling paper was mine.

19

DALTON AND I sat there for an entire hour after seeing *Spenser Q. Collins of Chicago, Illinois* scribbled on that writing tablet. It seemed unreal, impossible. We just sat there like two village idiots trying to figure out how in any universe my name could be written on that page. Finally, Dalton wrapped the book up and we retreated to our separate corners of campus.

The next day, I went to the Lowell House Library, determined to find out about Mike Donahue. If I could show that Donahue was once an employee of the Abbotts, it would implicate Collander Abbott even more in both Donahue's death and his son's disappearance. This could be the centerpiece of the puzzle.

After more than an hour on the computer, Ms. Kilcourse finally found something. Donahue's obituary had been written in a small paper called the *North Adams Transcript*. His family had immigrated to this rural northwestern Massachusetts town at the turn of the century. He had two sisters who were still alive, and a brother who had died in a boating accident. Donahue served as an army cook in World War I, then worked in several hotels in Boston before joining the Delphic Club as a steward. He had never been married and was survived by his parents and two sisters. That was it. There was no mention of the Abbott family. It had been presented and accepted that Mike

Donahue was just a small-town kid of Irish immigrants who met an untimely death.

THE NEXT COUPLE OF DAYS, I lumbered through a mental fog. Donahue was a dead end, but there still was the mysterious succession book with my name on the back plate. I carried a copy of the religious passage with me, and several times an hour, I'd slide it out from my notebook and stare at it, trying to imagine where it might've come from and why the Ancient Nine made it their creed. If there had been even the slightest reference to the date or a relevant historical event, I might've been able to figure it out, but there was nothing but those eighty-five words. I was going to need help, but I had to be careful. The best and safest place to start would be one of the reference librarians at Widener.

After a quick lunch at the Union, I climbed the wide concrete steps of Widener. Most students were either in class or heading to lunch, which meant the reference desk would be empty. A thin woman with short curly blond hair and a tiny nose looked up at me as I approached the desk. Her reading glasses hung on a necklace made of oddly shaped turquoise stones.

"My very first customer of the day." She smiled. "How can I help you?"

"I'm trying to figure out the source of a passage," I said. "And I've no idea where to start."

"What kind of passage is it?" she asked.

"Religious."

"Is it Scripture?"

"I don't think so. More like an oath."

"Do you have it with you?"

I handed her the creed. She lifted the oval glasses to her nose and read the passage. The expression on her face turned from intrigue to concern.

"This seems very old," she said. "The spelling and grammar are extremely arcane. But I'm afraid without any kind of reference or notation, this might be almost impossible to trace. Is there anything else about the passage that you know that might help identify it?"

I shrugged my shoulders. "This is it," I said.

"Where did you find it?" she asked.

I was prepared for that question. "Written on a piece of paper, but the rest of it was torn away."

She pulled out her keyboard and said, "This is gonna be tough, but let me do a quick search." For the next fifteen minutes, she entered different combinations of the words into the search engine. When nothing worked, she shook her head and said, "Religion is way out of my area of expertise. You need a religious scholar. Have you tried someone from the Divinity School?"

I shook my head. "Who do you suggest?"

"Start with one of the reference librarians over at the theological library. They see a lot more of this type of material than we do. If they can't help you, then I'm sure they can send you to someone who can."

I thanked her, left the library, and began heading back to Lowell through the Yard, but the clanging bells of Memorial Church changed the course of everything. I turned toward the church.

Reverend Leonard S. Campbell was the distinguished minister of Memorial Church and the Plummer Professor of Christian Morals at the Divinity School. He also happened to be the most visible African American at Harvard, a frequently quoted biblical scholar, and a highly sought-after lecturer even for matters beyond the scope of his religious expertise. Campbell was small in physical stature but towering in academic pomposity and intellect. Born and raised in Boston, he spoke with a New England accent whose hard corners had been elaborately rounded by his grandiosity and a vocabulary that left even the most skilled lexicographers baffled. He was the longest-serving minister of Memorial Church, a feat made more dramatic only by the fact that he had been the only African American ever to hold this critical post in what was considered to be Harvard's spiritual center. He was a Baptist preacher by training, and his scholarship had produced an entire shelf of acclaimed books and essays.

Once I reached his office, his secretary informed me that he was having a late lunch at home. I'd have to hurry if I wanted to catch him before he left for a trustee meeting at MIT.

After a short bike ride, I stood in front of Sparks House, a daffodil yellow brick Georgian revival mansion auspiciously located between the Science Center and William James Hall.

A dour-looking middle-aged woman in a white-and-crimson uniform answered the door. She was holding a small potted plant that looked like it hadn't been watered in months. I gave her my name, and she allowed me to enter with the admonition that appointments were the norm to see Reverend Campbell.

I stepped in and watched her disappear up a red-carpeted curved staircase. It felt like I was standing in a museum gallery. Oddly shaped mirrors, drab landscapes, portraits of genteel white women, and gold accents covered the wallpapered foyer. It was exactly the kind of place I imagined Campbell would live, tastefully ornate without being flamboyant, the décor conveying a deep sense of tradition and history. He definitely knew his Rembrandts from his Renoirs and felt as comfortable quoting from Plato as he did Genesis.

The woman returned minutes later, having exchanged the potted plant for a large crystal vase of sunflowers. Their bright colors did nothing to improve the sullenness in her eyes.

"You're in luck," she said. "The minister has finished lunch and is up in his study. He will see you briefly."

I followed her to the second floor and down a short hallway full of polished wooden furniture and colorful lamps. The house was rather large, but so much of its space had been taken up with furnishings and knickknacks that it felt curiously small and intimate. She had led me into the study and quickly disappeared. The enormous volume of books that filled the warm room overwhelmed me. They were stuffed into ceiling-high bookcases, haphazardly stacked on tables, and even piled against the wall in one corner of the room. And where there weren't books, there were picture frames. An entire gallery of them had been spread about the tables, the bookcase shelves, and even the mantelpiece. There must've been hundreds of them, everything from elaborate silver frames to intricately carved wooden designs. A large male bust stood in front of one window, a graduation cap on its head and two medals hanging around his neck.

Reverend Campbell sat in a rust-colored Asian print tapestry chair with nail-head trim. The glow from the burning logs in the emerald fireplace danced in the round lenses of his glasses. He was wearing a gray pin-striped suit and white shirt and holding a small stack of papers. I had never seen him without his clergy collar. A faded wool Harvard–Yale game banner hung on the wall behind him.

"How may I help you, young man?" Campbell said with his aristocratic inflection.

"I'm Spenser Collins, class of '91," I said. "I had a question about the source of a religious passage, and I hoped you might be able to help me."

"A piece of Scripture?" he said.

"I'm not sure, sir."

Campbell rested his papers on a nearby table. "Might I take a look?" he said.

I took the folded piece of paper from my backpack and handed it to him. He read it carefully, then looked at me with a curious expression, deep wrinkles coursing across his forehead. He shook his head softly. "This obviously isn't an original," he said.

"No, I copied it."

"May I see the original source?" he asked.

"I no longer have the original."

The intensity of his stare made me feel naked. "The truth, sir, is that I'm not at liberty to say where I copied that passage," I said.

After a pause he said, "That's fine. I respect your desire for discretion." He cleared his throat. "Well, this most certainly is not Scripture, but it appears to be Scripture-inspired. It could be seventeenth century, but I can't be sure about specific dates without further analysis. The tone is very strong, even defiant, possibly the words of a Crusader. But without more to go on, that last opinion is nothing more than speculation." He glanced over the passage again. "It's an intriguing collection of words. How vital is it that you identify its intended meaning?"

"It's not for a paper or anything, so it's not that important," I said. "More a matter of personal curiosity."

"Don't dismiss the importance of this discovery simply because it's not part of a course," he said. "Obtaining knowledge for one's own personal intellectual enrichment is also one of the highest academic merits. That's how scholars are made." He held up the passage and said, "May I keep this for a short time and further investigate?"

"Absolutely," I said. "Should I leave you my contact information?"

"That won't be necessary at all," he said with an easy smile. "I'll be able to find you with little effort."

BASKETBALL PRACTICE came and went in a haze. Mitch and Coach were back on the court together for the first time and it was as if nothing had ever happened. I tried my best to focus, but I was too numb to feel fatigue or excitement or anger or anything else, for that matter. I just went through the motions, and everything reminded me of that little blue book. Standing there at the foul line, I'd look up at the rim and the small square painted on the backboard and suddenly, as if hallucinating, I'd see my name scrawled across it the same way it had been on the tablet. Five players on the defensive squad, five steps of the succession plan. Nine points on the scoreboard, nine basketballs in the carriage, and nine players from the women's team stretching on the sidelines as our practice began winding down—I saw nines everywhere.

After practice, we went over to Kirkland House for dinner, and I don't remember much about that either. Then Roz Minter showed up with some of her volleyball teammates and every guy in the dining hall practically snapped his cervical spine to get a look at her. That I remember. And on the back of her jersey, a big fat old nine.

I was cutting across the MAC parking lot when an idea suddenly jumped in my head. If the Order of the Ancient Nine really had been modeled after the British Order of the Garter, wouldn't they share similar missions and traditions? Maybe learning the history of the Garter would help me understand the history of the Ancient Nine and explain the mysterious passage they had adopted as their creed.

I dropped my gym bag off in my room and headed straight to Widener. There was a long line assembled at the reference desk, so I decided to start the search on my own. I got on the computer and immediately found three books that explored the history of the Order of the Garter from its inception to the present. I copied down their titles and call numbers and ventured off to the stacks.

I set up shop in a carrel on the third floor next to the only radiator that seemed to be working. I began my hunt for the three books and managed to find all three within half an hour, all on different floors and brought my treasures back to the desk and began the slow task of combing through them and taking notes on anything that might be relevant to the Ancient Nine. The largest of the three seemed most relevant. It was titled *The Institution, Laws, & Ceremonies of the Most Noble Order of the Garter.* It had been originally published in 1672, but this copy was a reprint published in 1971. The spelling and letters were Medieval, but I was able to make out most of what had been written. Chapter V contained the most important information.

THE MOST NOBLE ORDER OF THE GARTER WAS FOUNDED BETWEEN 1344 AND 1348 BY KING EDWARD III. IT'S CONSIDERED TO BE ONE OF THE OLDEST AND MOST IMPORTANT ORDERS, DEDICATED TO THE PRINCIPLES OF SERVICE AND CHIVALRY. THE VICIOUS AND BLOODY RELIGIOUS CRUSADES OF THE MIDDLE EAST FREED THE WARRIOR CLASSES FROM THE CONSTRAINTS OF A FEUDALISTIC SOCIETY AND BONDED THEM IN A UNIFIED MISSION TO FIGHT FOR THE SUPERIORITY AND GROWTH OF CHRISTIANITY. THE ORDER OF THE GARTER BROUGHT TOGETHER TWENTY-FIVE OF THE COUNTRY'S MOST INDOMITABLE MILITARY LEADERS UNDER THE COMPANIONSHIP OF THE SOVEREIGN KING. THIS SECURED A NEW FELLOWSHIP IN THE SERVICE OF AN ALMIGHTY GOD, THE VIRGIN ST. MARY, AND ST. GEORGE THE MARTYR.
STAYING TRUE TO THE RELIGIOUS ASPECTS OF THE

MISSION, THE ORDER ADOPTED ST. GEORGE AS ITS
PATRON SAINT AND CONSTRUCTED ST. GEORGE'S
CHAPEL, WHICH IS STILL LOCATED IN THE LOWER
WARD OF WINDSOR CASTLE. THE KING HAD A TWO-
HUNDRED-FOOT DIAMETER TABLE ERECTED FOR THE
KNIGHTS TO CONVENE AND FEAST. THE CHAPEL HAD
BEEN USED FREQUENTLY AS A PLACE OF WORSHIP,
BUT ACTIVITIES SLOWED DOWN IN THE 1700S,
PICKING BACK UP IN THE MID-1900S WHEN KING
GEORGE VI REVIVED THE DORMANT ORDER AND
HOSTED ANNUAL CEREMONIES IN THE CHAPEL. TO
THIS DAY, ON A SPECIFIC DATE EACH JUNE, THE
MEMBERS OF THE ORDER MEET IN THE STATE
APARTMENTS OF THE UPPER WARD OF WINDSOR
CASTLE, THEN PROCESS ON FOOT THROUGH THE
CASTLE TO ST. GEORGE'S CHAPEL, WHERE THEY
PARTICIPATE IN A TRADITIONAL RELIGIOUS SERVICE.
AFTERWARD, THEY TRAVEL BACK TO THE UPPER
WARD OF THE CASTLE VIA CARRIAGE AND ENJOY
A LARGE CELEBRATORY LUNCH.

GREAT ATTENTION TO DETAIL AND EXPENSE WENT
INTO DESIGNING THE GARTER AS WELL AS OTHER
PARTS OF THE CEREMONIAL DRESS SUCH AS THE
SURCOAT, HOOD, COLLAR, AND MANTLE. THE GARTER
WAS CONSTRUCTED OF BLUE VELVET ADORNED
WITH GOLD AND PRECIOUS STONES. A GOLD BUCKLE
HAD BEEN AFFIXED AT THE END SO THAT THE
KNIGHTS COULD FASTEN IT ABOUT THEIR LEGS.

Then I found a section in one of the books that focused on nomenclature. This
was the first material connection I could make between the Order of the Garter and the Order of the Ancient Nine. I continued taking notes.

It's tradition that the Knights Companions of the Garter are allowed to place "Sir" before their forenames and in the case of the Lady Companions, they can use "Lady." Knights and Ladies are also allowed to use the letters "KG" and "LG" after their written names.

This could explain why in the succession book Uncle Randolph had *Sir* in front of his name and the *KG* after it. I left the stacks and went down to the basement of the main library and called Dalton.

"I think I have something," I said.

"Where are you?" he asked.

"At Widener, reading about the Order of the Garter."

"I already looked at that stuff."

"I know, but we weren't paying attention to the history and traditions," I said. "It turns out that King Edward III and his knights formed this order not only for military purposes in the spirit of King Arthur and the Round Table, but for religious reasons. They believed they were defending the will of God as his faithful servants."

"Okay, so what does that have to do with the Ancient Nine?" Dalton said.

"The whole business of chivalry and knighthood came from the tradition of the medieval Crusade, when the Christians practicing Catholicism set out on military expeditions to defeat and convert non-Catholic forces and other religious movements they considered to be heretical. The wording in that religious passage we found in the book has the character and conviction of the Crusader ideology. The Crusades spanned two hundred years of some of the bloodiest fighting."

"So, you think the Ancient Nine have a religious mission?" he said.

"Why not? It seems like they adopted a lot of other things from King Edward's Order, including nomenclature like the 'Sir' in front of your uncle's name and the 'KG' after it. The Knights Companions used these attachments as a means of distinction. I think the creed might have something to do with their religious beliefs.

"Dunhill said something about a rift between Abbott and his father over religion. Maybe this had something to do with the son's obsession with the chamber."

"All kinds of possibilities," Dalton said. "The closer we get, the more questions we find. I need a break. I'm heading to the Hong Kong to meet some guys for drinks if you wanna come."

I wasn't in the mood for big scorpion bowls of cheap alcohol and punch, so I left Widener and headed to the Tasty for a bite.

The Tasty was the true late-night nucleus of the Square. A twenty-four-hour grill in the tradition of the great American diner and no bigger than a walk-in closet, this narrow greasy spoon had served the best and cheapest hamburgers and milk shakes in Harvard Square for close to seventy-five years. Its customer demographics changed as the day wore on. Locals and highbrow professors occupied seats at the runway chrome countertop until well into the afternoon. Then, as night fell, sleepy local drunks sat shoulder-to-shoulder with raucous students looking for their fill of grease and cheap calories before calling it a night.

It was standing room only when I walked in. Charlie manned his position behind the countertop, quietly taking orders, flipping burgers, and mixing milk shakes. He almost always worked by himself, a quiet man with thick wire-rim glasses and receding hairline. Whether you were a Nobel Laureate from the economics department or sanitation worker, he addressed everyone the same way—"What'll it be, chief?"

I ordered a bacon double cheeseburger with the works and a bag of fries. I had just found a space against the back window small enough to squeeze into when I heard my name. I peered through the crowd and saw Stromberger standing in line.

"How's the research going?" she asked after fighting her way to my seat.

"I'm making a little progress," I said.

"I thought of something the other day," she said. "It's kind of crazy, but don't laugh at me. What if nothing really happened to Abbott that night at the Delphic, but instead he ran away, and his father actually knew this?"

Dalton and I hadn't considered this angle. That would explain why the family mysteriously didn't seem to press for answers or even come to campus.

"Maybe they quietly shipped him off to some place like Europe, where he lived the rest of his life."

"But why?" I said.

Stromberger shrugged her shoulders. "Lots of reasons. He could've been running from something bad in his past," she said. "Or maybe there was some dark family secret they wanted to hide."

In my mind, I ran through the pieces we had assembled. Dunhill had confirmed that Abbott actually made it in. He also said that Sampson was watching from an upstairs window. The case file in the Boston Police Department archives said that not long after the police questioned the girlfriend of Sampson's cousin about Sampson's alibi on that Halloween night, the girlfriend and the cousin were found shot in the head on the wharf. The cousin had twenty-five thousand dollars in his pockets. What if that was Sampson's money? And what if Sampson had gotten the money from the Delphic or Abbott? Hush money.

There was another possibility. Abbott starts searching the club and actually finds something. Sampson catches him and learns that Erasmus is the son of Ancient Nine Knight Collander Abbott. Sampson then offers his silence and the kid to the father, for which he's compensated a large sum of money—at least twenty-five thousand dollars. Even with Sampson paid off, Abbott is still worried his son could be killed for breaking into the chamber, so he quickly and quietly relocates him.

"You need to find out more of the history of Abbott's disappearance and if there was anything going on in the local community to find him," Stromberger said. "Check with the Cambridge Historical Commission. The university has been here so long that the history of the school and town are pretty much one and the same. I have a good contact over there if you need it. They're a little slow, but reliable."

AS I SLID INTO BED, I had flashbacks of Uncle Randolph lying in his bed in his silk pajamas, frail and tired. I rolled over, picked up the phone, and dialed Dalton's number.

"Did I wake you?" I asked.

"No, I just got in," he said. "I was playing beer pong in the basement of the Owl Club."

"I think Brathwaite knew your uncle was going to die."

"Everyone did," Dalton said. "Uncle Randolph had been sick for a while."

"No, I mean, Brathwaite knew *exactly* when your uncle was going to die."

There was a moment of silence before Dalton said, "Wait a minute, Spense. You think Brathwaite killed Uncle Randolph?"

"Or knew that someone else was going to kill him," I said. "Do you know where Brathwaite lives and where he works?"

"Not off the top of my head, but I can find out pretty quickly," Dalton said. "Give me a sec."

I heard drawers being opened and closed, the shuffling of papers.

"His office is in New York City," Dalton said. "I'm looking at a copy of Uncle Randolph's will and the attorney's letter."

"What about his home?"

"It doesn't say, but there's an after-hours contact number for him. It's a 203 area code, which is Connecticut. That could be his home number."

"Let's call it," I said.

"It's one thirty in the morning."

"No one will know it's us. We'll make believe we dialed the wrong number. Do you have three-way calling?"

"Hold on."

The phone clicked over into silence; then moments later, I could hear the ringing tone of a third line.

"You there?" Dalton asked.

"Yup."

The phone rang at least seven times before someone picked up.

"Brathwaite residence," a groggy woman's voice answered.

"Sorry, wrong number," Dalton said before disconnecting the line. When we were certain she was off the line, Dalton said, "Okay, so what does that prove?"

"Nothing yet, but we need to make one more call," I said. "Conference us in with a Connecticut operator."

"Hold on," he said.

Moments later, the line was ringing again.

"I'll speak this time," I said.

The operator answered shortly.

"I have a phone number, but I need to know what part of the state it's located in," I said. "Could you give me that information?"

"What's the exchange?"

"Seven six one."

"One moment, please."

There was a long pause punctuated by the sound of typing.

"That would be the town of Wilton," she said.

"Thanks for your help," I said.

Dalton disconnected the line.

"Do you know where Wilton is?" I asked.

"Never heard of it," Dalton said.

"Hold on, Percy keeps a road atlas in the front closet." I said. "Let me check."

I found the atlas tucked away on the top shelf underneath his squash rackets and a tall stack of *The Economist* magazine.

"How far is New York City from your uncle's estate?" I asked.

"All depends where in the city you're talking about and when you're traveling," Dalton said.

"Let's say Brathwaite was in his office when he got the call your uncle had died," I said. "How long do you think it would take him to drive there?"

"At least forty-five minutes, probably more," Dalton said. "Traffic is heavy that time of day, especially getting out of town."

I flipped open the atlas and found Wilton, Connecticut. It took me several pages and a few adjustments to get the estimated distance.

"It would take about fifty minutes to get from Brathwaite's home in Wilton to Wild Winds," I said. "And that's being conservative."

"Okay, so what does that prove?" Dalton said.

"When Muriel ran to the gate, she said that once your uncle died, they called the special number like they were supposed to, and Brathwaite arrived in twenty minutes in a sedan. It would've been impossible for Brathwaite to drive from either his home or his office and reach the estate in twenty minutes."

"Brathwaite must've already been on his way."

"That's right, unless you want to believe he just happened to be on a scenic drive through the neighborhood."

"Brathwaite killed Uncle Randolph."

"Or he sure in hell knows who did."

Dunhill's ominous baritone voice came back to me. *I think you boys should leave well enough alone. You open too many doors and you might find skeletons. You open the wrong door and those skeletons might end up being yours.*

20

❧

THE NEXT COUPLE of days I felt like I was stuck in a holding pattern. I hadn't heard anything from the club about whether I had made it to the next round, and there hadn't been any word from Reverend Campbell about the religious passage. I had placed a call to Stromberger's contact at the Cambridge Historical Commission, but she hadn't gotten back to me either. I was still trying to piece together why the firm that had been listed in Collander Abbott's bio in the alumni directory was the same firm listed in the succession book, the first notification contact in the event of a member's death.

Tired of making no progress on the Delphic or Ancient Nine, I threw my energies elsewhere. I plowed into a paper for Mettendorf's class, even taking the time to create an entire outline, something which I rarely did. I called Ashley twice, each time leaving a message with her mother, but neither time getting a return phone call. I found myself eating all over campus, hoping I'd see her in one of the dining halls, but my search produced no sightings of the girl who was slowly and painfully stealing my heart.

A letter from my mother arrived with a hundred-dollar check that couldn't have been timelier. I called her, and we talked for about an hour, mostly about classes, my eating habits, and the basketball team. I gave her a brief explanation of the Delphic, leaving out information that would have led to questions

I couldn't answer. We discussed the costs of membership, and she wasn't sure it was something my father would have supported. He had left money in an account for me from one of his relatives, who had given it to him with specific instructions that it be used only for my college education. My father put it in the bank and never touched it; nor did my mother after his death. My mother would never tell me the actual amount, but I knew it was enough to cover the remaining portion of tuition that financial aid didn't cover and a monthly allowance that she rationed very carefully.

No sooner had I rested the phone on the cradle than it began ringing again. It was Thaddeus Claybrooke, chairman of the Delphic punch.

"I know it's short notice," he said. "But I'm calling to see if you can make dinner this Thursday at nine o'clock."

"Sure, I can make it," I said.

"Nine o'clock in New York City."

"Did you say *New York City*?"

"Yup. We're inviting three punchees to be our guests at a New York dinner. We'll fly everyone down, spend the night, then fly back first thing the next morning. The club takes care of everything."

I almost dropped the phone. I couldn't believe that they were going to fly three of us to New York just for dinner.

"We're planning on leaving at seven, but if that's cutting it too close, Delta has a seven-thirty shuttle."

"The later one would be better for me. I'll come right after practice."

"We'll meet in front of the clubhouse at six fifteen. Remember to wear a blazer and tie, but bring something to change into. We're definitely going out afterwards. You ever been to New York City?"

"Never."

"Then you're in for the night of your life."

IT WAS A CLEAR, crisp Cambridge night, and small packs of students huddled in front of their entryways, taking smoking breaks. Others trudged back from the libraries, heavy backpacks slung over their shoulders, their faces long and exhausted. I grabbed a hot Sicilian slice and a can of fruit punch from Pinocchio's, then headed toward the river. Dalton sat on the steps of the Newell Boathouse when I arrived.

"Let's walk and talk," he said, rising to his feet. "The wind coming off the water is whipping the hell out of me."

We headed out east along the river, the lights of downtown Boston beaming in the distance. We walked down Storrow and past the immaculate Georgian brick buildings of the business school.

"I started working on the first line of the poem," he said. "Waldorf is a tiny rural village in the southwest part of Germany. It's in a shallow valley about six miles west of the Rhine River. There's nothing special about the village except it's been around since the mid 600s A.D. That's about all I could find. There's not much written about it. The population isn't even a thousand people."

"Maybe somewhere there's a listing of all the graduates by their hometowns," I said. "We can see if any lived there."

"Already tried that," Dalton said. "I went to the alumni office to check their records. They only have the graduates listed by class or last name."

We crossed the street and started along the winding path behind the dark courtyards of the river houses. We passed underneath the shadows of the new Leverett Towers, then the sprawling buildings of old Leverett. Dalton slowed down when we neared the long, immaculate house that bore his family's name.

"Why is all this stuff about the Ancient Nine so important to you?" I asked.

He walked closer to the Winthrop courtyard and clasped his hands around the locked wrought-iron fence.

"I've been fascinated by rumors of the Ancient Nine for a long time. When I was about thirteen, I saw something else I wasn't supposed to see. I saw Uncle Randolph kiss another man."

"As in his lover?"

"Not that way. One summer I was upstairs at Wild Winds, sitting in that same window that you were in the other day," Dalton said. "I was looking at the boats coming down the river, when I saw Uncle Randolph and another man sitting in the rock garden. They were talking for a while, then when the man got up to leave, Uncle Randolph kissed the man on both cheeks, then kissed him on the forehead."

"Did you tell anyone?"

"I didn't say anything for almost two years, then one night Aunt Teddy flew up here for some art auction and stayed with us at the house. When she and I were alone, I told her what I had seen. That's when she explained everything to me. Well, at least everything that she understood at the time. He never told her all the details."

"Why didn't you join the club yourself?" I said. "With your name and connections, they would've let you in easily."

"They would've let me join the club, but I never would've been inducted into the Ancient Nine. There's supposed to be a rule that the bloodline to the Ancient Nine must be pure. I was Uncle Randolph's great-nephew, not his son or grandson. I've always known that my best chance of cracking their brotherhood would be from the outside with some help from a partner on the inside."

"And I'm that partner," I said.

Dalton turned, put his hand on my shoulder, and looked me in the eyes. "Only if we can get you behind that big blue door on Linden Street."

THE WALK BACK to Lowell House was dark and cold. Windows in the river houses had steamed up against the chilled air. The few souls willing to brave the frozen temperatures walked briskly and with determination. My conversation with Dalton and the prospect of attending the Delphic's New York dinner had my head spinning. I remained hopeful that Campbell would figure out the meaning of the creed, another big piece of the puzzle.

The Lowell entryway was empty. Not even the smokers who normally gathered there for study breaks were willing to fight the chill. I was eager to get back to the room to see if Ashley might've left a message. It had been days since we last spoke, and I ached to see her again. I turned down the stone path and descended the steps into the east courtyard. I was only feet away from my entryway when someone stepped in front of me, so close that I could smell his cologne—seasoned wood and aged tobacco leaves.

"Good evening, Mr. Collins," the man said.

He was at least six-foot-five and dressed in a ski jacket. When I saw the tight baseball cap, I knew it was the same guy who had followed me to the *Crimson*. His hands were jammed deep in his pockets.

"Who are you?" I said, keeping my eyes on his hands.

"Milton Brathwaite," he said. "Attorney for Mr. Randolph Winthrop."

"Mr. Winthrop is dead," I said.

"Yes, but his affairs are still a matter of my concern," Brathwaite said. "And obviously to others."

"What do you mean?"

"You and Dalton seem to have a special interest in Mr. Winthrop's private matters."

"I don't know anything about Mr. Winthrop's personal business," I said.

"Really?" Brathwaite said, his right hand moving in his pocket. "What were the two of you doing at Wild Winds the day Mr. Winthrop died? You both were in his bedroom, then you went into town."

"Dalton and I were just visiting his uncle," I said. "They were very close."

He moved in front of me and blocked my passage. I looked around him to see if anyone else might be coming. Witnesses. My chest tightened.

"What did you take?" he asked.

"I didn't take anything," I said.

"So, it was Dalton?"

"He didn't take anything either. What do you want from me?"

"Whatever you took from Mr. Winthrop."

"I've already told you that I didn't take anything."

"And I don't believe that."

I heard voices entering the courtyard. Two guys laughing. This was my opportunity. I took a quick step to pass him, and then quickly walked toward my entryway door. He didn't move.

"Be careful, Mr. Collins," he called after me. "You've already been warned nicely."

I fumbled with my keys in the darkness and finally got the entryway door open. Not until I had made it into my room and double-locked the door did I realize that I was breathing again.

21

"BRATHWAITE WAS HERE!" I said.

My hand was still trembling as I held the phone.

"Where?" Dalton said.

"Inside the east courtyard here at Lowell. He stopped me as I was heading to my room."

"Holy shit! What did he say?"

"He knows the two of us were talking to your uncle just before he died. He knows we went into town. He knows we have the book."

"No, he *thinks* we have the book," Dalton said.

I explained my exchange with Brathwaite.

"What are we gonna do?" I asked.

"Move faster to keep ahead of them. Keep trying to figure out what happened to Abbott and find out the meaning of that creed. The fact that he showed up is proof how important the book is."

"If he tells the Delphic members that we have the book, they'll cut me from the punch."

"He'll never tell them about the book," Dalton said.

"Why?"

"Because then he'd be signaling to the undergrad members that the Ancient Nine exist."

FOR MOST OF THURSDAY, I felt like a kid watching the second hand of the clock on Christmas Eve. Time dragged. When I wasn't thinking about the Delphic, I was thinking about Ashley Garrett, and it was killing me that she hadn't returned my calls. The upperclassmen had always told us our greatest pickup line for the next four years would be the address of the Harvard house we lived in and our graduating class number behind our names. But they never told us what to do if our Harvard standing had the opposite effect. Dinner and a movie on my best behavior, and just like that, she disappeared from my life. It was over a week since I'd talked to her, and it finally settled in that it was very likely I'd never hear from her again. Besides that, I had too much pride to keep chasing her. So, shock is a mild description of what I truly felt when I ran into her on the first floor of our entryway seated on a small chair we kept outside our door. She was casually turning the pages of a small book.

"Ashley!" I said. "What are you doing here?"

"Happy to see you too," she said, closing the book and standing. "I was trying to get some work done."

"Yeah, but here?"

"I'm working over at Quincy House today, and my shift doesn't start for another hour. I didn't have anywhere else to study, and this seat was empty."

"I called you twice last week, and you never returned my calls."

"I've been really busy with work and classes." She picked up her bag and slung it over her shoulder.

"A quick callback still would've been nice," I said.

"Are we gonna stand out in this hallway all day, Harvard, and have this conversation, or are you gonna open the door?"

I reached down and unlocked the door. She followed me inside, but took only a couple of steps before stopping.

"Not what I expected," she said.

"Come in and have a seat," I said. "I don't bite."

She sat on the far couch, making it clear she would maintain her physical distance. "Your taste isn't too bad," she said. "Did you do the decorating or a previous girlfriend?"

The truth was that one of Percy's maids had come up and arranged everything the first week we moved in. The only thing I was responsible for was the candlestick on the mantelpiece that my high school science teacher and her husband had given to me as a graduation gift.

"I take offense to the question and implication," I protested. "Some of the greatest interior designers have been men, thank you."

"Sure, and they were raised on the South Side of Chicago, played basketball, and got a Harvard degree to learn how to match color swatches," Ashley said. "Nice try, but I don't think so. This is definitely a woman's touch."

"It's a mistake to underestimate my decorating talents." I smiled.

"Difficult to underestimate something that doesn't even exist," she said. "Anyway, I came over to see if you had any plans for Saturday night."

"I'm completely free."

"I have two tickets to the New Edition concert in the Garden. It's their 'Heart Break Tour.' I thought if you weren't busy, you wouldn't mind *meeting* me there."

"Will this qualify as a date?"

"No, it's a meeting."

"Okay, fine. Then I'm not going."

Neither of us spoke, and I pretended to be looking for something in the bookcase. She looked at me and tapped her foot. After some time, she said, "Well, I don't want to throw this extra ticket away."

"That would be a terrible waste," I agreed.

Finally, she said, "I have to warn you in advance that these aren't the greatest tickets in the world, but they're the best I could do. The seating is probably a lot different from what you're used to."

"I've never even been to a concert there before," I said. "I'm happy just getting into the arena. What I didn't tell her was that I'd be willing to sit on the damn roof just to be next to her at a concert.

She folded her arms across her chest. "And just because this is a date, it doesn't mean you can take liberties."

"Me take liberties?" I said, throwing up my hands. "Thought never crossed my mind."

I DIDN'T WANT to raise any suspicions from my teammates that anything out of the ordinary was happening, so instead of taking a shower once I got back to my room, I took it with the team, changed into a pair of jeans, then rode the hell outta my bike back to Lowell to get changed for the night. On my bed, I had already laid out Dalton's blazer, a shirt that I ironed that morning, and one of Percy's ties that I found in the back of his closet. It was a wide dark-blue silk tie with small yellow and silver paisleys that gave it a little pop. It was active, but not too loud. I had played in state championship games in front of fifteen thousand screaming fans and sunk two game-winning free throws with three seconds left on the clock. I'd given my high school valedictorian speech while being filmed by one of the local news stations. But never before had I been so nervous and excited as I was now, getting ready for the trip to New York City. Before I was dressed and out the door, I was sweating so badly, I applied a couple of more swipes of deodorant, changed into a second undershirt and retied my necktie five times until the dimples in the knot were perfectly centered and the end just grazed the top of my belt. I grabbed my overnight bag and ran out the door.

As I shot across Mt. Auburn and up Linden, I noticed a black stretch limousine parked across the street with its hazards on. The driver stood outside with his hands folded behind his back. I spotted three blue blazers huddled in front of the Delphic mansion. I recognized the lone punchee, a short, muscle-bound varsity wrestler whom everyone called Buzz. He was in the Army ROTC, a program that had been so controversial during the Vietnam War years, it was banned from campus. Harvard undergrads were still allowed to enroll, but they fulfilled their cadet duties a mile down the river on MIT's campus.

A large Delphic member standing closest to the door stepped forward and extended his meaty hand toward me. He had that uncomfortable look most big guys have when they have to comb their hair and dress up. "Hutch," he said. "Welcome to the New York trip. Hope you're ready for a good time." Hutch must've been running six foot four, 250 pounds, all shoulders and chest with an infectious smile as big as he was wide. You could easily imagine him comfortably planted in front of a big-screen TV with a six-pack, watching a football game. He looked like he'd already had plenty of adventures in his young years.

As introductions were being made all around, I felt a pull on my shoulder and turned to find the limousine driver reaching for my bag. With a slight bow, he took my bag, hurried back across the street, and loaded my gear into the limo. So, this was how these guys rolled.

"You ever been to New York before?" Hutch asked.

"My first time," I said. "I'm looking forward to it."

"You're from the Windy City, right?"

"Born and raised."

"Chicago's a great city," Hutch said. "I have cousins out there. But New York is a completely different beast."

"Are the women as pretty as everyone says they are?" Buzz asked.

"Prettier," Hutch said, wiping his forehead. The temperature hovered around freezing, yet he was sweating like he had stepped into a sauna. "Don't get me wrong, you can find beautiful women everywhere. But there's just something about a New York woman that's hard to explain. Besides, and all the top modeling agencies are there, so it's crawling with stunners."

The blue door to the clubhouse opened, and out walked a kid straight from the pages of an L.L.Bean catalog. He wore a madras blazer and a navy blue Delphic bow tie covered with gold torches. His vintage wool gabardine pants were cuffed half an inch too short with pleats deep enough to hide a roll of quarters. He didn't wear any socks with his rustic burgundy penny loafers, the heads side of the pennies showing in the slits. It had to be Thaddeus Claybrooke III, proud descendant of a Mayflower family, and every bit the pompous rich kid Dalton had described. He had the look of a person accustomed to being in charge.

"Welcome, gentlemen," he said. "I'm Clay. Where's Carderro?"

We all looked around.

"He's not here yet," Hutch said. "He was supposed to be coming right over from tennis practice."

Claybrooke looked down at his watch and announced, "He has three minutes and thirty seconds to get here or we roll without him. We have important activities waiting for us in the great city of New York, gentlemen."

"Here he comes," Hutch said. He cuffed his hands to his mouth and yelled, "Way to go, Cards, my boy!"

I was happy to see him also. A familiar face might help untangle the knots in my stomach. I felt sure that Cards and I were destined to become friends. We had too much in common not to be. Two guys from the wrong part of town who had no business getting mixed up in this world of secret codes and blue bloods.

Cards was out of breath when he reached us. "Hey, guys," he said. "Thanks for waiting. Practice was a bitch today. But I'm here and ready to go."

"Almost left you," Claybrooke said. "For the record, it's usually not good form for a punchee to keep the members waiting."

"Cut the shit, Clay," Hutch said, grabbing Cards in a semi–bear hug around his shoulders. "We're all here to have fun. The team is assembled, so let's go off to war."

And with that pronouncement, we loaded into the back of the limousine, where plenty of beer and iced champagne awaited us. Not surprisingly, Hutch snapped off a beer cap with his teeth, while Claybrooke went directly for the bottle of champagne. Cards and I begged off, but Hutch assured us that when we got to New York, our abstinence would be short-lived. As the limo driver whipped us down Storrow Drive, I looked at the Harvard buildings growing smaller in the distance and felt a creeping guilt over the fact that my family thought I was tucked away in the corner of some library, studying to make the dean's list, when here I was in a limousine heading to some fancy dinner in New York City. As excited as I was, I couldn't stop thinking about the Sunday-night FBT discussion. My emotions were at war. Was I somehow betraying the many generations before me, thousands of nameless people who fought and sacrificed to break down barriers so that I could attend Harvard? Now, here I was—excited and participating in a night like this, which was based on the very principles of exclusion they had sacrificed so much of their lives to bring to an end. I wondered what my father would think. These were the times that I really missed him. Usually I could figure things out on my own, but there were moments that I longed for his counsel, a steady hand to show me the way.

The limo driver squeezed into the small artery streets that fed into the Sumner Tunnel. We made it to the airport with forty minutes to spare, and a uniformed airport official met us as we got out of the limousine. He personally escorted us ahead of other waiting passengers and through the security checkpoint. Exhausted from practice and anxiety, the only thing I remember about that flight was putting on my seat belt before we took off and leaning back against the headrest. The next thing I knew, we were skidding into La-Guardia Airport.

22

❦

MY LOVE AFFAIR with New York City began the second I stepped off the plane. Before I even saw my first building or my first New York City taxicab, I knew I would live there for the rest of my life. Even in the airport, everything was fast and fashionable, men in pin-striped suits and leather trenches, women wearing flamboyant hats and big jewelry. New Yorkers were their own breed and brand. They looked confident and savvy, people who could survive anything, anywhere, anytime. Even the shoeshine boy had attitude, standing there against his chair, hands hanging out of his pockets, his head cocked to the side with a toothpick rotating in the corner of his mouth.

We walked down the steps to baggage claim, and were met by a sea of drivers, most of them foreign looking. Hovering above the others, however, was a giant. Dark-skinned, with closely cropped hair, he had shoulders so wide, they looked like someone had stuffed tires in his sleeves. This mountain of muscle held a sign that had CLAYBROOKE written across it. We all gathered around him, and he introduced himself as Hugh Samuels, but preferred to be called by his nickname, Tiny. He offered to take all our bags at once—which I'm sure he could've done, along with every other bag in the airport—but we declined and followed him outside. An entire row of taxis was lined up along the curb, picking up passengers, then speeding off toward the exit. It was surreal, standing there and looking at a classic New York symbol that I had seen only in pictures. I wanted to jump into the back of one and yell out the address through the glass partition like I had seen actors do in the movies. But dreams of a wild taxi ride would have to wait as Tiny led us to a stretch limousine that was even longer and shinier than the one we rode in Boston.

The limo had three televisions, a full bar, enough champagne to open a liquor store, and panels of lights that could change from red to green to white with just the flick of a switch.

"Welcome to the Big Apple, men," Claybrooke said, a glass of champagne teetering in his hand. "I want to tell you a little about our host tonight. Mr. Weld Bickerstaff, class of '53, is third-generation Harvard and descends from a long line of prominent Gas men. Until last year, he was the chairman of Merrill Lynch. A couple of years ago, *Forbes* magazine listed him as the sixth-wealthiest man in the country. But even more impressive, an article in *Playboy* claimed his fourth wife, Dominique, to be his greatest asset. Bickerstaff is one of our most loyal alums and has thrown the New York punch dinner for the last ten years. He's a great man with a heart as deep as his wallet. He bleeds Delphic blue, so you have him to thank for everything that happens on this trip. He's given us Tiny for the night as well as the influence he wields in this great city. Forget about Harvard and term papers and anything else that'll distract you from the adventures that await us. Tonight is all about networking with one of the country's wealthiest men and taking New York for all it's worth. But remember one thing, lads—what happens in New York, stays in New York. So, raise your glasses to Bickers, the Big Apple, voluptuous Dominique, and the eternal life of the Gas."

The roar that erupted threatened to blow the sunroof off the limo. We all knocked back our glasses of bubbly, and the bottle made another round.

"What's up with this Dominique?" Buzz asked Brandon Pollack, the member sitting between us. Pollack was the son of a famous movie director who had also gone to Harvard, but had been a member of the Fly Club. Pollack had seen and heard it all, whether playing basketball in the backyard of his family's Beverly Hills estate or watching Sharon Stone lie topless by his family's pool.

"If sex were an artist and painted a self-portrait, it would look like Dominique Cardona Bickerstaff," Pollack said. "He found her down in Venezuela on a trip with his third wife to see Angel Falls."

The limo pulled onto the Triborough Bridge, and I had my first real look at the world's most famous skyline. It was breathtaking, more concrete and glass in one condensed area than I had ever seen in my life. The lights flickered against the sky like fireflies on a clear summer night. Then I saw the building that would forever come to symbolize the city for me. It was in midtown, much taller and different from the others around it. Its lighted gothic arcades, symmetrical and iconoclastic, lined the spire all the way up to its highest point. While I knew nothing of architecture, I was certain that this was an important building. It looked like a lithe ballerina compared to the others that were masculine and clunky. I had seen it several times in a movie, but I never knew its name.

"What's that building over there?" I asked Hutch. "The one with the lighted spire."

"The Chrysler Building," he said. "Isn't she a beauty? Built by the automotive tycoon Walter Chrysler in the 1930s and at one point the tallest building in the world."

"Until General Motors got in the picture," Claybrooke interjected. "One of the GM executives hated Walt Chrysler, so he changed the plans on his own building that was under construction and beat the Chrysler by just over two hundred feet. It's over there with the red, white, and blue lights on the tower. The Empire State Building." It was an impressive building, lurking there in the sky like a bully in a crowded schoolyard. But I couldn't keep my eyes off the Chrysler.

We finally made it into Manhattan, where the yellow taxis zipped around us, cutting each other off as they dipped and dived to pick up passengers. The first thing that hit me about New York was all the concrete. It was nothing like Chicago, a city of parks and trees built around the expanse of Lake Michigan. Instead, New York was a grid of long, broad avenues running in parallel lines up and down the island with narrow horizontal streets connecting them. The city looked old and dirty with large garbage bags piled up on the curb, waiting to be picked up in the morning, graffiti-scarred edifices crumbling onto the sidewalks, and rusted fire escapes zigzagging beneath rows of smoky windows. I was struck by how each block seemed to be different from the next. A row of immaculate brownstones with artistic lighting fixtures might sit adjacent to a street full of dilapidated tenements with broken doors and taped-up windows.

"Mr. Bickerstaff has been nice enough to offer us the entire suite of bedrooms on the third floor of his apartment," Claybrooke announced. "So, we'll put our things away, have dinner, and then go back upstairs to change for our night out. And as a legal precaution for the club, I must remind all of those who are underage that we do not encourage the consumption of alcoholic beverage amongst minors." He winked at us and smiled, and we downed another round of drinks.

The limousine turned onto storied Fifth Avenue. To the right stood a wall of darkness as the tree-lined border of Central Park broke only for a few blocks to showcase the imperious Metropolitan Museum of Art and its colorful exhibit of banners flapping in the night breeze. To our left, towering apartment buildings loomed, and ornately uniformed doormen peered behind tall glass doors, assisting residents out of dark sedans, dutifully carrying leather-strapped shopping bags and large packages into the well-appointed buildings. Most of the lobbies boasted impressive crystal chandeliers, polished wood, and elaborately designed wallpaper. Mercedes and BMWs and other foreign cars sat double-parked against the curb, their hazard lights blinking, their drivers standing outside at the ready.

The limo pulled up to a gray marble-tiled building with a long green awning that reached from the lobby to the curb. No sooner had Tiny stopped than two doormen in matching uniforms opened our doors and then stepped aside, their white-gloved hands bent behind their backs, their heads bowing each time one of us climbed out of the backseat. Their deference was embarrassing, and I looked at the others to see if they too felt uncomfortable. Claybrooke, of course, was out front, nose in the air, acknowledging the men only by handing off his overnight bag, while the rest of us gladly carried our own.

"I'll be here when you're done with dinner, Mr. Claybrooke," Tiny said. "Shall I restock the bar in the meantime?"

"A few more bottles of Dom Pérignon would be great," Claybrooke said. Then he turned and looked at Hutch. "And a couple of cases of Amstel Light for the brute."

We followed Claybrooke into the shiny, wood-paneled lobby. Everything looked expensive, from the slip-covered furniture surrounding the long glass table to the marble sculptures resting in the mahogany niches. The concierge picked up a phone behind his desk and said something into it before escorting us into an elevator. The lift operator welcomed us and already knew our destination. A large mural of angels and rolling hills covered the ceiling, and a velvet couch sat along the back wall. I wasn't sure if the couch was meant to sit on or if it was just there for decoration, so I took a cue from the others and remained standing.

Within seconds, we were in the foyer of what can only be described as a mansion in the sky. A chandelier large enough to light up a football stadium hung from the ceiling in front of a peach marble staircase that disappeared somewhere near the domed ceiling. An enormous painting hung on the left wall, and a fresco half its size occupied most of the right wall. It was the most intimidating display of opulence I had ever seen.

"Hey, boys!" a voice echoed from the other end of the long hall. A dark figure made its way toward us while two others trailed behind. *"Mi casa es su casa,"* the man said as he reached us, letting out a boisterous laugh that raced around the foyer, then rattled up the stairs.

Weld Bickerstaff was nothing like I had imagined. His long red hair, tinged with streaks of gray, was neatly tucked behind his ears and curled just above his shoulders. An army of freckles poked through his deep tan and spread across his cheeks. He had heavy bags under his eyes, as if miniature pillows had been slipped under his skin. He was military stocky and wore a pair of jeans that looked tight enough to constipate him. Under his deep chocolate suede blazer, he wore a French blue shirt opened enough to show a mat of red whiskers crawling up his chest. He held a tumbler full of what looked like vodka and soda and three olives. A man's man. A young Vietnamese man and woman who looked like they could pass as brother and sister stood behind him with welcoming smiles.

Claybrooke stepped forward. "Good evening, Mr. Bickerstaff," he said, extending his hand.

"Mr. Bickerstaff?" the man said, looking wide-eyed over his shoulder. "Who's that?" He let out another howl that sent a flash of red across his cheeks and said, "I'm Mr. Bickerstaff to these two behind me. But to my fellow brothers of the Gas, I'm Bickers."

Claybrooke nodded and smiled, as did the rest of us. I already liked the man.

"Haven't we met before?" Bickerstaff said, stepping closer to Claybrooke and looking him over.

"Yes, sir, I was here two years ago for my punch dinner. I'm Thaddeus Claybrooke, '89."

"That's right, I remember," he said. "You told me about your great something or other crossing over on the *Mayflower*." Claybrooke released one of his smug grins. "Your people were upstairs eating filet mignon while mine were down below, knifing each other for greasy scraps," he said. "Last time you were here, you were a little uptight." He reached up and pulled Claybrooke's bow tie until it unraveled. "This time, loosen up a bit. You're a member now, so no need to kiss anyone's ass."

The rest of us, feeling safe with Bickerstaff as a buffer, joined him in another hearty laugh, then introduced ourselves to him in order.

"Leave all your bags right here," he said. "Tran and Huang will take them up to your rooms. We're gonna set you up on the third floor. Each of you will have your own room to accommodate any company you might have later." He winked and laughed, then said, "Now, let's get something to eat. I'm starving."

We followed him down a series of wide hallways and through a cluster of sumptuous rooms that had been tastefully decorated with sleek furniture and expensive art. We finally reached a large dining room dominated by a long pink marble table. The combination of polished silverware and brilliant light made the table look like it was littered with diamonds. Two black women in uniforms different from the ones worn by Tran and Huang showed us to our seats and began fussing over us right away. I was terrified that I was going to do something embarrassing, like use the incorrect fork or pick up a dinner roll from the wrong plate. So, I resorted to my safety plan—follow the movements of someone I knew would do everything right. I scoped out Claybrooke, who, of course, was prominently seated to Bickerstaff's right, his bow tie gone, but his shirt still closed to the top button.

"I hope you boys are hungry," Bickerstaff said, nursing a fresh drink. "I had them search halfway around the world to get you some quality meat. We got some beef from Argentina and lamb from Australia. Have one or both. It's your choice. And don't be shy. We ordered enough to feed an entire battalion."

I didn't doubt it. I leaned over to Hutch. "Where's Dominique?" I whispered.

"Oh, don't worry." He smiled with a slow nod. "She'll show."

There was the sound of silver on glass, and we all turned to see Bickerstaff standing at his seat. "First round of jokes of the night, fellows," he said. "A young woman brings her fiancé Marcus home and is excited to introduce him to her parents. The father is sitting in his study smoking a cigar and reading the newspaper. Like any good father, he says to Marcus. 'So what exactly is it that you do?'"

"'I'm a biblical scholar with a special focus on translations of the New Testament,' Marcus says."

"The father replies, 'That is commendable, Marcus, but you plan on marrying my daughter. How are you going to buy her a house and feed her?'"

"'Not a problem at all,' Marcus says. 'I study the Bible and Scripture assures me that God will provide.'"

"The father puts down his newspaper and says, 'That is well and good, but I'm sure you plan on giving me grandchildren. How do you plan on paying for their education?'"

"'Not a problem at all,' Marcus says. 'I study the Bible and Scripture assures me that God will provide.'"

"The father sits upright in his chair. 'A young family needs things like health insurance and a steady supply of food and other household items. How will you pay for all of this?'"

"'Not a problem at all,' Marcus replies. 'I study the Bible and Scripture assures me that God will provide.'"

"The father has had enough and goes into the kitchen where his wife is putting the finishing touches on dinner."

"'So what's he like?' the wife asks anxiously."

"'Well, he seems to be a fine boy,' the father says. 'I just met him and he already thinks I'm God.'"

We picked up the heavy silverware and got down to the business of eating.

Hutch elbowed me in the side. She walked toward us in a silver, shimmery, formfitting dress with a plunging neckline that showed off the bronzed skin of her ample cleavage. Her long black hair had been pulled back from her sun-soaked face, exposing a pair of large teardrop diamond earrings that shone like mini flashlights. The first two words that instantly popped into my mind—*flawless* and *goddess.*

Bickerstaff stood and the rest of us followed.

Bickerstaff cleared his throat and said, "Gentlemen, my lovely wife, Dominique Cardona Bickerstaff. My most valuable treasure."

She smiled, and I swear I had to hold on to the back of my chair to keep myself from falling. Those turquoise green eyes set against that dark skin was like God saying, "If you ever doubted my ability to perform miracles, you will never doubt me again."

One of the servants pulled her seat out for her, and at Bickerstaff's suggestion, the rest of us went around the table, offering our names and hometowns. She nodded her approval and then to the surprise of everyone but her husband, offered to tell a joke of her own. She formed her words with that thick Venezuelan accent, which made the delivery all the more wonderful, and zipped a practiced joke about a young nursing student and involuntary muscle contractions.

When she finished, the room erupted in applause and Bickerstaff raised his glass. And that set the tone for the evening. "Domi," as she liked to be called, may have looked like some delicate South American princess, but she kept up with us every step. She cursed as well as Bickers, enjoyed every dirty joke we told, and was openly flirtatious.

I was having an extremely difficult time keeping my eyes off her. "You don't think it bothers him even a little that every guy in here is undressing his wife with their eyes?" I said to Hutch.

"Not at all," Hutch said. "He's completely secure." I looked down, and there he was in the middle of another story, one hand gesturing in the air, the other holding on to what must've been his fifth vodka tonic. "Besides, why do you think he brought her back from Venezuela? It wasn't for her advice on his stock portfolio."

The meat came out, several trays of it, piping hot and succulent. Then came the vegetables, an entire garden's worth.

"You fellas ever hear of the great Teddy Kennedy story?" Bickers called out from his end of the table. "It's a testament to the power of money, even at a school like Harvard. When he was a freshman, I was a sophomore. He liked to party and chase the girls even back then. So here comes exam time and he has to take his Spanish A final. One of Teddy's football teammates had a roommate, a guy they called El Señor, a skinny kid from the Bronx who was a master of Spanish. Teddy was a great athlete, very smart but not exactly the most diligent of students. So, on a whim, someone suggested that he have El Señor take the exam for him.

"So, El Señor agrees to do it and reports to the examination room and starts the test. Problem is, the guy proctoring the exam recognizes El Señor and knows damn well he wasn't enrolled in an entry-level Spanish course. It wasn't five minutes after the exam had ended that Teddy got a call from Dean Leighton's office. Nailed him to the wall. They didn't permanently expel him like they would've if you or I had done it, but they kicked him out and told him they'd consider his readmission after a year off. He enlisted in the army during his time off, and sixteen months later, he went back to campus as a full-time student living in Winthrop House like his brothers before him. He went on to join the Owl Club, and the Pi."

"Is that really true?" Pollack asked.

"Damn right it is," Bickerstaff shot back.

"How do you know it's not just part of the Kennedy legend?" Claybrooke asked.

"Because I was El Señor," Bickerstaff said with a wide grin. "And the sonuvabitch never spoke to me again. He said I was a piece of shit for turning him in, which of course, I didn't. I just got caught."

"You think he's telling the truth?" I whispered to Hutch.

"Every word of it," Hutch said. "But he didn't finish the story. Bickers was coming home one night from the Tasty about a week after that, and a group of thugs beat him so badly, they knocked him unconscious. That's how he got that scar underneath his left ear."

"A very naughty girl," Cards whispered. "She's getting a kick outta Pollack and Buzz looking down her dress."

"I can't stop looking at her either," I said.

"None of us can. And she knows it."

After we had gotten through dessert and another round of drinks, Bickerstaff looked down at his watch and suggested we get upstairs and change. "Now the real fun begins, gentlemen," he said with a smile wide enough to swallow the room. He told us that Tiny was ours for as long as we wanted him, and the doormen had been instructed to give us full access to the building. He reached into his pocket and pulled out a wad of hundred-dollar bills big enough to choke an elephant. He handed it to Hutch, and told him to give us "the time of our life." He delivered a parting joke about two monks in a Mexican whorehouse, then put his arm around his trophy and marched off down the hall. It was the last we would see of the great Weld Bickerstaff, class of '53.

23

OUR FIRST STOP was Oliver's, a small preppie bar in the section of the city that Claybrooke called the Upper East Side and Hutch followed up with "a place where you'll find a lot of *his* kind running around in boat shoes." We stepped through the heavy oak door and found pristine blond girls in bright argyle sweaters flirting with country-club guys with upturned collars. Claybrooke spotted a group he regularly summered with in the Hamptons. The rest of us sidled up to the bar, and Hutch ordered us a round of shots, peeling a bill off Bickerstaff's wad of cash.

"So, what were you and Domi the Divine talking about all night?" Hutch asked Pollack. A question the rest of us had been dying to ask.

"The usual." Pollack shrugged. "The economy, political unrest in North Korea, and new efforts to preserve the Amazon jungle."

"Bullshit," Hutch said, slapping Pollack on the back and sending him stumbling against the bar. "You were so far down her dress, I can see her panty marks around your neck."

"She's one helluva woman," Pollack said, shaking his head. "I talked to her through the entire dinner and can't remember even half the things she said."

"You should've gotten her to come out with us," Buzz said.

"Don't think I didn't try," Pollack said. "She said the next time we came down to give her a call and she'd be willing to show us *her* side of the city."

More preppies strode in with their wrinkled khakis and starched blazers and a whole bunch of attitude. Hutch bought a second round of shots before announcing it was time to leave. We turned and found Claybrooke whispering in the ear of some prissy blonde sitting on his lap. Hutch walked over and Claybrooke refused to get up, so Hutch grabbed him by the back of his collar and told him that he was coming with us or getting left behind. Seconds later, we were jumping in the back of the limo, Claybrooke yelling at Hutch about messing up his rap, Hutch yelling back at him that he couldn't mess up something Claybrooke didn't have.

"Where to next?" Tiny said through the partition.

"The Pink Bitch," Hutch said.

"Do we have to go there again?" Claybrooke sulked. "I hate that place."

"It's about the team, Clay," Hutch said. "Their trip won't be complete unless they experience the Pink Bitch."

The limo flew down a long avenue as we passed skyscrapers, crowded restaurants, and dark bars, eventually stopping at a red light across the street from a crowd of people who looked like they were just leaving a formal. The men wore tuxedos, white silk evening scarves, and black cashmere coats while the women sparkled in elaborate ball gowns and long fur coats. They stood under a large steel-and-glass awning that stretched from the side of the building to the curb. An entanglement of limousines and chauffeured sedans snarled the northbound lanes of Park Avenue. This was the image I had always had of New York City.

"What's that building over there?" I asked.

"The Waldorf Astoria," Claybrooke said. "One of the city's most famous landmark hotels. That's where kings and presidents stay when they come to town."

I looked back at the art deco hotel and the flurry of activity bustling in the lobby and spilling into the streets. Then it struck me. *A son of Waldorf not far from the Rhine.* Was it possible the Waldorf in the poem was the same

Waldorf of this hotel? It couldn't be a very common name. I made a mental note to look into it once I got back to Cambridge.

Several minutes later, we headed into a gritty working-class neighborhood. "This is the East Village," Hutch explained. "No argyle or buckskins in this part of town. This is where it gets real."

Tiny maneuvered the limo down several narrow streets. Gone were the scrubbed buildings and wide sidewalks of the Upper East Side. We now passed rows of squat tenements that looked old and tired, rusted signs hanging lopsided above crammed storefronts.

"Stop here, Tiny," Hutch called out. "We'll walk from here." Tiny pulled the limo to a stop just a few feet into the street.

"Why did you tell him to stop?" Claybrooke asked. "The bar is all the way down the block."

"Because I'm not stupid enough to pull up to the Pink Bitch in a limo," Hutch said. "That's enough of a reason for someone inside to wanna kick our Ivy League asses."

I looked down the street and understood exactly what he meant. A long chain of Harleys was lined up in the middle of the block, their polished chrome handlebars shining under the streetlights. We marched off toward the official start of what Bickerstaff had called the fun part of the evening. The front window was made of thick black glass blocking out the bar's interior, and the big steel door had the bright pink letters *PB* painted on it with the silhouette of a naked woman. Hutch pulled open the door, and it seemed like we had walked into the middle of a rock concert and strip club all rolled up in one. There were bodies everywhere, a sea of tattooed, ponytailed men covered from head to toe in black leather and silver chains. Women wore tight pink T-shirts and lots of lip gloss. Motorcycles hung from the high ceiling along with helmets, leathers, boots, and Harley-Davidson paraphernalia. The floor was covered with wood chips and sawdust.

Hutch elbowed a path for us through the crowd, carving out a spot in the middle of the bar with its long stainless-steel top and pink track lights running underneath it. The four bartenders all looked like they could be *Playboy* centerfolds. Skimpy bikini tops, tight leather miniskirts, and biker boots strapped just above their knees—everything was hot pink. They screamed and poured, smiled and flirted, and every fifteen minutes, one of them would jump up on the bar to dance, ripping off her skirt and revealing a bikini bottom that was nothing more than a tiny slit of fabric held together by a precarious knot. After the dance had ended, she'd pick up a pink cowboy hat, then strut her wares the entire length of the bar as patrons whistled and pelted her with balls of money that she happily caught in the hat.

"Welcome to the Pink Bitch," Hutch said, passing out a round of shots. "No place like it anywhere in the world. If you can't find what you need here, you can't find it anywhere."

By this time, most of us were starting to feel the effects of the alcohol. I was feeling good, confident I hadn't made a fool of myself at Bickerstaff's dinner table, and happy that Hutch had insisted we leave Oliver's and cut our teeth on the Pink Bitch.

Pollack nudged my shoulder. "What do you think about those two over there against the wall?" he said.

I followed his finger and immediately saw what had gotten his attention, one a brunette with enormous breasts, the other a strawberry blonde with bright blue eyes. They stood against the wall, shaking their heads to the music and sipping Guinness. They smiled at us when I looked over. I kept my eyes on the brunette.

"So, what do you think?" Pollack said.

"They could be fun," I said.

"You game?"

I took another pull of beer and looked over at them again.

"What do we have to lose?" I said.

"Which one you want?" Pollack said.

"I'll take the brunette."

"Perfect, 'cause I'm feeling vibes from the blonde. Whatever you do, don't tell 'em we go to Harvard. Just say we're from out of town."

"Copy that."

We cut our way through the mass of sweaty bodies. Pollack, a handsome-enough guy and much smoother than I would've expected, cozied up to the blonde while I slid over to the brunette. They were all smiles.

"What's going on?" Pollack said.

"Nothing much," the blonde answered. "What's up with you guys?"

"Just trying to have a good time," Pollack said. "What are your names?"

The blonde smiled. "Cindy."

"Becky," came the brunette.

"I'm Brandon," Pollack said. "This here is Spenser."

I nodded. They were two knockouts, and I couldn't believe our luck of reaching them before anyone else did. "Nice to meet you both," I said.

"Where are you guys from?" Becky asked. "You're not from around here."

"How could you tell?" Pollack said.

"You don't have the look." She smiled. "Too clean."

"I'm from L.A.," Pollack said.

Their eyes moved to me. "Chicago," I said.

"What brings you to the city?" Cindy said. I thought I heard traces of an Eastern European accent.

"We're here on a little business, a little pleasure," he said nonchalantly. "How about you guys?"

"Jersey," Becky said. "And we're here all for pleasure."

"Then no need standing around empty-handed," Pollack said. "Let's get you some more drinks."

They looked at each other and giggled. "Two mojitos," Cindy said.

Pollack went to collect the drinks, leaving me with the lovelies. I tried looking Becky in the eyes, but I was having a difficult time not staring at her gigantic chest. Her T-shirt had J-U-I-C-Y spread across it in small crystals, and the fabric was under so much tension, I thought the I was going to pop off and hit me in the face.

"I've never been to Chicago," Becky said. "Is it as cold as everyone says it is?"

"The winters can be hard," I said. "But you get used to it after a while."

"You ever see a Bulls game?" Cindy asked. "I don't know a lot about basketball, but I love Michael Jordan. He's so cute."

"I've been to a couple," I said. "But it's the toughest ticket in town. They're sold out three years in advance."

"I saw him once in an airport," Becky said. "He wasn't all stuck up like some of those other athletes. He signed autographs for everybody."

"You guys come here a lot?" I asked.

"Every couple of weeks," Cindy said. "But Thursdays are the best nights. Everyone comes for the midnight countdown."

"What's that?"

"At twelve, they play 'Midnight Cowboy' and everyone sings along, drinks a shot when it's done, then kisses the person next to them for an entire minute."

I looked down at my watch. It was a quarter to twelve. Our timing couldn't be more perfect. Pollack returned loaded with drinks. He handed them out and we toasted to new friendships formed at the Pink Bitch as well as Joni Mitchell and her classic "Midnight Cowboy."

Becky moved closer to me and I could feel her on my arm. She stood on her toes and said, "So, how long you boys in town for?"

"Just till the morning," I said.

"Where ya staying?" Cindy asked.

"At a friend's place," Pollack said.

"What do you say we go back there after this and really party?" Becky said.

New York was fast becoming my favorite city. I looked over at Pollack, and he too had made his move. Cindy was running her hands through his hair and he was leaning into her ear whispering something that was making her laugh. How in the hell could we get so lucky?

I looked down at my watch. "Let's wait till after midnight, then we'll leave," I said.

"Can Cindy come along?" she asked.

I looked over at Pollack, who had his hand around Cindy's waist and his face nestled in her hair. "Of course," I said. "It looks like that was probably their plan anyway."

The music suddenly got louder, and another bartender jumped up on the stage. Free shots were being passed around, and everyone started singing the words to "Midnight Cowboy." I didn't know all of them, but I knew enough to fake it. It was one of the craziest things I had ever seen, burly biker dudes tilting their heads back and screaming their lungs out, women in their tight tees parading around to the pleasure of roaming hands. Then the song finally ended, and everyone downed their shots before the kissing began. Becky was a spectacular kisser, and her tongue was remarkably strong. She placed one hand behind my head and rested the other between my legs. My response was immediate. I opened my eyes for a brief moment and saw Pollack enjoying Cindy's full attention. I saw Hutch across the room getting some action.

A loud horn blew to let us know the minute was up, and the entire bar rocked with a deafening explosion of whistles and applause. Pollack and I locked eyes and exchanged the nonverbal equivalent of a high five.

"Ready to go?" Becky whispered in my ear.

I looked at Pollack, and he gave me the let's-get-the-hell-outta-here nod. I turned back to kiss Becky, and that's when I felt it. I thought it was her pocketbook at first, but then I looked at her shoulders and there wasn't a strap. I thought it might be something in her hands, but her hands were around my waist. I reached down in the dark, moving my hands around, trying to find it. I did. I screamed. Becky backed up against the wall, a look of horror stretching her eyelids to the top of her forehead. I tried to say something, but my mouth wouldn't form words. So I just screamed again.

I looked over at Cindy. I could tell by the look on her face that she knew what had happened. Pollack put his arm around my shoulder. "You all right, Spenser?" he said.

"Holy shit!" I yelled. "We have to get the hell outta here! Now!"

"What's wrong with you?" he said. "Things are going great. Cindy wants me to take her home. Chill before you mess us up."

I grabbed Pollack by the collar. "They're guys," I said. "They're not girls."

He pushed my hand away. "What the hell are you talking about?"

"Becky and Cindy are guys! They're not girls. They're guys dressed up like girls."

"You're drunk, Spenser." He laughed, throwing his hand around my shoulder. "We got two of the hottest girls in here. You're drunk. Stay cool."

I reached around Pollack, grabbed Cindy's hair, and tugged it. She screamed and fought me, but I managed to fling the wig to Pollack.

"Holy shit!" he yelled. He threw the wig back at Cindy, and stood there frozen, a look of horror contorting his face. Becky screamed, and suddenly three guys with heavy beards, black bandannas, and tattoos riding up their biceps suddenly surrounded us.

"They won't leave us alone!" Becky yelled. Cindy had gotten the wig back on with one hand and held the other across her chest.

I quickly searched for Hutch or Buzz, but they weren't at the bar. I looked at the three bears surrounding us and thought how much this was going to hurt. Pollack was already backed up against the wall, and they were closing in on us. I had my hands ready to block my face. Suddenly I heard, "You boys wouldn't be lookin' for a fight, now, would ya?"

We all looked up at the mountain of black flesh. There was Tiny, nose flared, the veins in his neck standing up like lead pipes. The area around us had cleared into a circle, and everyone was waiting to see what would happen next. I could see Claybrooke and Hutch fighting their way through the crowd. The three bears took one look at Tiny, then raised their hands in surrender and backed up.

"Understanding is a wonderful thing," Tiny said. He turned to us. "You guys wanna stay or go?"

"Go," Claybrooke said. "I'll get my ass fried if one of our punchees gets hurt or ends up in jail tonight."

Tiny plowed a way for us through the restless crowd, and when we got outside Hutch turned to Pollack and said, "What the hell happened in there?"

"Misunderstanding," Pollack said.

"Dude, what did you do to those girls?" Claybrooke said. "They were screaming like someone was trying to kill 'em."

When Pollack turned and looked hard at me, I knew it would remain our secret. "I didn't mean to," he said. "And let's leave it at that."

We climbed into the back of the limousine, and Hutch gave Tiny our next destination, the Lion's Den. Then he turned to Pollack and me and said, "I hope you animals can behave yourselves at this next spot. I happen to have a good reputation in there."

I tried pushing out of my mind the fact that I had just kissed a guy who had also felt me up, but every time I looked at Pollack, the horror kept flooding back.

In a matter of minutes, a panorama of flashing neon lights flooded over us, and I knew that we were in Times Square, the heartbeat of the city and a reason why they said it never slept. A collage of people packed the sidewalks, and brightly lit stores remained open, hawking I ♥ NY paraphernalia.

"Couple of rules, gentlemen," Hutch said. "First of all, there's no touching the ladies unless they invite you to do a little exploring. If you put your hands on them without permission, you'll get tossed by security. And don't think because it's dark you'll get away with it. They have cameras everywhere. Second, no getting up onstage and joining the fun, I don't care how much some chick turns you on, stay in your seat and let them come to you. Third, you can go back to the private rooms, but no more than two at a time. Last, have fun. I have the money to take care of everything."

Hutch led the way to the entrance, where two greasy-looking guys in black pin-striped suits and white alligator shoes immediately opened the velvet ropes as we approached.

"These guys are pros," Buzz said to me. "We just walk right in here, and they start taking care of us."

"It probably doesn't hurt having a couple of thousand of Bickers's dollars burning your pocket," I said.

A girl in a tight leather dress with a neckline running down to her exposed navel showed up out of nowhere. She said something to a woman behind the cashier and led us through a set of double doors. A long stage with two poles anchored the center of the room. An Asian woman wearing only an orange wig and a matching G-string crawled on the stage, and every time she opened her legs, the guys sitting in the front row would let out a cheer as if their team had just scored a touchdown. She expertly held her pose spread-eagle on a bed of dollar bills.

Topless women mixed drinks at a bar along the wall near the entrance, and I noticed several smaller dance floors with spotlights, poles, and curved ladders. The girl escorted us to an elevated VIP area to the right of the stage that was guarded by two iron-faced security guards who robotically moved to let us pass.

Hutch took a seat in the center of the table, and the rest of us fanned out on the sides. Buzz sat to my left and Pollack to my right. Cards and Claybrooke sat on the other side of the table. No sooner had we gotten comfortable than a beautiful black girl in a skintight leopard print dress showed up at the table with a bucket and two bottles of champagne. She introduced herself as Jaguar and told us that she'd be our exclusive waitress for the night. In addition to the champagne, Hutch ordered a bottle of Grey Goose vodka.

Pollack leaned over to me and said, "You all right?"

"As long as I don't think about it," I said.

"Good, we'll act like it never happened," he said. "Our secret." We shook hands underneath the table.

"At least here we can see what we're getting," I said.

"My thoughts exactly," he said with a laugh.

The lap dances started immediately, a parade of naked women, each impossibly beautiful. They snaked and crawled, gyrated and slithered, moving their bodies in ways I never thought possible. Old Bickerstaff was probably out cold by now, but he was with us in spirit. With his cash, six very horny college boys were living out every pimple-faced adolescent's dream. Even Claybrooke joined in the fun. In fact, he and Cards were the first to take a trip to the private room, followed by Buzz and Pollack. I was getting close to being completely wasted, so I backed off the vodka and started drinking water.

At about three o'clock, Cards leaned over to me and said, "I gotta go to sleep. If I stay up any longer, I'll be dead in practice tomorrow."

"Same here," I said.

"You think it'll look bad if we call it quits?"

I looked at the members, each with their own woman riding their thighs and feeding them chocolates. "I think they have a lot more important things to worry about than us turning in early," I said.

"Look at Buzz," Cards laughed.

The tough wrestler from Iowa was slumped in his chair, shirt completely unbuttoned, his body motionless as drool puddled on his chest.

"Maybe we should take him home too," I said.

So, Cards and I stood up, walked over to Buzz, and helped him to his feet.

"Where you boys going?" Hutch asked.

"Back to the apartment," Cards said. "If I don't get some sleep, I'm gonna pass out during practice tomorrow."

"You sure you wanna call it a night already?" Hutch said. "We're gonna hit an after-hours spot next."

I couldn't believe what he had just said. Wasn't three o'clock already after hours? We begged off, and Claybrooke, even with a Russian version of Dolly Parton attempting to smother his face, had the wherewithal to remind us that we were his responsibility and he needed to make sure we returned to Cambridge safely. He instructed us to take the limousine back to the apartment then tell Tiny to return and pick up the rest of them. So, with Buzz's arms slung over our shoulders, the three of us stumbled out of the Lion's Den and fell into the backseat of the waiting limo.

Tiny drove us to the Bickerstaff manse and informed us that he would be back first thing in the morning to take us to the airport. Somehow, we found our way upstairs to the third floor of the apartment. Buzz threw up all over the bathroom floor, and we did the best we could to clean up before putting him to bed.

The combination of the darkness of the hallway and my head spinning like a dreidel made finding my room a bit of a challenge. The first two I tried were wrong, and the third was occupied. As I was about to close the door, I heard somebody ask, "Who's there?"

I could tell by the accent that it was Dominique Bickerstaff.

I thought about pretending like I hadn't heard her, but instead I whispered, "Spenser Collins. I'm sorry to bother you. I'm looking for my room."

"This is your room," she said. "Come in quickly and lock the door behind you. I've been waiting for you all night."

I'm still not exactly sure what went through my mind, but in my condition, it wasn't anything rational. I stood there for a second, trying to clear my head, fighting to make sense of what I should do. She beckoned me a second time, and I surrendered. That night, thirty-five floors above New York City, overlooking a sleeping Central Park, Dominique Cardona Bickerstaff made a boy from the South Side of Chicago feel like a man.

24

❦

WHEN I STUMBLED into Lowell House the next morning, there were two messages waiting for me on my answering machine. The first was from Ashley, telling me where and when to meet her for the concert on Saturday. She left a not-so-subtle hint that she was going to arrive early and at the very least I should be on time. Hearing her voice made me feel guilty about my drunken New York escapades. The next message was from Reverend Campbell. Hearing his mighty baritone voice bounce around my small room made me feel like God had descended from the heavens and knocked on my door for a chat. He wanted to meet first thing in the morning at his house before his day of lectures and meetings began. He'd be waiting for me at precisely nine o'clock after his breakfast. I looked at my watch only to find that I had less than six minutes to get there.

I quickly changed into a pair of khakis so that I wouldn't be sitting in Campbell's house in the same jeans I had worn in a strip joint several hours earlier. I biked over to Sparks House, doubled over and out of breath by the time the front door opened. The same dour-faced woman led me through a maze of rooms before entering a large salon with heavy antique furniture and forest green wallpaper. The room had been decorated with a distinctly aristocratic flair, earth tones and dark wood, and a Persian carpet that covered most of the hardwood floor. A large portrait of an old African American man, perhaps a relative of the Reverend, hung over the fireplace. Ceiling speakers emitted soft classical music, and I found Reverend Campbell seated in a high-backed tufted leather wing chair with a tea service next to him. He was tapping his foot as he wrote something in his appointment book. He looked up when I walked into the room.

"Come in, Mr. Collins," he said, closing the book and standing. We pumped hands and I was surprised by the strength of his grip. "Can I get you anything to drink?" he asked.

With the pain knocking around the back of my head, the last word I wanted to hear was *drink,* even a nonalcoholic beverage. I had already popped several aspirin, but the jackhammer was still pounding the base of my skull.

"I'm fine," I said, waiting for his direction before taking a seat next to him. The chair was a lot more comfortable than it looked.

"I wanted to get back to you about that mysterious passage you left with me last week," he said. "Quite an odd little thing."

"What do you mean by odd, sir?"

"I couldn't recall having read it before, so I reached out to some of my colleagues at the Divinity School. A couple of them took a turn at it. They think it might be something from seventeenth-century Puritanical literature."

"Is that what makes it odd?" I said.

"No, that makes it rare," he said. "But what's so odd is that some of our research faculty couldn't place it, even after consulting several sources. And I might add, these are some of the greatest biblical scholars in the world."

These were not the words I wanted to hear, but I also wasn't surprised. I knew that trying to identify the source with so little to go on would be a long shot. "So, you think it's untraceable?" I asked.

"Nothing's untraceable." Campbell smiled. "It just means the search might be a lot more difficult than I first anticipated." He took a sip of tea, and I noticed the small gold signet ring on his right pinky, just like the one Percy wore. "Tell me something, Mr. Collins. How does it come to be that a biology concentrator from the South Side of Chicago who plays on the basketball team happens to find such an obscure passage?"

His eyes bore down on me, and his tone was definitely less inquisitive than it was accusatory.

"Like I said before, sir, I copied it down," I said.

"Yes, I remember you saying that. But you also declined to identify the source from which you copied it. Would you like to tell me what's really going on?"

I shifted uncomfortably in my seat. I definitely wasn't prepared for this line of questioning.

"Mr. Collins, I've been at this university for the better part of three decades," he said. "I've seen and heard a lot in my tenure. As the minister of Memorial Church, I've been able to do much more than teach Scripture and ethics. I have become a confidant to many students who have sat exactly where you are right now and opened up on a variety of topics. The best teachers are also the best listeners, and I'd like to think that over the years I've earned my stripes with the students on this campus. You might consider these things and choose to trust me."

I felt like calling a time-out and running to phone Dalton to see what I should do. But I knew Dalton would vehemently forbid me from naming the book. We still didn't know the boundaries of the circle of knowledge or whom it included. I had to tread very carefully here.

"I found this passage in a dead man's journal," I said, splitting the truth. "But if you don't mind, I prefer not to discuss his identity. I'm a little sensitive about it."

"That's certainly your prerogative, Mr. Collins, and I respect that," Campbell said. "But might I ask if this was a religious man?"

"I never know what someone means when they use the word 'religious,'" I said. "He believed in God and the importance of faith, but if you mean did he go to church every Sunday and pray before he went to bed every night, I honestly don't know."

"But he was a Christian man, no?"

"Yes, I'm certain of that."

"Was he a collector of rare manuscripts?"

I was starting to get really nervous about where this was going. Campbell's cunning could be as effective as it was stealthy.

"I really didn't know him well enough to answer that question," I said. "I probably never should've looked through his journal, but I did. Curiosity got the best of me."

"You're an excellent student with a strong academic background," Campbell said. "You have won the respect and admiration of some very important people around here. I'm not saying there's a problem, but I just wanted to make sure you weren't in any kind of trouble."

"I'm fine, sir," I said. "Other than all the work for Mettendorf's class, everything is good."

"Yes, Harvey's courses tend to be a challenge even for our brightest students," he said. "What remains to be answered is how much of the difficulty is the material or Harvey himself." He smiled softly. "That last comment is between you and me."

Campbell then reached down and pulled open a drawer in the table beside his chair. He picked up a folded piece of paper and handed it to me. "This is for you," he said. "When all my other queries didn't yield anything, I turned to one of my oldest friends for help. Here's his name and phone number."

I opened the piece of paper—*Dr. Charles Davenport, Professor Emeritus, HDS.*

"Professor Davenport is one of this school's true gems," Campbell said. "He's written more analyses of seventeenth-century religious literature than any person alive. He's slowed down a little the last couple of years, but he's still active, giving lectures at universities around the world. I faxed him a copy of the passage, and he thinks he might be able to help you."

"When should I call him?" I said.

"Anytime. He's expecting to hear from you."

I tucked the slip of paper in my coat and stood. "Thanks for all your help, Reverend Campbell," I said. "I'm grateful you took the time to look into this for me."

"I'm always here to help." He smiled. "Good luck with the round ball this season. And for God's sake, please beat those damn Princeton Tigers this year. My cousin teaches philosophy down there, and I can't stand another year of him calling and gloating over a Princeton victory."

"Don't worry, we have an answer for them this season," I said. "We've got a freshman from New York who's one of the best recruits in the league. With him clogging up the paint, we're a much better team."

Campbell stood and smiled once more. "Yes, I've heard about that young man. Rumor has it, he's as talented a boxer as he is a ball player."

I can't even say that I was surprised that Campbell had heard about the punch. It seemed to me there was very little he didn't know.

25

THE RENOWNED CHARLES Davenport answered his own phone, something that was surprisingly common amongst Harvard professors. The school's philosophy was that teachers were there to educate the students, and however prominent they might be in the academy, they should remain accessible to those who ultimately gave the school purpose. Davenport seemed genuinely excited when I told him my name and the purpose of my call. He instructed me to come over to his office right away.

Most of the Divinity School's buildings were located north of the Yard on Francis Avenue, tucked behind the science complex and across the street from the Organismic and Evolutionary Biology Greenhouse. The central building, Andover Hall, housed large lecture halls, administrative offices, and a chapel. I rarely had any reason to visit this part of the campus.

I found Davenport's basement office with little difficulty. His door was slightly ajar when I approached. I knocked softly and entered only after his invitation.

There were two things about Professor Charles Davenport that you'd never forget. He probably had the biggest ears of any man that's walked the face of the earth, long doughy flaps that fell beneath his jawline with a forest of hair growing out of them. Then there were those glasses, big and black and rectangular, made all the more prominent by his hairless dome. He vaguely reminded me of the legendary Chicago Cubs announcer Harry Caray. The office was ridiculously cold, darker than a mausoleum, and so crammed with books that I couldn't see the top of his desk or any other piece of furniture. He sat in a wooden chair propped over a manuscript in his lap.

"Move some of those things over there and have a seat," he said, pointing to a stool that had a stack of books on it as high as I was tall. "Excuse the mess, but this is what happens when you've been around as long I have."

I cleared off a spot, careful not to step on any of the piles of paper on the floor, and took a seat next to his invisible desk.

"Lenny called me last week and told me of your dilemma," he said, leaning back in his rickety swivel chair.

I was mesmerized by the hoard of diplomas and honorary degrees lining the walls.

"I'm sorry I couldn't get around to it earlier, but I've been fighting like hell to get rid of this damn cold," he said. "Anyway, I finally had a chance to sit down and take a good look at the passage. I was immediately intrigued. Where on earth did you find it?"

"In someone's journal," I said.

"Really?" He nodded his head slowly and frowned. "Just so I understand, was this someone's personal journal or was it a document someone had kept inside of the journal?"

"No, it was actually written in the journal," I said.

"And this person just gave you their journal to read?" he said.

"Not exactly," I said. "I found it by accident."

He leaned toward his desk and with his gnarled hands, wrote something in a notebook. He paused for a moment and thought about what he had just written, then bent down again and scribbled something else. When he was satisfied, he rested the pen on the desk and slumped back in his chair.

"What do you know about Puritanism?" he asked.

The question threw me. "Puritans, sir?" I said.

"Yes, early New England settlers that everyone talks about at Thanksgiving. How much do you know about their history?"

I shrugged. What the hell did I know about the Puritans? I hadn't really thought about them since Mrs. Tahan's fourth-grade history lessons. I finally blurted out, "They were simple people who came over to the New World on the *Mayflower*, landed on Plymouth Rock, and lived a strict life."

"That's a start." He smiled. "But do you know anything of their origins, things like why they even came into existence and what their mission had been?"

"To build a new life away from the bad politics of England?" I shrugged.

"The Puritans were an extremely religious people, young man," Davenport said. "They came here to escape religious persecution during the reign of Queen Elizabeth I. There was a growing number of people who felt that her ecclesiastical establishment was too political, too compromising, and too Catholic. I don't want to bore you with a history lesson, but suffice it to say, these dissenters were called Calvinists, early Protestants who believed in the absolute sovereignty of God's will. They believed that the Scriptures didn't sanction the state to create and organize bishops and churches, and they felt called to purify the church, thus the name Puritans."

"So, you think this passage has something to do with Puritanical beliefs?" I said.

"I don't think that, young man, I know it," Davenport said. "In style and content, the passage is Puritanical. Although they were but few in number, their zeal afforded them influence."

"Do you know where the passage comes from?"

Davenport stood, grabbed his cane, and hobbled toward the door and closed it. When he was back in his chair, he turned to me and in an almost conspiratorial tone said, "That's why I've been excited to meet you." His face turned suddenly dark and tortured. "These words come from the work of one of the most regarded authors of Puritanical texts. His name was Reverend John Downame, and his writings had enormous influence on early New England life. He was a giant amongst giants in religious thought and doctrine, and for his time, quite famous."

"But what makes this passage so important?" I asked.

"That answer lies in the source in which you found it," Davenport said.

I felt like grabbing the old man by his pointed shoulders and shaking him until he stopped talking in riddles. "Why is the source so important?"

"Because that passage comes from a book written more than three centuries ago. It's one of the most famous books in Harvard's history. In fact, many would say it *is* Harvard, and very few copies exist today."

"What's the name of it?"

"*The Christian Warfare Against the Devil World and Flesh.*"

"Why is it so important to Harvard's history?"

"Because of the old fire," Davenport said.

He paused and looked at me as if I should know which fire he meant. I didn't.

"Well, you do know of the three lies on the *John Harvard* statue."

I nodded. The "Statue of Three Lies" was requisite Harvard lore that all freshmen heard within a week of moving into the Yard. Just behind University Hall and prominently situated in the Yard was Harvard's most photographed landmark, a bronze statue of a man sitting regally in a chair, dressed in the day's finery. Daniel Chester French cast the statue in 1884, and then went on to create the Lincoln statue in Washington, D.C. The inscription on the John Harvard statue reads: JOHN HARVARD, FOUNDER, 1638. And not a single one of those words is true. Contrary to popular belief, John Harvard was not the founder of Harvard College. The Massachusetts Bay Colony established the small college, and only later was it named after John Harvard. Harvard was founded in 1636, not 1638, and the seated figure of the statue isn't a depiction of John Harvard. According to legend, when the statue was cast, no authentic pictures of John Harvard could be found, so Chester French used a student, Sherman Hoar, as a model.

Davenport continued his story. "Reverend John Harvard came from England to Charlestown, Massachusetts, in 1637. He died a year later. He left half his estate and all his books, about four hundred of them, to the nearby college, which had been founded the previous year and had been simply called the New College. Harvard's entire collection of books, along with the rest of the library, were stored inside Harvard Hall. In 1764, amidst the heavy winds and snow of a severe nor'easter, Harvard Hall caught fire and burned to the ground. It was devastating for the college, destroying furniture, pictures, wigs, scientific equipment, and clothing. But what really demoralized the school was the loss not only of its library holdings but also John Harvard's entire collection of books.

"The president and faculty were spiritually devastated, having lost the collection of its first and most important benefactor. But there was to be a miracle in one Ephraim Briggs, a senior who had checked out a book on October 14, 1763, for a maximum loan period, which at the time was three weeks. After the fire in 1764, Briggs finally got around to returning the severely delinquent book he had checked out almost a year prior. Miraculously, it was the fourth edition of Downame's book that had been published in 1634—*The Christian Warfare Against the Devil World and Flesh*."

"Where's that book now?" I asked.

"Displayed in a glass case in the entry of Houghton Library," Davenport said. "A security guard sits nearby. It's the only remaining book from John Harvard's collection and one of the most important books on religious doctrine in the world."

"Can anyone look at that book?" I asked.

"Sure, with special permission and close supervision," Davenport said.

"Then why's it such a big deal I have this passage when anyone can access the book?"

Davenport smiled. "Because the passage you have written there didn't come from the book on display in Houghton, the fourth printing. It could only have been copied by someone who had seen the extremely rare 1604 *first* printing. Only a few copies of that edition still exist in the world today. Harvard owns one of those copies"

Maybe I was still feeling the aftereffects of the New York trip, but I still wasn't seeing his point, nor could I understand how he knew the passage well enough to know it was from the missing pages of the 1604 book. "Can people look at that first edition?" I asked.

"Yes, but access is severely restricted."

"Then why is this passage such a big deal if people can still go to the library and look at it?"

"Because they can't. That passage comes specifically from pages 545 and 546, the only two missing pages in that book. Scholars and collectors around the world have been searching for those pages specifically from Harvard's copy for more than a century. And to this day, the whereabouts of those pages remains among Harvard's greatest unsolved mysteries."

ON MY WAY HOME from the Divinity School, on a hunch I took a detour and stopped at Robinson Hall in the northeast corner of the Yard. Robinson was the home of the history department, a gigantic brick building originally erected at the turn of the century to house the schools of architecture and city planning. Most undergraduates had little reason to visit the old building unless they were taking a history course or wanted a quiet place to study.

I climbed a long staircase and made a couple of turns, then found myself standing in front of a simple door with the word LIBRARY stenciled in small letters. I walked in, expecting to find a large, cavernous room full of musty old texts and bound periodicals, but instead I found myself in a converted classroom with long wooden tables, hospital-white walls, and rows of bookshelves extending along the perimeter of the room. A few students, their noses buried in books, sat at the tables, and a young woman with long black hair tied into a ponytail and a lime green turtleneck sweater sat behind the front desk. She was typing something into a computer and smiling at the same time. I figured her for a graduate student.

"How can I help you?" she said as I approached the desk.

"I'm trying to find out about disasters that occurred off the coast of Newfoundland," I said.

"What dates are you looking for?" she asked.

"I don't have any precise dates."

She nodded. "What kind of disasters are you talking about?"

"I'm not sure about that either. I'm trying to research a man who died in the waters off the coast of Newfoundland."

"Then maybe we could start a search with his name," she said, sounding more optimistic. She turned the computer screen around so that I could also see it as she typed.

"That's another problem," I said, starting to feel like an imbecile. "I don't know his name either. But I know his initials."

Her shoulders dropped. "This will be an almost impossible search," she said. "You don't have any real parameters to work with."

"Could I just do a search on Newfoundland and accidents?"

"Sure, but that would come back with everything both on land and water. I'm almost afraid to ask this, but do you know if it was a boating accident or plane crash?"

I lowered my head.

"In that case," she said. "The best you can do is to search some of the online catalogs and see what you find. If I think of something else, I'll let you know."

I took a seat behind a terminal in the small computer area and went to work. Entering *Newfoundland* as the search term brought back almost twenty pages of books and articles, so I restricted the search and added the word *disasters*. That cut the results to just a couple of pages. Most of the sources were books, but there were a couple of brief articles that caught my attention. The first was from December 2, 1938, in *The Fisherman's Advocate*.

> The people of the North side of Trinity Bay were shocked this week to learn of the loss of the schooner *Marion Rogers* whilst attempting to enter Trinity Harbour in the storm of Sunday night last. Seven men went to watery graves as a result of the loss of the schooner.
>
> The schooner struck the rocks near the Fort Point Lighthouse, at the entrance to Trinity, where there is also a fog alarm.
>
> The members of the crew were William Hogarth, Master, and his son Lester of Trinity East, Alfred Pitcher and son Simeon of New Bonaventure, T.B., William J. Butler, also of New Bonaventure, Ellis Butler of Port Rexton and Edward McGarth of Trinity.

Over the next several hours, I found three more articles, but it was the last one that I decided to print and take with me. It was from *The Winnipeg Evening Tribune.*

FOUR FISHERMEN ARE DROWNED ON BANKS

ST. JOHN'S, Nfld, July 8, 1927—Four Newfoundland fishermen have been drowned on the Banks, according to a report received at the Cape Race wireless station from the Canadian government steamer *Arras.* Those lost were Charles Williams and George Robert May of Fortune Bay, from the schooner *Donald A. Creaser,* and Martin Quann of Sagona, and Randolph Macon Strawbridge of Red Cove, from the schooner *Marian Belle Wolfe.* Quann's body was the only one recovered.

The tragedy occurred last Monday during a southeast storm which sprang up shortly after the dorymen left their vessels. Williams and May were lost sight of soon after they pushed off from the schooner in their dories, and were never seen again.

Quann and Strawbridge succeeded in reaching their trawls before the storm hit them, and were pulling in their catch when their dory upset. Quann's body was caught in the trawl and recovered, but Strawbridge was not seen again.

I kept looking at the name Randolph Macon Strawbridge. This had to be my answer. He had drowned in the waters off the coast of Newfoundland, and his initials matched the RMS at the bottom of the poem. But Strawbridge had died in July, and I had my doubts the waters were as icy in the middle of the summer as the poem had indicated. There was an easy way to know. I signed on to one of the Harvard databases and entered Strawbridge's name in the alumni search. I had my answers within seconds. Randolph Macon Strawbridge had never been a Harvard student, which also meant he had never been a member of the Delphic Club. I was back to zero as I left Robinson Hall that afternoon, but I was certain of two things: Decoding that poem was going to be more than extremely difficult; it was going to be near impossible. Second, the Ancient Nine's guile should not be underestimated.

26

HOUGHTON LIBRARY WAS the kind of stodgy affair that serious academics dream about, and most students avoid at all costs. Sandwiched between the more popular Widener and Lamont Libraries in the New Yard, Houghton was like an old piece of furniture in your living room that you walked by every day but never used. It enjoyed brief fame in the 1940s as the nation's first academic library specifically constructed to house rare books and manuscripts. It had also been an architectural wonder at the time. To house such a valuable collection, it had to be fire- and earthquake-proof. It was also the first library in the world to have built-in climate control.

I walked up the narrow steps and opened the doors to a dark, drafty circular lobby. A man in a wrinkled blue uniform and clip-on tie sat behind a small desk in the center of the marble floor. *The Boston Globe* was opened to the sports section and neatly spread on top of a pile of papers. He looked up when I approached and closed the paper. "How can I help you?" he said.

"I'd like to take a look at John Downame's *Christian Warfare Against the Devil World and Flesh*," I said.

He tapped the keys of the computer, then looked at me and said, "Did you make an appointment with any of the librarians?"

"I didn't know I had to," I said.

"For this book you do," he said. "We have the fire copy that's in the display case, and at least twelve others. But these books can be viewed only under supervision."

"How do I make an appointment?"

He reached for a clipboard on the desk. "Write your name and phone number here, and one of the reference assistants will get back to you."

"Are any of them available right now?"

"No, their appointments are full for the rest of the afternoon."

"How long will it take for me to get an appointment?"

"Not sure. Each reference assistant keeps his own schedule. Is this research for a senior thesis? That would give your request some priority."

I almost lied, but thought better of it. It wouldn't take long for them to figure out that I was only a sophomore. "No, it's just some independent research I'm working on," I said.

"Are you on a deadline?"

"There is some urgency."

"Then you should write down the reason for the deadline. That could also help give your request some priority."

"Where are these books kept?" I asked.

"Depends on the printing. The one saved from the fire is right over there. But the first printing is locked in the vault. Access is highly restricted, and access is typically limited to approved scholarly research."

I started to write my name and information on the sign-up sheet, but as I was finishing my phone number, I noticed there was only one other phone number in the column. It started with a 212 area code. The rest of the numbers were only five digits long, either beginning with an 8, which meant a student phone, or a 5, which meant a faculty or administrative office. Then I looked at the name in the entry. M. G. Brathwaite from New York City had signed in less than twenty-four hours ago.

I STOOD OUTSIDE the front door of Houghton, thinking of the possibilities. There was no way in hell it had been a coincidence that Brathwaite had gone to Houghton to conduct some type of scholarly research. What business would a lawyer have with a library that housed rare manuscripts? He was there because he knew Houghton would be the likely next stop in our pursuit. I figured he had come to accomplish one of two things. He wanted to check and see if we had accessed *The Christian Warfare,* suggesting that we had learned of its connection to the Ancient Nine's creed, or he had come to confirm for himself that what we were looking for was no longer in the book. Whatever the case, he was turning up the heat, which meant we were getting closer.

I hopped on my bike and decided I'd ride over to break the news to Dalton, but as I left the Yard, I got an idea. I turned toward the *Crimson* offices. A guy wearing the ugliest orange-and-green sweater I had ever seen was sitting at the front desk, reading a book and picking his nose like it was a sport. I asked him if Stromberger was in, and he went back to get her.

A couple of minutes later, she came bounding down the hall. She actually looked rested. "Hey, Spenser," she said. "How's the research going?"

"It's going," I said.

"Did you call my person at the Historical Commission?"

"I did, but she hasn't called me back."

"Don't worry, she will."

I waited for the kid in the atrocious sweater to walk out of earshot before I said, "I was stopping by to see if you knew anything about the Harvard fire of 1764 and the only book from John Harvard's original collection that survived."

"I've heard the story," she said. "A student took the book out several months before the fire, and returned it after the rest of Harvard's collection had burned. It was a religious book. I think it's over in Houghton."

"That's where I just came from," I said. "It's on display in the lobby. But I wanted to find out about an earlier edition of that book. It's in the Houghton vault."

"I don't really know anything about that," she said.

"The book that was saved from the fire was the fourth edition," I explained. "But Houghton also has a very rare first edition. There's some mystery about it missing two pages. I'm trying to figure out if that's true and what's so important about those pages."

"Did you ask one of the librarians over there?"

"I tried, but the security guard said that I needed to sign up and make an appointment. One of the reference assistants will call me when they have an opening. Seems like a pretty big deal, so I'm thinking the *Crimson* might've written something about it."

"Do you know if the book was acquired with the pages already missing, or someone clipped them afterwards?" Stromberger answered.

"That's what I'm trying to figure out."

"There's not much to go on," Stromberger said. "I can look in our archives and see if the *Crimson* covered it, but I'll have to figure out the right key words to use in the search. Our paper only goes back to 1873, so if this happened before then, we might not have anything."

"When could you take a look?"

"Probably later tonight. I have classes till four, and I have to meet with my advisor. I'll take a look after dinner. Do you think this book has anything to do with Abbott's disappearance?"

"I'm not sure. Every time I get close to figuring out one answer, another ten questions pop up."

I CALLED DALTON twice before practice, and both times his answering machine picked up and both times I left an urgent message for him to call me. By the time I walked into the locker room that afternoon, my headache had finally abated and my liver had worked the alcohol out of my system. Coach was in a rare good mood and put us through all the drills we liked. He didn't make us run a single wind sprint, and after an hour, he allowed us to divide ourselves up into teams and scrimmage for the remainder of practice. We were all very suspicious. He was actually making jokes and shadowboxing with guys on the sidelines. After a shoving match broke out between two of our big guys, he actually started taking bets on who would've won if it had been an all-out fight.

What made his behavior even stranger was that we had our first scrimmage against Boston University coming up in a week, a game that meant nothing for our season record, but everything for city bragging rights. Normally he would have worked the hell out of us in hopes we'd take our anger out on the BU team.

During one of the water breaks, Geilton and I met on the sidelines.

"What the hell has gotten into him?" I asked.

Geilton shook his head. "I have no idea. It's the first time in four years I've ever seen him act like this. It's scary."

"Have any of the assistant coaches said anything?"

"Nothing. They're acting like everything is normal."

I looked across the gym. Coach had his arm around Mitch's shoulder, and they were laughing about something.

"I don't like it," I said. "He's being too nice. That's not a good sign."

"Let's just ride the wave. Maybe the monster will be back tomorrow."

Coach blew the whistle, and with a good half hour left of practice, kicked us out of the gym. "That's it," he said. "You guys have been working hard the last couple of weeks. I'm calling practice early."

We just stood there and looked at each other. No one moved. It was like being a prisoner who's been locked away in the pen for twenty years and who sees the warden just walk up to him in the rec yard one afternoon, hand him the key to the front gate, and tell him he's free to go. Instead of sprinting toward his freedom, the prisoner stands there, trying to figure out if this is a trap. Is it better to stay locked up or risk getting shot in the back as he makes a run for it?

"What the hell are you standing there for?" Coach laughed. He blew the whistle to crack our stupor. "Practice is over. Go home, men."

Still no one moved. I looked at the other guys, and no one dared to be the first to leave the court. This had all the makings of a setup.

Geilton finally stepped up and said, "Everything all right, Coach?"

"Yeah, why wouldn't it be?" he said, shrugging his shoulders.

"Just checking, that's all," Geilton said. Then he turned to the rest of us and yelled, "Line up on the damn baseline!"

The rest of us looked at each other, then at Geilton as if he had suddenly gone mad.

"You heard me!" he yelled. "Get your asses on the baseline. We're gonna run five sprints before we leave. We have a game in a week, and we're not gonna be embarrassed like we were last year. This is where it starts."

Slowly we made our way to the baseline, cursing Geilton under our breath. Coach and the assistants left the court and walked upstairs to their offices, but we could see them looking at us out their windows. And I'll be damned if Geilton didn't run us harder than Coach ever had. When we had finished the five sprints, he called for another five before we dragged ourselves into the locker room.

"It was a trap," Geilton said apologetically as we all lined up in the shower. "He wanted to see if we'd walk off the court and take the easy way out. Today we showed him we're willing to go above and beyond and do whatever it takes to win. Trust me, we scored some points today."

His analysis was probably right, and we might've scored some bonus points with the coaching staff, but it was difficult not feeling a bit salty, having left half our lungs on the court. By the time we limped out of the locker room, the Coach's office lights were already turned off and he was long gone. He probably had a big fat grin on his face when he left the building. The cunning sonuvabitch had put a spin on something my grandfather had always preached. He almost killed us with kindness.

27

⁂

"I'LL BE OVER in ten minutes," Dalton said. It was a little after seven, and he had finally called me back. "Meet me out front. I'll be in my car."

"Where are we going? I have a ton of reading to do tonight, and I wanted to tell you about New York and my talk with one of the Divinity School professors."

"We'll talk about it in the car," he said. "I think we'll find Abbott tonight or what's left of him. Just be ready when I get there."

Before I could protest, he had already hung up the phone.

I put on my heavy coat and made my way to the front archway. It was mid November and the weather had taken a decisive turn, and it was downright cold. Thanksgiving was a couple of weeks away, which meant the rest of the campus would be empty while those of us athletes who were still in season would be spending another cheerless Thanksgiving night in the one dreary dining hall that drew the unlucky straw to stay open.

Dalton pulled up just as I stepped into the archway. He wore a thick black turtleneck sweater and sheepskin coat. I said my customary prayer before jumping into the passenger's seat. I had barely closed the door before he sped off, tires squealing, people on the sidewalks jumping back as the car's roar approached.

"So, you wanna tell me where we're going?" I asked once we had raced through a string of yellow.

"Rhode Island."

"Rhode Island?" I yelled. "Are you out of your damn mind? Stop the car right now! I'm not going to Rhode Island tonight!"

Dalton mashed the accelerator even harder as we rocketed through the narrow streets and finally climbed over Anderson Memorial Bridge and past the athletic facilities of Soldiers Field. He reached down and turned up the radio as if he hadn't heard a word I just said. I reached over and turned it back down.

"Are you gonna tell me what the hell is going on?" I said.

"We're heading to the old Abbott estate in Newport," he said. "It's only about an hour away, maybe less if we don't hit traffic."

"And what are we gonna do there?"

"A little excavating."

"Have you totally lost your mind? What do you mean 'excavating'?"

He hiked his thumb over his shoulder, and I turned to find two small shovels barely fitting across the backseat.

Then he said, "I made some calls yesterday while you were running around New York—which we still need to talk about, by the way—and I found out some interesting things about the Abbott estate. The Abbotts lived in one of the biggest mansions in Newport, which they had purchased from a Philadelphia coal family. They lived through the golden era of Newport society when all the big names like the Vanderbilts, Astors, and Dukes summered there in what they called 'cottages.' Collander Abbott bought the Breckinridge estate right down the street from the Vanderbilts' palace, the Breakers. Abbott didn't have Vanderbilt money, but he dumped a small fortune into the mansion, trying to rival the others.

"It took two hundred men almost three years to renovate the house and property. They called it Magnolia Woods because of all the magnolia trees Mrs. Abbott had planted around the property. Collander Abbott left specific instructions in his will that he be buried deep in the woods, underneath a certain tree. He was buried there first, followed by Mrs. Abbott, who died the following year."

Dalton turned onto the Interstate 95 ramp, and once he had cleared the tollbooth, shifted the car into warp speed.

"How did you find all this out?" I asked.

"I had a long talk yesterday with Aunt Contessa," he said. "She was Uncle Randolph's younger sister and spent most of her summers as a kid living on the Winthrop estate called Emerald Meadows, right next door to Magnolia Woods. She said Abbott and his wife spent a lot of their money and time trying to be accepted by Newport society, but to no avail. Only five people attended both their burials. Aunt Contessa was one of them."

I looked into the backseat again at the shovels and noticed two pairs of work gloves. "Are you planning to go to Newport to dig up the bodies of Collander Abbott and his wife?"

Dalton released one of his mischievous smiles. "Better than that. If Aunt Contessa is correct, we're gonna dig up the body of Erasmus Abbott."

WE ROARED INTO Newport in just under an hour. On the way, I updated Dalton about what had happened in New York, conveniently omitting "the kiss" from the story. We talked about Campbell, Davenport, and the passage, and agreed that whatever was going on, it definitely had something to do with religious doctrine. Dalton pulled into a single-pump gas station to fill up and get directions to Magnolia Woods. The chatty attendant informed him that the house was one of only a few of the original cottages that remained privately owned. Most of the mansions had been donated to the historical society and turned into museums. The Dann family, who now owned Magnolia Woods, opened the house for one week of the year to tour groups, but it was closed for the fall and winter seasons while the Danns lived on their estate in Barbados.

Dalton swung the car into the estate section of town and drove down the dark, tree-lined streets. We caught glimpses of the mansions, barely visible behind the tall gates and formidable hedges. He turned toward the ocean, and once we were in a small parking lot overlooking a beach, he turned off the car.

"This is where we get out," he said.

"I thought you had directions to the house?"

"I do. But we're not just gonna drive up to the front door and say, 'Hello, we're here to dig up a couple of bodies in your backyard.' We're gonna walk along the beach and enter through the back of the property."

Visions of us sitting in the Newport jail flashed through my mind. How was I going to explain to my mother that I had been busted for exhuming the bodies of a dead printing tycoon's family?

"Dalton, have you really thought this through?" I said. "There's a good chance that we could get caught doing this."

"There you go again, looking at things from the negative perspective," Dalton said. "We're *not* gonna get caught. Now, grab one of those shovels and let's get to work."

We walked for at least half a mile along a path that ran beside the ocean and overlooked several steep cliffs. Every once in a while, we could see lights from one of the mansions shooting into the sky. Dalton took out a piece of paper from his pocket, where he had diagrammed the properties. We had only another hundred yards before we reached the estate.

"How are we gonna find this burial site when we can barely see two feet in front of us?" I said.

"It shouldn't be too difficult," he said. "Aunt Contessa said it was under the widest tree in the woods, and it was easy to find amongst the others because one of the branches hung so low, it was like an arm reaching down to pick you up. She insisted that it's such an odd-looking tree, that it sticks out from everything else around it."

The path had ended, but we continued to walk along the ocean, scrambling with difficulty over a gaggle of boulders perilously towering over the whitecaps breaking below.

"This is where the property line starts," Dalton said. He pulled the diagram out again and confirmed our location. We walked until we reached a tall wrought-iron fence that dead-ended against an enormous tree. There was just enough space between the last fence post and the tree for us to slip through.

I was so nervous, my hands trembled. I couldn't stop thinking that if we got caught, I'd get expelled and there would be no medical school, no career in medicine, and no payback to my mother for all her sacrifices. Dalton didn't need to graduate from Harvard to have a successful life. His name and money could buy him anything he ever wanted and then some.

We walked into the heavily wooded part of the property, and at one point we got a full view of the house. It stopped me in my tracks. It was as if someone had stacked ten houses next to each other, then just knocked down the walls between them and made it one gigantic compound. I counted five dark rows of windows and at least twenty chimneys on the sections of the roof that I could see.

"What's wrong?" Dalton asked.

"If that's just a cottage, what do they call a house?" I said.

"And this isn't even the biggest cottage on the block," Dalton said. "The Breakers makes this look like a carriage house."

We walked deeper into the woods, and separated about ten feet from each other, figuring that would help us cover more ground and make us less likely to miss our target. There were all kinds of strange sounds, owls whooping in the branches above, four-legged critters scampering in the darkness. It was cold enough that the mosquitoes weren't out, but I could imagine what a feasting ground it must've been during the summer. After twenty minutes, we reached the fence at the other end of the property. We hadn't seen any tree even closely resembling what Dalton's aunt had described.

"This might be a lot harder than I expected," he said, taking off his gloves and leaning against the fence. "I didn't know we were gonna be searching a damn forest."

"It could take us days to find this tree," I said.

"Aunt Contessa said it was in the middle of the property," Dalton said, wiping his sweaty forehead with the back of his hand.

"Yeah, but how in the hell can we tell what's the middle? These woods could cover more than a square mile of land. And your aunt was here more than twenty years ago. Who knows how much things have changed since then?"

"I say we separate more and take another pass," Dalton said.

I remembered a movie I had seen where three kids were looking for a buried treasure in a campground. They eventually found it by marking off the property in evenly spaced sections.

"We could make a sectional grid," I said. "It took us about twenty minutes to walk across the entire property. So, let's move over another twenty-five feet, walk back in the same direction, then stop at about ten minutes. We'll do a ninety-degree turn either left or right and walk till we get to the other end of the property. That should help us sweep by the center. If we don't see it on that portion of the grid, then we'll turn around and walk back toward the other end."

"Sounds like a plan," Dalton said, pushing off the fence and grabbing his shovel.

We walked laterally about twenty-five feet from where we stood and separated from each other by twenty-feet this time instead of ten. Once we had marked off the distances, we slowly made our way back through the dense woods. Dalton called out twice, thinking he had found the tree, only to be disappointed when we got closer and realized that they were really two trees next to each other instead of one.

Each time we had a false call, we went back to our positions and restarted the sweep. After forty minutes, I was starting to lose hope. Then something up ahead on the left caught my eye. It was the silhouette of an enormous tree, about four times the size of the others and sitting by itself with a wide clearing around it. The closer I walked, the more massive it became. But I couldn't see the low-lying branch that Dalton's aunt had described. Was it possible that someone had cut the limb down or that it had broken off?

When I finally reached the tree, I began circling it, and then I saw it. The branch was as wide as the trunks of some of the other trees, curved down in a U with a considerable portion that was flat enough to sit on. It was the strangest-looking tree I had ever seen.

"Holy shit!" Dalton said, sticking his shovel in the ground as he stood next to me. "This is the craziest-looking tree I've ever seen. How in the hell does something grow like this?"

We both walked over to the branch and stood there in amazement. It looked like a human arm stretching out.

"So now we have to find the graves," Dalton said. "Aunt Contessa said

Mrs. Abbott had been buried underneath the tree on the right side of Mr. Abbott. The order had something to do with Scripture. Erasmus had been buried on his father's left."

"Let's do this in circles," I said. "We'll start tight against the trunk and walk around it until we meet. If we don't find any gravestones, then we'll step farther out and circle it again."

Starting up against the tree we walked the first circle but didn't find anything. We did this ten times, but there was no sign of a gravestone. When we were twenty feet away from the tree, Dalton stopped and said, "They're here, but we're doing something wrong."

"Maybe they're flat markers instead of vertical tombstones," I said.

"Possible," Dalton said. "Just seems strange a man as rich as Abbott would be buried without a tombstone.

"Maybe not," I said. "They knew that one day this property might be owned by someone not in the family. If they built a big monument to themselves, whoever bought the place might grow uncomfortable with a reminder of death so visible. So instead, the Abbotts decided to do it quietly with small, discreet plates. No one would really know, and they could remain here forever."

We walked back to the tree and started our circles again. This time, however, we used our shovels and feet to clear away the leaves and brush. It was going painstakingly slow until Dalton hit something.

"Jackpot!" he yelled.

I ran to the other side of the tree. He was on his hands and knees about ten feet away from the trunk, pulling and yanking at the weeds and gnarled shrubbery. I got down beside him and started doing the same until we had a clear look at the flat metal marker belonging to Elizabeth Abbott. It was remarkably simple.

ELIZABETH CHARLESWORTH ABBOTT

WIFE OF COLLANDER WENDELL ABBOTT

WOMAN OF THE WORLD

1888–1978

Dalton kept looking at the grave marker, then said, "Life is funny. Who would imagine that a woman with a life of such privilege and influence would be remembered by a small piece of bronze and twelve simple words?"

"Collander must be to her left," I said.

We moved over a foot, and after clearing away leaves and pulling at more weeds and overgrowth, we found the second plate.

COLLANDER WENDELL ABBOTT
PIOUS SERVANT OF GOD
1887–1977

Dalton and I didn't say anything, sensing how close we were to our answer. Another foot over and we began clearing away the brush. We scraped and pulled until we found it. It was smaller than the other two and carved in black marble.

ERASMUS DANFORTH ABBOTT
BELOVED LOST SON
1908–1927

"His plate is here, but it doesn't mean he was actually buried here," Dalton said. "This could just be a memorial to him."

"What if he really is down there?" I said. "Doesn't prove much."

"It means that Collander Abbott knew a helluva lot more about his son's disappearance than he was letting on."

"But it still doesn't prove that Erasmus was killed trying to break into the Delphic that night. He could've been kidnapped and killed at some other time, and the Abbotts just never made it public."

"Possible," Dalton said. "Or they knew who killed him and why and decided to keep their mouths shut about the whole thing."

"Or he's not even down there," I said. "Maybe it's just an empty grave."

"It's very possible they could've just put a plate here to honor him," Dalton said.

"First things first," I said, planting my shovel in the ground.

We went about our grim task, saying very little to each other, the screeching sounds of bats and birds and night crawlers echoing in the darkness. It took the better part of an hour, but I was the first one to hit something. I thought it was another rock, but when I tried digging around it, I only hit more of the hard surface. I got on my knees and cleared the dirt with my hands, and that's when I first saw the dull metal.

"You got it!" Dalton said, flashing the light over the dirt.

It was well past midnight when we had the entire casket unearthed.

"You want the honors?" Dalton said, planting his shovel into the mound of dirt.

"Let's do it together," I said.

We made signs of the cross, then reached down and pulled at the lid. It didn't open with the first tug, so we regripped and tried again. Still no give. Finally, we both stuck our shovels inside the seam and pried it open.

I wasn't sure what to expect, but I figured Abbott's skeleton would be a pile of dust after all these years. Then I had visions of a decaying body with maggots and other insects and a foul odor. But neither was the case. Instead, we found a small silver urn with bowed handles that looked like a golfing trophy.

Dalton reached down and lifted the urn.

Abbott's name, date of birth, and death had been inscribed.

He handed the urn to me, and I was surprised at how heavy it was, considering it was so small.

"Let's look inside," Dalton said.

As I turned the urn to remove the lid, something caught my eye. I took the bottom of my shirt and rubbed it across the face of the urn in hard, slow circles, then held it back up to the light.

"What does it say?" Dalton asked.

I immediately recognized the grammatical style and strange spelling. "You're not gonna believe it," I said. "I think this is part of the Ancient Nine's creed in the succession book."

"Are you kidding?" Dalton said, taking the urn back. He turned and read the words, then lifted the top and pulled out a small, tarnished silver box. Erasmus's initials were engraved in the top.

I slowly pulled back the lid and looked at a teaspoon of ash dust. "Something's not right," I said. "We didn't find any published reports about his body being found nor a burial. The Abbotts were hiding something."

"Or protecting a deadly secret," Dalton said.

WE HAD ALMOST finished covering up Abbott's casket when sounds trickled in from the other side of the woods. These weren't sounds coming from animals. The voices were heavy. There were several of them. One of the men was shouting out directions. I could see flashlights crisscrossing in the distance.

"Let's go!" I said to Dalton. "They know we're back here."

I grabbed my shovel and was about to make a run for it when Dalton grabbed me by the arm.

"We can't go back the way we came," he said. "We have a much better chance of making it onto the adjacent property."

He stuffed the urn in his backpack, grabbed his shovel, and pointed in the opposite direction.

"But how are we gonna climb the fence?"

"It must end somewhere."

The voices were closer now. The sounds of twigs snapped under heavy feet. Flashlight beams crisscrossed through the thick woods.

We ran hard and fast, their voices falling at our backs. Stray branches ripped at our clothes, and partially buried rocks twisted our ankles as we navigated the uneven ground. I almost fell a couple of times, but grabbed nearby trees to keep me upright.

Then Dalton suddenly stopped.

"What's up?" I said, out of breath, the taste of acid filling my mouth.

"Follow me," Dalton said.

We were about seventy-five yards away from the burial site. I could no longer make out the tree, but I could see the cluster of light beams in the area we had just left. Dalton squatted behind a large oak, then opened his backpack and lifted a pair of binoculars.

"Night vision," he said. "Forgot I had them. Five times magnification with a built-in infrared illuminator."

He made a couple of adjustments on the lenses and brought them to his face. We sat there for a couple of minutes, him looking back at the burial site, me looking at him wondering what he was seeing.

"I have to give it to him," Dalton said. "That sonuvabitch is relentless." He handed me the binoculars.

I adjusted them to fit my face. Brathwaite stood there in that same ski jacket and baseball cap. He was looking down at the graves and saying something to the other men. One man was short, heavy around the midsection, and wide in the shoulders. He carried himself like someone accustomed to manual labor. He had a flat nose and disheveled black hair. Unlike the other two men, he didn't wear a hat or gloves. I saw a gun in his hand. My body instantly tensed.

"The short one is carrying a gun," I said, still looking through the binoculars. "Brathwaite is saying something to him."

I couldn't see the face of the third man, whose back was facing me. He wasn't as tall as Brathwaite, but he stood several inches above the man with the gun. He had a cane in his right hand and a flashlight in his left. He was wearing a long heavy coat. Brathwaite pointed to something in the ground, when the third man moved enough for me to catch a quick glimpse of his face. I recognized him right away. His movements were slow and his expression somber. Stanford Jacobs was standing over the grave of Erasmus Abbott.

28

IT WAS ALMOST three o'clock in the morning by the time we pulled into Cambridge with the remains of Erasmus Abbott resting comfortably in the backseat. We decided it would be important to do a careful word-by-word comparison of the passage engraved on the urn to the Ancient Nine creed. It looked the same, but neither of us had memorized the text, and the arcane English spellings were so strange that it was difficult to tell if any of the words had been altered.

While the trip had at least answered one important question—whether Erasmus Abbott's body had ever been discovered—it still left a lot of others unanswered. Was he killed that night in the Delphic? Why hadn't his family been more open about what happened? Why hadn't the media covered the discovery of his body?

"We can forget about all the theories that Abbott was kidnapped or secretly sent away to live out the rest of his life in anonymity," I said. "The dates on the marker say he lived to be nineteen, the same age he'd been the night he broke into the Delphic."

"He was killed that night," Dalton said. "But how many people knew, and when did they tell his father?"

"They probably told him right away," I said. I bet Abbott knew Erasmus's death could expose the club's secrets, so he agreed to keep it all quiet and let the commotion slowly fade away. With his son already dead, what good would it do to also expose the Ancient Nine?"

"I'd buy that," Dalton said. "But why would he put that same inscription from the book on the urn? If these guys were so secretive about their brotherhood, then why take the risk of basically publishing the passage?"

"That's assuming the Ancient Nine creed and the urn inscription are the same," I said.

"Jacobs was a little bit of a surprise, but it all makes sense," Dalton said. "He's probably the Delphic's wealthiest member. He's old enough to know about these events, and an ideal member for the Ancient Nine, a man who some respect and others fear."

"Just makes me wonder about the conversation I had with him at the cocktail party," I said. "Showing me his art collection was a ruse to get me alone. Then he hit me with all those questions about my family, especially my father. What was it about my dad and his family that was so fascinating to him?"

"I wasn't convinced before, but now I am," Dalton said. "He was definitely digging for something."

"And he's obviously tight with Brathwaite."

"Tight enough to get up and drive an hour in the middle of the night to an old burial ground in the middle of the woods."

"Do you really think they would've shot us?"

"I hope not," Dalton said. "Maybe they want to scare us. Brathwaite thinks we have Uncle Randolph's book. Now he knows we have Abbott's urn."

"And both lead us back to the Ancient Nine."

"And them to us," he said. "We have to expand our thinking beyond the Ancient Nine. There's some kind of pattern with these religious passages. I keep feeling like all roads lead to that damn book in Houghton. I think we're closer than ever."

"And Brathwaite knows it," I said. "I can check HOLLIS tomorrow and see if there's anything on microfilm. I've found other old books that have been copied. If we're lucky, maybe *The Christian Warfare* was copied too."

"Maybe. But we'll probably still need to see the original book."

We reached Dalton's room, hiding the urn in his backpack. He went into the closet and stood up on a chair to reach the back of the top shelf, where he pulled out the little succession book. The urn had tarnished so badly, it was black, but the engraved words were still legible under the light. We placed the book and urn next to each other and read them both. I grabbed a sheet of paper and together we transcribed the wording on the urn.

> I will breake of my finnes by vntained repentance and turne vnto the Lord whom I haue offended, affuring my felfe that his mercies are infinite, and therefore he is redie to forgiue, and the merites of Chrift a full fatisfaction for all my finnes though many and hainous, and therefore in him I may bouldly challenge forgiueneffe as a thing of right appertayning to me.

I wrote down the transcription:

> *I will break of my sins unfeigned repentance and turn unto the Lord whom I have offended, assuring myself that his mercies are infinite, and therefore he is ready to forgive and the merits of Christ a full satisfaction for all my sins though many and heinous, and therefore in him I may boldly challenge forgiveness as a thing of right pertaining to me.*

Then we opened the succession book and looked at the Ancient Nine's creed on the back page:

heretofore I haue diſhonoured God by my ſins, but now I will giue him glorie in beleeuing and acknowledging his infinite mercie, goodneſſe, iuſtice, and truth in his promiſes; and ſecing by my ſinnes I haue crucified the Lorde of life, I will not ad hereunto this outrageious wickedneſſe, to tráple his pretious bloud vnder my filthie feete as a thing vnholy and of no worth, neither will I through my vnbeleefe make it to be ſpilt in vaine; but now with all care and conſience I will gather it vp as a moſt precious balme, and with the hand of faith apply it to thoſe greiſly gaſhes, and deepe woundes which ſinne hath made in my ſoule and conſience, and with this ſpirituall lauer I will waſhe my polluted ſoule till it bee thoroughly purged from all vncleaneſſe. And ſeeing I haue depriued my ſoule of that in herent rightcouſneſſe wherewith it was indued by creation, now I will apply thereunto a farre more excellent rightcouſneſſe by the hand of faith, euen the righteouſneſſe of Ieſus Chriſt God and man, wherewith being adorned I may boldy offer my ſelfe into the preſence of my heauēly father & receiue the bleſſing of euerlaſting happines.

"So much for that," Dalton said. "Two completely different passages, saying totally different things."

"True, but that doesn't mean they're not related," I said. "Look at the way the words are spelled and the sentence structure. They're both heavy on religious themes—sins, repentance, and spiritual obedience. They could be from the same source. This is why we need to look at that book."

WHEN I GOT home that night, I was surprised to find Percy sitting on the steps outside our entryway, smoking a cigarette. He was wearing a shrunken ratty blue Andover T-shirt, his silk pajama bottoms, and monogrammed slippers. His hair was a complete mess.

"What the hell are you doing out here so late in your pajamas?" I asked. "You're gonna freeze to death."

"Give me a break," he said, looking up at me momentarily, then resting his head on the railing. His eyes were red and swollen. I could smell the alcohol on his breath from several feet away. He was more than a little drunk. He was bombed.

"You're wasted," I said. "C'mon, let's go into the room."

"I'm not going anywhere," he said. "And I don't want any of your fake sympathy. I had a lot to drink, and I deserved every damned inebriating ounce of it."

I was cold and tired and in no mood for playing psychiatrist, but he looked so pathetic that I couldn't ignore him and go in. "What happened?" I said, sitting down next to him.

He took another pull on the cigarette, choked a little, and blew out a burst of smoke. "You don't care. No one cares. My life is gone to shit, and no one gives a shit." He let out a pitiful little laugh.

The poor guy was in the worst shape I'd ever seen him. He wasn't even wearing that damn pinky ring. "What the hell happened?" I asked.

"They're all a bunch of phony bastards," he stammered. "Every single rotten one of them is a no-good, sniveling bastard."

"You mind telling me who you're talking about?"

"The Spee," he mumbled. "Bunch of lying assholes. If I owned a gun, I'd go over there and shoot every last one of 'em, then find their mothers and shoot 'em too."

"Slow down, Percy," I said, wrapping my arm around his shoulders. "It's okay to be drunk, but you're talking real crazy right now. Tell me what happened."

"What the hell do you think happened?" he said. "They cut me from the punch. Two generations of Hollingsworth men have been members of that goddamn club, and I don't even make the final dinner. Can't be more of a loser than that."

I wasn't exactly sure what to say. With all his family money and Harvard lineage, I had figured Percy to be a lock to get into the Spee. "You don't need a club," I said. "It's their loss, not yours. You already have the Din and Tonics, and you're comping the Lampoon."

Percy just shook his head. "You don't understand, Spenser," he said. "You never will. Getting into the Spee was about tradition and putting my name up there next to my father and grandfather. Now I have to call my family and tell them I got rejected."

The light above the entryway door suddenly flickered out, and I could no longer see Percy, but I could hear him sniffling. He brought his hands to his face. It was difficult not feeling sorry for the guy, even if in the grand scheme of life, this didn't seem to merit such agony.

"C'mon, let's go in," I said, grabbing him by his shoulders. "You're gonna freeze to death out here, and if that happens, who knows what kind of room-mate I'll get stuck with."

Percy took one last pull on his cigarette and flicked it in the grass. I hooked him underneath his arms until he stumbled to his feet. It's strange how things turn out in life. A filthy-rich kid who I thought had everything imaginable, and who should've been feeling like the king of the world, was completely distraught about something that while important in the elite circles of soci-ety, in the grand scheme of life seemed inconsequential. And here I was, not even fifty dollars in my bank account, trying to make him feel like everything was fine with the world.

When I finally had him situated in his bed, I reached down and gave him a big hug. At first he kept his hands by his side, but then he squeezed me around the neck.

When we released each other, he said, "I don't know how I'm gonna tell my father that I didn't get in."

"Tell him the guys were complete assholes," I said. "And you didn't feel like they were worth the next two and a half years of your life."

He shook his head. "He won't buy that.'"

"Well, after a good night's sleep, I'm sure you'll think of something that'll work."

I was almost through the door when he said, "By the way, some girl stopped by to see you. A little girl with crooked teeth. Her name was something like Stromstein or Hamburger."

I laughed. "You mean Stromberger?"

"Yeah, something like that."

"What did she say?"

"Something about good news, and you should call her."

"Hey, what did you do with your pinky ring?"

He looked down at his hand, and waved it in dismissal. "I took it off and put it away."

"Why?"

"I've disgraced the Hollingsworth name. I'm not worthy of wearing the family crest."

When I got back to my room, I lay awake in my bed for almost an hour. All my life, I prayed to God that I would find a way to make my mother and myself rich. But that night, I realized being rich meant dealing with different but not necessarily easier problems. My grandfather was right. "Money can buy a helluva lot of things, but it can't buy real happiness."

29

BY THE TIME I finally reached the lobby of the Boston Garden on Saturday night, I felt like I had fought two wars and barely lived to tell it. The Red Line heading into downtown from Harvard Square was packed to capacity. I switched over to the Green Line, which was five-deep with everyone heading to the New Edition concert. The streets around the arena were so thick with bodies that we seemed to be moving like one giant organism funneling between the barricades and avoiding the police patrols sitting atop their gigantic horses. I figured I would surprise Ashley by arriving before she did, but I was only five minutes early by the time I squeezed my way through the doors. Even with all the chaos inside the lobby, it didn't take long for me to find her at our meeting spot underneath the hanging Larry Bird jersey.

"You're early," she said, looking down at her watch and smiling. Her hair was done differently, straightened and layered, then curled at the ends. She was wearing makeup and pink lipstick. I didn't think it was possible for her to look any more beautiful, but she had found a way to improve on perfection.

"I would've run here all the way from Cambridge if I had to," I said. "No way I was gonna be late."

"Good," she said, stepping close enough for me to smell her perfume—

sweet apple with a light sprinkling of cinnamon. "A gentleman never keeps his woman waiting."

"'His'?" I said. "It's nice you're finally admitting where we stand."

"Don't get too excited, Harvard," she said, folding her arms across her chest. "It was just a figure of speech. Let's get in there before it starts." We joined the crush of bodies moving slowly up the old ramps, finally squeezing through our gate and into the dark arena. I was pleasantly surprised at our seat location. I expected the nosebleeds, but we were in the lower half of the arena with a great view of the stage.

"You scored some nice seats," I said once we had gotten settled.

"We're not on the floor," she said. "But they're the best I could do. Dining services isn't exactly making me rich."

"These seats are perfect," I said. "Al B. Sure! was supposed to open, but heard some people saying he's sick tonight."

"Really? That's no fun. I love him."

"Well, maybe New Edition will sing more songs to make up for it," I said. "Have you been to other concerts here?"

"Only one," she said. "A couple of years ago, I won Prince tickets in a radio contest. My brother took me."

"I love Prince," I said. "How was he?"

"Incredible. Everyone kept saying he was only gonna play his new stuff, but he sang everything that night from 'Purple Rain' to 'Little Red Corvette.' Three full hours nonstop. No one wanted to leave."

A loud pop cracked over the sound system, followed by an electric hum and then total darkness. Silence blanketed the crowd. Drums were the first sound coming from the black stage, followed by the electric guitar and keyboard. Spotlights went up, and there they were in shiny silver suits with matching sunglasses and black fedoras. Within seconds, the crowd was rocking and dancing and singing the words to "Candy Girl," and the Garden jumped with the beat of the bass bouncing off my chest.

For the next two hours, it was one hit after another, and we never took our seats. Then they sang the emotional ballad "Is This the End," and all the girls, Ashley included, screamed like they were trying to make the roof collapse.

Other guys scooped their dates in their arms and kissed away most of the song, but while Ashley had allowed me to hold her close, I wasn't feeling that courageous yet, so I just swayed with her underneath my arm and took in the moment.

The song finally ended, and the houselights went up and people stood there in a delayed state of shock. Some of the girls were crying, the guys were yelling for more, and only smoke remained on the stage where the singers once stood. After twenty minutes of unanswered pleas for an encore, we slowly started filing out the doors. We still had a couple of hours before Ashley's curfew, so we decided to grab a bite at Uno Pizzeria. We took a crowded Green Line train from North Station into Kenmore Square, home of the towering Citgo sign, Boston's most famous landmark that sits atop the old Peerless Motor Car building.

We had a half-hour wait for a table, so we left our names and decided to take a short walk along Comm Ave. It was perfect weather for a brisk walk, and it felt good to have Ashley curled underneath my shoulder. Antique streetlamps along a path of towering trees and old wooden benches lit the median park along the wide avenue.

"So, what do you want to do with your life?" I asked. A horse-drawn carriage rolled by, the rhythmic clipping of the horse's hooves slapping the pavement.

"I want to finish this year with good enough grades to earn a scholarship to one of the big universities," she said.

"And beyond that?"

"I'm not gonna tell you."

"Why not?"

"'Cause you'll laugh."

"C'mon, I'm not gonna laugh. Scout's honor."

She stopped and turned into me. "Were you really a Boy Scout?"

"No, but some of my friends were, so sometimes I borrow their honor. Tell me. I promise I won't laugh."

She resumed her position nestled underneath my shoulder and we kept walking. We passed the gated townhouses of some of Boston's wealthiest families, and through the tall glass doors I could see doormen standing attentively at their posts.

"I bet all your friends want to go on to graduate schools and become doctors, lawyers, or businessmen," she said.

I thought for a quick moment. She wasn't too far off. I had one friend, Jack Madsen, who wanted to be a software programmer, but other than that, everyone pretty much had designs on one of the big three. The race had already started to see who would return millionaires by our tenth class reunion.

"So, what is it that you want to do?" I asked.

"Promise?"

"Cross my heart."

She grabbed my arm tighter. "I'd like to be a wedding planner."

I wasn't sure I heard her correctly. "Did you say a wedding planner?"

"See, I knew you'd laugh."

"I'm not laughing. I'm just making sure I heard you correctly."

"Well, you did," she said. "I want to help people with one of the most important days of their life. So many weddings are ruined by people who either don't know what they're doing or don't know how to make the most of a limited budget. I want to be the one who helps people get it right."

I was surprised, but there was no way I was going to show it. It was the first time that she had been vulnerable with me, and I was determined not to blow it.

"I've always liked weddings since I was a little girl," she continued. "They can be so beautiful and full of meaning. Think about it. There are billions of people in the world, and yet two people find each other through all of life's chaos and pledge themselves to eternal love. It's just so romantic."

I couldn't figure out how someone so young could've already given marriage so much thought. "You sound like you've been married before," I said.

"Don't be silly, Spenser," she said, hitting me on the shoulder. "Getting married isn't a prerequisite for appreciating the beauty of weddings. I watched Princess Diana's wedding on TV and cried for weeks. It was the perfect fairy tale."

"Have you told your mother about your career plans?" I asked.

"Are you kidding? You don't know my mother. If I told her that, she'd march me into a shrink's office to have my head examined. My mother has spent most of her life cleaning for rich people. She has it fixed in her mind that I'm gonna be a lawyer and work in one of those fancy glass towers. She doesn't want me to struggle like she has."

"Sooner or later you're gonna have to tell her," I said.

"Then I choose later."

"How do you get experience at planning a wedding?"

"It's a real business like anything else," she said. "I can do an internship or become an assistant."

We walked in silence for a few yards. "I don't know anything about planning weddings, but I respect you for finding something you want to do and following your dreams regardless of what everyone else thinks," I said. "That takes a lot of courage."

She looked up at me and said, "Do you want to be a doctor because of the title and money, or because you really want to help people?"

"I don't think anyone who wants to be a doctor doesn't have a strong desire to help others," I said. "But there's also nothing wrong with doctors wanting to make a decent living."

"As long as your heart's in the right place," she said.

I don't know what it was that came over me, but I stopped her right there and said, "Well, since we're on the subject of hearts, when will you put yours in the right place and be my girlfriend?"

A blank expression fell over her face, and she said, "But we haven't even dated."

"Earth to Ashley," I said. "These *are* dates. Dinners, movies, a concert. They're considered dates in the real world."

"I can't date you, Spenser," she said, looking into my eyes.

"You're afraid to give me your heart?"

"I'm afraid you'll crush it."

"Give me a chance."

"I can't."

"You can," I said. "We both know that you want us to be together as much as I do."

"We're too different," she said, looking away.

"That's bullshit and you know it."

"It's not—my world isn't anything like yours. We met because I'm the one who was *serving* you. Remember? You go to Harvard. I go to a community college."

"Forget about Harvard," I said. "A school doesn't make me who I am. Where I come from makes me who I am. I appreciate hard work. I know struggle. My family has problems just like everyone else."

She turned back to me and smiled. "You don't have a clue what real problems are," she said. "Trust me."

That's when I grabbed her by the shoulders and brought her into me, and before she could back away, I kissed her under those lamps on Commonwealth Avenue with the Citgo sign shining above us. At first, she resisted, but then she opened her mouth and wrapped her hands around my neck, and we stayed frozen like that as the wind blew in our faces and the cars raced by.

After we had separated and she had straightened her coat, she said, "Did I say you could do that?"

"You didn't have to."

We walked back to Uno's hand in hand and ordered a deep-dish pizza with everything on it. With the first kiss behind us, we were free to imagine things we had only danced around in the past, and we left the restaurant with our hearts as full as our stomachs.

"I'm not letting you go home by yourself tonight," I said, as we walked up to the crowded T stop.

"You don't have to let me," she said. "I'm a big girl. I can make my own decisions."

"It's wrong for me to let you go home alone this late," I said. "What if something happened to you?"

"I've done a good job getting home for the past nineteen years," she said. "I think I can manage one more night."

"You're so damn stubborn."

"No, the problem with you Harvard boys is that you're used to being with girls who do everything you say."

"You're not that tough," I said. "I kissed you tonight, and you weren't even willing to call this an official date."

"Little boys with big, tender egos." She smiled. "Don't fool yourself and think you just suddenly got your way. I've been wanting to kiss you since the first night I saw you in Eliot."

This time *she* grabbed me, and by the time our lips touched, I was completely under her spell.

WHEN I GOT BACK to the room that night, there was a message on the door from Stromberger. She would be editing stories all night at the *Crimson,* and I should call her whenever I got in. I checked to see if Percy was in his room, but it was empty. I looked at his desk and noticed the pinky ring was missing, which meant he was well on the road to recovery.

The phone rang about ten times before Stromberger answered.

"You told me to give you a call," I said.

"I'm up to my eyeballs in copy," she said. "But I've got good news for you. I might've found something about that book, or at least I'm on the right trail. There was a *Gazette* story in the forties about a string of burglaries involving the rare books collection. There's also an article in an old *Crimson* about a guy who tried to steal the Gutenberg Bible from Widener. I copied them for you."

"You wanna take a break and meet me at Elsie's?"

"I don't know if I can get out of here right now," she said. "I still have tons of work to do. I'm covering for one of the other editors who went away this weekend."

"It'll only take half an hour," I said. "Plus, it sounds like you could use the break. We'll have two big sloppy sundaes. My treat."

"You buried the lead." She laughed. "I'll meet you there in ten minutes."

ELSIE'S SANDWICH SHOP on Mt. Auburn Street was one of Cambridge's gastronomic landmarks, a homey little place that had been serving up its famous roast beef and hamburger sandwiches with Russian dressing for more than three decades. I snatched the last two empty stools before putting in my order for a chocolate fudge sundae with the works. Stromberger walked in wearing a long varsity swim coat.

"Where did you get that from?" I asked. It was one of those ankle-length hooded coats with a faux fur lining and large satin Harvard letters stitched across the back. It was one of the most coveted sporting paraphernalia items on campus.

"My roommate has two of them, so she lets me borrow this one," Stromberger said nonchalantly.

"Is she outta her mind?" I said. "That coat's worth a fortune."

"Why?" Stromberger shrugged. "It's just a coat. The lining isn't even real fur, and the zipper is always getting stuck."

And that's one of the things I liked about Stromberger. She had an uncanny ability to quickly put things into perspective and make molehills out of mountains.

"Someone broke into the equipment room last year and stole ten of them," I said. "Sold them for a two hundred a pop. They're the most important varsity gear to score, harder than a DHA sweatshirt."

"Anyone who'd pay more than fifty bucks for this thing needs to have their head examined," Stromberger huffed. She weaved her way to the counter, ordered her sundae, and returned. "Here's the first article," she said, pulling a folded piece of paper from inside her coat. It was from the *Crimson* and dated September 18, 1969.

BURGLAR SLIPS AS HE TRIES TO REMOVE
GUTENBERG BIBLE FROM WIDENER LIBRARY

A daring burglar came within inches of successfully stealing Harvard's Gutenberg Bible from its resting place in Widener Library on August 19.

He succeeded in foiling the library's alarm system, and removing the

Bible from its plastic display case, but appears to have slipped when he attempted to climb down a rope hanging out of a library window. He fell some 40 feet to the ground outside.

The burglary suspect, identified as Vido K. Aras, 20, of Dorchester was found unconscious outside the library in the morning with the two volumes of the Bible in a backpack beside him.

Aras is currently in Cambridge City Hospital suffering from skull fractures. He has been charged with breaking and entering and possession of burglary tools. In an interrogation by police, he is reported to have said that "somebody is going to take the rap besides me."

Harvard's copy is one of 47 known Gutenberg Bibles known to be in existence. The book was printed about 1455 by Johann Gutenberg, the inventor of movable type. For insurance purposes, the Bible is valued at $1 million but it is almost irreplaceable. The bindings of the book, which are not original, were damaged in the fall, but the pages are still in good condition.

Police believe that the suspect hid in the library until after closing time on August 19, then went on the roof, climbed down the rope to a window and broke into the Widener Room where the Bible is kept. He then removed the Bible from the display case and was attempting to climb further down the rope to the ground outside when he fell.

"It looks like a professional job all right, in the fact that he came down the rope," University Police Chief Robert Tonis said, "but it doesn't look very professional that he fell off."

The Bible had been given to Harvard in 1944 by the family of Harry Elkins Widener '07, who died in the 1912 sinking of the *Titanic*. Widener had been a rare book collector: his family donated his entire collection to the University, along with part of the money needed to build the library which now bears his name.

The attempt to steal the Bible is expected to spur work on new security measures, which had already been under consideration.

Another article in the *Boston Traveler* reported on a New York ring of book thieves who had been hitting major libraries along the East Coast, including Widener and its extensive rare book collection. Some observant book buyers noticed traces of library markings on some of the title pages of the stolen books and alerted police.

Stromberger returned with our sundaes, trying not to spill them as she worked her way through the crowd. "So, what do you think?" she said, shoveling a mound of ice cream into her mouth.

"Interesting, but they don't say anything about the specific book I'm researching," I said.

"No, but I figured you could use these articles as a base and branch out from there. If there were two cases of book thefts, no doubt there were others."

30

✤

I WASN'T THRILLED to be awakened early Sunday morning by the irritating sound of a squirrel scratching against the exterior screen of my bedroom window. I threw one of my pillows to make him go away, but he was back at it a few minutes later. So, there I was lying awake at seven o'clock on the only day I could sleep in late, staring up at the ceiling while a damn squirrel begged me for food. My thoughts turned to our trip to Newport the other night and the two surprises that awaited us.

I still couldn't figure out the meaning of the religious passages. Did they reveal the secret the Ancient Nine had vowed to protect? I reached over to my nightstand and read for the hundredth time the passage inscribed on Abbott's urn.

> I will break of my sins unfeigned repentance and turn unto the Lord whom I have offended, assuring myself that his mercies are infinite, and therefore he is ready to forgive and the merits of Christ a full satisfaction for all my sins though many and heinous, and therefore in him I may boldly challenge forgiveness as a thing of right pertaining to me.

I picked up the phone and called the operator and asked her to connect me to the office of Professor Charles Davenport. It was early, but a lot of old people started their day at the crack of dawn. The phone rang eight times before he picked up.

"Davenport," he said, out of breath.

"Sorry to bother you, Professor," I said. "It's Spenser Collins. I'm the under-grad who showed you that religious passage last week."

"Yes, Mr. Collins, I was wondering what happened to you," he said. "How are you making out?"

"I haven't gotten too far, but I'm working on it. I think I might've found another passage that's somehow connected to the first."

"Is that so? Where did you find it?"

"Engraved on an artifact."

"And what type of artifact was this?"

"Something like a silver bowl."

"That's peculiar," he said. "Do you have the bowl with you?"

"No, but I copied down the engraved words. I was hoping you might look at it and tell me what you think."

"What makes you think the two passages are related?"

"The language is almost identical, and the words are spelled in a similar style with old letters."

"Interesting," he said. "Maybe you should bring the passage by so that I might examine it more closely. I'll be in my office until four, then I have to go out for an appointment."

"I'll come right away," I said, jumping out of bed and hanging up the phone. I quickly threw on a pair of sweats and ran out the door.

"YOU REALLY HAVE no idea what you're looking at?" Professor Davenport said, removing the magnifying glass from his wrinkled face and resting the passage on his crowded desk. His words seemed innocent enough, but his tone was accusatory.

"It definitely seems related to the other passage I showed you, but other-wise I'm at a loss."

Davenport returned his heavy rectangular glasses to his face. "You're gaming me, Mr. Collins."

"No, I'm not, sir," I said. "That's all I know. I swear it is. That's why I've come to you for help."

Davenport eyed me for some time, then stood with the help of his cane and shuffled over to one of his bookcases. After emptying nearly an entire row, he found a folder and brought it back to the desk. He opened the folder and handed me two sheets of paper.

"Read these carefully," he said. "Slowly. Absorb the meaning, then tell me what you think."

I took the first sheet and studied the text. The words and spellings were identical to those contained in the passages Dalton and I had found. The tone was also similar, strong and determined, even militant at times. I could feel Davenport watching me, so I read each line twice before moving on to the next.

Of the meanes whereby we may be preſerued &c. **545**

my conſience, & therefore farre bee it frō me to load it with a farre more vnſupportable burthen I haue already too much diſhonoured my good God by my horrible ſinnes, and herefore I will in no caſe more diſhonour him, now then in committing all my other ſinnes, by denying his mercie, iuſice, truth, and euen the godhead itſelf; for what were this but being already in a burning feauer to caſt myſelfe into the fire, or being gone ouer the ſhooes in the filthie puddle of ſinne to plunge my ſelfe ouer head and eares, and euen to drowne my ſelfe in the bottomeleſſe gulfe of deſperation? Nay rather now I will breake of my ſinnes by vntained repentance and turne vnto the Lord whom I have offeded, aſſuring my ſelfe that his mercies are infinite, and therefore he is readie to forgiue, and the merites of Chriſt a full ſatisfaction :for all my ſinnes though many and hainous, and therefore in him I may bouldly challenge forgiuneſſe as a thing of right appertayning to me.

And thus are wee to reſiſt Sathans tentations and though wee be often foyled yet to riſiſt againe, in no caſe ſuffring him to plucke out our hand the fhield of faith, though he hath difarmed vs of the breft-plate of righteoufneffe ;for if once we be depriued of this part of this fpiritual armour wee fhall lie open to all his blowes and thrufts, vntil wee be wounded to the very death.

But most lamentable it is to fee the greeuous miferie

Of poore humbled finners wherinto they are brought through the violence of Sathans tentations ; for howfoeuer feeling the heauie waight of their other finnes they earneftly defire to be freed frō thē, howfoeuer being tormented with greeuous fmart of their other wickedneffe they hate and abhorre it, yet they eafily fuffer themfelues to bee plunged into defperation with euery friuoulous tentation ; and quietly offer their hands to be manacled, and bound in thefe giues of hell withoue refiftance. But let all fuch ftiree vp themfelues, and gather their oppreffed fpirites together, faying to their owne confiences I hate and deteft from my heart my former wickedneffe, and fhall I now entertaine a finne more horrible than all the reft;

the

It didn't take long before I realized why he had wanted me to read that page. I continued reading the rest of the words, then looked up when I was finished. "Does this page come from *The Christian Warfare* by John Downame?" I asked.

"Exactly," he said, seeming pleased that I was catching on. "Have you had a chance to look at it?"

"No, I've been waiting for an appointment with one of the reference librarians. The passage I found on the bowl matches the text in this first paragraph."

"What kind of bowl is it?" he asked.

"Silver."

"And how did you come across it?"

I was prepared for that question. "It was the craziest coincidence," I said.

"I just happened to be flipping through an old book, looking for clues to the first passage, and noticed it in one of the pictures."

"Do you have that book?"

"No, it was in a friend's room. Maybe I can get it if he hasn't returned it to the library yet."

"That might be rather helpful," Davenport said. "So, what are your interpretations of that first page?"

I was reluctant to answer out of fear of making a fool of myself. One of the world's greatest religious scholars was asking me my interpretation of something that I was sure he himself had spent many years analyzing.

"It sounds like the person has realized his sins and wants forgiveness for what he's done," I said. I skimmed over the passage for a second time. "We must keep faith in the goodness and will of God and resist the temptations of Satan, who strives to exploit our weaknesses and cause us to sin."

"That is a good literal interpretation," Davenport said, nodding slowly. "But what might it mean in the abstract?"

I shrugged. I didn't say something foolish.

"What do you know about King James I?" he finally asked.

"Not much," I said. "I know there's a version of the Bible named after him."

"That's a start," he said. "King James I was not very popular but still a powerful king in the mid-sixteenth to early-seventeenth century. He was the only son of Mary Queen of Scots and her second husband, Lord Darnley. Following an uprising, his mother was forced to abdicate the throne in favor of her son, James, who was crowned the King of Scotland at just thirteen months of age. When he turned thirty-six, his cousin, the first Queen Elizabeth of England, died, and he inherited her throne, becoming the ruler of two kingdoms. He was quite a controversial and at times vulgar man. He lived to be almost sixty, a great accomplishment in those disease- and war-ravaged times."

"But what does King James I have to do with these pages?"

"Go ahead and read the second page," he said.

546 Of the meanes whereby we may be preserued &c.

the burthen of my other finnes oppreſſe me and make me earneſtly to
defire eafe, and ſhall I adde a loade farre more intollerable to my
afflicted confience? I am filled with ſhame and confuſion becaufe by
my former finnes. I have dishonoured my gratious God and that I
continue more to dishonour him by doubting of and denying his
mercy, iuſtice, and truth in his promiſes? I have heretofore with *Iudas*
betrayed my Saviour Chriſt vtno the death, yea and with my finnes I
have whipped, mocked, and crucified him, and now hee hauing made
full fatisfaction for my finnes, and called me vnto him that he may
eafe me of this intollerable burthen, ſhould I wish *Iudas* refufe to
come defperately caſt of al hope of mercie and become mine owne
hangman? be it farre from mee, nay as I hate all other finners fo let
me hate this aboue all the reſt, in being more hainous then al the
reſt ; as I defire to be eafed and freed from the heavie burthen of
other my wicked-neſſ, fo I will with all my power refiſt Sathan when
he feeketh to loade me with this loade of defperation and being
farre more intolerable, heretofore I haue dishonoured God by my
fins, but now I will giue him gloerie in belieuing and acknowledge ing
his infinite mercie, goodneſſe, iuſtice, and truth in his promiſes,
and feeing by my finnes I have crucified the Lorde of life, I will not
ad herevnto this outragious wickedneſſe, to trāple his precious blood
vnder my filthe feete as a thing vnholy and of no worth, neither will
I through my vnbeliefe make it to be ſpilt in vaine ; but now with
all care and confience I will gather it vp as a moſt precious balme,
and with the hand of faith apply it to thofe greiſly gaſhes, and deepe
woundes which finne hath made in my foule and confience, and with
this ſpiritual laver I will waſhe my polluted foule till it bee thoroughly
purged from all vncleaneſſe. And feeing I haue depriued my foule of
that inherent righteouſneſſe wherewith it was inbued by creation,
now I will apply thereunto a farre more excellent righteouſneſſe by
the hand of faith, euen the righteouſneſſe of Iefus Chriſt God and
man, wherewith being adorned I may boldly offer my felfe into the
prefence of my heauēly father & receiue the bleſſing of everlaſting
happiness.

Laſtly

It wasn't long before I recognized the passage that I had brought to him last week, the Ancient Nine's creed.

"I don't understand," I said. "The last time we spoke, you said that people have been looking for those two missing pages for centuries, and that there were only a few copies of the first edition still in existence. But you have copies of the pages right here."

"Part of your education here, Mr. Collins, is to ask the right questions," he said. "But an even bigger part is to undertake the rigorous chores of scholarship to try to find some of those answers yourself. You seem to be an ambitious young man. Use that ambition to stimulate and satisfy your intellectual curiosity. These pages are copies made from microfilm, not the actual book. In other words, these are copies of copies. Anyone can get access to this information on microfilm, but no one has been able to find the *original* pages missing from the first edition in Houghton. Scholars have been trying to learn the fate of those pages for decades." He opened the folder and pulled out another sheet of paper and handed it to me. "Read this."

RLG's Eureka(R)—FIND Title christian warfare
AND Imprint Year 1604

Author: Downame, John, d. 1652.

Title: The Christian warfare. Wherein is first generally shewed the malice, power and politike stratagems of the spirituall enemies of our saluation, Sathan and his assistants the world and the flesh; with the meanes also whereby the Christian may withstand and defeate them. And afterwards more speciallie their particular temptations, against the severall causes and meanes of our salvation, whereby on the one side they allure vs to security and presumption, and on the other side, draw vs to doubting and desperation, are expressed and answered. Written especially for their sakes who are exercised in the spirituall conflict of temptations, and are afflicted in conscience in the sight and sense of their sinnes. By I. Downame preacher of Gods word.

Published: At London: imprinted by Felix Kyngston, for Cuthbert Burby, and are to be sold at his shop in Paules Church-yard at the signe of the Swan, 1604.

Physical Details: [24], 272, 271–366, 371–676, [2] p. 4°. Notes: With final errata leaf.

Signatures: [par.]4 A-2V8 2X².

Signatures from DFo.

References: STC (2nd ed.), 7133.

Notes: Microfilm. Ann Arbor, Mich. University Microfilms

International, 1982. 1 microfilm reel; 35 mm. (Early English books, 1475–1640; 1709:2). L.

Other Titles: Christian warfare.

Subjects: Puritans—Doctrines—Early works to 1800.

Christian life—Early works to 1800.

Location: British Library, London, England
Shelfmark: [Shelfmark not available]
Note: -A2–3

Location: Aberdeen University Library, Aberdeen, Scotland
Shelfmark: [Unverified]
Note: [Catalog match]

Location: Belfast Central Library, Belfast, Northern Ireland
Shelfmark: [Unverified]

Location: Belfast Central Library, Belfast, Northern Ireland
Shelfmark: [Shelfmark not available]
Note: [Contributor match]

Location: Oxford University Bodleian Library (includes The Vicar's Library, St. Mary's Church, Marlborough), Oxford, England
Shelfmark: [Unverified]
Note: [Catalog match]

Location: York Minster Library, York, England
Shelfmark: XV.I.15
Note: tp. damaged, -4p.l.

Location: Folger Shakespeare Library, Washington, District of Columbia
- Shelfmark: STC 7133
Note: HH74/16. Vellum binding, with remnants of ties. MS. notes on back fly-leaves. Provenance: Harmsworth copy
Location: Harvard University Libraries, Cambridge, Massachusetts
Shelfmark: [Unverified]
Note: lacks Mm8 [Catalog match]

Source: English Short Title Catalogue.
Record ID: ESTCS1536

When I had finished, I asked, "What does this list mean?"

"Have you ever heard of the English Short Title Catalogue?" he said.

"Never," I said.

"It's the world's largest and most important electronic database containing bibliographic records for books, pamphlets, broadsides, and songs published in Great Britain or her dependencies in any language. It is therefore the best source for materials published in the English language from 1473 to 1800. If any library in the world holds a particular title, it would be listed here. As you can see, there are only eight libraries in the world, including Harvard, that have a first edition of *The Christian Warfare*. But despite the existence of these other books, our edition is uniquely of interest."

"Why?" I asked.

He lowered his voice to a whisper. "Because of those two missing pages."

"Are these two pages not found in the other seven copies?"

Davenport took the papers out of my hand, placed them back in the folder, and closed it.

"The answers are out there for you, Mr. Collins. But you must be willing to work a lot harder to find them."

31

DALTON AND I agreed to skip the dining hall and have lunch at a favorite restaurant in the Square, a small greasy spoon called Leo's Place, which for my money had the best short-order cook in town. Tucked away between the STA travel offices and a CVS pharmacy, Leo's was passed over by most students, who were unaware that they were walking by one of the best meals Cambridge offered. I was already seated at the long yellow Formica countertop when Dalton walked in.

"Smells great in here," Dalton said. "All these years I've lived in Boston, and I never knew this place existed."

"A lot of people don't," I said, walking up to place our order. "That's what's so nice about it. The regulars are die-hards and the owners treat us like family."

Rafi and Rich Bezjian were two hardworking Armenian brothers who took over the shop from Leo back in 1982, and through grit, great customer service, and simple, delicious food had won the hearts and stomachs of a clientele that included everyone from locals to senior administrative university deans to a sprinkling of celebrities. We ordered a couple of cheesesteaks and fries and took a seat in the window. The sun pouring through the glass felt good.

"Well, it's safe to say that you're no longer in the Delphic punch," Dalton said. "I'm sure Jacobs took care of that right away."

"We both knew I was a long shot from the beginning," I said. "It sucks, but life goes on."

"And so does our search for the Ancient Nine's chamber," Dalton said. "Just because they won't let you in, doesn't mean we're not getting in."

"It's gonna be almost impossible now," I said.

"There are other ways of getting in," Dalton said.

"They sure in hell aren't legal."

"No, but they could be effective."

"Care to share your genius plan?"

"Not yet." Dalton smiled. "I'm still working on the details. Speaking of which, I've been thinking a lot lately about Moss Sampson."

"What about him?"

"I've been trying to figure out what his role might've been in all this."

"He probably killed Abbott," I said. "Dunhill saw him in the window that night."

"Yeah, I know, but it just seems too convenient," Dalton said. "The one guy with the violent past killing Abbott's son."

"If he didn't, then who did?" I said.

"Why not one of the members?"

"Because the regular members presumably didn't know anything about the Ancient Nine or their secret chamber. If one of them had caught Abbott, they would've assumed Abbott had broken in just to pull a prank. That wouldn't be a reason to kill him."

Dalton thought for a moment. "I still think it wouldn't hurt to get a better idea of what happened to Sampson," he said. "He's a valuable link, and he just suddenly disappears. What did he know? Where did he go? How did he die?"

"Let's say we did find that stuff out. How could that help?"

"I'm not exactly sure, but it might give us better insight into what happened that night."

"My bet is on *The Christian Warfare*, if Brathwaite hasn't done something with it," I said. "Once we get a look at the book, I think it'll help direct our search."

"If we can understand what the hell the damn thing is saying," Dalton said. "The English is so old, it's like reading hieroglyphics."

"I went to see Davenport this morning in his office," I said. "I wanted him to look at the passage that was engraved on Abbott's urn and tell me what he thought."

"You didn't tell him where you saw it!" Dalton said, slightly rising from his stool.

"Of course not. I'm not stupid enough to admit that we *illegally* exhumed and carted away someone's ashes."

"Then what did you tell him?"

"I lied and said I was flipping through a book in a friend's room and saw the passage engraved on a silver bowl. Don't worry, he bought it."

"So, what did he say about the passage?"

"Not much, actually. He showed me two pages from the book and asked me what I thought. Both passages were on those pages."

"Pages from *The Christian Warfare*?"

"Yes, but not from the 1634 fourth edition that was in John Harvard's collection. Davenport had copies of the two pages from the rarer 1604 first edition."

"I thought those two pages were missing."

"They are. But his pages came from one of the remaining books that's not in Houghton. He said the 1604 edition is available on microfilm and his pages were made from one of the remaining books in England. But what I don't get is why he insisted that I need to see the original book if he already had copies of the missing pages."

"Doesn't make sense to me either. Nothing is making sense anymore. What's so important about those passages that the Ancient Nine would adopt some of the words as their creed and Abbott's family would engrave the other on his urn?"

"That's why I wanted to talk to you. Davenport suggested that the literal translation of the words is not what really matters. There's something unique about the first edition book here at Harvard that makes these two pages more special than in the other books around the world."

"So, Harvard doesn't have the only copy of the first edition?"

"No, there are seven others. There's a total of eight first editions left. Three copies in England, one of which was used to make the microfilm, two in Ireland, one in Scotland, one in D.C., and the one here in Houghton. But Davenport made it very clear that even with the other copies available, researchers and scholars around the world have been focused on the one here at Harvard with the two missing pages."

"Doesn't make sense to me," Dalton asked.

"There must be something about the actual missing pages."

"Did he say what it was?"

"He wouldn't tell me."

"Why not?"

"He said I needed to work harder to find some of my own answers and satisfy my intellectual curiosity."

"Jesus Christ! Why won't the old geezer just come clean?"

Rafi brought over our cheesecakes and drinks, and we went right to work.

"On another note, I kissed her last night after the concert."

"No way!"

"Yup. Right on Comm Ave near Kenmore."

"I thought she didn't want to date a Harvard man."

"She doesn't. In her mind, it was just a kiss."

"Women and their mind games. If you score, it'll be one of the all-time greatest scoops."

As we dusted off the rest of our cheesesteaks, I updated him on the articles Stromberger found about the book heists. He told me his plans to go back down to Wild Winds to keep digging.

"I'M LOOKING FOR ARTICLES about rare book thefts at Widener," I asked Lucy Tyler, the brunette member of Lamont Library's dynamic reference duo.

"How can I help you?" she asked in a slightly raspy voice.

"I'm looking for articles about rare book thefts at Widener," I said.

She wrinkled her forehead and cocked her head to the side as if she didn't hear me. "Did you say book thefts at Widener?"

"Yes. I have copies of *Crimson* articles from 1932 and 1969 that cover book thefts. I wanted to see if there were any others."

"Is this for a paper you're writing?" she asked.

"Just some research I'm doing on international biblioklepts," I said.

"Do you have those articles from the *Crimson* with you?"

I handed her the articles.

"I'd heard about the Gutenberg case, but I hadn't heard about this New York thievery syndicate," she said. "I'm not surprised. A large and open library system like Harvard's is very vulnerable to thefts."

"Is it possible to find out if anyone ever stole the book *The Christian Warfare*?" I asked.

"The one in our special collections in Houghton?"

"Exactly."

"It might be best to ask one of the research assistants over there," she said. "They can probably tell you more about it than I can." She looked down at a schedule and said, "Oh, they're not open on the weekends. Let me just do a quick search in our databases and see if anything comes up."

After a few minutes of typing, she said, "I don't see anything specifically regarding the book that you mentioned. I tried several key word combinations, and nothing has come back. I wish I could be more helpful."

32

ON A HUNCH, I decided to try the Boston Public Library. I took the Green Line to the Copley Plaza branch. I wasn't expecting the mass of people that awaited me. It took almost an hour to find a reference librarian who could help me. He was a short man with foppish sandy brown hair, reading glasses hanging around his neck, and a plaid shirt tucked neatly into his beige chinos. His eyes widened when I told him the subject of my search. He found the summary of an article from the *Boston Post* that talked about book thefts at Harvard. It was written on October 17, 1931. Joel Williams, a Harvard graduate and resident of the nearby town of Dedham, stole almost two thousand books from Widener and was caught when he had the audacity to attempt to sell two of them to a bookstore in Harvard Square, only yards away from Widener. Williams eventually admitted his crimes under intense questioning and was sentenced to two years of hard labor. There was no mention of the specific titles he had stolen or their presumed worth.

"We have that paper on film," he said. "That was a major paper." He wrote down the call number. "Let's go take a look."

We took the elevator to the third floor and walked to the section of the library that housed long rows of metal filing cabinets and an entire room of viewing machines. Most of them were occupied.

"This is the cabinet," he said, pulling out the top drawer. There were only two boxes inside. He picked them up. They weren't the dates I needed. "Strange," he said. "This drawer should be completely full." He pulled out the second and third drawers. They were full. The librarian walked me back to his desk and scanned through several screens before shaking his head.

"I have really bad news," he said. "That film is lost. We renovated the library several years ago and stored many of the old films. When the boxes were returned from storage, two were missing. Unfortunately, the film you're looking for was in one of those boxes."

I couldn't believe my bad luck. Thousands of rolls of old film, and the one I needed was one of the few that got lost. I would have to go directly to the paper.

"Do you know where the paper's offices are?" I asked. "They must have their own paper on film."

"They would if they still existed," he said. "The *Boston Post* folded in October of 1956."

HARVARD'S MORE THAN one hundred libraries were spread across several campuses in buildings that most of us didn't even recognize. Pusey Library was one of them and it housed the University Archives with a reading room situated at the end of a long, carpeted hallway, next to one of the world's most admired map collections. Other than the staff, there was no one around for miles, but the archivists still spoke in hushed tones. This was a subterranean gold mine for serious research and my next best hope after striking out at the Boston Public Library. A bookish-looking woman with salt-and-pepper hair and a pencil stuck behind her right ear offered a smile as I approached the front desk. The name PEGGY was etched into her nameplate. Once she entered my ID into the computer and assigned me a number, I asked her about biblioklepts from the thirties involving Widener.

"That's an interesting request," she said, nodding her head. "I've been here for fifteen years, and this is the first time someone has asked about that."

I explained to her the contents of the article describing the attempted burglary of Widener's Gutenberg Bible. She did a search for other burglaries. There wasn't any mention of *The Christian Warfare*, but she found the summary of the *Boston Post* article on Joel Williams.

"Can we get the entire article?" I asked.

"Possibly," she said. "We have so much material in our repository, most of our collection is kept off-campus, and it might take a few days to get it here. But it's possible we have it downstairs." She typed more into the computer, then scowled. "Unfortunately, this is off-site. It'll take two or three days to get it here."

I took a moment to think.

"Do you know when microfilm came into existence?" I asked.

"Not offhand, but I'm sure it's not too hard to find out. I'm certain the technology has been around since the mid-1800s."

"But when do you think the technology was widely available for commercial purposes like recording books and newspapers?"

"Much later, I would presume," she said. "Maybe turn of the century, probably even later than that. In the beginning, it was being used only in select centers throughout the world, then as the process improved, others began to use it."

My reasoning was pretty straightforward. The succession book was dated 1936. So some time before 1936, they had either seen Harvard's 1604 first printing of *The Christian Warfare*, had gotten ahold of the other few copies that were in Europe, or they had seen the microfilm. In any case, it all came down to timing.

"I have the title of a book, and I know that it's also available on microfilm," I said. "Is there any way you can check and see who made the microfilm and when?"

"This is really something one of the reference librarians at Widener or Lamont should be helping you with," she said. "I'm an archivist." She looked around, then said, "But it's not busy today, so I'll give it a shot."

I gave her the title and author of *The Christian Warfare*.

She worked the keyboard expertly over the next several minutes, then said, "That recording was done by University Microfilms International. They're out in Michigan. But it doesn't give the production date."

"Are they the only ones who made a microfilm copy of that book?" I asked.

"I'm pretty sure," she said. "You're talking about a book from the early 1600s. There are very few remaining copies of a book that old that can be photographed."

Then I thought of another way to get to the date. "When did that company start making microfilms?"

She flipped through a couple of more screens. "It says here the company was founded in 1938 by Eugene Power, who was racing against the clock to protect and preserve Britain's scholarly treasures during the war." She stopped reading aloud and instead started mouthing the words to herself. She bunched her face up into a frown. "That's ironic," she said.

"What?"

"The first microfilm they made was of Early English Books, the ongoing microfilm edition of the Short Title Catalogue I and Short Title Catalogue II. So, that means *The Christian Warfare* was probably one of the first books they actually photographed. What a coincidence."

"But they did it in 1938, right?"

"At the earliest. That's when the company opened."

And that gave me my first elimination. The Ancient Nine couldn't have gotten the passage from a microfilm copy, because the succession book was dated two years earlier, 1936. So that meant the Ancient Nine had either seen the Harvard 1604 copy of *The Christian Warfare* before the two pages had been stolen or they had seen one of the other seven copies of the intact books.

Another thought occurred to me. Maybe there was a record of when the 1604 book had been acquired and its condition. If two pages were missing before Harvard acquired it, that important detail would have merited recording. I walked up to the front desk and waited for Peggy to get off the phone.

"Does the library keep records of all the books they acquire?" I asked.

"Sure, but the type of record kept depends on the value of the book and the era," she said.

"What are those records called?"

"Accession records."

"Can they be seen?"

"Sure, they're open to the public."

"How do I get the accession records for a rare book that was donated around the turn of the century?"

"All the rare books and manuscripts are stored in Houghton," she said.

"I know, but Houghton wasn't built when the book was donated."

"Hmm, that's a tricky one. In that case, we would likely store the records. It really depends. Back then, all the records were handwritten. With the construction of all the new libraries and the transferring of books, things got somewhat disorganized. Houghton keeps some of the records, Widener has some, but we keep a vast majority of the older donations."

"What about *The Christian Warfare*?" I asked.

She smiled. "Let me check." She typed into the computer, and scribbled something down on a piece of scratch paper. She turned to the bookcase directly behind her and pulled out several binders until she found the one she wanted. "This will tell us something," she said, leafing through the crinkled pages.

I tried following what she was doing, but the numbers and librarian notations read like a foreign language. So, I just waited for her to finish her search.

"Today's your lucky day," she said. "We have those records downstairs. I'll have someone go down and get them for you."

I was proud of myself as I sat down at the table. Reading the accession records could go a long way in helping me figure out the ownership history of *The Christian Warfare* and whether those two pages had gone missing before or after the book entered the Harvard system.

Ten minutes later, I saw the runner who had gone to retrieve the file. She returned empty-handed. I got up from my seat and met her at the front desk.

"There's nothing there," she said to Peggy.

"Are you certain?" Peggy said.

"I checked everywhere."

"Maybe it was misfiled."

"I thought the same thing, so I checked all the records. They're all on the same shelf in the subbasement."

"That's strange," Peggy said. "Where else could it be?"

The runner shrugged her shoulders.

"This is highly unusual," she said. "Let me go down and take a look with you." She turned back toward me and said, "Please be patient. Every once in a while, a file gets misplaced."

I nodded, with a sinking feeling. Could it be just bad luck that the record of the one book that might hold the answers was missing? Or was something more sinister at work? The events of the last couple of weeks persuaded me of the latter.

A few minutes later, Peggy was back behind the front desk frowning at the computer monitor. I knew it was bad news.

"I don't understand what happened," she said as I approached. "I checked the entire room, and it wasn't there."

"Maybe someone borrowed it," I said.

"Impossible," she said. "You can't borrow from our files. We don't lend things out like the circulating libraries. You can sign things out only to be viewed in this room." She worked on the computer a little more. She paused and said, "Even stranger, it was here two days ago." She wrote down a number on a piece of paper. "A visitor signed it out at ten forty-three in the morning."

"What's that number you just wrote?" I asked.

"The ID of the person who requested it," she said, walking to another computer. "I can't give you the name, but let me see who it is."

When she put her head down, I slid around the side of the counter just enough so that I could read the monitor as she typed in the ID number. Within seconds, the name and address popped up: Godfrey Channing, 108 Brattle Street in Cambridge. I didn't recognize the name, but the address practically jumped off the screen. It was the address of the Delphic cocktail party, the home of Stanford L. Jacobs III.

"JACOBS RESIDENCE," A woman answered.

I was back in my room and had dialed the number Jacobs had written on the business card he gave me the night of the cocktail party.

"May I speak to Mr. Channing, the secretary," I said in a nasally disguised voice.

"I'm sorry, but Mr. Channing is currently out," she said. "May I take a message?"

"Do you know when he'll be back?"

"Who may I ask is calling?"

"It's a personal call."

"Mr. Channing doesn't receive calls on this line," she said. "You've called a private number."

"I see. This is the only number I have for him."

"Mr. Channing will be back within the hour." She gave me the main house number and asked me to use it when I called back. She seemed slightly annoyed.

"Thank you very much for your help," I said. "Next time I'll be sure to use the right number."

"That would be appreciated," she said. "And just as a point of clarification, I'm Mr. Jacobs's secretary. Mr. Channing is his butler."

33

"SPENSE, GET THE hell over here," Dalton said.

I was lying in my bed, looking at the digital numbers of my clock burn in the darkness. It was 2:35 A.M. I thought I was dreaming. I wasn't sure how the phone had gotten into my hand.

"Spense, are you there?" he said.

"What's going on?" I said.

"Someone broke into my room."

"It's two thirty in the morning, Dalton."

"They took Abbott's urn."

Those four words sat me up.

"What?"

"I went to look at it after I got home from the Hong Kong," Dalton said. "It's gone."

"Jesus Christ!"

"Did they take the succession book?"

"Nope," Dalton said. "I'm sure they were looking for it, but I hid it in my bedroom at my parents' house."

"I'm on my way."

❧

DALTON WAS SITTING in the middle of the common room on the floor with his legs crossed. His eyes were glazed, and he had a blank expression on his face. He hadn't yet taken off his jacket and hat. A small lamp on the mantelpiece was the only light on in the room.

"Are you all right?" I asked, extending a hand to help him up.

"A little shaken up, that's all," he said, looking toward his room.

"Where are your roommates?"

"Asleep."

"Are they missing anything?"

"I don't know. Their doors were closed when I got home. I was out scorpion bowling at the Kong."

He grabbed ahold of my hand and stood up. His legs were wobbly as he fell back on the couch.

"You're drunk," I said.

"Not too drunk to know someone's been in my room. And they knew what they were looking for."

I followed Dalton across the common room and into his bedroom.

"What the hell!" I said, panning the room. It looked like a cyclone had blown through. The desk drawers had been pulled out and turned upside down on the floor. Most of his books had been snatched from the bookcase and piled up on the floor. His closet door was open, and the clothes had been balled up and scattered across the room.

"The urn was hidden in the bottom of my closet," Dalton said. "I don't think anything else is missing. My grandfather's watch was right there in the open and wasn't touched."

"And you're sure the succession book wasn't here?" I asked.

"Positive. Right after you told me Brathwaite had stopped you in your courtyard, I took the book to my house and hid it there."

Dalton walked to his desk and lifted the phone.

"What are you doing?" I asked.

"I'm calling University Police," he said.

"The hell you are," I said, snatching the receiver from his hand and placing it back in the cradle. "What exactly are you going to tell them?"

"Someone broke into my room."

"And stole an urn that *we* stole from a grave?"

Dalton rested his head against the wall and covered his face with both hands. "I'm not thinking clearly," he said.

"You're not thinking at all. Take your clothes off and go to bed. You need to sleep off all those scorpion bowls before you do something stupid."

"They're out there waiting for us."

"I think they've been out there waiting for us since the very beginning."

"What do you mean?"

"You said it yourself that first night we talked about the invitation to the cocktail party. You said it doesn't make a damn bit of sense why I would get punched by the Delphic. I'm completely the opposite of what they're looking for in new members."

"I wasn't knocking you, Spense, but I said that because you don't fit their club image."

"Exactly," I said. "Whoever punched me had specific intentions. They wanted to monitor my movements for some reason. It's the only way to explain a lot of stuff that happened. For example, how did Brathwaite know I was at Widener that night he followed me to the *Crimson*? Why was Jacobs asking me all those personal questions at the cocktail party? How did he know things about me that I had told very few people?"

"But of all people, why you?" Dalton said.

"And why was my name in the back of your uncle's succession book?"

TWO DAYS LATER, Peggy Rosendale from University Archives left a message on my machine. The microfilm I had requested finally arrived. I skipped lunch and biked over to Pusey. Save for an old woman with her face buried in an oversized book, the reading room was empty. Peggy had the film waiting for me when I arrived. I loaded it into a viewer. The newspaper was so dark and the print so faded that I could barely read certain portions. But I could clearly see the pale, youthful face of forty-nine-year-old Joel Clifton Williams. He wore large round glasses and a felt fedora and looked more like an absentminded professor than he did a book thief. The headline was plastered across the page.

HARVARD BOOK THEFTS SOLVED

———

Dedham, MA, October 17, 1931. 1,804 Volumes Stolen from Widener Library Found in Dedham Home of Joel C. Williams—Graduate of College and Holder of Two Degrees Is Arrested

———

Claims He Purchased Books—Apprehended When Trying to Sell Them in Harvard Sq.

The first couple of paragraphs opened like an item in a local police blotter:

Trapped by an alert clerk in a Harvard Square bookshop, where he is alleged to have attempted to sell stolen volumes, Joel Clifton Williams, 49, Harvard graduate, holder of two degrees, and a highly respected lifelong resident of Dedham, was taken yesterday by Dedham and Cambridge police, who have charged him with the larceny of 1,804 volumes from the famous Widener Library at Harvard.

———

BOOKS WORTH $100,000 STOLEN

Thefts from the Widener Library during the last 10 years, in which books worth more than $100,000 have mysteriously been taken from the shelves, were partially solved, police believed last night, with the removal of a five-ton truck load of volumes, many of them rare, from Williams' home in Dedham. The recovered books have a valuation of about $25,000.

The article went on to explain that Williams once served as an instructor at the exclusive Groton preparatory school and he claimed to have been a principal at several prominent high schools. Then it spelled out the details of his demise.

> Williams is declared to have denied to police that he stole the books, declaring that he bought them from a mysterious man named "Hendricks," whom he often met by appointment in Harvard Square.
>
> He was unable to give the first name of the "seller." The Harvard graduate's home was found filled with books, nearly 3,000 volumes in cases and on shelves. He told police that he was a book-lover.
>
> The downfall of the scholarly appearing ex-schoolmaster came Thursday when he appeared at Phillips' Book Store, Massachusetts Avenue, Cambridge, in the very sight of Widener Library, and offered to sell two books to a clerk.
>
> The books were almost instantly identified as two of the missing Widener volumes, an examination showing where attempts had been made to remove identifying marks, according to the police.

Williams received both Master of Arts and Master of Education degrees from Harvard. He had been stealing books from Widener for eight to ten years but stopped after a turnstile was erected near the exit, where guards had been specifically installed to inspect suspicious bundles. When Williams was told by police that he was to be locked up, he asked if he should bring his nightshirt, then inquired about the accommodations at the Cambridge lockup.

Williams's deceit, while grand in the scale of its accomplishment, was simple in its methodology. The entire time books had been mysteriously disappearing from Widener, he had been wandering about the library, exercising certain privileges that were denied even to enrolled undergraduates. He was well known to the library staff, always carrying his briefcase and even greeting them with a pleasant "good night" as he sauntered past university security guards with some of the library's most valuable books. The article mentioned that Williams had snatched at least one complete set of books on a naval topic, but it didn't specifically name any of the other titles he had stolen. Was it possible that Joel Williams had stolen *The Christian Warfare* and clipped those two pages?

THREE DAYS LATER, I found myself waiting outside the locked doors of Houghton Library. I had skipped that morning's organic chemistry lecture, which was like committing heresy for a premed student. I couldn't concentrate on anything but the missing pages and the Delphic. At precisely nine o'clock, the lock clicked back and the same security guard whom I had encountered on my first visit opened the door.

"How can I help you today?" he said, taking a seat behind the small desk in the middle of the cold lobby. He was out of uniform, instead sporting a blazer a couple of sizes too small and a pair of wool trousers that were badly in need of a hem job.

I looked toward the glass-encased bookcase on the left and spotted my target. A crimson leather box with bright gold lettering boldly announced its legendary contents—John Harvard's *Christian Warfare*.

"I'd like to speak to one of the reference assistants," I said.

"Do you have an appointment?" he said, opening the top desk drawer and pulling out a clipboard.

"No, but I figured since it was first thing in the morning, they wouldn't be busy yet. I came last week and signed up for a session, but no one has called me. The deadline for my project is almost here."

"ID?" he asked.

I showed him.

"I'm really not supposed to do this," he said. "They're very strict about schedules. But let me see if someone can help you."

I held my breath as he picked up the phone and gave someone my name, then repeated almost verbatim what I had told him. He nodded his head a couple of times, then hung up the phone.

"They don't normally make exceptions like this, but Thomas Forde, one of the reference assistants, is willing to meet with you. His first appointment isn't for another hour."

"Thanks for your help," I said, quickly heading toward the glass doors.

"Hold on," he called out. "You need to sign in and get a key for a locker before you can enter the reading room. All items except for the books and papers that you carry in your hand must be kept outside and locked up. You can retrieve them when you leave."

I signed the sheet, and he directed me to the other end of the lobby and into a small room containing two rows of standing metal lockers and a wobbly coatrack leaning against the wall. I stripped myself of all the prohibited items, then with a pad and couple of pens walked back across the lobby toward the reading room.

"There's a buzzer located on the left wall," he said. "Press it once, and someone at the desk will let you in."

I did exactly as he had instructed, and a few seconds later the lock released. I took a deep breath as I walked into one of the greatest houses of rare books and manuscripts in the world. Five long immaculate tables lined the room on a floor waxed to a mirror shine. Floor-to-ceiling windows were symmetrically spaced along the walls with the open blinds admitting a rush of sun that brightened the airy room.

"Spenser, my name is Thomas Forde," a man called out as I stood just inside the entrance. "I'm one of the reference assistants. How can I help you today?"

I turned toward a large, polished semicircular reference desk. Like everything else in the room, it looked like it had been built with great effort. The man standing behind it wore small oval glasses and had shoulder-length graying hair that was parted straight down the middle with little attention to style. His faded corduroys and wrinkled oxford belied his crisp and efficient voice.

"I'm doing some research on the book *The Christian Warfare*," I said, walking up to the desk. "I was hoping to take a look at it."

"Is this your first time here at Houghton?" he asked.

"Yes," I said. "Professor Davenport from the Divinity School told me that this is the place where I can actually read that book."

"What he told you is absolutely correct," Forde said. "We know Professor

Davenport quite well here. We have several editions of the book you've mentioned. Which one would you like to see?"

"I thought I'd start with the 1634 edition."

"The one from John Harvard's personal collection?"

"Exactly."

"It's one of our most requested books," he said. "We typically show it by appointment only, but there's no one here right now, so I can get it for you without too much trouble. Even though it's locked in the case just outside, I still need you to fill out a call slip for documentation purposes. Our collection is also open to the public at large, so we must keep traceable records of who has seen which items."

"Of course," I said. I filled out the requested information.

"And that will be your last usage of a pen," he said with a tolerant but stern smile. "Only pencils are allowed inside the reading room. You can pick this up on your way out." He handed me two pencils in return for the pens. "Now, if I could see two forms of identification. I need to enter them into the computer."

I gave him my license and school ID and wondered if a blood test and eye scan would be next.

"If you'll have a seat, I'll be right with you," he said.

He disappeared through a door behind the desk, and I got comfortable at a table in the corner of the room. Shortly thereafter, another man, younger, taller, bearded, emerged through the same door Forde had exited. He sat behind the desk, and I caught him sneaking glances in my direction as I waited.

I looked around the room at the oil paintings hanging high on the pastel green walls. Of the portraits of eight men and one woman, I was surprised that I actually recognized a few of their faces. Teddy Roosevelt, hanging prominently on the center wall, was the most recognizable. I also recognized Charles Sumner, the namesake of Boston's Sumner Tunnel. A painting of Henry Wadsworth Longfellow, once a professor at the college, hung adjacent to a circular glass clock.

The security guard got up from his desk and walked to the front door and locked it. Forde promptly emerged from a small door in the center of the lobby and walked to the glass cabinet. He pulled out an oblong brass key that unlocked the cabinet, and carefully extracted the large leather box from its perch. Not until he had safely returned through the central door did the security guard unlock the front door and take up his position behind the desk.

Forde returned to the reading room and sat behind the reference desk. He and the other man put on white gloves, then slowly pulled out the oversized book. Their movements were precise and delicate. Once the book had been secured and freed from its packaging, Forde wrote something on a sheet of paper in front of him, grabbed another pair of gloves from his desk, then walked toward me. I sat there frozen in disbelief. I was seconds away from putting my hands on the book on which Harvard's entire legacy rested.

"Please pull the cradle toward you so that I can rest the book in it," Forde said, standing over me.

Once I had the foam cradle situated in front of me, Forde gently rested the book in its arms and handed me the gloves.

"Please touch the book only with gloved hands, and keep the book in the cradle at all times," he said. "This helps prevent the cover from getting scratched, and it protects the spine. As you can imagine, these pages are extremely brittle, so your care in turning them is also appreciated. Do you have any questions for me?"

I was almost too nervous to say anything, let alone touch a book that was three and a half centuries old.

"Can I open it?" I said.

"All yours," he said. "I'll be up at the front if you need any more assistance. Happy reading."

For the first five minutes, I couldn't bring myself to touch it. I just sat there and examined the cover, faded brown leather with no title or publication markings. Then I slowly ran my hand along the soft cover, stopping to appreciate the indentations, little nicks, and areas where the leather had been pulled and stressed. I noticed what looked like water marks, small, darkened areas that made me picture the legendary John Harvard himself spilling some of his drink while reading himself to sleep.

I looked up toward the reference desk. Forde was busy on the computer, and the other reference assistants had disappeared somewhere in the back. I opened the cover and at once appreciated the book with its interior battered and scratched. The leather was still crudely affixed to the board by some type of dense adhesive that surprisingly was still doing a decent job of holding everything together. A handwritten bookplate announced that it had once belonged to John Harvard's personal collection. The title page was equally scarred, but still very legible and in excellent condition. I ran my hand over the thick paper, which had darkened considerably around its edges. I hadn't expected to be so dazzled by its incredible history both known and unknown.

I slowly turned to the first page, read it carefully, and moved on to the next. I was surprised that the ink had remained incredibly legible over these hundreds of years, and though the words were sometimes difficult to make out because of the strange letters, I was finally able to read Reverend John Downame's original Puritanical masterpiece. I spent the next hour sitting there in the calming silence of the reading room, turning those old pages, absorbing the fiery words of an obviously spirited and opinionated preacher. "Allow your mind to abstract," Davenport had said to me in his office. So I sat back in the cushioned seat and closed my eyes, trying to think of what might have been so important about the words on these pages that an exclusive brotherhood of affluent men would adopt them as their creed and an eccentric millionaire would have them engraved on the urn of a son who might've been murdered.

34

I WAS SUDDENLY awakened by the sound of a heavy door closing. I looked up and found the reading room bustling with bursts of quiet but frenzied activity. At each of the tables at least a couple of people sat hunched over, reading books and manuscripts propped up in the foam cradles. They furiously scribbled notes in their writing pads, some even tapping away into their laptops. Forde was still seated behind the reference desk. I looked up at the clock and realized I had been asleep for just over an hour. The sun beat heavily through the open blinds. *The Christian Warfare* was still in front of me, comfortably resting in the cradle. I got up and walked over to Forde.

"How's everything going?" he asked.

"Great," I said. "Am I allowed to keep this book a little longer and look at another one at the same time."

"Sure. You're permitted to have three items out simultaneously. Do you have the title?"

"It's the same book, but I want the 1604 edition."

Forde wrinkled his forehead. "That's the first edition."

I nodded my head.

"Normally, I'd have you go to the electronic catalog and find the call number," he said. "But I've retrieved the book so much for Professor Davenport lately that I have it memorized."

"When was Professor Davenport in here last?" I asked.

"Sometime last week," he said.

Forde wrote down the number on a call slip and disappeared through the back door, and a female assistant replaced him at the desk. Her badge read VALERIE DUPONT. "Where exactly are all these rare books and manuscripts kept?" I asked her.

"Downstairs in the basement," she said. "Some in the stacks, but the more valuable items are stored in the vault."

"Where were the rare books kept before Houghton was built?"

"The Treasure Room in Widener."

"And before Widener?"

"Probably Gore Hall. That used to be the school's central library. It was demolished to make way for Widener."

"Do you know when Gore was demolished?"

"Not offhand, but give me a second." She picked up the phone and dialed a number. After a short conversation, she said, "The books were evacuated from Gore Hall, then it was demolished in 1913. Widener opened in the fall of 1915."

"I wonder where they kept the rare books collection during that two-year gap?"

"I don't know."

Forde reemerged from the back door, carrying a small book wrapped in parchment. Judging by its size, I was certain he had retrieved the wrong book.

"This is the book you requested," Forde said.

I reached my hand out.

"I'll have to carry it over to your working area," he said.

When I was seated again at the table, Forde walked over and carefully placed a small piece of felt inside the cradle before he rested the book in its arms.

"And you're sure this is the first edition of *The Christian Warfare*?" I said. I was having trouble reconciling the physical differences between the two editions. The 1634 book was almost four times the size and contained a lot more pages.

"This is definitely the first edition," he said. "The later edition that you looked at before has more than a thousand pages. This one has only six hundred seventy-six pages. Well, actually only six hundred seventy-four because two pages are missing. Please be extremely careful with this book. The pages are extremely brittle, and it's one of the most valuable books in our collection. Unlike the book you looked at earlier, I can keep this out of the vault for only two hours at a time."

I nodded my head, and quickly turned my attention to the book with Davenport's encouraging words ringing in my ears. Just as I had with the other book, I made a point of studying its physical characteristics first. It was no bigger than my hand and covered in a chestnut brown calfskin leather. Like the 1634 edition, there was no title on the cover. What I saw instead stunned me. I sat there and stared at it, forcing myself to believe what was in front of me.

I immediately recognized the Latin words around the coat of arms: *Honi Soit Qui Mal Y Pense*—"Shame to Him Who Evil Thinks." They were the words of England's most noble Order of the Garter, words Dalton and I had deduced were an inspiration for the Order of the Ancient Nine. This was a big break. I scribbled some notes in my pad, and then opened the cover. The interior was deeply weathered, the leather stretched and strained around the pointed corners and flat edges. Most prominent was a rectangular bookplate that had been glued onto the board. The design was some type of ethnographic artifact and there was the name of the owner typed underneath it:

Lawrence Waters Jenkins
Ex Libris

I wrote the name on my pad. Then I lifted up the free end of the bookplate, and I swear my heart froze when I saw the handwritten note underneath it.

From the library of King James I, title page torn

I kept looking at the words, even mouthing them as I followed the curve and dip of each letter. I wanted to make sure there was no other way to interpret what I was reading other than that King James I had actually owned this book himself. The power of that possibility paralyzed me. I didn't understand why Davenport had quizzed me about my knowledge of King James I and his insistence that I see the actual book. Now it made sense. He knew exactly what I would find, and like any good Socratic teacher, he didn't want to steal the thrill of the discovery. My skin tingled.

I looked at the reference desk. They were busy helping other patrons. I lightly ran my gloved fingers across the same pages that had once been touched by one of Europe's most powerful monarchs and whose name was associated with one of the most enduring translations of the Bible. I looked over at the title page, which while slightly torn along the top edge as the note had said, it was mostly intact and the words completely legible. Could the death of Erasmus Abbott and the mission of the Ancient Nine be explained somewhere within these 674 pages?

I turned the book over and examined the back cover. It was identical to the front, the same coat of arms surrounded by the garter's motto. I then looked on the inside of the back cover and found a different bookplate design, this one also identifying LAWRENCE W. JENKINS as the owner, but also giving his hometown of Salem, Massachusetts. Who was this man who had once owned one of the world's rarest books and then donated it to Harvard?

"I have your answer," a voice said over my shoulder.

I looked up and found Valerie standing over me.

"While Gore Hall was being demolished, all the books had to be temporarily stored, so they devised a plan to spread them out all over the university," she said. "Some books went to the lecture halls in the Yard and the Freshman Union, but almost two-thirds of the collection, including the rare books, went to Randall Hall, which had been in use as a dining hall."

"Where's Randall Hall?" I asked.

"*Was* is more like it," she said. "It used to be on the corner plot where William James Hall now stands."

I lifted up the bookplate on the front page. "Am I reading this correctly? Was this book really in the personal library of King James I?"

"Absolutely," she said without hesitation. "It's one of the greatest bequests to the library's collection in the last century. That's a handwritten notation by one of the old librarians. Someone would've written that only after making certain it was verified. We don't write in books like that anymore, so it was definitely recorded a long time ago, probably at the time of acquisition."

After she left, I went back to the book, turning the thick pages, marveling over the antiquity of the typeface and the way sentences were constructed. Though the pages had been printed on a press, the words still looked like they had been written by a calligrapher. I turned very quickly to the five hundreds, then slowed when I neared the missing pages. I read page 544, then turned the page. It jumped to 547, as I had expected it would, but what surprised me was the condition of the slit of paper that remained from the page that had contained 545 on the front and 546 on the back. It wasn't as if the page had been torn out and a jagged edge left attached to the binding. Instead, the page looked as though it had been meticulously cut with a razor. As I touched the remnant, I closed my eyes and thought about the photocopies I had seen in Davenport's office. *Abstract the mind.* In just a couple of hours, I had a page full of notes and hopefully several new pieces to the puzzle. The central question, however, remained. What was specific to those missing two pages that would drive someone to deface one of Harvard's most precious rare books? I closed my eyes for the next several minutes as my mind struggled with the possibilities. Was there a code to a royal treasure? Was there a secret they didn't want exposed? Were there words printed only on the pages of this book copy that weren't printed in others?

"I'm sorry, but time's up." I looked up at Thomas Forde, and then down at my watch. Exactly two hours. "I'm gonna have to take the 1604 book back."

"Can I ask you a question before you take it back?" I said.

"Sure."

"I think I know the name of the person who donated this book, but how do I make sure it was really that person?"

Forde opened the cover. "This bookplate lists Lawrence Jenkins," he said. "But that doesn't necessarily mean he was the one who actually donated it. In situations like this, we'd have to locate the accession records and see what was written."

"What kind of information would be written in those records?" I asked.

"Depends," he said. "Some of the records are very specific while others tend to be extremely general. It all comes down to when the book was donated and who actually recorded the acquisition. Of course, we didn't have computers back then, so unfortunately, some of the records for the older items in our collection have either been lost or misplaced."

Or stolen, I thought to myself. I still hadn't heard from Archives if they had found the missing records. "Couldn't you just type the name Lawrence Jenkins into one of the databases and see if he was the donor?" I asked.

"If only it were that simple." Forde smiled. "Sometimes we keep donor files, but depending on how far back the gift was made, we might not have the file any longer or it could be buried somewhere in Archives. Sometimes we can find out information about the donor from an accession number or the shelf list record." He examined the inside of the front cover. "Well, here's one of our answers already. This handwritten number indicates that someone from Widener assigned it to this library. This is how they used to code their books. So, the book was acquired prior to the opening of this library in 1942, when the rare books, manuscripts, and map collections were transferred here from Widener. But this also means that we wouldn't have the accession records, because they're too old. You'd have to either go to Widener to see if they still have them, or better yet, check with Archives. Many of the old records are stored in their depository."

So far, Archives had proved to be a dead end. "When can I come back and look at this book?" I asked.

"It needs to be in the vault for two hours," Forde said. "There's already another request for it in the queue. Unfortunately, you'd have to come back another day."

"The electronic catalog says that there are two missing pages from the first edition, but it doesn't say what happened to them," I said. "Now that I see the book, I realize that it's one physical page missing with 545 on the front and 546 on the back. Do you know anything about them?"

"No more than anyone else," Forde said. "But over the years, there have been all kinds of stories about what had been written on them. Ask a hundred different people, and you'll get a hundred different answers."

"Is there one story you believe more than the others?" I pressed.

"Sure. I'm obviously not as much an expert as Professor Davenport, but I did my thesis on the Kings and Queens of England. James I was a major figure. He presided over the 'golden age' of Elizabethan literature—Shakespeare, Donne, Ben Jonson, and the like."

Forde shrugged his narrow shoulders. "My guess is that while it was widely known at the time that King James was bisexual, those pages contained definitive proof in the King's own hand."

35

TWO DAYS LATER, I walked into the Archives reading room and stood in front of Peggy and her automatic smile. I was blinded by her bright yellow sweater, hot pink corduroys, and green duck boots. They still hadn't been able to locate the accession records. I told her that I had the donor's name and address.

"Maybe he was an alumnus," she said. "Let's check the directory."

She walked to a small bookcase behind the desk and quickly pulled out a thick book with a fading red cover. The words HARVARD ALUMNI DIRECTORY were still visible despite the wear. I held my breath as we searched through last names beginning with J. We found him within seconds. Lawrence Waters Jenkins graduated in the class of 1896. She wrote the name down on a call slip and disappeared through a door marked STAFF ONLY.

I went through the timeline as I waited. In 1604, Reverend John Downame writes one of the pioneering doctrines on Protestantism and Puritanical ideals, a call to break with Catholicism and practice "pure" Christianity to fight off the temptations of the devil. A copy of that book ends up in the private library of King James I. Over the years, the book is sold who knows how many times until it's acquired by Lawrence Jenkins, Harvard class of 1896. Assuming that Jenkins donated the book after he graduated, then it would've joined the library collection in Gore Hall sometime between 1896 and 1913.

When Gore was demolished in 1913 to make way for Widener, it would have been transferred to Randall Hall. In 1915, when Widener opens its doors, the rare books are transferred from Randall to the Treasure Room in the new library. *The Christian Warfare* stays there for the next twenty-seven years until Houghton is built in 1942. The Ancient Nine's 1936 succession book includes a creed taken directly from *The Christian Warfare*, which means they saw the text before it went to Houghton. During those years, hundreds, if not thousands, of people would've had access to *The Christian Warfare*, especially at a time when security was practically nonexistent. So, everything seemed to boil down to two critical questions: Who removed those two missing pages? And why?

"Good news," Peggy said, returning from the back with a thin manila folder. "They found this downstairs in the stacks."

She took a seat next to me, and I realized that she was equally intrigued by the mysterious circumstances surrounding *The Christian Warfare*. But before she could open the folder, the phone rang, and she reluctantly went back to the reference desk. The folder contained three old newspaper clippings. The first was from *The Boston Globe*, 1961.

L.W. JENKINS,
MUSEUM HEAD
49 YEARS, DIES

PEABODY, Apr. 21—Lawrence W. Jenkins, 88, director emeritus of the Peabody Museum in Salem, died last night at his home, 35 Newcastle Rd. Mr. Jenkins retired from the museum in 1949 after 49 years as its curator.

A native of Salem, he was graduated from Harvard in 1896. He was a charter member of the American Assn. of Museums; a fellow of the American Anthropological Society; a member of the Society of Nautical Research of London, of the American Antiquarian Society and Massachusetts Historical Society; the Colonial Society of Massachusetts, and the New England Historical Society. He also was a member of the Essex Institute in Salem, serving as its vice president from 1925 to 1951.

Mr. Jenkins enlisted in the First Corps of Cadets in Boston in 1892. In World War I, he joined the 15th Massachusetts State Guard, retiring in 1920 as a lieutenant colonel. He was also a member of the Sons of the American Revolution and clerk of the Salem Marine Society for 25 years.

Funeral services will be held at 2 p.m. Monday at the First Unitarian Church, Salem.

I read through the other obituaries, which reported similar information. On rereading the *Boston Herald* clipping, something caught my eye. In the third paragraph, the bit about the Colonial Society of Massachusetts stood out. I had seen that name before in another newspaper clipping. I kept repeating the name until the image popped in my mind. Collander Abbott's obituary. It had been listed under his many civic activities. I remember wondering to myself if they reenacted events like the Puritans landing on Plymouth Rock.

I walked over to a computer and started searching for information on the Colonial Society of Massachusetts. It didn't take long for the computer to retrieve the information. The society was founded in 1892 as a nonprofit educational foundation to promote the study of Massachusetts history from the earliest settlement through the first decades of the nineteenth century. Its membership was originally limited to descendants of the Massachusetts Bay Colony or Plymouth colonists, and the number of resident members had been capped at two hundred. Its stated chief business was publishing documents related to the early history of Massachusetts. Much of its work was carried out in its headquarters in a Boston landmark building at 87 Mt. Vernon Street. It was one of only a few remaining private houses built by the legendary architect Charles Bulfinch.

Then I thought about the passage engraved on Erasmus Abbott's urn and the Ancient Nine creed. Was it just a coincidence that those passages came from a rare historical book that was once owned by Lawrence Jenkins, Collander Abbott's fellow Colonial Society member?

Peggy returned with the 1901 and 1906 class bulletins, two thin, cloth-bound books that had the years stamped on the cover. "Sometimes major gifts from alumni were announced at their reunions. So I thought these might help."

I turned the pages to the class of 1896 section, but there wasn't any mention of Jenkins or his donation.

"Bingo," she said. She had been looking through the 1906 book. "It says here, 'Mr. Lawrence Jenkins made the auspicious donation of a fully preserved 1604 first edition of *The Christian Warfare* on the event of his tenth-year reunion.'"

I now could tighten the timeline by ten years. Someone had very neatly cut out those two pages between 1906 and 1936. But the two critical questions still remained: Who and why?

I CAUGHT UP with Dalton after practice that night, and we talked about everything that I had discovered. He was planning on flying down to New York the next afternoon to have another look around Wild Winds. After we had finished talking, I studied for a couple of hours in the room, standing up while I read Kant to keep myself from falling asleep. I was in a solid groove when Percy came home, eager to talk about how he had gotten into the Lampoon and how much better he was feeling about the Spee Club rejection. As happy as I was that his life had been restored, when he knocked on my bedroom door for the fifth time that night looking to chat, I decided to finish my reading at Lamont.

Midterms were only ten days away, which meant a packed library. I found a tiny stall on the second-floor mezzanine and set up camp like everyone else. With my headphones blocking out the noise, I got through my Orgo problem set rather quickly before taking out my biology text and getting to work on Mendelian genetics. After reading a couple of chapters, Ashley came to mind, and I started thinking about her birthday in two days and what I would get her. Ms. Garrett had told me in confidence that Ashley had never wanted a party growing up, and how Ms. Garrett now regretted that she had obliged. I didn't have much left in my bank account, but I wanted to somehow make this a memorable birthday for her.

On my first hourly break, I went upstairs to find out whatever I could about Forde's revelation that King James I was rumored to be bisexual. I looked through a couple of encyclopedias, but they steered clear of the topic of his sexuality, instead focusing on his political accomplishments and policy miscalculations during his reign. But then I came across a couple of essays and a book that had been written about his life. Unlike the encyclopedias and earlier writings, they confronted the issue head on.

James I was suspected of being homosexual as early as his teenage years, when he supposedly entered into an improper relationship with his older cousin, Esmé Stuart—Seigneur d'Aubigny who was the Duke of Lennox and a French courtier. The Scottish nobility and court disapproved of the relationship and eventually arranged the kidnapping of King James, during which time he was forced to issue a proclamation against Esmé, who eventually fled Scotland. While James had seven children with his wife, Anne of Denmark, he was also known to have had close and intimate relationships with several men.

The author went on to assert that one of the King's closest advisors, George Villiers, whom the King made Duke of Buckingham, was the great love of his life. The King argued in front of the Privy Council that not only did he love Villiers more than anyone else, but he had the right to do so. King James put Villiers in charge of foreign policy, which according to most historians turned out to be a considerable mistake. Some accounts even had King James publicly calling Villiers his wife. I finished reading several more essays regarding King James's sexuality, and returned to the reading room. I felt like I had done enough work to report back to Davenport. I was hopeful that he would now help me connect the dots.

THE FOLLOWING AFTERNOON, I found Professor Davenport sitting at his desk in the basement of Andover Hall, wearing what was most likely the same corduroy suit. As I walked into the cramped office, he was struggling to keep his balance as he reached for a book on the top shelf with his cane.

"Let me get that, Professor," I said, rushing into the room and leaping over the stacks of papers on the floor.

When he turned toward me, he lost his balance and almost toppled over before dropping his cane and grabbing on to the bookshelf.

"Perfect timing," he said. "That book up there is giving me fits."

I helped him out of the chair, then stepped up and reached back to retrieve the book. It was a 1905 guide to early churches. I handed it to him before squeezing into a seat near his desk.

"How goes the research?" he said after catching his breath.

"I know a lot more than I did the last time I was here," I said. "And I actually looked at *The Christian Warfare.*"

He strained his muscles into a smile. "Indeed, you have made progress, young man," he said. "And I would assume that you've answered some of your own questions." He slid his chair close to me with great effort. "Let's talk about what you've found."

I pulled out my pad and quickly skimmed my notes. I had highlighted my short list of questions for quick reference. I decided to discuss my findings in reverse order. "I was looking into the life of King James," I said. "I hadn't known that he was bisexual."

"A fact that has been known since his reign," Davenport said. "And he was not the first monarch to have such a liberal sex life. The monarchists of the day were scandalized by the *public* revelation of the King's personal indiscretions. He had become, by default, the symbolic leader of Christianity. Ironically, his aberrant behavior flew in the face of Christian principles as spelled out in the Bible. You must also remember that King James had been baptized Catholic but raised by tutors, the most influential being a staunch Protestant Calvinist by the name of George Buchanan. He was kidnapped early in his reign for a year when his sexual relationship with Stuart was discovered. His captors forced him to denounce his lover, who was a Roman Catholic and believed to be influencing his policy. History shows that James was one of the most intelligent men ever to ascend the throne, and he immortalized his legend by commissioning a new Bible translation bearing his name. To this day, the King James version is still one of the most widely used Bibles in the world." Davenport took a sip from a coffee-stained mug on his desk. "So, what did you make of the book?"

I looked down at my notes. "I found out that the 1604 edition of the book was donated by an alum named Lawrence Jenkins. He was a graduate in the class of 1896 and the former curator of the Peabody Museum in Salem."

"Good work, Mr. Collins," Davenport said. "Yes, Jenkins was a great historian in his own right and an immense collector of historical documents, books, and artifacts. I had the opportunity to meet him once. He was an extremely prominent and philanthropic man who served Harvard and this state very faithfully."

Davenport explained that Jenkins was aware that the John Harvard book wasn't a first edition. As a serious collector, with tenacity and deep pockets, he finally tracked down and acquired a first edition for his personal collection. I shared my discovery that Jenkins was acknowledged for his book donation on his tenth reunion. I didn't share with him how I had triangulated the dates the pages must have gone missing, because if he asked me about the 1936 date, I'd have to reveal the Ancient Nine's succession book.

"The reunion bulletin said that Jenkins donated a fully preserved book," I said. "Do you think that was accurate?"

"I'd bet my life on it," Davenport said confidently. "It's unlikely a collector of Jenkins's stature would purchase a book with missing pages, especially since there are other complete copies in existence."

"I looked through the 1604 edition," I said. "From what I could tell, it looked like someone had meticulously cut those pages with a razor. The other pages before and after it were in perfect condition."

"Those pages were definitely targeted, and whoever did it knew what they were doing," Davenport said.

He talked about the infamous Williams case and how he had met the man on several occasions in the library. Then he recounted the attempt on the Gutenberg Bible. "And those are just the cases we know about," he said. "With a library system that has over six million books, I'm sure there have been probably hundreds, if not thousands, of thefts."

I looked down at my list of questions. "That explains opportunity," I said, "but I still have a problem with motive."

"I'm listening," he said.

"There are seven other copies of the first edition."

"That's correct."

"And there are microfilm copies of the first edition available to everyone."

"That's correct also."

"Why would someone steal those specific pages when other copies of those pages existed?"

"Very nice, Mr. Collins," he said. "You've arrived at one of the most critical questions. You must stretch your mind." He tapped his arthritic finger against his temple. "You're halfway there. There'd be no reason for someone to steal those pages, since the text could be acquired elsewhere. So why take them?"

I shrugged. "It wasn't a random act of vandalism. Maybe there was something on those specific pages that wasn't in the other books."

Davenport nodded slowly, and the aged leather seat squeaked underneath his frail bones. "Someone must've gone through considerable effort and risk to steal those pages. You're asking the right questions."

"This book is special for two reasons," I thought aloud. "First, it was King James's personal book, and second, two pages have been stolen from it. There must be a connection."

"You're thinking." Davenport smiled. "How about this? A book from a private library might mean that private notes were written in it."

"King James wrote something on those pages," I said.

Davenport nodded with another easy smile.

"What do scholars think he wrote?" I said.

"Depends on whom you ask." He reached down to his desk for another gulp of coffee. "I've spent a great deal of my professional life pursuing those two pages and their importance," he said. "My first wife almost left me over them, but that's another story for another time. I believe the King wrote a poem on either one or both of those pages." Davenport leaned forward in his chair, nostrils flared. "Make no mistake, young man," he said. "This poem was like no other. Many of us believe that this poem could've been his own admission of sorts of his homosexuality. A very valuable piece of history that scholars have been seeking for centuries."

36

I WAS FEELING proud of myself as I boarded the train in Harvard Square with a dozen pink roses, a box of Godiva chocolates, and Prince's *Lovesexy* CD. I had called Ms. Garrett to set it all up. Ashley wouldn't be getting home from class until seven thirty that night, which meant I had more than enough time to get to her place in Roxbury before she got home. I purposely hadn't called her earlier in the day, hoping that she would believe I had forgotten her birthday. I could barely contain my excitement thinking of the look on her face when she walked through the door and saw me sitting there with her birthday presents. I had willingly emptied my bank account, knowing that the smile on her face would be worth every penny.

I had carefully written down the directions from Ms. Garrett. I took the Red Line to Park Street, made a couple of transfers, and then got off on a busy street on the edge of Roxbury. As I found myself on a five-minute walk through a run-down neighborhood of vacant lots and dilapidated tenement houses, I started worrying that I had either made a mistake in taking the directions or missed a turn. I couldn't imagine Ashley living in this kind of neighborhood. It reminded me of the toughest parts of southwest Chicago that even I had always avoided. Stripped, rusted cars sat on lopsided cinder blocks, and groups of teenagers in baggy coats and tilted baseball caps clustered on the corner, staring menacingly as I passed. I was about to turn around and walk back to the train station, but then I saw Shirley Street and hooked a right as Ms. Garrett had instructed.

Multifamily shoebox houses lined the narrow sidewalks. They looked old and badly in disrepair, chipping paint on crumbling façades, hanging wood slats blowing in the wind, holes in windows closed with black electric tape, and many of the front doors reinforced by a heavily fortified exterior screen door. Most of the streetlights were out. The farther I walked, the more I understood why Ashley had always been so determined that I not escort her home.

I finally reached her house, a modest two-story building with yellow vinyl siding whose color had faded in some places and thick patches of dirt had collected in others. A broken-down van sat in the alley adjacent to the house, and the front porch listed slightly to one side. I climbed the uneven steps and found her last name underneath the second of two buttons. I pushed it, and moments later a faint buzzer sounded. I opened the front door and entered a dark, cold foyer. A steep set of rickety steps led to a door on the second floor. I scaled the steps with their worn carpet and as I neared the top, the door quickly opened. A tall woman in a simple black skirt and red blouse stood framed in the entrance. She and Ashley could've easily passed for sisters.

"Nice to finally meet you, Spenser," she said. "I've heard so much about you."

"Thanks for allowing me to come over," I said, stepping into the apartment, where I was immediately filled by the sweet aroma of a freshly baked cake. The rooms were tiny, but they were immaculate and filled with pride. It suddenly dawned on me that in many respects, this four-room apartment had more dignity and grace than any of the mansions I had visited the last couple of weeks. The Garretts made the most of what little they had, and for that I had enormous respect.

I immediately felt comfortable with Ms. Garrett, which was unusual for me since I had never been big on the parent thing. I always believed that once you met the girl's parents, if anything went wrong in the relationship, the guilt would only be magnified. But Ms. Garrett reminded me a lot of my own mother, young and attractive, left alone to raise a single child under difficult financial circumstances, yet hopeful that hard work and strong faith would lift her family beyond their present condition.

By the time we heard Ashley putting her key into the door, Ms. Garrett and I had become fast friends, and our small surprise party had been arranged. The chocolate cake with twenty candles had been placed in the middle of the kitchen table surrounded by my flowers and gifts. I squeezed into the living room and waited while Ms. Garrett met Ashley at the door.

I heard them exchange greetings; then moments later Ashley walked into the living room. I was standing next to the door and yelled, "Happy Birthday!" when she walked in.

A look of shock exploded behind her eyes. I expected her to laugh or smile, but she did neither. Instead, she bunched her forehead into a frown and said, "What are you doing here?"

"It's your birthday," I said. "I wanted to surprise you." I rested my hand on her shoulder, but she knocked it away.

"You didn't ask if you could come over," she said.

"It wouldn't've been a surprise if I did," I said.

"You should've asked me first," she said, dropping her book bag to the floor. "I don't like these kinds of surprises."

Ms. Garrett had been standing there quietly in the doorway. She finally stepped in and said, "Ashley, Spenser called me yesterday, and we thought this would be a nice way to celebrate your birthday since you've never had a party before."

"Well, it isn't," she said. "If everyone wasn't so busy planning things behind my back, then I could've had something to say about how I wanted *my* birthday to be celebrated."

I was happy Ms. Garrett was standing there, because at the moment I was speechless.

"Where are your manners, Ashley?" Ms. Garrett said firmly. "Birthday or no birthday, Spenser is still a guest in this house and you will treat him as such."

"This was a terrible idea," Ashley said behind clenched teeth. "You don't just go to a person's house without asking."

I started feeling like someone had swung a bowling ball and hit me right in the gut. How could something that seemed so right end up being so wrong? I wanted to crawl into a hole somewhere and die.

"I have a cake for you in the kitchen," Ms. Garrett said.

"And I brought you presents," I said.

But Ashley just stood there with her hands folded across her chest. She frowned at her mother, and then turned to me. "Thank you, Spenser, but I've had a long day, and I don't want a cake or presents. I just want to be left alone."

"I'm sorry," I said, backing up out of the room. "I thought this would make you happy. I'll go."

"Don't, Spenser," Ms. Garrett said.

But Ashley didn't ask me to stay and I could see it in her eyes that she wanted me gone. Maybe even out of her life altogether. Too embarrassed to prolong the agony, I quickly thanked Ms. Garrett, took a look at the presents sitting on the kitchen table, and raced down the steps and into the cold night. It wasn't until I was outside that I realized tears were racing down my face in buckets.

TWO DAYS FOLLOWING the debacle with Ashley, Dalton and I agreed to meet in one of the draft studios of the Carpenter Center, one of the most controversial buildings on campus. Built by the French master architect Le Corbusier, it had been reviled by the traditionalists for its modern, geometric design, which lacked any connection at all to the classic Georgian brick buildings that characterized Harvard architecture. Critics had described it as "two elephants copulating," but it was built for the visual arts, and given that group's proclivity for all things eccentric and unique, they couldn't have been more thrilled to call the peculiar-looking building home.

We found a small unlocked room at the end of the floor squeezed between the janitor's closet and the exit stairwell. A row of light boxes lined the back wall. Dalton took out the photo he found tucked away in a box in the basement of Wild Winds. It had been sticking out of a small book, the 1950 Delphic Club directory.

"Let's look at the photo first," Dalton said. Dalton removed the black-and-white photo from an envelope in his backpack. The three torches were centered in the bottom edge. He brought the loupe to his eye.

"I think they're wearing some type of powder," he finally said. "Their skin color is too perfect."

I looked over his shoulder and immediately counted the figures. There were nine of them.

"There's the reflection," Dalton said. "I can just make out his forehead and one of his eyes. Something is covering the rest of his face."

He finally handed me the loupe. I started with the five men who were seated. They were all wearing dark clothes and ties with some type of decorative brooch clasping their capes in front of their necks. They held up lighted torches in their right hands. Their legs were all crossed the same, the right ankle over the left. Then I looked into their pale somber faces. I moved to the standing men who were dressed the same as those seated. They had torches held high in their right hands and their left hands resting on the right shoulders of the men sitting beneath them. No one smiled.

I scanned the perimeter of the photo, picking out the face Dalton had mentioned in one of the windows. I knew right away it was a black man. He was mostly obscured by a rectangular object, but one of his eyes and part of his nose and mouth were visible. His muscular neck plugged into a broad shoulder. What was he doing there?

"Are you thinking what I'm thinking?" Dalton said.

I nodded. "This could be the Ancient Nine."

"And from the looks of it, they're involved in some kind of ceremony."

"But why would they let someone photograph them?" I said. "It totally violates their secrecy."

"That's true," Dalton said. "But the secrecy isn't violated if the person who photographed them already knew they existed."

My mind suddenly made the connection. "Moss Sampson?" I said, grabbing the loupe and looking at the photo again.

"Bingo," Dalton said. "He'd be the only one they'd trust. He was their enforcer, the protector of their secrets. He could be the one who killed Erasmus Abbott that night."

"So, they trust Sampson with everything," I said. "But then he kills Abbott."

"And then they pay off Sampson to keep their secrets protected, and he quietly disappears."

We both looked down at the photo again.

"You think they're sitting in the Delphic courtyard?" Dalton asked.

"Maybe," I said, looking at the picture again. "I was only there for about forty minutes before we left for the outing, so I don't remember a lot. But the way this picture is taken and those columns in the background make me think they were sitting underneath the portico attached to the back face of the mansion."

"We need to be certain of the location," Dalton said. "If we can confirm where this picture was taken, we might be able to confirm the location of the chamber."

"We can't just walk back into the courtyard," I said. "It's locked and completely fenced in."

"But the Bureau of Study Counsel building isn't," Dalton said. "And its upper floors look over the Delphic courtyard. We just need to find a window with a view."

I thought about the article I had read on Vido Aras, the Dorchester man who almost got away with the Gutenberg Bible by hiding in the building near the end of the day. Once everyone left for the night, he emerged.

"Where's the book?" I said.

Dalton reached into his backpack and pulled out a thin blue book with gold lettering.

THE
DELPHIC CLUB
1950

I pulled back the cover, and the first page contained an old black-and-white photograph of the mansion in winter. The black gate surrounding the mansion was much shorter than the one that guarded it now, and there weren't any trees or shrubs hiding the first-floor windows. Piles of snow covered the sidewalk and street, and one of the gates of Harvard Yard was barely visible in the distance. The book began with a short foreword, followed by a list of three trustees. I recognized two of the names, Stanford L. Jacobs III and Collander Abbott. The last name was Guyton Jennings. The next several pages gave a detailed history of the club and how it had grown from the 1846 Charter of the Delta Phi Fraternity with a small rented room on Brattle Street into the exclusive Delphic Club and its mansion at 9 Linden Street.

The next few pages described the responsibilities of the trustees who officially constituted the Delphic Trust. The trust not only held the title to the club property, but also held and managed the endowment funds. A detailed history spelled out how the trust funds were acquired and which members had made donations. A special provision had been set forth that the income earned from the endowment would be used to help defray the costs of membership fees for those students who might need assistance. The remainder would be used to cover land taxes and other operating expenses.

"Turn to page eighty-three," Dalton said.

I flipped through the thick pages until I had settled on a listing of the classes of 1922 and 1923. I ran my finger down the list and was only halfway through the page before I spotted what had also caught Dalton's attention. Robert Mead Swigert, Board of Governors 1915, 240 Park Avenue, New York City.

"Who is he?" I asked.

"Beats the hell outta me," Dalton said. "But remember the RMS we were trying to figure out. Well, this fits perfectly."

"Yeah, but I'm sure if I looked through the rest of these names, I could find others with the initials RMS."

"You sure could," Dalton said. "There are seven others."

"So why are you stuck on this name?"

"Because of his street address," Dalton said. "His is the only one with the number 240 in it, which makes it a perfect match for RMS 240."

I looked down at Swigert's entry, wondering who this man had been and how or why he might be part of this mysterious poem that could unlock the answer to so many questions.

37

❧

TUESDAY NIGHT WAS one of the most embarrassing nights of my athletic career. For the first time since I had been at Harvard, we played to a standing-room-only crowd. When I rode up to the back of the gym an hour and a half before game time, I could see people lined up all the way from the box office in front of the building, into the parking lot that ran up against the football stadium, and onto the sidewalk underneath the steps of Blodgett Pool. Seeing the massive waves of people entering the facilities complex sent the adrenaline surging. When I opened the back door where the players always entered, a rush of wet heat hit me in the face. The bleachers were packed all the way to the top row, and the band was already banging away, trying to keep the restless crowd entertained. This was only a scrimmage, but the Boston University Terriers had a six-foot-eight sophomore forward who was one of the best players in the country. He was so dominant that many were convinced he would skip out on his last two years of school and enter the NBA draft once the season was over.

The energy in the locker room matched the intensity in the gymnasium. Run-DMC blasted out "My Adidas," and guys punched their fists against the metal lockers. When Coach came in, everyone settled down. He scrapped his usual pregame routine of methodically reviewing our offensive and defensive plays, and instead spent twenty minutes sitting on a stool in the middle of a circle, talking in a low voice about what it was like growing up the son of a garbage truck driver in a community of doctors and lawyers and three country clubs. It was all about embracing a position of disadvantage rather than fearing it. "Underdogs play the game not for championships or trophies that end up dusty and forgotten on a shelf," he said. "They play the game to protect their honor."

I looked around the room when he finished his speech, and I swear half the guys were tearing up or trying not to. I was somewhere in between.

We went out on the court the most fired up we had ever been before a game. Even Morrissey, the smallest and most congenial guy on our team, was so charged up that in the lay-up line he kept looking across the other side of the court at the much taller and stronger BU players, talking trash about what we were going to do to them once the game started. We had to reel him in a couple of times, afraid he might start a melee before the first whistle had even blown. Our fans, normally quiet and mildly interested, were surprisingly boisterous as the band whooped them up by playing our fight song—"Ten Thousand Men of Harvard"—as courageously as they played it at the always-spirited ice hockey games. Even I got caught up in the moment and started believing that we could actually beat the Terriers.

That pipe dream lasted about as long as a Miami rain shower. The humiliation started at the opening buzzer. One of their shorter players jumped up against our seven-footer for the tip-off and not only did he win control of the tap, but converted it into an immediate fast break and a two-handed reverse dunk that even our fans couldn't help but cheer. And the rest of the game was all downhill from there as they tortured and decimated us on our own court in front of what felt like half the population of Boston. By halftime, they had more than doubled our score, and we sat in the locker room dazed and embarrassed by the pounding. It was the first time I had ever felt like taking off my uniform and surrendering. Basketball had been an important source of pride for me, especially since my mother had always told me how proud my father would've been to see his son play and love the game as he had. Tonight was an embarrassment for me on a much more visceral level.

The second half started off better than the first because they played their second team and we kept in our first. Coach continued to rant and scream on the sidelines like a lunatic, and our fans started cheering for anything, regardless of how small, that went well for us. Mitch blocked the shot of a guard almost half his size, something that he should've been able to do blindfolded, and judging by the crowd's wild applause, you would've thought he just made a half-court shot backwards.

Coach pulled me after my fourth foul, and as I sat on the bench seething, my eyes drifted into the bleachers. That's when I spotted her. Ashley was sitting there in the middle of the crowd, composed and beautiful and expressionless. I wished I could've shriveled up and died right there. I was praying that she had just walked in, but I knew damn well that she had seen every second of our beating. Our eyes met across the gym, and I slumped in my seat as if that would make me invisible. It was the first time I had seen or heard from her since the birthday disaster.

The final horn sounded, and we limped into the locker room on the wrong side of a fifty-point thrashing. Coach was too embarrassed and upset to talk to us, so he sent Zimowski in, who made a valiant effort to remain positive. But nothing he said really mattered. It was like telling a painter who had lost both his hands in an accident that at least he still had his arms.

I took my time showering and changing, hoping that Ashley would get tired of waiting and leave. She didn't. She was sitting by herself on the bottom bleacher when I walked out of the locker room. She greeted me with a kiss on the lips.

"Maybe we should lose more often," I said, walking her out the back door and into the cold. She wrapped her arm around mine as we headed toward the river. The crowds had dissipated, and the grounds were empty.

"You played hard," she said.

I knew she was trying to lift my spirits, but those were the most dreaded words an athlete can hear after a bruising defeat.

"We got crushed, Ashley," I said. "You don't have to sugarcoat it. Doesn't make it any better. Just call it like it is."

"But you never gave up," she said.

The second most dreaded set of words.

"Please, Ashley, we played like shit," I said. "I know you're trying to be supportive, but sympathy isn't gonna change the fact that we just got our heads handed to us on our own court in front of thousands of people. The papers are gonna kill us tomorrow."

"Then what do you want me to say?"

"The truth."

"That you sucked."

"Yes."

"That you guys looked like children playing against men."

The brutal honesty felt good. "Yes."

"And that I could've played better than half your team."

I stopped at the foot of Anderson Memorial Bridge. "Now, let's not get carried away," I said. "We agreed on honesty, not creativity."

We walked up to the top of the bridge and stopped to look along the river. The night was clear, and we could see all the way to the Citgo sign towering above the buildings of downtown Boston. A small stream of cars raced along Storrow and Memorial Drives, and the Harvard houses on the banks of the Charles lit up the dark sky. Hundreds of small windows glowed like rows of prayer candles burning at the altar. A lone sculler glided his boat in the black water. His movements were rhythmic and efficient, perfectly matching the tranquility of the still night.

"You're being too hard on yourself," Ashley said. "BU is a top Division One team. How do you expect to compete with a school that offers athletic scholarships?"

"That's a tired excuse, and you know it," I said. "Tonight was an absolute embarrassment. I don't care how much better another team is, there's no reason to play like we did. They came into our house and made us look like a high school team. We're not gonna win every game, but I be damned if we have to play like a bunch of pansies. That's why I'm so mad. We played like we knew we couldn't win."

She ran her hand over my head, and it felt good having her touch me like that. "I've never seen you so angry before," she said. "I thought you were going to hit the ref when he called that fourth foul on you."

"Trust me, I thought hard about it," I said.

We stood there silent for a moment, the sound of the water slapping against the concrete posts of the bridge. The cut of the wind made my eyes water. I spotted the lights of a helicopter in the distance as it swept over the downtown skyline.

"At least you looked cute in your shorts," she said, wrapping her arm around my waist and squeezing me. "A couple of the girls next to me were talking about you the entire game. I didn't know you had such a big fan club."

"That makes two of us," I said.

"They kept going on about how good-looking you were and how much they wished they could go out on a date with you. I was having a hard time keeping my dinner down."

"Stop trying to make me feel better."

"You said you wanted the truth, right?"

"More than I want sympathy."

I found a rock on the railing of the bridge and threw it side-armed into the water. It was a perfect skimmer, hopping four times on the water's surface before disappearing. She squeezed my arm tighter, and I felt the anger drain out of my body. We stood like that for a couple of minutes before I said, "Somehow standing here with you makes everything else seem so unimportant."

"Do you mean that?" she asked.

"Of course I do."

I grabbed and held her from behind. Then when I looked down at her, I could see that she was crying. "What's wrong?" I said.

"Nothing."

"Nothing? You're crying."

"No, I'm not. It's just the wind making my eyes water." She turned away from me, but I could still see the tears sliding down her face.

"You're breaking our promise to each other," I said. "We agreed never to tell lies, regardless of how tough the truth."

She turned and faced me. "Okay, fine. There's something I should tell you, but I don't want to."

The ominous tone of her voice made my stomach tighten. My mind raced through all the bad possibilities. I just knew she was going to say that she was hooking back up with an old boyfriend or she was dying from some incurable disease. I tightened my stomach for the blow. But she kept looking at me without saying anything.

"Godammit, Ashley, what is it?" I said.

"I can't," she said. "I'm afraid."

"Jesus Christ, Ashley. You should know by now that you can tell me anything. I can handle it."

"You swear?"

"Scout's honor," I said, crossing my heart.

That brought a small smile. "But you were never a scout."

I wondered how someone could look so beautiful even when they cried. She looked up and closed her eyes. Then when she opened them, she said, "I love you, Spenser Collins."

I had a temporary moment of dissociation where I felt like my body and its senses were completely disconnected. A fog passed through my brain. Then the words finally sank in, and I brought her into me. Hard.

"I've loved you since the minute I first saw you," I said.

Then I kissed her like I had never kissed anyone before.

38

THE DELPHIC NEVER told me that I had been officially cut from the punch, but they didn't have to bother. Dalton and I were certain that Brathwaite and Jacobs had seen to it that my name was quickly removed from consideration. It felt bittersweet. I knew from the beginning I was a long shot to make it all the way through, but after getting this far, I had actually believed it was possible. I already had visions of what the rooms upstairs looked like, with their antique furniture and polished oak bookcases. I would be the first poor kid from the South Side of Chicago to have his name engraved alongside the chosen progeny of the most elite families in the country. A teenage fantasy swallowed whole by old-world reality. I didn't want to admit it, but after all that I had been through, the rejection stung. How could I not take it personally?

For those lucky punchees who remained, the clubs had entered the no-contact period, which meant the clubs couldn't contact any of the punchees until the entering class had been elected.

This was also one of the most important weeks on Harvard's social calendar for reasons that had nothing to do with the final clubs. An entire week of parties and pep rallies would lead up to the 105th installment of the Harvard–Yale football game, which Harvard was hosting. BEAT YALE signs and Harvard banners blanketed the venerable brick buildings in the Yard, while businesses in the Square hung up Harvard posters in their windows and offered special Game-week discounts to college ID holders. Even our curmudgeonly professors showed some school spirit, taking every opportunity during their usually somber, no-nonsense lectures to poke fun at the Yalies and triggering a round of applause amongst those of us unaccustomed to seeing their playful side.

Major papers across the country ran stories about the Game's long-standing tradition as the front pages of *The Boston Globe, The New York Times,* and *The Washington Post* displayed pictures of successful middle-aged couples wrapped in traditional raccoon fur coats, tailgating behind shiny Range Rovers and long Mercedes-Benzes.

Game day was ideal football weather—chilly but not too cold, overcast but no real threat of rain. As the sun climbed higher, thicker waves of fans flooded the narrow streets of Cambridge. This was more than a football game; it was an absolute spectacle. More than seventy thousand people, not all of them planning on actually watching the Game, took over the streets running from the Square all the way down to the river and over into the Soldiers Field. I met up with a couple of my teammates, and we joined the march of bodies to the stadium. A walk that normally took ten minutes took almost half an hour. We arrived to find ourselves in the midst of one massive fall picnic. Millionaire alumni sipped champagne and vintage Bordeaux as their argyle-sweater-wearing classmates tossed footballs and Frisbees on the freshly cut lawn.

The luminaries had already claimed their real estate. Senator Ted Kennedy, class of '54, and his clan held down a prominent position in the first parking lot, eating on linen-covered tables while being served by two women in dark uniforms. I couldn't help but think of Bickerstaff and that Spanish A final exam.

Ninety-eight-year-old and onetime political scion Hamilton Fish III, class of 1910, sat in a wicker chair in the south parking lot, bundled in several layers that included a hand-sewn Harvard quilt from another era. He patiently received a long line of well-wishers waiting to kiss the ring. There had even been sightings of Vice President George Bush, now President-elect Bush, Yale

'48, and his army of Secret Service agents. He had been positioned east of the stadium under a tent that had been secured with a ring of state trooper cruisers and long black SUVs with multiple antennae sticking out from the hood. An ambulance, a requisite part of the vice-presidential motorcade, idled nearby.

The actual outcome of the Game itself was of little consequence, except the bragging rights it brought the victor. I quickly learned that this was not Alabama versus Ohio State. For this contest, the numbers on the scoreboard would always take a backseat to the numbers that really mattered—like how many presidents the colleges had put into the White House or how many justices they sat on the Supreme Court. Harvard was far ahead on this score: 6–3, thanks to Bush's recent win over Dukakis. Many people never even bothered leaving the tailgates, and most of those who did only entered the stadium at halftime, when their champagne had run dry or their canisters of caviar were empty. This crowd even cheered differently. They didn't yell and clap like most football fans. Rather they spoke complete, grammatically correct sentences, saying things like, "What a magnificent play!" and "Thrash them, Harvard!" Sometimes it was difficult to tell if they were watching a football game or croquet match.

My most enduring image of the crowded stadium came after a second-quarter touchdown by running back Tony Hinz which cut Yale's lead to three points. When the Harvard side of the stadium rose in unison, it was not to clap, but to jingle car keys in a massive show of approval. I watched in awe as thousands of Jaguar, Mercedes, and Rolls-Royce keys dangled in the air as the band ripped into an exuberant rendition of "Ten Thousand Men of Harvard."

For those interested enough to keep score, we lost the Game that year by nine points after the Harvard offense failed to convert a defensive fumble recovery into a score. The stadium emptied after the final whistle, and the real parties began as alumni flooded back across the river into the Yard and upperclassmen houses sprawled along the winding banks of the Charles. They roamed nostalgically with their children and grandchildren in tow, pointing out where they had roomed and promising the younger generations that they too would fulfill their destiny on these hallowed grounds.

By Monday, the expensive European cars and limousines had vacated campus, and those of us who remained took our time to recuperate from the long weekend. Most of us skipped classes that morning in a post-Game tradition, not rolling out of bed until late that afternoon. Thanksgiving break started on Wednesday and most of campus was already getting a jump on the holiday and heading out of town. That night, Dalton and I were back behind the locked door of the study room in the Lowell House tunnels. He had the enlarged photograph of the Ancient Nine and a copy of Moss Sampson's old police file.

"It's still hard to tell if it's him," Dalton said over my shoulder as we compared the blown-up photograph that had the man's reflection in the window with Sampson's prison photograph.

Dalton held up a paper full of handwritten notes from the police file. "It says here that he came from Beulah, Mississippi, then he moved to a town called Rosedale, where he worked as a short-order cook at the White Dog Tavern."

"Talk about a weird coincidence," I said. "My father was from Beulah, Mississippi. The name stuck with me. My mother once joked that we had more people living on our block in Chicago than the entire population of Beulah."

"Maybe your father knew Moss Sampson," Dalton said.

I shrugged my shoulders. "I doubt it. Sampson was probably much older than my father. They probably didn't live in Beulah at the same time."

"Do you ever speak to your father?"

"Never. But my mother said they were a small family. She met them once when my father took her home, then didn't see them again until his funeral. His parents died young. One of his relatives let him some money. That's about all I know."

Dalton looked down at his notes. "It says that Sampson spent time in the Mississippi State Penitentiary for murdering two people. The governor granted him clemency in 1923 after the ACLU argued he had been coerced into a confession. He moved up here to Dorchester, leaving his girlfriend and son back in Beulah."

"Makes you wonder if the members knew his history before they hired him to work at the Delphic."

"Unlikely. It was the early 1900s. They didn't have computers or fax machines. Everything was in paper files. It was easy back then to just pack up, move away, and start a new."

I thought about the last line of the poem. *Now stands as our protector with loyalty and pride.* Then there were those letters RMS. "Could the poem be talking about Sampson?" I said. "*Our protector with loyalty and pride.*"

"But the second line doesn't fit him," Dalton said. "*Brother in the Gas of standing quite fine.* He wasn't a member."

"Maybe we're reading it too literally," I said. "He could've been a brother in a figurative way. He was the only other person who knew their secrets. Look at those initials. RMS. Moss Sampson."

"What about the R?"

"Maybe he didn't use his first name, like G. Gordon Liddy or H. Ross Perot. He could've gone by R. Moss Sampson."

"I still like Robert Meade Swigert, down on Park Avenue," Dalton said. "It makes more sense for the poem to talk about one of the members. Besides, how would Sampson get up to Newfoundland, and why would he go there?"

Swigert still seemed too convenient. Were we willing to accept him as the answer because we had grown tired of running into dead ends?

"Everything doesn't have to fit so easily," I said. "This is a code created by a group of extremely intelligent men. They wouldn't make it easy."

"My vote is still with Swigert over Sampson," Dalton said. "In order for all of the lines to make sense, it must be a Delphic brother."

I looked down at the photographs. Sampson looked like a brawler. He had a shaved head with big black eyes and a boxer's jawline. His neck was long and thick, and even though he was wearing a jumpsuit in the picture, you could see the mounds of knotted muscles in his shoulders.

"Last night I snuck into the Bureau of Study Counsel building," Dalton said. "Don't ask me how. Anyway, I found one window that had a decent view of the Delphic courtyard. That picture was definitely taken behind the mansion."

"Which means it's most likely the chamber is somewhere inside."

39

BAM! BAM! BAM! It sounded like someone was attacking my door with a battering ram. I jumped out of bed, realizing that it wasn't a dream, but someone actually pounding on the front door. The clock read 3:00 A.M. I turned on my lamp and ran into the common room. Percy's bedroom door was still closed. He must've taken his anxiety pills before he went to sleep, or the racket would have woken him too. A cold gust of wind swept in as I opened the door. Several red faces sat atop big, puffy ski jackets. "What's going on?" I said. I recognized Hutch, Duke, and Pollack. Before I could register the other faces, they rushed me to the couch and piled on top of me. Graydon Brimmer pushed his way through the mass of bodies and freed me enough so that I could breathe.

"Spenser, on behalf of the Delphic Club, I take honor in announcing your election into the hundred and third neophyte class of the Gas."

Another round of cheers went up, and they piled on me again in a crushing heap. Then after we had rolled around on the floor for a few minutes, they lifted me up and Brimmer handed me a small envelope. "This makes it official," he said.

I opened the envelope and read the letter.

The President and Members of the Delphic Club
are proud to announce the official election of
Spenser Q. Collins, this day, November 29, 1988.
We would be pleased to receive a written notification
of membership acceptance in the lounge of the
Hasty Pudding Club at 12 Holyoke Street
between 9:00 A. M. and 12:00 noon today.

I went numb. How did this happen? None of it seemed real. I could feel the beginning of tears forming behind my eyes, and I hoped like hell I could hold them back till the guys left.

Someone produced a shot glass and bottle of blue alcohol.

"Delphic tradition," Hutch said, handing me the glass. "Down in one."

I threw it back to more cheers as the alcohol burned the back of my throat. I was given a firm round of handshakes before they headed to the door to go wake the next elected neophyte. Hutch was the last to leave.

"Listen, Spenser," he said. "I told you before that everyone really likes you. The club has a lot of cool guys, and you'd fit right in. I know this is a really big decision, but we hope you'll deliver an acceptance later today. You'll make a great Gas brother."

"Why does the notification have to be written?" I asked, pointing to the line in the election letter.

"It's not a big deal," he said. "We do this because some punchees get elected into more than one club, so the acceptance letter is the official documentation of their selection. But remember, you have to be there by twelve. That's an interclub council rule. A minute late, and your election is automatically nullified."

"Don't worry," I said. "I'll be there."

He reached out and gave me a bear hug before he left. I went back to my room and called Dalton, who was in equal disbelief. After an hour of staring up at the stars through my window, I fell asleep with the election letter safely tucked under my pillow.

＊

I WOKE UP later that morning to the chiming of the ten o'clock bells. I sat down to my computer and started typing my acceptance letter. I wasn't sure what to write, but an hour and seven drafts later, I came up with something I thought was adequate.

> *I, Spenser Q. Collins, do hereby accept election into the Delphic Club on this day, November 29, 1988. I am aware that my acceptance forfeits the possibility of joining any other final club. I also accept the responsibilities and privileges attached to my acceptance.*
> *Sincerely,*
> *Spenser Q. Collins*

Satisfied, I threw on my sweats and left my room in more than enough time to arrive at the Hasty before the noon deadline.

BY SEVEN O'CLOCK that night, the newest class of Delphic members had already packed the basement. Drinks and hors d'oeuvres covered the long, narrow table, and a raging fire popped in the fireplace, thawing our frozen limbs. I was happy to see Jon Carderro and Buzz, but I was equally happy not to see Satch Washington, who had obviously been cut. After almost half an hour of somewhat giddy mingling, Graydon Brimmer and Oscar LaValle turned off the TV and called the meeting to order. Brimmer gave us a short introduction, and then Oscar pulled out a small, tattered book and began reading a long list of club rules. The first dealt with women's access to the clubhouse. He called it the "No Women Rule," which had a long list of specifications of when women could enter, which door they had to use, and which rooms they couldn't access. Any member breaking this rule would be expelled on the third violation.

Oscar continued reading the long list of rules and their corresponding fines, mandatory meetings, and the dress code for Wednesday-night dinners.

Nonmember males who attended the college were allowed access to the basement only if accompanied by a member. Harvard male graduates were allowed into the main rooms of the clubhouse only after their ten-year reunion. Servants were never to address us by our first names, and socializing with them was strictly prohibited. No photographs by nonmembers were ever allowed in the clubhouse.

Oscar then turned the program over to Carlyle Emmerson, the treasurer.

"I'm sure most of you know by now how wealthy this organization is," Emmerson began. "So, let's start right out with the big-ticket items. What I'm about to tell you is for your ears only. If it is discovered that you've shared this information with anyone, you'll forfeit your participation. It's a Delphic tradition that dates back to the early 1900s. Due to the generosity of living and deceased alumni, a special endowment has been created that calls for a one-million-dollar gift to each member upon graduation, paid out in installments."

I strained forward, unsure if I actually heard what he had just said correctly. There were a couple of other gasps in the room. A few neophytes laughed skeptically.

"No, it's not a joke, men," Emmerson said. "You will all be given a small package right after commencement exercises in the Yard. This package will contain an account number and the necessary documents and instructions to retrieve your graduation gift. I must remind you that you've sworn an oath to the club that what we discuss tonight is never to leave these four walls. Any violation will result in the member's termination and the permanent ban on any direct bloodline relatives from ever being admitted to the club."

I was glad to be sitting, because my legs felt like jelly. One million dollars. How could this be true? I was going to have a million dollars in the bank when I graduated? Could I tell my mother, or would that be violation? The announcement fogged my head, and the rest of the meeting was a blur.

Keys to the front door would be distributed on initiation night, as well as the security code to the alarm system. We had a month to pay the fifteen-hundred-dollar initiation, and dues would be billed monthly. Three black-tie affairs, which many prominent graduate members attended, would be held throughout the year. While the graduates picked up the bulk of the costs, the undergrad membership would still be assessed a small portion of the tab. Lunches were served every weekday except Wednesday, because we had our weekly club dinner that night. After we finished a question-and-answer session, Oscar opened a large box and handed out our silk club ties—navy blue with small gold torches sewn into the fabric. They were to be worn at all semiformal club functions and Wednesday-night dinners. Ermenegildo Zegna–designed spring ties were available for purchase for seventy-five dollars.

I had no idea how much the tally for these costs would run, but I was practically having an anxiety attack. There was no way I could afford any of this, and I had no idea where I could even go to borrow this kind of money. I had already spoken with my mother, who agreed to use a small amount of the money my father had put away, but I'd have to get a work-study job to pay the rest.

Brimmer spoke last. "Brothers, I want to make something crystal clear," he said. "This is not a fraternity, and we don't expect it to be treated like one. We are a final club, and we expect our house and everything in it to be treated accordingly. A lot of great men have occupied the same chairs you sit in now, walked the same halls and dined at the same tables. Remember that as you gather around those long oak tables upstairs. Out of a hundred and fifteen punchees, just the few of you were selected. It's our hope that we chose well. Initiation dinner will be held in December. Upstairs remains off-limits until you're officially initiated." He then rammed the heavy gavel onto the table. "This first meeting of the one hundred third neophyte class of the Gas is adjourned."

40

DALTON AND I had continued puzzling through the poem, but our best efforts produced only disappointing results. We decided that the first line dealt with the person's place of origin, *A son of Waldorf not far from the Rhine*. Waldorf, it turns out, was a small hamlet in Germany nestled between Heidelberg and the Rhine River. The third line had given us the most trouble, *Downed off Newfoundland in waters icy and wide*. Even after spending countless hours reading about the history of Newfoundland and its sea-weathered people, this line had us stumped. Without knowing which specific year to research, we were left with a long and complicated history that stretched all the way back to 1497, when the navigator and fisherman John Cabot sailed into a sea so full of fish that they could be taken "not only with the net but also a basket in which a stone is put."

We were certain that Moss Sampson had been born in Beulah, Mississippi, and it was unlikely he had ever even been to Germany, but we agreed that he could still fit the last line, *Now stands as our protector with loyalty and pride*. He could be the *protector* of their chamber and secrets. But we had yet to come up with an explanation for the *R* in front of his name. If this had been an ode to their former confidant, it was a strange way to remember him.

I recited, wrote, and sang that damn poem and still got no closer to making sense of those four jumbled lines.

ON THE FIRST WEDNESDAY in December, I got a call from Claybrooke.

"Spenser," he said between clenched teeth. "It's Claybrooke from the Gas. The final dinner and initiation are set for Friday night at eight. Black-tie. Someone will pick you up at six o'clock at your room. They'll bring you over."

Luckily, it was over our bye-week, so we didn't have a game that weekend.

"What's gonna happen?" I asked.

"All I can say is you'll have lots of fun. And make sure you wear the oldest tux you can find. Nothing too fancy."

An *old* tux? That seemed strange.

"Good luck, Spenser," he said, then was gone.

I ran into a couple of other neophytes in the Yard that afternoon heading to class, and they had the same unanswered questions. One of them had a brother who was a member of the Fox Club, and he told him initiation rituals varied between clubs. His advice had been to eat a little pasta an hour before the pickup time because it was going to be a long night before we got a chance to eat. The only thing predictable about initiation night was that it would be totally unpredictable.

FRIDAY FINALLY ARRIVED, and I'm not too proud to admit that I hadn't been that nervous since I played Moses in a Sunday-school play in front of the entire church. Finally, I would be allowed upstairs in the legendary rooms of the Delphic mansion. I didn't know what awaited me, because like everything else thus far, the evening's plans had been shrouded in secrecy. Two days ago, Percy and I had gone to Keezer's in Central Square, a resale shop that sold and rented discounted new and used tuxedos. We found a used tux that was a little big in the waist and shoulders, but for twenty dollars, I couldn't complain. I purchased my first real bow tie, as Percy insisted it would be bad form if I wore one of those cheap clip-ons. "A real bow tie is what gives the tux its character," he insisted.

I was also nervous as hell on many fronts. First, I had no idea what they had in store for us. Second, I worried about Brathwaite and Jacobs and whether tonight was their time to strike. No better place to deal with me than somewhere in their fortified mansion. At precisely six o'clock, after twenty exhausting minutes of trying to knot that damn bow tie with Percy's help, there was a loud knock at the door. When Percy opened it, Hutch, Duke, and Pollack stood there, wearing enormous smiles, tuxedos, and overcoats.

"You ready, buddy?" Hutch said, throwing his arm around my shoulders. "You've got a big night ahead of you."

"Ready as I'll ever be," I said, reaching for my coat and heading for the door.

"Not so fast," Duke stopped me. He reached in his pocket and pulled out a black piece of cloth. "We've got to put this blindfold on first."

"Are you serious?" I asked.

"As a heart attack." Hutch laughed. "Don't worry, all the other neophytes have to do the same thing. Initiation-night tradition."

"Well, okay," I conceded, turning my back to them.

"Don't worry, Spense," Hutch said. "We've got your back."

"You're now one of us," Pollack said.

Once Duke had tightened the blindfold, they made sure I couldn't see anything. I already felt dizzy, and we hadn't even left the room. They grabbed me by the arms and led me out the door into the crisp night.

"Okay," Duke said. "The other neophytes standing here are also blindfolded. Lift your hands so we can put them on the shoulders of the person in front of you."

I did as I was instructed and felt my hands resting on someone much shorter.

"Who's this in front of me?" I asked.

"Dylan Parkhurst," Hutch answered. "You're the fourth in the group."

"Who else is here?"

"Kasey Benton and Buzz Malloy."

It was not lost on me how ridiculous we must've looked, standing there blindfolded in our tuxedos with our hands on each other's shoulders.

"Just keep your hands on the person's shoulders in front of you, and everything will be all right," Duke assured us. "Don't forget, the other guys are depending on you. If one falls, you all fall. That's how a brotherhood works."

As we slowly stumbled out of the courtyard, I could hear the muffled laughter of passersby. The members laughed also, only adding to the absurdity of it all, and I felt like a helpless jackass. We ambled through the front archway and down Holyoke Street. Then we crossed Mt. Auburn, and I could tell we were marching up Linden Street. I was sure we were heading into the clubhouse until I heard the busy sounds of Mass Ave, which meant we had walked past it.

"Okay, we're going up a lot of stairs now," Duke said. "Go slowly. Trust the neophyte in front of you."

We started the long ascent, one step at a time. When we finally reached the top, we were all panting. I knew we had just climbed the Widener steps. There was no other climb in the Yard that long and steep.

"Time to show Harvard your killer moves," Pollack said.

They took off our topcoats and tux jackets and placed plastic bowler caps on our heads.

"We're gonna play some music, and you must dance in place. You're on the edge of a high platform, so there's very little room. If anyone stops dancing before the music ends, we'll start all over again. When the music stops, you must turn around, drop your pants, and give us the biggest moon of your life. Am I clear?"

The four of us grumbled our acceptances. I kept praying to God that my naked butt wouldn't end up on the front page of the *Crimson* tomorrow morning. My mother would have a conniption.

The music started and we began dancing. I thought we might get away without attracting a crowd, but soon a loud chorus of clapping and whistles accompanied us. After several minutes, the song stopped, and although it took every ounce of willpower for me to do it, I turned around, unclasped my waistband and dropped my pants. The crowd, of course, went wild, and once the cold air stung my ass, I scrambled like hell to get my pants up.

Minutes later, we were back in formation, down the steps, and on the march. I heard the sounds of cars honking and braking. We walked up a short flight of steps, through a door, and into a lobby. I thought we had entered one of the houses. Keys rattled and another door opened. My frozen fingers and feet welcomed the rush of heat.

"You guys are doing a great job," Duke said. "Now it's time for a drinking mission. We're gonna fill a glass with Jack Daniel's, and you have to take a swig before passing it to the next person. But you must swallow before you pass it on. The anchor will be the last person to get the glass. That's Parkhurst. He must finish whatever is left in the glass in one sip. If he can't finish, we switch anchors and start all over again. Thirty seconds or less—otherwise, we fill her back up till you do it right, like real Delphic men."

I heard the wet gulps of the lead-off drinker. "This shit tastes like battery acid," Buzz complained to the laughs and cheers of the members.

"What's this?" Kasey asked. "A pitcher. He took a swallow, then passed the glass to me.

After I had swallowed as much as I could and was about to pass it on to Parkhurst, Duke yelled, "Time's up. You didn't make it. If you spent less time talking and more time drinking, you would've finished. Gotta do it all over again. Dylan, you're first this time. Spenser, you'll take over as anchor. They shuffled our position in line.

"Okay," Duke called out. "Go!"

The room fell silent as Dylan began to drink. He choked a little, letting out a heavy panting sound when he had finished swallowing. Kasey was next, and it seemed like he had finished his portion without any snags.

"Fifteen seconds!" Duke yelled.

I could hear the gurgling sound of Buzz drinking. Then I felt the tall glass in my hands, but to my relief, there wasn't much in it.

"Five, four . . ."

I quickly tipped the glass back, opened my throat, and chugged down what was left in the glass. Just as Duke reached one, I raised the empty glass in victory.

"Way to go!" Hutch yelled. I could feel his heavy hands on my shoulders.

"I'm gonna puke, guys." It was Kasey Benton. I felt the same way, but didn't admit it. Two guys ran to Kasey's side and grabbed his arms, but they still wouldn't let him take off his blindfold. I heard them stumbling out of the room, opening a door, and then the unmistakable sound of vomit hitting toilet water.

Once Kasey was cleaned up and led back into the room, Pollack said, "To cap off the festivities here, we're gonna review the alphabet, boys and girls. Kasey, you'll be excused for this one. This is a mission of speed. The first two to say the alphabet backwards without mistakes will be the winners. The last one will do a shot."

Once Pollack had counted down from five, the mumbling and stuttering commenced as the alcohol began taking its toll. Buzz and his intrepid steel gut was the first to finish, and I pulled up a close second. Parkhurst was still trying to get beyond M by the time Pollack called it off. It all seemed a lot funnier once I realized that I wouldn't be the one drinking the shot. Parkhurst got stuck with the shot while the rest of us slid back into our seats and took a much-needed break.

"It's after seven," Hutch announced to the other members. "We'd better get to the club. The other groups are probably back already." We stumbled back down the stairs into the cold night. The sounds of passing cars and pedestrians grew louder as we made our way across the busy street.

The combination of the alcohol and the blindfold sent my head spinning. We walked a short distance before I heard Pollack say, "Everyone's meeting in the basement."

They led us several more feet, took a hard right, then guided us down a couple of steps and into what I presumed was the alley on the side of the Delphic. The old door creaked on its rusted hinges; then someone rested their hand on top of my head and guided me underneath the doorjamb.

"Can we take our blindfolds off now?" Parkhurst asked.

"Not yet," Duke said. "We have to wait until everyone's here."

Laughter and spirited voices echoed in the darkness. As we made our way toward the pool room, the door opened behind us and another group of neophytes entered the basement. They sat us down next to each other in front of a giant fire. We listened as members compared stories and notes on what their respective neophyte groups had done. It sounded like we actually had an easier time of it than the others.

They finally stood us up and one by one freed us of the blindfolds. The rush of light was sudden and dizzying at the same time, but after two hours of darkness, it was a relief to rejoin the visible world. The basement was packed with tuxedo-clad members, all wearing large silver medallions hanging on blue satin ribbon necklaces. The same medallion Uncle Randolph wore in the photo Dalton found at Wild Winds. They cheered and applauded, then joined in song as we stood and accepted their hands in brotherhood.

Brimmer got up on a chair and instructed us to line up in the back of the room. The fifteen of us stood shoulder-to-shoulder before the lights were turned off. Someone lit a round of candles, and suddenly the cramped room with its dark oak and stone walls took on the aura of a midnight séance. The other members cleared a space in front of us. Brimmer remained on the chair, holding a bottle of blue liqueur and a shot glass.

"Gentlemen, you are now ready for the Delphic flaming shot. Set all fears aside as you watch and listen to your noble heritage. There have been generations of great men before you who for more than a century have stood as you now stand on the auspicious occasion of initiation. Heroic and courageous, committed to the bonds of brotherhood, most loyal disciples of the Gas, your distinguished ancestors, men who have served this club with honor and distinction, have also downed this flaming blue liquid—Delphic blood. Brother Hutch will proudly show you the custom of your fabled lineage."

The room filled with applause as big Hutch stepped up on a chair next to Brimmer and bowed to the crowd. Brimmer poured the blue liqueur into the shot glass and handed it to Hutch. Someone standing nearby lit a match and set the drink on fire. The sudden burst of flames lit up Hutch's face before he raised the glass above his head in a toast, tilted his head back, and poured the fiery blue liqueur into his mouth. In seconds, he had swallowed the Delphic blood, and his hands went up in victory as Brimmer dabbed his face with a towel.

Kasey Benton was the first neophyte lifted to the chair. Brimmer poured the liqueur into the glass, passed it to him, and then Claybrooke lit it with a match. Kasey stared at the flame for a moment as everyone yelled, "Drink, neophyte! Drink, drink, neophyte! Drink!" Kasey tilted his head back, closed his eyes, and downed the flaming shot. Two members had taken positions on chairs behind him and immediately reached out with their towels to dry his face. You could see in his eyes a moment of disbelief that he had actually downed the drink without injury. He broke into a smile, and the crowd chanted his name.

Buzz was next, and without hesitation, he stepped up on the chair, accepted the drink, and threw it back without fear. I only prayed that I could be so smooth as they lifted me up above the crowd. I took the glass, put on a brave smile, and looked into the flame. Hutch gave me a tap of encouragement on the shoulder; then in one motion I put my head back and poured the burning liquid into my mouth. It was hot going in, and I had visions of flames covering my face, but within seconds, my throat felt the warmth as the bitter liquid moved down the back of my throat. Towels smothered my face, and I shouted more from relief than a show of bravado. Chants of my name bounced off the walls, and I threw my fists up in victory.

Parkhurst was up next on the chair, and I could tell by the look on his face that he wasn't thrilled to drink the blood of his brethren. He accepted the glass, stared blankly into the flame, and then raised it to his mouth. He poured back the sizzling liquid, but instead of it going into his mouth, most of it splattered on the sides of his face, sending rivulets of flames from the corner of his mouth down to his chin. For a brief moment he sported a flaming goatee, and silence fell over the room as he wildly slapped his face, trying to put out the flames. The two members standing behind him went into action, burying his face in towels, muffling his screams. I was certain that he had been burned, but seconds later, his face emerged unscathed, only the collar of his shirt slightly charred. A thunderous round of cheers exploded in the room once it was obvious that he would be fine. Once Parkhurst realized his great escape, he started hugging Hutch, and the two fell off the chair only to be caught by the circle of men surrounding them.

Order was restored; then they separated us into groups of three, re-blindfolded us, and arranged us in a single line at the door. Every few minutes, a group was led away from the room and escorted down the hallway. The rest of us waited patiently to discover our fate. I was in the third group, and when we started moving, I feared we were heading back outside.

"This is a narrow staircase," a voice informed us as we were led through another basement door. "You have to get on your hands and knees and crawl up. No standing allowed. After ten steps, there's a sudden turn to the right, so be ready."

We weren't going outside, but finally heading upstairs into the clubhouse. I didn't know who else was in my group, but we cautiously crawled up the stairs, and after we reached the tenth step, they stood us up, maneuvered us through a hard turn, walked us a few feet, then put us back on our knees for another set of stairs. I could hear distant laughter and faint applause from the rooms above us. Once we had reached the top of that stairwell, they lined us up and took the first one in our group away. A few minutes later, I felt someone grab my arm.

"Don't worry," someone whispered. I could tell it was Duke. "Hold on to me and you'll be fine." The voices were louder now, and several people were yelling instructions. There was a lot of muffled laughter, and I could only make out bits of what was being said. "All you have to do is take a step forward and stand still," Duke said. "But it's important you don't move around. Stand in the same spot."

Once the door opened, I followed Duke's instructions. I felt like I had walked into a furnace. As the door slammed behind me, everything had fallen silent, and suddenly I was drenched in sweat. I stood stock-still, fearful that if I moved, I might touch whatever was generating the tremendous heat. My breathing became more difficult, and my head felt like it was stuck in a vise. I concentrated on my balance, but my body swayed back and forth. I thought I heard voices, but I didn't know if they were real or if I was hallucinating. Any moment, I thought I might pass out. Then I suddenly felt a gust of cool air as the door opened and the voices returned. They chanted my name and hit me on the shoulder. "Great job, Spense," Duke said. "You're almost home."

Someone else grabbed my arm and said, "Walk slowly and follow me." I felt carpet under my feet, then the hardness of a tiled floor.

"What's your dominant hand?" he asked.

"Right," I said.

"Okay, then we'll roll up the left sleeve."

Once he had taken my cuff link out and rolled up my sleeve to my elbow, another voice said, "Here's the deal. I want you to put your hand in this water, move it around, and squeeze whatever you feel."

"What am I squeezing?" I asked.

"Don't worry about that," he laughed. "Whatever you feel, squeeze it until we say stop."

Then I heard another voice say, "The camera's ready."

I felt my hand being lifted, and suddenly immersed in cold water. I could tell that it was a toilet bowl, and I almost vomited at the thought of what I was soon to feel.

"Open your fist and feel around," one of the voices instructed. "It's time to squeeze for gold. Use your left hand, because later you need to eat with your right."

As hard as I tried to open my hand, I couldn't bring myself to do it. The thought of grabbing feces had paralyzed me. I took deep breaths to prevent myself from vomiting.

"Come on, Spenser!" they yelled. "Squeeze it, baby! Squeeze it!"

I held my breath as if that would make it feel any better, then I opened my hands and searched the bowl, finally meeting something of a slimy consistency that made me jump and lift my hand out of the water as soon as I felt it. The roar of laughter filled the room.

"Get back in there and get your dinner," someone said, forcing my hand back into the bowl.

I clenched my teeth and found the slimy matter. I suddenly felt faint. I squeezed, and whatever it was oozed through my fingers. It was the most disgusting thing I had ever done in my life. I was squeezing someone's shit. I lifted my hand again.

"Not good enough," a voice said. "You stop only on our command." Someone squirted my face with cold water. "Put your hand back in there."

So, I did.

"Now, doesn't that feel good?" someone said in the midst of all the laughter.

There was a flushing sound, and the water circled my hand and carried away the slime between my fingers.

They pulled me to my feet, took me over to the sink, and put a bar of soap in my hands. I scrubbed so hard that I broke a nail. They moved in and stopped me, because I would've stayed at that sink all night. Someone grabbed me by the arm and guided me up another flight of stairs, and into a room where voices were echoing off the ceiling.

"Wait here," he commanded. "We have to finish downstairs with the last guy in your group." I heard him walk away, and I was tempted to peek from the blindfold to see where I was. But within seconds, voices broke the silence, and I heard footsteps approaching on the hardwood floor.

After the last neophyte in our group had arrived, they walked us into another room, where the soft sound of a crackling fire blended with the muted tones of a television. The members sat us on thick leather sofas and chairs and seemed to ignore us as they drank, laughed, and talked amongst themselves.

I felt someone's hand on my shoulder and a voice say, "How ya holding up, Spense?" It was Hutch.

"I'm still alive," I said.

"Hang in there, buddy," he said. "You're in the home stretch. You'll be fine." He tapped my shoulder and walked away.

Every few minutes or so, they called the name of a neophyte and escorted him out of the room. Finally, my name was called, and two people grabbed both my arms and helped me to my feet. They walked me out of the room, down a quiet hall, and into another room. The door closed behind me.

Hands went to work on the back of my blindfold, and I opened my eyes into a dark, candlelit room. Brimmer and two older men I had never seen before were standing above me on a short rectangular table. Both gray-haired men wore white dinner jackets with the Delphic torches on their bow tie and cummerbund. A large fire jumped at their backs and cast their shadows against the dark walls. They instructed me to step up on the table.

"Welcome, Spenser," Brimmer said. "This is Mr. Ward Purnell, class of '51, our graduate president." A tall man with thin, oval-framed glasses slightly nodded his head in acknowledgment. His countenance was only made more serious by his square face. His thick gray hair had been meticulously combed backwards. "And this is Mr. Conrad Goodhue, our graduate secretary," Brimmer said. The short, plump man bowed graciously. His skin glistened under the glow of the fire.

"Congratulations on making it to this point, Spenser," Mr. Purnell said. "This is your official swearing-in ceremony. Before I read you the club oath, I'm going to let you read it to make sure you're fully aware of the obligations. You are about to make a lifelong commitment, so I suggest you read and understand the entire pledge before you take it."

Purnell handed me a small book with a leather cover that bore a faint resemblance to *The Christian Warfare*. The pages were old and delicate.

I, (name of neophyte), hereby accept lifetime membership into the Delphic Club of Harvard College. As a member, I promise to forever hold the name and spirit of the club in the highest regard and remain loyal to its principles, practices, and secrets. I shall in no way cause harm to the standing of the club or my brethren, nor shall I do anything that will in any way blemish its most honored reputation as long as I shall live. I pledge to faithfully abide by its laws and continue the most noble traditions of those great men who have gone before me and walked these hallowed halls. This, I do solemnly swear on the day of our Lord, December (day, then year), so help me God.

I handed the book back to Purnell and nodded my acceptance.

He said, "Place your left hand on the Bible and raise the first three fingers of your right hand to represent the torches of the Gas."

I followed his instructions, repeating the oath in slow, deliberate fragments. When I had finished, Mr. Goodhue handed me another book whose royal blue cover and pages had been embossed with the Delphic torches. The date had been printed in the top margin, and I could see the signatures of the other neophytes who had gone before me. I immediately recognized the triangular *J* of Jonathan Carderro. This book contained the signatures of some of the world's most powerful men, and I was overwhelmed with the realization that mine would be with them.

Goodhue handed me a heavy silver pen, and the three of them watched in silence as I signed my name into Delphic history.

"Congratulations, Spenser," Purnell said. "As graduate president of the Delphic Club, I officially accept your oath and welcome you to the brotherhood of the Gas." He handed the book to Brimmer, grabbed me by the shoulders, and proceeded to kiss me on both cheeks and then finally on my forehead. Goodhue did the same and Brimmer followed.

Purnell reached back on a shelf behind him and produced a thin box. He removed the lid and pulled out a medal.

"Spenser, this is your official Delphic medal," he said. "Wear it to all major club dinners and functions with pride and a great sense of history. Honor and cherish and protect it. Once I lay this around your neck, no one else is ever to wear it, and it shall be buried with you to accompany you in the life hereafter."

I examined the front of the brushed silver medal, three raised torches under which THE DELPHIC had been carved. He turned it over so that I could see my name, which had been engraved above the year of my graduation. He hung it around my neck, and the three of them clapped softly. It was official. I was a member of the Delphic Club.

"Congratulations, Spenser," Brimmer said, offering his hand. "I know you're getting tired of this, but we're gonna have to put the blindfold back on. It's only for a little while longer." I snatched my last glimpse of the large dark room with its English oak paneling, massive gilt-framed paintings of the somber faces of my now brothers. I wanted to record every detail. Someone led me out of the room and instructed me to wait.

The distant sound of applause erupted from somewhere below. I thought about the poem. *Now stands as our protector with loyalty and pride.* Footsteps approached; then someone grabbed my arm. "It's your turn next, Spenser." It was Pollack.

"What now?" I asked.

"Hang in there," he said. "You're almost home."

He guided me down a flight of steps and into another room. I could feel the presence of others as he led me across the creaky floorboards. Some whispered my name as I passed.

"Here we go," Pollack said, pulling me to his side. "Take a big step up and then another. Don't worry, I'm holding on to you." I followed his instructions. They turned me around and tapped me on the back.

"Are you ready, Spenser?" Pollack said. Then he whispered. "You've come a long way since the kiss at the Pink Bitch."

That brought a smile to my face. "Ready as I'll ever be," I said. His hands wiggled my blindfold free.

41

"GENTLEMEN OF THE GAS. I now present to you Spenser Q. Collins, our newest brother."

The blindfold fell, and my eyes blinked at a sea of tuxedo-clad men standing beneath me.

"Long live the Gas!" was the collective cheer as the room exploded into applause and whistles. I stood there, looking out over generations of Delphic men as they puffed long cigars and raised their glasses in a toast.

After two months of speculation, my eyes finally took in the dark walls that more than a century ago had been rescued from an English castle and shipped across the Atlantic. The room was thick with tradition, aged by countless nights such as these, heavy with cigar smoke and memories of years that had long since passed.

It was almost too much to take in at once, the dancing fire and deep leather couches surrounded by ornate wing chairs. Ornaments lined the mantelpiece underneath a memorial inscription that had been carved into the wall. The famous Delphic collection of cockfight paintings hung on the right wall over a wide mahogany table that had been covered with several leather-bound magazines.

Peering over the crowd, I could see into the adjoining room. An antique ceiling lamp swung over the massive pool table. Heavy satin curtains blocked the windows from curious passersby, and it was then that it sunk in that I had finally penetrated this closed world.

As the applause and cheers began to abate, Pollack nudged me out of my reverie. It was time to step down and rub elbows with my brothers. They greeted me with warm embraces and firm handshakes. Though I hadn't met all of them during punch season, each member welcomed me as if we were old friends.

As they brought the next blindfolded neophyte into the room, I made my way to a corner to observe the remainder of the ceremony. The words, gestures, dress—everything was steeped in such rich traditions, protocols followed to the smallest details. For decades, these initiating rituals, jokes, and laughs had been enjoyed on this special night. The faces had changed over time, but many of the surnames remained the same. Children, grandchildren, nephews, and great-nephews all continued their family's residence in privilege. It was humbling to see these successful and prominent men, masters of their class, return to their old stomping grounds to cheer and applaud a group of brash college students at 9 Linden Street.

After all the neophytes had been introduced, Brimmer stepped up on the table. "Neophytes of the Delphic Club," he said. "On behalf of the graduate and undergraduate membership, I welcome you to our most honored family. You shall sign your first commemorative poster as a member of the Gas to mark the occasion for generations of great men who will surely follow you." We were promptly lined up in the back of the room. The older members watched on with pride as we signed our names to a colorful poster of a man in a tuxedo leaning over a bar ordering a drink.

The party moved out of the reading room and into the front foyer. It felt good to finally stand on the other side of the big blue door. Four imposing columns anchored the room with a set of curtained French doors that led out into the courtyard. A large light in the middle of the ceiling hung from a brass chain, surrounded by a metal crown that looked like it once might've been part of a lost treasure. Lightbulbs encased in glass torches lit the corners of the room.

I looked at the faces of the men, both young and old, certain I would find Jacobs prominently at the center of attention. But he was conspicuously absent from the festivities. I wondered if he and Brathwaite were somewhere upstairs, plotting their next move. Maybe they were hidden in the chamber, watching all of us on surveillance cameras.

I walked over to the carpeted staircase and noticed the first poster of hundreds that I would soon discover. This one commemorated a biannual New York dinner that had been held on April 4, 1986. A painted Statue of Liberty was holding three torches, while a banner at her feet waved THE DELPHIC CLUB in gold letters. Approximately one hundred signatures were scribbled with pride, marking the members' attendance at the exclusive gala.

"What's the purpose of these?" I asked one of my new brothers who happened to be standing next to me.

"Well, it's more tradition than anything else," the short man said. "I'm Fritz Simington, class of '56."

We shook hands.

"At each major dinner and black-tie affair we hold throughout the year, we have these posters drawn to commemorate the event," he said. "Everyone in attendance signs their name and class year. The poster you just signed in the reading room will be signed by the rest of the members here tonight, then framed and hung somewhere in the club. You'll see tons as you walk around."

The party continued upstairs and I followed the rest of the group. Wooden-framed black-and-white photographs of the members covered the walls. The year of each picture was engraved in the bottom of the frame.

"Official club photo taken each year in the courtyard," Fritz said. "Oldest I've ever seen is from 1891. It's still hanging upstairs."

It was an eerie feeling, passing these hundreds of youthful faces who once had been standing and playing where I now stood. Time had relegated them to mere footnotes in the club's long history. That would be the fate of all of us assembled that night, regardless of how vital and strong and indomitable we felt. As we neared the second floor, I froze in front of the first black member. It was a 1976 photograph. I quietly paid homage to this pioneer. I couldn't even imagine the difficulties he must've faced being the first, how lonely he must've felt. I wondered who he was and what he did. Now my face would hang on these same walls. I wanted future neophytes to see me and hear my story, a most unlikely member who had done his best to open the doors and positively change the culture.

We took a right at the top of the stairs and walked through a set of open double doors and into a cavernous ballroom. Gigantic stuffed caribou heads hung conspicuously from the rafters. Along the dark walls, over the mantelpiece, on top of the piano, heads of deer, buffalo, and bison startled the unsuspecting eye. The older members volunteered stories of the adventurous hunts and courageous expeditions that brought these animals to 9 Linden Street. Narrow tables stretched the length of the room, dressed with white linen tablecloths, black champagne bottles, long candles, and ornate china. Dry logs crackled in the fireplace as the room began filling with the laughter and cheer of Delphic men.

A head table had been set up in the front of the room. A long line of uniformed servants dutifully stood at the ready.

I joined Hutch at one of the long tables. A stocky, round-faced man stood with his head held back and tapped a knife against his wineglass. A hush fell over the room.

"May I have your attention, please," he called out in a crisp, distinguished voice. "For those of you who don't know me, my name is Ellsworth Stohler, class of '79, and I'll be serving as your toastmaster for the evening."

"Did you mean '59?" someone yelled from across the hall, breaking up the gathering into fits of laughter.

Once the noise had settled, Stohler raised his glass and said, "The dangers of my job. But I remain fearless and loyal in my service to you tonight. Now, as I was saying, my name is Ellsworth Stohler, the graduate treasurer as well as tonight's toastmaster, and we have a great evening planned for you. The first order of business is properly welcoming the neophytes to their final dinner." On cue, the rest of the members took to their feet with their glasses raised. Stohler then said, "In these blessed halls legions of great men have come before you and many generations shall walk in the footprints that you leave behind. You now stand on the shoulders of those brave souls of Delta Phi and claim your rightful place amongst a celebrated pantheon of yesterday's fallen heroes, today's carriers of the torch, and tomorrow's leaders. Drink long and deep, my neophyte brothers, and know that you'll always have a home at the Gas."

"Hear! Hear!" the crowd roared, and we celebrated our first of many Delphic toasts.

"So, what do you think so far?" Hutch asked. He was seated to my right. "Is this great or what? Tonight, you'll eat and drink like a king."

"I had no idea what to expect," I said. "It's a really awesome feeling to be finally sitting here."

Salads were served, wine and champagne glasses were noisily brought down on the tables, and just as everyone dug in, a commotion sounded across the hall. A graduate was standing on his chair, banging his knife against his glass. Swinging the knife and cursing, he fought off the members who were attempting to bring him down. His long dark hair had been tucked behind ears, his bow tie hanging over his shoulder, and his speech badly slurred.

"That's Clarke Meriwether," Hutch said. "Don't worry, he's always out of control. Every year, he finds a way to make a fool of himself. This is my third initiation dinner, and I've never seen him leave one of these things sober. He walks in the door wasted." The rest of the hall quieted as the members smartly decided to give Meriwether his space rather than risk decapitation. Meriwether announced he had a joke about three horny secretaries who were sitting in the bathroom. He started out strong, but midway through the delivery he fell apart, and the rest of what he said was completely incomprehensible. But the room still erupted into a raucous applause and Meriwether took a bow, which sent him tumbling into the arms of those standing beneath him.

"Who is he?" I asked.

"Graduated ten years ago," Hutch said. "His family has been in the club since the mansion was built. He comes from a big mining family out of Pennsylvania. His grandfather left ten million dollars' worth of stock to the club. So, let's just say that the trustees have ten million reasons to be very tolerant of him."

We feasted on Cornish game hens, steamed asparagus, and potatoes.

Following dinner, an assortment of desserts was served with coffee and cappuccino and after-dinner liqueurs. Stohler stood on his chair at the head table and called for our attention. He formally introduced the rest of the graduate members seated next to him and announced their positions within the club hierarchy; then he began the tradition of post-dinner jokes. In fact, people had been telling jokes throughout dinner, all of them sexual in nature. Some of the jokes even made me uncomfortable. I wondered how the female staff felt, hearing these raunchy stories, no consideration at all that they were present.

That's how we spent the next forty-five minutes, drinking and telling jokes and passing around boxes of Cohiba cigars that had been illegally smuggled from Cuba through London and specially wrapped in Delphic parchment.

Tradition dictated the final joke of the evening be told by the oldest member present, so ninety-two-year-old Wallis Cabot slowly rose to his feet with the help of two canes and the hands of the members seated next to him. His voice was weak, but his joke was strong. He delivered a flawless rendition of a story about a construction worker who accidentally walks into a sperm bank. The applause was immediate and heavy, and a gleam came to Cabot's eyes as the magic of youth had returned, even if just for a fleeting moment.

A piano sounded in the corner of the hall as one of the younger graduates banged away on the ivory keys. Everyone formed a circle around the room, and Stohler stood holding an enormous silver bowl with two ornately curved handles. It looked like a replica of the Wimbledon trophy.

"What's going on now?" I asked Hutch.

"The cup song," Hutch said. "We close out every dinner by singing this song as the cup is passed and we drink to brotherhood."

> *Stroll again down Linden Street*
> *When you're far away,*
> *Just let your memories guide your feet*
> *And look forward to the day*
> *When the crowd has reassembled and the cup shall pass.*
> *Land or Sea,*

Wherever you may be,
Drink a toast to the Gas.

Chestnuts bloom on Linden Street
With the dawn of spring
And you'll recall their fragrance sweet
As you raise your glass and sing
To the days we've shared together, brothers class by class,
Land or sea,
Wherever you may be,
Drink a toast to the Gas.

That simple song filled the hall, the silver cup was passed, and members took their drink for the Gas. When Cabot took the ceremonial last drink, more applause knocked against the ancient walls, and the room fell into a mass of congratulatory hugs and handshakes and another round of cigars.

"The women should be here in about half an hour," Hutch said. "So how about seeing *your* club before the party starts?"

"Let's do it," I said, feeling strange hearing him call it my club.

He took me through the entire clubhouse. The oath had been given in the library underneath original portraits of various U.S. presidents and prominent club graduates.

A large photograph of an elegantly dressed man hung conspicuously over the mantelpiece.

"Who's that?" I asked.

"John Jacob Astor IV," Hutch said as we walked up to the portrait. "He was a member in the late 1800s right along with J. P. Morgan. At one point, his great-grandfather was the country's richest man, right alongside the Rockefellers. He donated many of these books from his private library."

There was an enormous TV room furnished with a six-foot-wide television screen and a cadre of Bose speakers scattered around the room. He continued the tour, showing me the sauna where they made us stand in the oppressive heat, the locker room where I had squeezed what was a banana in the toilet, and their own full-sized squash court. The entire time, I couldn't stop thinking of where the chamber was hidden and if the Ancient Nine were inside it, watching our every move.

He led me down a narrow staircase lined with commemorative posters from the early 1900s. It deposited us into a small room with a smoked birch countertop. The dim lighting and drab colors combined with the cigars brought to mind an English gentlemen's club. The bartender, a short stocky man with a bulbous snout of a nose and meaty hands, served drinks with a flourish.

"That's Roscoe," Hutch said. "He's been here for over forty years. One night when it's not so busy, you gotta hear some of his stories. He was here the night Kennedy and some of his friends from the Spee broke into the basement. He's seen and heard it all."

Just over the liquor chest, five cards had been framed against a red mat. It was a royal flush: A, K, Q, J, 10. Underneath the cards was a big signature I couldn't read and the date April 10, 1959.

Hutch saw me staring at the cards. "That's the most famous poker hand in Delphic history," he said. "Bickerstaff beat some oil heir with it for fifty thousand dollars and a new Porsche. The old-timers call it the Poker Game of the Century. One day get Roscoe to tell you about it. He was serving drinks that night."

Hutch pulled me into the next room, where lunches were served. It was full of long oak tables and medieval wooden chairs with stuffed leather seats. On one side of the room a fire roared in a glass-encased fireplace. A tribute had been inscribed in the panel above the mantelpiece with the years 1941–1945 and a list of graduate members who had fallen in World War II. The carved letters had been positioned between two torches and inlaid with gold leaf. An excerpt from Laurence Binyon's poem "For the Fallen" gave it a surreal quality.

THEY SHALL NOT GROW OLD,
AS WE THAT ARE LEFT GROW OLD:
AGE SHALL NOT WEARY THEM,
NOR THE YEARS CONDEMN.
AT THE GOING DOWN OF THE SUN

AND IN THE MORNING, WE WILL
REMEMBER THEM.

A Delphic dish rested on the mantelpiece in a holder that read:

SET OF DELPHIC CLUB CHINA
GIVEN BY HIS PARENTS
IN MEMORY OF
RALPH BLAKE WILLIAMS III '55 1933–1963

He pointed to an intricately carved shelf that ran along the ceiling. I noticed it as soon as we had walked into the room. "Those porcelain steins and silver tankards are a big part of the club's history," he said. "The two sitting in the far corner belonged to Napoléon Bonaparte before he was exiled to the island of Elba. Gifts from the Morgan family. They come down only once a year during our midwinter dinner in February. The undergraduate and graduate presidents always use them for the first toast."

Everything in the mansion had its own story, small pieces of history delicately woven together. We walked across the foyer and into the billiards room. A long oar hung over the double door. It had been covered with a thick coat of varnish and the words:

UNDEFEATED CREW 1938 VARSITY BOAT RACE
NEW LONDON, CT JUNE 24

"Charles P. Thorpe, class of '62."

I turned to find a tall man with dark, perfectly coiffed hair; a long, pointed nose; and thick black eyebrows. Hutch had struck up a conversation with another alum.

"Spenser Collins, class of '91," I said.

He threw a stiff right hand in my direction.

"Welcome to the Gas," he said. "You'll relish this night and this club for the rest of your life. Except for choosing Harvard over Yale, joining the Gas was the most important decision of my life. I got into the Pork and the Fly, but I knew this was where I belonged. There's a sense of family here the other clubs just don't have. I haven't missed an initiation in twenty years."

"Charles, old boy," a man with the most perfect set of teeth I had ever seen called out from across the room. He held a cigar in one hand and a drink in the other.

"Chip?" Thorpe exclaimed. He turned back toward me. "I've gotta run along, young man, but remember what I said. Treasure every minute you can spend here. The years will speed by, and one day you'll look up and not know where they went." He skipped off to embrace his old friend.

I spent the next fifteen minutes drifting from one conversation to the next; then Oscar LaValle hailed me down and asked me to follow him to the president's office. Situated in the back hallway, the office was full of more old photographs and club memorabilia. He opened a safe and pulled out a walnut box filled with gold, rectangular keys. Three torches had been engraved into one side of the key. The number *235* had been stamped underneath. He opened a dense book and had me sign next to the number. Next, he handed me a copy of the membership directory and explained they called it the Delphic Bible because it contained the names, addresses, places of employment, and private phone numbers of all the graduates.

"You'll find alumni living all over the world and working in every industry from filmmaking to garment factories," Oscar said. "Call 'em up, tell 'em you're a Delphic man, and they'll take care of you. But don't leave the book lying around where outsiders can see it. A couple of years ago, some reporter from the *Crimson* got ahold of a copy and ran a big story about it. They published the names of our most prominent members, calling them elitists and accusing them of hiring discrimination because they gave preferential treatment to their Delphic brothers. Our lawyers eventually made the stories go away, but the optics weren't good for the club."

I tucked the directory under my arm and assured him that I would keep it well out of anyone else's reach. He led me to the front door and showed me the elaborate alarm system and had me practice entering the security code. A white keypad had been affixed to a wall just inside the foyer, between the big blue door and an inner door. A five-digit code had to be punched twice; then within five seconds a hidden buzzer over the second door had to be pushed. Failure to enter the right code twice or pushing the buzzer after the five-second period had elapsed would trigger the alarm inside the club and one at the Cambridge Police Department. There was also an emergency button hidden underneath the mail slot. In the event a member ran into trouble at the front door, it could be pushed to set off an alarm.

When we walked back into the club, we stepped into a whirlwind of activity. Oscar told me that they had staggered the arrival of the girls. Wellesley girls first, followed by the invited Harvard girls, and last a sorority from Simmons. The staff worked feverishly to clear the rooms as the DJ started spinning records, and a team of bartenders put the finishing touches on a champagne ice fountain. The graduates made the last of their toasts, then wished us luck on our evening conquests before leaving us to fulfill our destiny as Delphic men.

42

❧

A WEEK OF lunches and visits to the club brought me no closer to discovering the secret chamber. I found myself worrying about Brathwaite, Jacobs, and the flat-nosed man holding the gun. Where were they, and what were they plotting? I tried putting them out of my mind, but it was impossible. I noticed every shadow walking home at night from the Yard. I made sure I always left practice with a teammate, so I had company heading back over the river. Despite our fears, Dalton and I continued our search. Several times, I had climbed the rickety stairs to the third floor in the middle of the night when no one else was there. I examined every room in the mansion except for the steward's tiny office. After flipping every switch and banging on every wall, there was no indication of a chamber. For hours on end, I hid in the dark shadows, waiting for something to happen, but there was only silence.

One night while I was upstairs, I heard a couple of members enter the mansion and shoot a couple of games of eight-ball on the first floor, but they left within an hour. On another night, three members stopped by for a sandwich and a couple of games of backgammon in the reading room, but they left without a mention of anything unusual. None of them ever came up to the third floor.

Then something happened. One night, on my way home from studying at Lamont, I stopped by the club to grab a snack and catch the last quarter of the UNLV–Georgetown game. I ran back to the kitchen, picked up a ham and cheese sandwich, and headed upstairs to the third-floor TV room. I noticed a streak of light breaking into the dark stairwell on the mezzanine landing.

I continued up the stairs slowly, and when I reached the third floor, I noticed the door to the library was closed. This struck me as odd, since I had never seen the door closed. Just as I put my hand on the knob to open it, I heard several voices from within engaged in lively conversation. I withdrew my hand and rested my ear against the door. The voices were muffled, but I could tell they belonged to older men.

I could feel my heart beating in my mouth as I knelt down and put my eye to the keyhole, straining to look inside. In the center of the floor was a circle of middle-aged and elderly men clad in tailed tuxedos, white vests, top hats, black capes, and white satin gloves. They held up their outstretched arms, locking hands with each other. In the middle of the circle, Stanford Jacobs stood on a chair, facing another man of equal height who looked to be in his early fifties. Jacobs held a torch in one hand and an open book in the other. They were dressed like the men in the photograph Dalton had found in Uncle Randolph's attic, the men we assumed were the Ancient Nine. It was difficult for me to see the other faces, but I recognized Charles Thorpe. I was changing my position for a better angle, hoping I might recognize some of the members I had met on initiation night, but the room fell dark. Jacobs continued to hold the torch.

I stood up and tiptoed to the adjacent TV room, not believing my luck. This had to be the Ancient Nine. There was no other explanation. It was highly unlikely any students would be in the clubhouse that night, as we were nearing the end of the semester and everyone was stuffed into the libraries, cramming from shared class notes and old exams. So, I kept the TV room lights off and went to the corner nearest the library wall and sat on the floor. As I hoped, the grated vent carried in the faint voices from the other room.

"My brothers, we are gathered here tonight in the name of the most noble Order of the Ancient Nine," Jacobs said.

"God save the King," came the unified response.

"We are here to induct our fellow brother, Theodore Stickney, into our most privileged circle. Let it here be known that by unanimous vote of the most noble Order, Ted shall gain the full rights and privileges of an Order Knight. Ted, upon this night, you shall become bound by a most sacred covenant, one that will follow you to your grave and follow your soul into the ever after."

"God save the Gas," came the unified response.

There was a shuffling sound, and I could hear the dragging of chairs. Jacobs's voice returned. "Ted, please put your left hand on the Bible and raise your right hand. Repeat after me. I, Theodore Stickney, hereby accept the terms and conditions of membership into the most Noble Order of the Ancient Nine. I solemnly swear never to discuss the private affairs of this group with any nonmember of the Ancient Nine, including family, friends, business concerns, and other members of the club. These secrets I shall take with me to my grave and beyond. If I should violate this covenant, so shall my soul perish. So help me God."

Stickney's finishing of the oath was followed by the soft applause of gloved hands. More chairs were dragged across the floor, along with the sound of champagne corks being popped.

Jacobs's voice took over again. "Ted, these words I shall soon say to you must be memorized and never written down. Never forget them, for they will guide you in the spirit of the Order. There was a moment of silence before Jacobs said, "A son of Waldorf, not far from the Rhine. Brother in the Gas of standing quite fine. Downed off Newfoundland in waters icy and wide. Now stands as our protector with loyalty and pride. RMS 240."

The chatter quieted as Stickney slowly repeated the same poem Dalton had found inside the succession book—the same poem we had spent the last several weeks on, trying to decode its meaning without any success. I listened carefully to see if Jacobs would give a full explanation of its meaning. Instead, I heard, "A toast to our newest member." It was the distinctive voice of Charles Thorpe rising above the sound of clinking glasses. The room filled with commotion as the men congratulated the newest Knight.

Laughter and animated conversations ensued; then suddenly the noise disappeared. I kept my ear pinned to the vent, but there was only silence. What could they be doing? I couldn't even hear their footsteps on the hardwood floor. For thirty minutes I strained to hear anything, but it was as if they had suddenly vanished.

I quietly rose to my feet, then tiptoed to the library. The door was still locked. I knelt and looked through the keyhole. Nothing. The lights were still off, the candles had been snuffed, and the room was completely empty.

I returned to the TV room and took my position at the vent. I was scared as hell someone might come in and catch me there, but I was too close to back away. If necessary, I would pretend I had fallen asleep. I would do whatever it took, but I wouldn't be stopped now. In the quiet darkness, I waited for the slightest movement from the other room. For three long hours, I heard nothing but the hollow sound of air blowing through the metal vent. Then I heard voices. But they were distant, not close as they were before. I ran to the balcony next to the library and looked out the large bay window and into the courtyard. That's where I saw them, shaking each other's hands and walking toward the exit on the northern side of the mansion. But they were in regular clothes with jackets and hats. Gone were the tuxedos, capes, and top hats. I was completely confused. How did I miss them walking out of the library? I should've heard some sort of commotion as they left.

I ran back to the library and tried the doorknob. Locked. How was this possible? I looked through the keyhole. Empty. The candles were gone, the smoke had cleared, and the chairs had been returned to their original places, as if no one had been there. When I felt certain the club was completely empty, I sneaked downstairs and out the back door.

"HELLO."

"Dalton, wake up!" I said.

"Spenser?"

"I just got back from the club."

"What the hell? It's almost four o'clock in the morning. What were you doing there so late?"

"I think I saw the Ancient Nine tonight!"

"What are you talking about? How the hell is that possible?"

I told him about finding the lights on in the library, hearing voices, how they were dressed, Stickney's initiation, the poem, and their disappearance for several hours.

"And you're certain the library was locked?" Dalton said.

"A hundred percent. They didn't leave through that door."

There was a long pause before Dalton calmly said, "It's gotta be in there, Spense. There's no other explanation. The chamber must be somewhere off that library."

THAT WEEKEND WAS Princeton–Penn weekend. Unlike other Division I schools, most of our games were played on the weekends to reduce the time we missed from classes. So, we played in pairs based on geographic proximity. Yale and Brown played on the same weekend, as did Cornell and Columbia. Dartmouth, which is in Hanover, New Hampshire, is the closest to Cambridge, so they were our partners.

We resented being treated like a high school varsity team, but there was nothing we could do. The big conference teams flew around the country in commercial planes while we piled into chartered buses with seats that barely reclined, driving through the icy New England countryside staring through frost-covered windows.

However, the Princeton–Penn trip was always the best of these sojourns. Not only was Princeton's field house enormous, but the stands were always packed too, and the campus was fanatical about their Tigers. This year included a bonus. Model and actress Brooke Shields had just graduated, but it was rumored she still attended many of the home games. Even the coaches seemed excited about the possibility of catching a glimpse of the leggy Calvin Klein model, though they'd never admit it.

After the Princeton game on Friday, we usually ventured to Philadelphia, where we played Penn Saturday night in the Palestra, one of basketball's oldest and most storied arenas and the site of the first NCAA championship in 1939. Penn fans always packed the musty gymnasium, standing in unison as they sang their fight song, which ended with a salute to the Penn banner hanging from the rafters.

Ashley picked me up in her mother's little Bug and drove me to the Cage, where the buses were waiting. She had baked me a small canister of chocolate chip cookies and made several of my favorite roast beef and cheese sandwiches for the long ride to Princeton. She had applied to BU, Tufts, and UMass and was expecting to hear the decision on her acceptance on Friday or Saturday, so I gave her an extra kiss for luck, then boarded the bus.

These were our two biggest games of the year. Princeton was in first place, and we were only one game behind. Penn was a close third. Coach boarded the bus with Matilda, an old broom that had been around since the forties, and held her up for us all to see. No need to explain to us. When Matilda had been taken down from her display case in the lobby of Briggs, that meant we were expected to sweep the weekend and return to Cambridge sitting on top of the Ivies.

Princeton, as always, was a hard-fought game. They ran their traditional slow-down offense, full of quick passes and backdoor cuts, a methodical game plan that lulled opponents into passivity before going on the attack. We ran the opposite kind of offense, lots of running and fast breaks, quick shots and monstrous slam dunks in the open court. Brooke Shields was seated in the middle of their student section, another weapon of distraction in her tight Calvins and black cowboy boots. She had a gaggle of girls around her who were equally leggy and beautiful, prompting several of our guys to openly question their choice of colleges.

We played them even until the half, and during the third quarter the score remained tight. Mitch was having an unbelievable game with more than twenty points and ten rebounds and no sign that any of their big men could stop him. Geilton had shut down their point guard, who was averaging close to eighteen points a game, and both head coaches had already gotten technical fouls for arguing calls with the referees. We ended the fourth quarter tied and headed into a contentious overtime period that almost erupted into a bench-clearing brawl when one of their bruisers undercut Mitch as he went up for a dunk. The Princeton player was ejected from the game, Mitch sat out for a couple of minutes while our trainer had to retape his ankle. He returned and continued to punish them down in the low post. Geilton won the game for us on a buzzer-beating three-pointer that their head coach, Pete Carill, hotly contested but the referees held up. It was thrilling not just to win the game, but also see their typically obnoxious fans quietly file out of the arena with their Princeton banners dragging and their heads hung low. Brooke, however, looked just as beautiful in defeat.

Saturday night, the Palestra was jumping the minute we walked into the building. It was still more than an hour away from game time and most of the stadium's seats were already filled. Their band played everything from James Brown's "Gonna Have a Funky Good Time" to Queen's "We Will Rock You," and their cheerleaders led the growing crowds through a round of spirited fight songs. We were still riding high from last night's overtime win at Princeton and walked onto the court with more confidence than I had ever seen in my teammates. There was a hunger in their eyes and a determination in their clenched jaws, and I knew long before the opening tip-off that we were going to win that game.

I had the best game of my career that night, hitting double digits in both points and assists, and Mitch continued his tear, racking up another twenty-point game and fifteen boards. Everyone seemed to be having career nights, with little Morrissey even getting in on the action and picking up eight points and two steals. By the time the final buzzer sounded, the boisterous Quaker fans had been silenced and we swept our way back to the bus with Matilda. We pulled out of Philly late that night sitting in first place for the first time since I had been at Harvard. I wondered if Reverend Campbell was already on the phone gloating over our victory with his cousin at Princeton.

WHEN I CRAWLED into my room after the six-hour bus ride home, the light was blinking on my answering machine. Ashley was speaking so quickly that I could barely understand what she said. The gist of it was that she had gotten into both UMass and Boston University, and both schools had offered scholarships that would cover most of her tuition. I went to sleep that night feeling life just couldn't get any better.

43

"**THE WAY TO** get into the chamber is probably buried in one of those damn books," Dalton said.

We had just sat down to French toast and hickory-smoked bacon at Leo's Place. It was late Sunday morning and the winter's first snowfall had just descended on our sleeping campus.

"Why are you so certain our answer is in one of the books?" I asked.

"Because it's been right in front of us the entire time, and we've completely missed it," Dalton said. "It's all about books and literature and religion."

I scooped up a healthy serving of French toast wedges, dipped them in the pool of syrup, and took a big bite.

"Think about it," Dalton said. "A rare seventeenth-century religious book, two missing pages, a succession manual, a code buried within a poem, and an induction ceremony in the library. This is all about books."

"There must be five thousand books or more in that library," I said. "It could take me weeks to go through all of them. For you to help, I'd have to sneak you upstairs when no one else was around, then pray like hell we don't get caught."

Dalton looked up from his plate and smiled. "Start praying."

After I returned to my room, I pulled up the blinds to let in what little sun cut through the heavy clouds. Percy had gone to meet Hartman at Quincy House, and only the hissing steam of the old heaters emanated from the common room. I sat back on the couch and thought about what was in store for us later that night. Getting into the club wouldn't be a problem, but making sure no one else came in while we were there would be a real challenge. If I got caught sneaking Dalton upstairs, at the very least I'd be kicked out, but then I thought about Erasmus Abbott and realized that might be the smallest of my worries.

AT TWO O'CLOCK in the morning, while the rest of the campus was ensconced in heated rooms and down comforters, Dalton and I met at the bottom of Linden Street clad in dark sweat suits and black skullcaps pulled down just above our eyes. We walked to the Delphic and down the alleyway to the servants' entrance. Dalton brought an industrial flashlight, and I brought two candles and matches just in case the batteries went dead.

I unlocked the creaky door to the back hallway. Once inside, I punched the alarm code in the keypad. As the old floorboards cracked under our feet, we worked our way down the hallway, through the kitchen, then up the back stairs to the third floor. The mansion was empty, so we quickly moved through the dark hallways and spacious rooms, and finally into the library. I locked the door behind us and wedged one of the chairs underneath the knob for added security.

Dalton lit the long candles, which flickered in the draft seeping through the chattering windowpanes. "When you checked this place, did you look behind the books?" he asked. "If they didn't go through the windows or a door, they had to go through the ceiling or behind the walls."

"I guess," I said. "But I'm not sure. I just heard them through the vent in the TV room."

"I'll start on the upper level while you start down here," Dalton said. "Look for any book that has something to do with Germany or whose author's initials are RMS. Read each title carefully. They wouldn't have made it easy."

For the next two hours, we removed and replaced the books, flipping through the pages, running our hands along the back of the shelves to see if there was a secret compartment or faux wall. As we pored over everything from early Russian literature to French poetry born out of the Revolution, our weary arms and strained eyes faithfully kept to the mission. When we had gone through half the shelves and had come up empty-handed, we took a break on the sofa.

We were feeling defeated, not saying much as we looked around the darkness. The silence was occasionally punctured by the stress sounds of twisting tree branches fighting the howling winds. Then I saw it. I wasn't certain until I aimed the flashlight at the painting.

"What are you doing?" Dalton said.

"Follow me," I said, getting up and walking over to the mantelpiece.

When we were standing in front of the portrait, I asked, "Do you know who that is?"

"No clue, nor do I give a damn," he said. "We have several more thousand books to go through, and the sun will be up in a few hours. I couldn't give two shits about some old portrait."

"That's John Jacob Astor IV," I said. "He was one of the early members. I saw his name in one of the old club directories. He was the recording secretary in 1885 and 1886."

Astor was dressed in a gray wool topcoat with a black fur collar. He was standing on the bow of a ship looking into the turbulent water with a pensive expression on his face. He had a long nose, a thick black mustache that was slightly curled at the ends. Long, well-groomed sideburns dropped beneath his ears.

As I further scrutinized the painting, I saw the three letters that had been haunting us for weeks and felt a jolt of electricity shoot through my body. There, along the starboard side of the ship and barely legible: RMS. The name that followed those three letters, which was barely visible, provided the breakthrough: *Titanic*. It all started to come back. The RMS *Titanic*. What most people didn't know was that RMS stood for Royal Mail Steamer, something I discovered when I wrote a sixth-grade school report on the *Titanic*. The *Titanic* had been built as the largest moving object ever created to carry passengers and mail across the Atlantic.

Dalton stood too far away to notice the faint letters in the bottom of the painting.

"It was here the entire time, and I missed it," I said. "'A son of Waldorf not far from the Rhine.'"

I walked to the bookcase adjacent to the door and pulled a volume of the 1938 *Encyclopedia Americana* and the second volume of the 1968 edition.

"Are you going to let me in on the big secret?" Dalton said.

"When I was down at the New York dinner, we passed by this fancy hotel," I said, flipping through the 1938 encyclopedia. "Tons of people in tuxedos and ball gowns were outside getting into limousines. Claybrooke said it was called the Waldorf Astoria. The Waldorf part caught my attention, but I didn't pay any attention to the Astoria. I meant to look it up when I came back, but forgot about it."

There wasn't an entry for the Waldorf Astoria, but I found several entries for the Astor family. I looked at the second entry for John Jacob Astor IV. I found what I read aloud:

> American capitalist and inventor, fourth of the name, nephew of John Jacob the third, and son of William: b. Rhinbeck, N.Y., 13 July 1864; d. at sea (*Titanic* wreck) 15 April 1912. He was graduated from Harvard in 1988. He was the manager of the Astor properties in America; a director in many banking companies, and member of various clubs and social organizations. He built in 1897 a very costly hotel, the Astoria (named after the famous fur settlement of 1811), on Fifth avenue, New York, adjoining the Waldorf built by his cousin, William Waldorf, the two being joined as the **Waldorf-Astoria**.

I picked up the 1968 volume and read from that one.

> In the Spanish-American War, Astor made his yacht available to the U. S. Navy, outfitted an artillery battery at a cost of over $100,000, and served in Cuba as a lieutenant colonel. Besides the Astoria, he built the Knickerbocker and St. Regis hotels, New York City Landmarks. He

actively directed the family fortune and was a director of such companies as Western Union, Equitable Life Assurance, the Illinois Central
Railroad, and the Mercantile Trust Co. He died on April 15, 1912, when
the steamship *Titanic* struck an iceberg and sank in mid-Atlantic. Soon
after the catastrophe, his wife, who had been saved from the *Titanic*,
gave birth to an heir, John Jacob Astor 5th.

"Genius," Dalton said. "Astor also fits the second line perfectly: 'Brother
in the Gas of standing quite fine.'"

I pointed to the portrait. Along the starboard side of the ship were the letters RMS.

I walked over to the bookcase where I had first started my search and
rummaged through the pile of books on the floor until I found an odd, oversized bundle of pages. It wasn't exactly a book, but the pages had been bound
tightly together. I brought it over to Dalton who recognized my point immediately when he read the top of the page.

"In 1985, Congressman Jones from North Carolina put forth a report to
support making the *Titanic* an international maritime memorial and to create international agreements on exploration and salvage of the sunken ship,"
Dalton said.

"And that report isn't in this room by accident," I said. "None of this
is. Think about it. The RMS *Titanic* sank into the icy waters off the coast
of Newfoundland. My sixth-grade teacher, Mrs. Milton had given me
an A minus, because I forgot to include how long it took for the ship to
sink."

"What's the answer?" Dalton said.

"Two hours and forty minutes."

"You did it!" Dalton screamed, grabbing and hugging me. "We were completely on the wrong trail with Sampson and Swigert. This poem was an ode
to Astor."

I looked up at the portrait. "And a reminder to the Knights where their
secret chamber was hidden," I said. "'Now stands as our protector with loyalty and pride.'"

| 99TH CONGRESS
1st Session | HOUSE OF REPRESENTATIVES | REPORT
99–393 |

THE R.M.S. "TITANIC" MARITIME MEMORIAL ACT OF 1985

NOVEMBER 21, 1985—Committed to the Committee of the Whole House on the State of the Union and ordered to be printed

Mr. JONES of North Carolina, from the Committee on Merchant Marine and Fisheries, submitted the following

REPORT

[To accompany H.R. 3272]

[Including cost estimate of the Congressional Budget Office]

The Committee on Merchant Marine and Fisheries, to whom was referred the bill (H.R. 3272) to designate the shipwreck of the *Titanic* as a maritime memorial and to provide for reasonable research, exploration, and, if appropriate, salvage activities, having considered the same, report favorably thereon with amendments and recommend that the bill as amended do pass.

The amendments are as follows:

Strike out all after the enacting clause and insert the following:

SECTION 1. SHORT TITLE.

This Act may be cited as "The R.M.S. 'Titanic' Maritime Memorial Act of 1985."

SEC. 2. FINDINGS AND PURPOSES.

(a) FINDINGS. —The Congress finds that—

(1) the R.M.S. *Titanic*, the ocean liner which sank on her maiden voyage after striking an iceberg on April 14, 1912, should be designated as an international maritime memorial to the men, women, and children who perished aboard her;

(2) the recent discovery of the R.M.S. *Titanic*, lying more than 12,000 feet beneath the ocean surface, demonstrates the practical applications of ocean science and engineering;

(3) the R.M.S. *Titanic*, well preserved in the cold, oxygen-poor waters of the deep North Atlantic Ocean, is of major national and international cultural and historical significance, and merits appropriate international protection; and

(4) The R.M.S. *Titanic* represents a special opportunity for deep ocean scientific research and exploration.

(b) PURPOSES.—The Congress declares that the purposes of this Act are—

(1) to encourage international efforts to designate the R.M.S. *Titanic* as an international maritime memorial to those who lost their lives aboard her in 1912;

(2) to direct the United States to enter into negotiations with other interested nations to establish an international agreement which will provide for designa-

71–006 O

I steadied the flashlight on Astor's face, slowly working my way down. We examined every brush stroke and color change, from the texture of his slicked-back hair to the subtle wrinkles pulling at the corners of his eyes. Then I flashed the light on the top button of his coat and motioned for Dalton to take a step closer. Our faces were only inches away from the canvas. I worked the light down his coat from the first to the second button, but when I reached the third button, I stopped.

"Why did you stop?" Dalton said.

"Look closer," I said. At a quick glance, this button looked like the others, but on closer inspection there were subtle differences. The other buttons were a solid black with streaks of silver running through them. But the third button was different. It was solid black, no streaks.

I rested the flashlight on the mantelpiece while Dalton brought over two chairs. We stood and carefully grabbed the heavy wooden frame and slowly lifted it off the hanging pin. Once we had it secured, we carried it across the room and rested it on the table. I picked up the flashlight and scanned the wall. There it was, right in the middle of the oak panels, a tiny black button that was serving double duty as the third button on Astor's coat.

"I can't believe this is happening," Dalton said. We stood there for a while, focused on the button. He finally said, "Go ahead and push it. You're the one who figured it out."

I stepped closer to the button, but started to have second thoughts. "I'm not sure this is such a good idea," I said. "How do we know this thing isn't alarmed? They wouldn't leave the chamber so vulnerable."

"There's no guarantee that pushing this button will put us right into the chamber," Dalton said. "This could be just a first step of many."

"Maybe we should go home, think this through, and come back later," I said.

"Hell no! We worked too hard to get here. I'm not turning back now. If you wanna leave, go ahead. I'll do it myself."

I thought about that Halloween night in 1927. Dunhill left Abbott and had lived to regret it. I wasn't going to make the same mistake. Then I started having flashbacks of initiation night and my standing there in front of Brimmer and Purnell, swearing my oath. How ironic that I was going to break the oath in the very room where I had been sworn to uphold it.

"What the hell," Dalton said, and before I could stop him, he reached up and pushed the button. Nothing happened at first, so we just stood there looking at the wall, then each other. But just as he lifted his hand to push the button again, the center of the wall divided, and the two halves drew away from us. My chest tightened.

"Holy shit!" Dalton said.

I aimed the flashlight into the darkness. Dalton took a couple of short deliberate steps forward, and I followed close behind. When we were no more than five feet inside, the walls closed behind us.

"This is crazy," Dalton whispered. "Damn. We found it."

"It feels like a dungeon," I said, flashing the light around our small enclosure."

Wispy cobwebs dangled from the corners of the black walls. It was damp and musty. I slowly panned the flashlight, starting on the left wall, then working my way to the right. It wasn't until I moved across the center panel that I saw a hunched figure standing in a small doorway.

"Shit!" Dalton yelled, jumping back.

I hit my head against the back wall. I shined the light directly in the man's face as he shielded his eyes with his left hand. He was wearing heavy black rectangular glasses and was gripping a cane in his right hand. An entangled network of blood vessels coursed underneath his translucent skin.

"If you would spare me the light, Mr. Collins," he said. "My eyesight is bad enough already."

"Professor Davenport?" I said, moving the light down from his face.

He nodded his head slowly. "And a good evening to you also, Mr. Winthrop."

Dalton looked at Davenport, then at me. "You know him?" Dalton said.

"So do you," I said. "This is Professor Davenport from the Divinity School. The one who's been helping me with the passages."

"If you care to follow me, I'll explain everything," Davenport said.

He turned and started walking through the small door.

Dalton and I looked at each other, then walked across the concrete floor and followed him through the crooked doorframe. He hobbled a few feet down a narrow hallway, then grabbed a lantern hanging on a nearby wall and fiddled with a knob until the light came on. At the end of the hallway, he led us down a small rickety staircase, then paused at the bottom of the steps and punched a code into a keypad attached to the door. Next, he lifted up a metal flap and held his thumb in a black box for a few seconds. A series of lights flashed underneath the box; then we heard the loud sound of a lock unclasp and the heavy steel door spring open. He pushed the door open with his cane, and we followed him down another short hallway. We came to a third door, where he stopped and stood facing what we thought was a peephole. But when he pushed a small white button against the wall, a red laser shot from it and into his eye. The scanner glowed for no more than a couple of seconds before going dark.

The second door popped open, and we followed him into a wide room with a low ceiling. Two standing lamps burned against the back wall.

"Welcome to the chamber, gentlemen," Davenport said. "The reward for your admirable efforts."

Dalton and I stood just inside the door and slowly took in the dark room. The walls were a deep mahogany and lined with tall wooden chairs whose backs rose to pointed spears. A series of colorful pendants hung above each chair as well as a column of black-and-white photographs pressed in gold oval frames. All white men, most of them middle-aged or older. None of them smiled. Gold was everywhere—picture frames, lamps, candle holders, vases, tables, even the massive chandelier hanging in the middle of the ceiling was covered in gold leaf. A bookshelf with glass doors ran along the entire back wall, stuffed with books and gold trinkets. There was an elevated platform in the center of the room and a tall glass enclosure that had been roped off like a piece of art in a museum exhibit. A dark maroon Persian rug covered the floor.

"Please have a seat, gentlemen," Davenport said. "It's been a long night for all of us."

Dalton and I eased back on the long sofa that squeaked as we settled.

"So, this is the chamber," Dalton said. "And you're the old man everyone says leaves the clubhouse late at night."

Davenport opened a large snakeskin humidor on the table beside him and pulled out a long cigar. He unwrapped it, took his time smelling the tobacco, and clipped one end and moistened the other with his lips before lighting it.

"Yes, this is the chamber, Mr. Winthrop," he said between puffs. "You saw it diagrammed inside the succession book you took from your uncle."

"How did you know we had that book?" Dalton said.

Davenport took a long pull on the cigar, blew a heavy cloud toward the ceiling, and smiled. "I know almost everything," he said. "At least as it pertains to the Order."

"You've known what we were doing since I walked into your office with the passage," I said.

"Before then," Davenport said. "When Lenny called and told me a student had shown up on his doorstep with this mysterious religious passage, I knew the two of you had betrayed your word to Randolph and opened the book. Any student who possessed a copy of that passage must've seen the Creed."

"You knew my Uncle Randolph?" Dalton said.

"Since I was almost your age. He was a good and noble man, so noble that in the end, he was more worried about your lives than his."

"How are you connected to all this?" I asked. "Are you a Knight also?"

"Far from it," Davenport said. "I was once employed by the club a long time ago. I was born in Germany and came here via Great Britain. My mother and I moved to America when I was only ten years old for fear Germany would destroy England. She worked on the docks selling odds and ends to the men when they came in from a day out on the ocean. When I was thirteen, I got a job here at the club as an errand boy. They paid me well, ten dollars a week."

"Were you working here on Halloween night of 1927?" Dalton asked.

"No, but I wish I had been," Davenport said. "I might've been able to save my friend's life."

"You knew Erasmus Abbott?" I said.

"Never met him in my life," Davenport said. "I was referring to Samps. At least that's what I called him. He went by the name Moss Sampson, but that wasn't his real name either."

Dalton and I shot glances at each other.

"His birth name was Tyrone Sampson Ludley," Davenport said.

"How well did you know him?" I asked.

"As well as anyone could, I guess," Davenport said. "Samps was a very quiet man. Didn't open up much about his private life. He started out as a third porter and worked his way up to captain. He was a good man and an even better friend. He taught me a lot about life."

"What happened to him?" I asked.

Davenport shook his head and looked away. He took a moment to gather himself.

"Samps was in the wrong place at the wrong time," he said. "He told me he saw the two boys that night when they climbed over the fence. He was up in his room when he heard the noise. When they landed in the courtyard, one stayed behind while the other broke in through the kitchen. Samps went down to see what was going on, but by the time he made it to the kitchen, the kid had already made it upstairs. Then Samps heard some knocking coming from one of the rooms on the third floor. He realized the intruder had made it up to the library. When he opened the door, he found the kid standing against one of the walls, tapping it with a hammer. He was looking for a way in.

"Samps yelled at him to stop, and that's when the kid turned and rushed Samps with the hammer raised above his head. Samps started fumbling in the dark for the light switch, but the kid kept coming at him. Fearing for his own safety, Samps met the kid's charge, tackled him, and knocked the hammer out of his hand. They wrestled on the ground for a while before the kid finally broke free and ran out the door."

"Did he know it was Collander Abbott's son?" I asked.

"Not at the time. But he knew the kid wasn't just a common thief. He had bypassed several rooms filled with very expensive items and made a beeline for that wall in the library. It was obvious the kid knew things that he shouldn't have, so Samps ran after him into the dark hallway and grabbed him from behind. There was a dumbwaiter at the end of the hall that went from the kitchen all the way up to the fourth floor. The servants used it to transport food for the dinners in the banquet hall. Samps grabbed the kid from behind and they tumbled to the end of the hallway. Too late. The dumbwaiter's door was still open. Samps tried to stop him, but he fell through. Samps described it as the most desperate scream he'd ever heard. There wasn't a night that went by that he didn't have some kind of nightmare, hearing that cry, then the thud of Abbott's body hitting the bottom of the shaft."

"So, it was an accident," Dalton said.

"It was more than an accident, Mr. Winthrop," Davenport said. "It was a tragedy of the greatest proportions, and one that was completely avoidable. Two innocent people lost their lives that night because of the secrets in this room. The events of that night changed me and everyone else who knew about it, forever."

Davenport rested his cigar in the ashtray, then stood with the help of his cane and hobbled toward us with great effort.

"And now, Mr. Winthrop, your visit has come to an end," he said, extending his hand. "There are a few housekeeping items that Mr. Collins and I need to discuss privately."

Dalton and I locked eyes before Davenport led him out of the room.

44

"WELL, I THINK it's time I showed you something," Davenport said. "Tonight, I want you to leave here with everything."

He disappeared through another door in the opposite corner of the room. He soon reappeared carrying a small leather box. He hobbled over and handed it to me.

"You've worked very hard since the cocktail party invitation arrived under your door," he said. "They tracked every move you've made, from finding the original Abbott article in Widener to the books in Houghton, then the Jenkins donor file in the University Archives. Your progress was steady and thoughtful. They've been as impressed by your tenacity as they have been fearful."

"If they knew I was getting closer to the truth, why didn't they stop me?" I said.

"Everything is not as it seems," Davenport said. "You're alive because they're afraid of the uncertainty your death would bring."

"Uncertainty?"

"It will become much clearer when you peruse the contents of that box."

I ran my hand over the thick, pebbled leather. "What's inside?" I asked nervously.

"Your legacy and destiny," he said.

I slowly lifted the lid. The contents were wrapped in plastic bags. I pulled the first one out and felt a small metal object attached to a beaded chain.

"That was one of Samps's army tags," Davenport said. "He always wore two of them. The only time I ever saw him take them off was when he gave one to me before he left the club for good."

I examined the stainless-steel tag through the plastic. It included the pertinent information—name, social security number, blood type, and religion. I ran my finger over a big dent just off center.

"That saved his life," Davenport said. "Some drunk in a bar in Mississippi shot at him after he thought Samps was looking at his woman. That dog tag deflected the bullet into his right shoulder. Just a quarter of an inch lower, and that shot would've gone through the center of his heart."

I pulled out the second bag. It was a black-and-white photograph of a skinny boy who couldn't have been more than seven. He stood against a porch with his hands in his pockets. He was squinting from the sun and smiling wide.

"That's him in front of his grandparents' house," Davenport said. "The only picture he had of himself as a boy. He kept it in a Bible his grandmother gave him at his baptism."

I looked down at the picture. He was a cute little boy with skinny legs and socks gathered at his ankles. I imagined him playing baseball in the summer or buying penny candies at the general store. His clothes were tattered and too large for his tiny frame, but he stood proud in front of the camera. A child's innocence.

I pulled out a long manila envelope next. Its edges had curled.

"Don't open that now," Davenport said. "I want you to save that for when you're back in your room. But make sure you open it alone, not even in the presence of Mr. Winthrop."

"What is it?" I said.

Davenport looked away, then closed his eyes softly. "What I've lived so long to be able to pass on."

I looked at the nondescript envelope and felt its thickness. It contained paper.

"There's something else you need to see before you leave," Davenport said.

He lifted himself from the chair and made his way across the room. He moved slowly but with determination. As I followed him into the center, I looked at the high-backed chairs lined against the wall. They were like the hard wooden celebrant chairs found in the pulpit of an old English abbey, their arms linked to each other and fluffy blue velvet cushions propped up in their seats. Brass nameplates were attached to the high backs, and I recognized some of the names. There was Randolph Winthrop's stall next to Collander Abbott's, which was next to John P. Morgan Jr. Theodore Stickney's nameplate hung above Uncle Randolph's, which meant he was the new occupant of the stall. One lone chair set apart from the other eight, centered on the back wall. It was much bigger and more ornate with two crossed swords hanging above it. The Sovereign's chair, I assumed. In the diagram, it had been marked with an S. John Astor's nameplate was the first in the column, and Stanford L. Jacobs III sat on top.

"Whatever happened after Abbott fell down the shaft?" I asked.

"Samps panicked," Davenport said. "Rightfully so, given the circumstances. He called the undergraduate president of the club, a guy named Sinclair Cripps. Cripps rushed over from his room, and when Samps told him what had happened, they got the graduate president on the phone, a mean sonuvabitch by the name of Earl Murdoch." Davenport pointed at the end stall on the right wall. "That was Murdoch's chair over there," he said. "Murdoch showed up, and Samps begged them to call the police and tell the truth—that it had all been an accident and that Abbott had attacked him with a hammer. But Murdoch wouldn't hear of it. Instead, he threatened Samps and made him promise never to mention a word of what happened to anyone or he would have him tried for murder. Samps was nobody's fool. He knew he didn't stand a chance as a black man against someone as powerful and vindictive as Murdoch. Regardless of the evidence, any jury in the country would've convicted this large, muscular black man of killing this small, rich white boy."

"So, what did he do?" I asked.

"What any smart man would do," Davenport said. "He wrote down an account of what happened that night, including his knowledge of the chamber and its contents, and found himself a sympathetic lawyer who agreed to take his case in the event the club or Abbotts ever pursued legal action against him."

"Did they go after him?"

"They couldn't. They'd risk exposing themselves and all their secrets buried back here. Murdoch got Collander Abbott on the phone that night, and together they cleaned everything up."

"Abbott knew what had happened the whole time?"

"Of course, he did, and he was part of the cover-up."

That explained why there was so little press coverage, and why Collander Abbott had remained so silent even in the face of his own son's death.

"He put the Ancient Nine before his son," I said.

"He didn't see it that way," Davenport said. "His son was already dead. Mr. and Mrs. Abbott were truly crushed. They were never the same. But nothing was going to bring him back. Exposing the club and this chamber would bring only more turmoil. He kept his oath."

A mounted glass enclosure sat opposite the chairs. Davenport walked closer to the ropes surrounding the glass enclosure, beckoning me to follow him.

"Don't get too close," he warned.

When I was standing next to him, he tapped his foot on a small metal pedal in the floor, and suddenly the glass case was awash in light. Four spotlights in the ceiling shone down on a single piece of paper vertically suspended in glass, the base engraved with the words LONG LIVE THE GAS. Davenport didn't have to tell me what I was looking at. Here at last were the missing pages of the 1604 first edition of *The Christian Warfare*. I leaned forward for a closer look.

"No!" Davenport yelled, releasing his cane and throwing up his arm to block me. "Don't get any closer than that! The alarm is still on."

I looked down at the ropes and around the glass enclosure, but I didn't see any wires or cameras or anything, for that matter, that might indicate it had been alarmed.

"It's all infrared," he said. "You get an inch closer, and we'll both be dead within seconds. Once the alarm is triggered, it activates the pneumatic vacuum seal. In less than thirty seconds, the air gets sucked out of here and the rooms are sealed off. Once the process is activated, it can only be stopped by entering a code over there. He pointed his cane to a far wall. "I'm no longer fast enough to make it over there in time."

I backed up several feet from the ropes.

"It's been here the entire time," I said. "And this is why you were the only person Reverend Campbell contacted about that passage from *The Christian Warfare*."

"Page five hundred forty-five on the front and five forty-six on the back," he said. He picked up his cane and walked over behind the Sovereign's chair. He opened a small compartment in the wall and pushed several buttons. "It's all right now," he said, walking back to me. "The alarm is disengaged."

I walked up to the glass enclosure and looked down at a piece of a legend more than three and a half centuries old.

"Those pages changed my life forever and inspired me to seek justice for Samps," Davenport said.

"What happened to him?"

"He told me all that had happened. They paid him a small fortune to leave. Then they asked me to take over back here. They doubled my pay, made me sign a stack of confidentiality papers, and agreed to send me to school. This single sheet of paper before you is what inspired my interest in theology. I not only wanted to understand the words themselves, but more important, their significance to nine men willing to commit murder to protect their secrets. I met Samps a few months later in the Commons. I didn't know it would be a goodbye. He was dead two weeks later. They killed him. I never had any hard evidence, but there's no doubt in my mind. I did some checking on my own. The police said there was no need to investigate his death. They claimed he suffered a heart attack during his sleep. The coroner's office never performed an autopsy, even though it was customary to perform one for a sudden, unexplained death like that. I was persistent. I'll never forget what the medical examiner said to me the morning I visited him. 'We were notified of the death and that the body was coming in. It never arrived. When I checked back to find out what happened, I was told the body had already been cremated. Peculiar.' That last word struck me. They killed him, and had it covered up. I will never be convinced otherwise."

I waited a moment to take it all in. I suddenly felt chilled. "Why are you still here after all these years?" I asked.

"When you've seen what I've seen and heard what I've heard, you never really leave," he said. "I'm here because of a promise I made to Samps. And I'm grateful to have lived long enough to fulfill that promise."

"You wanted me to find the chamber the entire time," I said.

"Very much," Davenport said. "But it was also important to the Ancient Nine that you found it on your own. If I had given you the answers right away or helped too much, they would've known. Whether it was at Houghton or the Archives or the burial site at the old Abbott estate in Newport, you left a trail that proved you were doing it on your own. And in all honesty, I wanted to know for myself that you had true rigor, before I gave you what's in that envelope."

I walked around the enclosure to see the back page. I recognized the words of the Creed and those engraved on Abbott's urn. But even more telling were the words that had been handwritten inside the right margin. The ink had faded into the page, but the carefully formed letters of King James I were still legible.

> *My Dearest Esmé:*
> *And shall I then like birde or beast forget*
> *For anie stormes that threatning heauen can send*
> *That obiect sweete, wheron my hart is sett*
> *Whome for to serue my senses all I bend*
> *My inward flame with colde it dothe contend*
> *The more it burnes, the more restrain'd it be*
> *No winters frost, nor sommers heate can end*
> *Or staye the course of constant loue in me.*

This was the hard evidence. King James I, one of the most powerful monarchs in history, a towering Christian leader who had the world's most popular Bible translation named after him, admitted that he had a homosexual relationship with his older cousin, Esmé Stuart. While the admission itself was not a surprise, having it written in his own hand made it an extremely rare and valuable document.

The lights in the room suddenly dimmed and the page evaporated in the darkness. Davenport was back at the wall, fiddling inside the compartment behind the Sovereign's chair. As soon as he stopped, the entire east wall slid back. Without turning around, he said, "Join me."

I stood up and followed him toward the missing wall. When we crossed the threshold, the room flooded with light. I stood there speechless for several minutes, trying to take in all that was before me. Describing it as breathtaking would be just a start. The room was not only twice as large as the chamber, but it was also the most decadent construction I had ever seen in my life. The walls were made of gold in which jewels were embedded throughout the entire room. Gold figurines ran along the entire border of the elaborately designed vaulted ceiling, gleaming with candelabras that bounced light and gold in one fiery glow. Each wall had a large painting gloriously perched in its center so that observers would be dazzled by their size and baroque frames. The floor was a complicated pattern of mosaics in gold and amber hues. Save for the two fancy tables and a few uncomfortable but expensive-looking chairs, the room was otherwise empty.

"This is what they've really fought to protect all these years," Davenport said, his voice echoing off the walls.

"A gold room?" I said.

Davenport chuckled softly. "Much more than that," he said. "Come, let's sit. I'm tired."

We moved deeper into the room and sat on two of the chairs. They were stiff, but the seat cushions molded around my body, making it surprisingly comfortable.

"Filled with real horsehair," Davenport said. "No detail was spared when they built this room."

"This doesn't seem real," I said.

"In a way it isn't, but in other ways it is," Davenport said. "What do you know about World War II?"

"Very little," I said. "I studied some of it in high school in Mr. Muchanski's history class, but a lot of it I've already forgotten."

"This room is a replica of the fabled Amber Room," Davenport said. "The real Amber Room has been missing since 1944. Another masterpiece lost to civilization. King Frederick William I, King of Prussia, had it built and installed in his home, the Charlottenburg Palace. He then gave it to Russia's Peter the Great in 1716. It was a peace offering. The room had amber wall panels, ornate gold leaf designs, and semiprecious stones. It was an international sensation. When Hitler invaded the Soviet Union in World War II, he commanded his soldiers to steal the room, along with many other artworks, and take it back to Germany. It's never been seen again. One of the great art mysteries of the modern era."

"Why did they build this replica?" I asked.

Davenport pointed his cane toward the portrait of a man imperiously staring down on us. His eyes were dark, his jowl full, and his shoulders broad. He looked important and mean, a man who was accustomed to getting his way. I imagined his voice was deep and somber.

"That man is John Pierpont Morgan Jr," Davenport said. "He was obsessed with art as most of the wealthy were at the time. Art was a way to show status. People couldn't see what was sitting in your bank account, but they could definitely see what was hanging on your walls. The Morgan family was right up there with the Vanderbilts and Rockefellers. They were obsessed with art and historical treasures. Morgan wanted to replicate the room that had captured the world's admiration for centuries. So, long before the original room went missing, he built his version here next to the chamber. Some say he spent ten million dollars in materials alone. Doesn't sound like a whole lot of money in today's terms, but back then it was an astronomical sum to pay for just a room."

I studied Morgan's portrait, but was still having a difficult time trying to comprehend why someone would spend so much money and go through so much effort to build a room so grand, only to be hidden behind the walls of an old mansion.

"Is it true this building was one of the first to have lights in Cambridge?" I asked.

"Correct," Davenport said. "His father was friends with Thomas Edison. This friendship is why the family's New York City estate became the first electrified residence in the world. Morgan's money built all of what you see around you."

"But why build it hidden here when he could've built it anywhere in the world?" I said.

"Because he regarded this as the safest place for his secrets," Davenport said. He pointed to the wall on the left. "Let's go take a look at that painting."

We made our way across the room. The odd painting was intensely colorful. A partially visible house sat on the left side of the frame and the vast expanse of the canvas was covered with bright flowers and trees with serpentine trunks. A barely clad Jesus figure with his arms stretched as if on the cross was prominently placed in the middle of the painting. Directly underneath his hanging feet was a pale-faced woman completely covered in a blue robe. His feet almost touched her head.

"Klimt," Davenport said, his eyes poring over the painting in awe as if he had just seen it for the first time. "Gustav Klimt. One of the greatest Austrian painters to have ever lived. Also a true cultural revolutionary during his time. What you're looking at is his famous *Country Garden with Crucifix*. Painted in 1911 or 1912."

"What makes it so famous?" I asked.

"Beyond its artistic value and it being one of his classic landscapes, this is considered by the rest of the world to be a lost masterpiece."

"Lost?"

"Goes back to World War II," Davenport said. "The Nazis were losing badly and knew the end was near. Stalin and the Soviets were punching through the German lines surrounding Berlin. The German forces were in a dramatic retreat. Immendorf Castle was in the southern part of Vienna. It had been captured and controlled by the German SS, who had turned its large rooms into a safe haven for valuable art they had looted throughout the war. Hitler wanted to build a museum that had the greatest collection of masterpieces in the world. Among the hundreds of stolen paintings stored at Immendorf, thirteen had been Klimt's. As the Germans were surrendering the war to the Allied forces, an SS unit blew up the castle upon their retreat just to be spiteful. A massive trove of art treasures, including the Klimt paintings, were destroyed. This is one of them."

"So, if the original was destroyed, then this is a reproduction, right?"

"No, this *is* the original. It was never destroyed. What the Germans destroyed was a reproduction."

"So how did the original end up here?" I asked.

Davenport turned and slowly walked across the room to another painting. I followed. "Not too close," he said, putting his arm up to stop me. "It's best when you stand a few feet away. You can take it all in better that way. This is truly the pièce de résistance."

It was a landscape of a busy city square with vivid images. It looked like time stood still. A group of men huddled in one corner, a man and his dog nearby. A child played not too far away, while others walked through the square. The buildings looked old but sturdy, the center one a bell tower stabbing the sky.

"Canaletto," Davenport said. "One of the most revered Venetian painters of the eighteenth century. This one is the *Piazza Santa Margherita*. It was once owned by a Jewish art dealer in the Netherlands before the Nazis invaded and stole it."

"How did this one get here?" I asked.

Davenport walked me back across the room, where we returned to the ornate chairs. His body was tired, but there was so much life in his eyes. He took a deep breath and leaned back.

"Mr. Collins, I need you to listen carefully," he said firmly. "The secrets in this room have been buried for decades because of their darkness and the power of the men they involve. You are young, but you must understand the weight of the information I'm about to share." He paused for a moment, then continued. "Morgan's father was an industrious man with his hands in all kinds of businesses, from railroads to electricity. He made money any way he could, and the more he made, the more he wanted. Junior inherited not only his father's fortune, but also the drive to be wealthy almost beyond measure. His pursuit of wealth led him to alliances with some of the most morally corrupt men in the world.

"Morgan's companies as well as other prominent American companies basically funded the Nazis. This is not something many people want to talk about. But these companies—Morgan's being the lead—provided loans and other types of assistance to a young revolutionary by the name of Adolf Hitler. This small unknown young man had begun rising to power after what most Germans thought were unfair concessions they were forced to make at the end of the First World War. Without getting into all the details, a director of one of Morgan's banks, a guy by the name of Charles Dawes, created a plan to help Germany pay back the war reparations they had agreed to pay for their role in the war. Germany was given as much as two hundred million dollars in loans, half of which was provided by Morgan's banks. In effect, Morgan and others in the American finance industry stabilized Germany's failing economy. Money continued to flow over to Germany, and some of that money was channeled into the Nazi Party to finance an increasingly popular Hitler, who was championing German purity and extreme nationalism. Morgan's banking company was not only paid significant interest on these loans, but they also bought great control of most of German industry, ironically, owning or funding the very same companies that built tanks, planes, and munitions that would be used against our Allied forces in World War II. Morgan knew where his money was going, but turned a blind eye to it in the name of profit."

"But that doesn't explain how these paintings got here," I said.

Davenport raised his hand. "One of Hitler's early propagandists was a guy named Ernst 'Putzi' Hanfstaengl. He was a German American. His father was a German art publisher, his mother an American. He spent his early years in Germany before moving to the U.S. He attended Harvard and graduated in the class of 1909. He started out working for the American Embassy in Germany as a liaison, but began to admire Hitler and fell under his spell. He also happened to be a very good piano player, and Hitler loved that about him.

There was no denying that Putzi was a Nazi sympathizer, but what few alive today know is that he and Morgan actually knew each other."

"But Morgan was the class of 1889 and Putzi was class of 1909," I said. "Their years here didn't overlap."

"That's correct," Davenport said. "But they met several times after Putzi graduated. Secretly. Morgan was aware of Putzi's reputation, and he knew that any public meeting of the two could be detrimental to his reputation and his business, so they met here. It was perfect. Putzi being seen on Harvard's campus was nothing out of the ordinary, so no suspicions would be raised. Once he was here in Cambridge, they could easily slip him in and out of the chamber late at night. There's a hidden stairwell behind the walls that leads from the chamber into a tunnel that opens up through a grate in the far end of the courtyard, behind the back hedges."

Now it made sense why I didn't hear the Ancient Nine leave through the library that night. They left through the private stairwell and exited through the courtyard.

"Morgan's father left him fifty million dollars," Davenport continued. "But the Germans brought him the kind of money he had never seen before. He loved this room and these paintings. The Klimt belonged to his father, who kept it in his master bathroom at his mansion in New York City. He wouldn't hang it in one of the public rooms for fear of someone discovering that it was a stolen masterpiece. The very day Morgan got word that his father had died during a vacation in Italy, he had the valet take down the Klimt, wrap it up, and ship it here to be installed in this room."

"How did the Canaletto get here?" I asked.

"That came much later," Davenport said. "Putzi knew about Morgan's obsession with rare art. So, he used back channels to get Morgan the stolen painting. A gift from the Führer himself. As fate would have it, after it was installed, Morgan got a chance to see it only once before he died of a stroke in Florida."

"With all due respect, it's hard to believe a family as wealthy and American as the Morgans was tied to Nazi Germany."

"And they weren't the only ones," Davenport said. "Very powerful men, titans of industry, even leaders of this great university. The connections are deep and wide and convoluted. Morgan was a brilliant man. He kept his circle close and he made it worth their while to protect his secrets."

"How?"

"The way people respond to most. Money. Lots of it. He set up a trust which is now worth almost three hundred million dollars. Everyone benefits from this trust, and you will too once you graduate and receive your gift. Many have heard rumors that the club is rich, but few truly know how rich it really is. The clubhouse, the staff, the paintings on open display throughout the mansion; those are valuable, but nothing like what's back here, this gold and amber room, the endowed trust, the Nazi-looted treasures, and the secrets that tied them all together. You must remember, these men are bound together forever, complicit in keeping these secrets, and beneficiaries of what these secrets have produced. If one fails, they all fail, the risk from exposing their complicit malfeasance too great to measure. And so the bond has never been broken."

We sat there in silence for the next few minutes as I looked around the sumptuous room, unsure of when or if I would ever see it again, and wondering what it now meant that I knew the buried secrets of the Ancient Nine.

"It's late," Davenport said, finally standing up and hobbling toward the exit. He beckoned me to follow. "You must be out of the club before the staff arrives."

We walked back into the chamber, and the wall closed behind us, hiding Morgan's Amber Room. We stood in front of the glass case.

"How did the missing pages get here?" I asked.

"That's a question I've never been able to answer," Davenport said. "The display was already set up by the time I took the job. They've never discussed in front of me how it actually got here. But I remember what Collander Abbott said to me the last initiation dinner he attended. He was old and dying from bone cancer, but he wanted to come back to this chamber one more time. He stood right where we stand now and said, 'The whole of Christianity will forever be indebted to the nine men who put God ahead of family and personal jeopardy to guard this document and the dark secrets that could irrevocably stain Christianity.' I don't know if I'd take it that far, but at the time, it was inconceivable to these very religious men that the namesake of modern Christianity was not only homosexual, but there was hard evidence to prove it. They couldn't erase the historical rumors, but they could at least hide some of the physical proof. Rather than destroy the pages, they kept them back here as a symbol of their conviction and a reflection of the power they had to do so."

"But why have they allowed me to live and discover all of this?"

Davenport paused and carefully chose his next words. "Because killing you could've cost them everything."

I BARELY REMEMBER my feet touching the ground as I raced back to Lowell House. I slipped into my room and locked the door behind me. My fingers tingled as I pulled the shade down over the window and turned on the desk lamp, I pulled the lid off the box. I looked at Moss Sampson's military tag again, then at his boyhood picture, which I took out of the bag and propped up on my desk. I carefully opened the last bag and pulled out the long envelope.

The edges were worn and slightly frayed. A couple of smudge marks were visible on the back flap, and a tiny grease mark stained the upper right corner. It seemed ordinary enough. I took a pen off the desk and slid open the flap, then reached inside and pulled out the folded papers.

The first sheet was a note written in black marker. The handwriting was neat and careful.

> Spenser,
>
> If you are reading this letter, then all has gone as planned. I have shown you the chamber and told you about my dear friend Moss Sampson, who is also your great-uncle. I've waited a very long time for you to hold these papers. Knowing that they are in the hands of their rightful owner, the most important part of my life's work is now done.
>
> What I didn't tell you is that the papers in this envelope have made

you a wealthy young man. I cannot tell you which choices you should make from this point on, but I can tell you to proceed with great caution and trust few. You have proved your rigor through this process. Money has an insidious way of making decent human beings behave in a most indecent way.

The Ancient Nine have made you a member of the Delphic Club in order to watch your movements more closely. Be certain that one day they will groom you to become a Knight of the Order. Do not be swayed by their generosity and charm, for their evil and cunning have no limits. Do not be flattered into complacency. Find good counsel that will guide you on this treacherous and winding path. Above all, remember the sacrifice that has been made so that you now might find yourself in this position of privilege. I have done what I can do, and now you must carry on and ensure that Samps, your great-uncle and my dear friend and mentor, did not die in vain.

—Charles Davenport

I read the letter a second time and couldn't make sense of him calling Moss Sampson my uncle. I felt dizzy and short of breath at the same time. How was this possible? I opened the other two sheets of paper—thick parchment with a stamped seal and several signatures lining the bottom of the pages. I read each sentence carefully, disbelief growing as the words ricocheted in my head. I held in my hands the last will and testament of Tyrone Ludley, a.k.a Moss Sampson. In simple language, he had bequeathed all his earthly possessions to any living male relative who could prove his bloodline and had possession of the document that I now held.

The second sheet of paper shocked and confused me even more. I looked at the deed and title to the land and building at 9 Linden Street. Moss Sampson's name had been typed on the owner's line. It was to remain in his possession until his death and passed on to his designated male beneficiary. If there were ever an intent to sell such assets, a first offer of sale had to be made exclusively to the trustees of the Delphic Club at a price no greater than 20 percent above fair-market value. There was, however, one important stipulation. If any of Sampson's male descendants joined the ranks of the Most Noble Order of the Ancient Nine, all rights and claims to the mansion and its surrounding property would immediately revert to the Delphic trustees in exchange for one U.S. dollar.

This is why they had not killed me, and why my name had been proposed in Uncle Randolph's succession book. This was why Jacobs knew so much about me the night of the cocktail party and why he had pressed me about whether I had been in contact with my father's side of the family. They knew my bloodline to Moss Sampson, and they knew what it could bring me as well as them. This also explained the money my father had been given by a relative with the instructions for it to be used only for my education. Despite great need, my mother said he had never spent any of it. Uncle Moss knew they would bring me to Harvard. They had been recruiting me before I even arrived on campus.

I heard Davenport's calming voice. *These men are bound together forever. Complicit in keeping their secrets and benefits of what these secrets have produced. If one fails, they all fail. And so the bond has never been broken.*

My chest expanded with pride as I thought about my father and Uncle Moss, both strong, wise men, my history and bloodline. I was overcome with emotion as I realized how the courageous decisions they had made so many years ago at some of their most challenging times were now going to make life easier for me and future generations of the Collins family.

In the darkness of my room, while the rest of the campus slept under a chilled Cambridge night, the buried truths had emerged. For more than a century, the secrets of the Ancient Nine, the missing pages of *The Christian Warfare*, the deaths of Erasmus Abbott and Moss Sampson, and two of the world's most significant lost art treasures have been buried behind the walls of the Delphic mansion, concealed underneath layers of oaths and deceits— that is, until now.

EPILOGUE

❦

TWENTY-FIVE YEARS ago, I stood just as he now stands, blindfold wrapped around my eyes, my tuxedo soiled and wrinkled from the initiation rituals. I can only guess what's going through his mind at this precise moment, but I'm certain that his concerns and fears are much different than mine were so long ago. I was alone, a foreigner in a new world that mysteriously embraced me. I pictured him laughing with confidence during the exploits of pre-initiation, waving his hands in the air, dancing blindfolded on the Widener steps.

"Gentleman, I now present to you Quentin S. Collins, our newest brother. Long live the Gas!"

His blindfold fell, and the room quickly filled with thunderous applause. I had purposely assumed a position in the back so that I could take the moment in its entirety. Most of all, I wanted to see him in full, standing on that same table I once stood, looking over the crowd that cheered and welcomed him into the brotherhood.

I felt the tears coming, but this time I refused to stop them as I did so many years ago. They felt good on my face, warm and heavy, salty when they collected in the corners of my mouth. I looked at his face, youthful and strong, handsome beyond what I could ever hope for one of my children. He had

Ashley's eyes and nose, even her curly hair. I tried to convince myself that I had contributed something, but it was obvious whose chromosomes had dominated. His younger brother and sister got the best of both of us, but all three of them had Ashley's stubborn determination.

Quentin flashed that big smile that always made my heart flutter. Then he waved to his new Delphic brethren gathered beneath him. He found me in the back and the smile grew impossibly wider. I returned his wave as I wiped away tears. He stepped down into the waiting arms beneath him while I hung back. As he received the congratulatory hugs and pats, I looked around the room. The mansion hadn't changed much in the last two and half decades. The pair of Napoléon tankards still sat in their corner on the long shelf high up near the ceiling. The commemorative china set donated by the parents of Ralph Blake Williams III still shone on the mantelpiece, and the walls remained dark and sturdy, full of stories about young boys who had bravely become men only to become boys again. But the faces had changed dramatically. There were several African Americans both in the neophyte class as well as the graduate members saluting them. There had even been high-level conversations about allowing women to finally join our ranks.

I wasn't sure how much I was going to tell Quentin. As the son of a graduate member, his path into the Delphic had been so much different from mine. One day I would have to sit him down and tell him that the comforts he and his siblings had enjoyed all their life had not only been due to my success as a surgeon and his mother's prosperous bridal business, but because of two brave men from an out-of-the-way town in Mississippi. I would show him that childhood picture of his great-great-uncle, Moss Sampson, then tell him how a poor boy from the Deep South, who once mopped these floors and polished the same oak tables he'd be sitting at for Wednesday-night dinners, had the courage and foresight to stand up to a group of powerful men who would eventually kill him.

I followed Davenport's advice and found counsel that had no connection to Harvard or any of the clubs. It had been an uncomfortable meeting with their representatives, but in the end, we reached an amicable agreement. I signed over the property and clubhouse to the trustees, and in return, they were extremely generous in their financial settlement and commitment to be more inclusive as they elected new members. What I wouldn't sign, however, was the gag order that prevented me from ever speaking about the secrets hidden within that chamber. The missing pages from *The Christian Warfare*, the tragic story of Erasmus Abbott and Moss Sampson, as well as the dogged curiosity of his godfather, Dalton Winthrop, were all a part of Quentin's legacy, a history that he had a right to learn, and no agreement would ever take away from him.

"I'm proud of you, son," I said to him as we embraced in the back of the room on the other side of those curtained windows.

"It's great to have you here for this," he said. "Too bad Mom couldn't've seen it all."

"Club rules," I said. "But don't worry. We'll tell her every detail when we get home."

Quentin smiled. "Almost every detail," he said.

DALTON WAS WAITING for me at the bottom of Linden Street in front of the Lampoon Castle. Gray had begun to speckle his closely cut blond hair, but his eyes were as blue as hot tropical water and as youthful as that first day we met in Memorial Hall. His handsomeness had withstood the punishing assault of time, and regular exercise kept his lean body tight and capable. Elsie's and the Tasty had gone the way of expensive rents and new development, but we were happy to settle on Tommy's, still serving the best New York–style pizza in all of Boston. It was almost midnight and the restaurant was packed. And while the jukebox had been replaced with a machine half its size that played CDs instead of records, not much else had changed.

"How was it?" Dalton asked as we cut into a large cheese pie.

"More emotional than I thought it would be," I said.

"Brought back a lot of old memories?"

"Some good, some bad."

"How was Q?"

"A champion."

"Any of the old guys still around?"

"Jacobs is gone. Thorpe was hobbling along on two canes, but the man re-members everything. Bickerstaff was there, looking strong as an ox. He's on his fifth wife, who's not much older than the kids in here."

"You happy with your decision to give it all back?"

"It was the right thing to do."

"Have you told Q the story?"

"Not yet. I will at the right time."

We finished off the pizza and our discounted two-liter soda. Once we had gotten tired of seeing our own mortality reflected in the young faces around us, we settled the check and headed outside. Dalton had replaced his Aston Martin with a black Bugatti. We folded into the bucket seats. I imagined what Erma would say, seeing us squeeze into that car.

"You still driving like a damn maniac?" I asked, strapping on my seat belt.

"Gave that up a long time ago." Dalton smiled. "Kids have a way of changing your priorities."

The Bugatti engine suddenly growled, and that mischievous smile re-turned on Dalton's face. The first push on the accelerator snapped my head back against the seat. Within seconds, we were racing through the narrow streets of Cambridge on our way to the Winthrop mansion on Beacon Hill. Just like old times.

ACKNOWLEDGMENTS

✤

I STARTED WRITING this book a very long time ago when the idea was fresh in my head and I still had a mastery of the Harvard geography and history that would be critical in getting this as right as possible. I don't remember all the names, but I want to thank the Harvard librarians and those librarians at the University of Chicago who endured my endless questioning and hypotheticals as I dug into the research minutiae. A shout-out to the professors in the Classics department at the University of Chicago who opened their doors and helped me understand the Latin phraseology I had encountered. I also want to thank my agent Mitch Hoffman, who believed in this project from the beginning, championed this book, and had the patience and determination to see it through. Thanks to Daniel Hutchinson, in memoriam, a big guy with a big heart who was a big reason why I joined the Delphic Club in the first place. I will never forget how he welcomed me, the most unlikely of punchees. And as always, an extra-special thanks to my A-team, who cheer me on and encourage me endlessly, inspiring me to always chase my dreams and try new things, regardless of how crazy they may sound—Declan, Dashiell, and Tristé.